THANKSGIVING

By the same author

Novels

A Girl for the Afternoons
Southern Cross

History

The Railway Navvies:
A history of the men who built the railways

Passage to America:
A history of emigrants from Great Britain and Ireland
to America in the mid-nineteenth century

The Liners:
A history of the North Atlantic crossing

Collected journalism

The Only True History

The Scented Brawl

Biography

Providence and Mr Hardy

THANKSGIVING

Terry Coleman

HUTCHINSON
London Melbourne Sydney Auckland Johannesburg

Hutchinson & Co. (Publishers) Ltd
An imprint of the Hutchinson Publishing Group
3 Fitzroy Square, London W1P 6JD

Hutchinson Group (Australia) Pty Ltd
30–32 Cremorne Street, Richmond South, Victoria 3121
PO Box 151, Broadway, New South Wales 2007

Hutchinson Group (NZ) Ltd
32–34 View Road, PO Box 40–086, Glenfield, Auckland 10

Hutchinson Group (SA) Pty Ltd
PO Box 337, Bergvlei 2012, South Africa

First published in Great Britain 1982
© Terry Coleman 1981

Printed in Great Britain by The Anchor Press Ltd
and bound by Wm Brendon & Son Ltd,
both of Tiptree, Essex

British Library Cataloguing in Publication Data
Coleman, Terry
　Thanksgiving.
　I. Title
　823'.914[F]   PR6053.0419
　　ISBN 0 09 146530 3

For Vivien

CONTENTS

PART ONE

1	The Archbishop's Palace	11
2	The Last of England	24
3	The Crown of Thorns	36
4	The Lands of Promise	53
5	Thanksgiving Becometh Saints	69
6	The Wedding over the Brook	77
7	Harvest Home	86
8	The Child and the Unicorn	100
9	To Cherish and Maintain Entire	115
10	The Snow Never Cold	121

PART TWO

11	The Woman Apart	137
12	A God-Drunken People	150
13	Manhattan Island	162
14	The Summer Garden	169
15	The Seventh of the Seven Seas	179
16	Fires Quenched by Blood	187
17	Gone To Breuckelen	200
18	Another Country	215

PART THREE

19	The Reef	231
20	The Discovery	245

21	The Caress	252
22	The Mandarin's Robe	262
23	Starved Rock	269
24	The Wilderness Wooing	279
25	Divide the World	287
26	The Tower of Babel	295
27	The King's Comet	308

PART FOUR

28	The Departure of the Gods	323
29	A Few Songs Sung	338
30	The Flight to St Germain	346
31	The Needle in the Rose	360
32	To Vindicate His Father's Fame	374
33	The Letter	389
34	The *Royal Charles* and Sir George	394
35	The Palaces and Dungeons of the Heart	406
36	Good Night, Manhattan	419
37	The Heavens Infinitely Higher	427

A Note and Acknowledgments   443

PART ONE

1

THE ARCHBISHOP'S PALACE

Wolsey Lowell sat very upright on a carved oak settle in the great hall of the archbishop's palace at Scrooby, waiting.

As the girl sat she felt against her body, through the fabric of her plain grey stuff dress, the raised pattern carved on the settle back. It was familiar to her. She slipped her right hand between her back and the wood of the settle, and touched with her fingers the relief of roses, vines, and clusters of grapes carved by an unknown carpenter three hundred years before and polished to smoothness by the use of generations. She thought of the grapes, vines, and roses as hers, she knew them so well. Following the pattern was something she had done since she was a little girl. Now, not looking back, she traced with her hand the curve of the vine as far as the first cluster, and counted the grapes with the touch of her fingertips. Twenty grapes to the first cluster, seventeen to the second, and so on. Her touch was delicate by instinct. Then she folded her hands in her lap again, and glanced up. The light of the south windows fell upon her head, but she seemed not so much illuminated as irradiated from within.

Wolsey was a slender girl of seventeen, slim-breasted, not tall, but strong, a brown-complexioned girl. She wore her hair swept aside from a broad forehead, and let it fall across her shoulders. Her eyes were green, the eyelashes strikingly long, and her eyebrows dark, darker than her hair. 'Ah,' the village women said of her, 'she holds her head well, that one.' No one had ever called Wolsey a pretty girl. Few had ever failed to see that she was often beautiful.

She waited in the warm afternoon, pleasantly conscious of the coolness of the settle against her back, and surrounded by dead magnificence. The place was, after all, a palace, but its use and power were long gone. Banners hung in the still air from high beams, but their colours were faded and their edges frayed and tattered. There were the tatters of the ensign of England, the St George's cross. The cross had once been red against a white ground, but now showed only as a deeper stain of grey against a mud-grey ground. It was a deserted palace in a village, whose inhabitants knew a little of its history from their grandparents. All that was known about the St George's flag was that it was made of Danish dog's hair, the finest and strongest cloth to make a flag. It may have been true. That flag had survived better than the others. Next to it hung the royal arms of England, the personal banner of the sovereign, but the flag drooped as if it were dead, and the royal leopards of England hung lifeless in embroidered rags upon it. Then there was a banner that had once been the bishop's, and once red, bearing upon its face two cross keys worked in silver thread. Most lifeless of all, and suspended directly over the girl as she sat, was what remained of a shallow-crowned, wide-brimmed hat, so decayed that it was transparent as the light caught it. It had been of scarlet silk, but the colour was so far gone that what remained were predominantly the natural tints of the raw silk before it had been dyed – the pale orange, isabella olive, and sea green of the strands as they had been spun by the Piedmont silkworms. Inside the hat, as if to construct a skull where a man's head had once been, the spiders of nearly a hundred years had spun their webs, which were now so dense that they appeared more substantial than the fabric of the hat itself. And behind the hat hung another banner. Most of the day it stayed in darkness, catching the light only at this hour, approaching three o'clock in the May afternoon. At that moment the light from a clerestory window caught the banner and showed it to have once been golden, though its gold shreds were now blackened and tarnished, only a few patches of rusty redness showing what they had been.

This place had been a palace when a palace was needed there. Scrooby was a village on the Great North Road from London to York. A princess of England, on her way to Scotland to marry beneath her, had once stopped there. It was remembered in the folk history of the place that her name was Margaret, that a horse in her entourage kicked and killed a man, and that an equerry tossed a gold coin to the new widow while she was still stooping over her man's body. She had cursed the equerry and spent the gold to erect a tombstone commemorating the occasion of her husband's death, 'Kicked by the horse of Margaret, princess of England.' The stone had toppled in a gale only a year before this story begins. And a king had stayed unwillingly at the palace. Henry VIII, benighted on a tedious journey to York, inflicted himself and an escort of five hundred men and one hundred horses on the hospitality of the steward, and all the wine laid down in the cellars, fifty years in the collecting, was drunk in a night. But of course the palace was principally the archbishop's, who needed it there because Scrooby was in good hunting country, with more deer to hunt than parishioners with souls to minister to. But the last time an archbishop had come to Scrooby to hunt was beyond the memory of man. The archbishop now stayed at York, or even in London. The glory of the place was past. Or rather, the only glory of the place that afternoon was a brown country girl of seventeen, as she waited for the clock in the outer court to strike three.

The hour chimed, and as it did she looked up, not so much because of that sound as because she sensed some movement in the gallery two hundred feet away, at the end of the hall, where musicians had once played while hunting archbishops feasted on abundant venison. But there was no further movement, if indeed there had been a movement at all. She waited on. But her senses had been right. In the obscure heights of the gallery there were two men. The younger one was Francis Wheaton, in his mid-twenties, a tall, proud man, honest by principle and unyielding in his honest belief. The other was William Brewster, thirty years older, a man who had done great things in the world and remained honest in spite of it. They had both been regarding Wolsey as she sat far away and beneath them.

The older man said quietly, 'That is the girl.'

The younger man asked, 'She has Latin, you say, Mr Brewster; and Greek, and can read Hebrew?'

The older man smiled. 'Well, so far as that goes, she is a better scholar than I am, Francis. Her father taught her. He was a priest of this parish. I knew him well. He died when his daughter was nine or ten. Her mother had died the year before that. When he was dying, I gave him my word I would look after his daughter. In a way I stand in trust for her. After he died, I taught her myself as far as I was able. Then I saw to it that she was taught by the canons at York. Her father wished it.'

'She will come with us, Mr Brewster?'

'She will answer for herself.'

Brewster called down to her. 'Wolsey.'

'Yes?' she replied, looking up but not seeing him.

Brewster moved forward to the gallery rail, disclosing himself and his companion. 'We are here. We shall come down.'

Francis Wheaton had been a scholar of St John's, Cambridge, and could have had a fellowship if he had not disqualified himself from holy orders by holding and tenaciously putting forward the view that the supposedly reformed Church of England was no better than the church as it had been unreformed, ninety years before, when an Englishman owed spiritual allegiance to the Pope. Wheaton was a Puritan, who wanted to purify the church of all its old trappings. He wanted no bishops in England, no ceremony, no vestments, and no prayer books – and all remained. That they did remain, he thought the work of Satan. William Brewster was a wiser man. He had served the old queen, Elizabeth. He knew the court, and if his own religious leanings had not leaned just too far, his career would have flourished. Brewster was a Puritan, too, but he had seen too much of the world, seen the rise and fall of too many other men, and known their minds too well, ever to be *certain* in any matter that he was right. He would have liked a middle way. He would not easily damn a man or a belief, but he would say he desired to learn further or better what the true will of God might be. He was a mild man. But Wheaton loved controversy. He also regularly recognized, deplored, and tried to mend the sin of pride which lay in his soul. And was it a flash of pride he felt, or just surprise, when Brewster did not present this country girl to him – because she did look a country girl in spite of her learning – but rather presented him to her? And though she had begun to rise as the two men approached her across the hall, it was plain that she was rising for her old mentor Brewster, who motioned her to stay seated. So, she was no country girl.

When Wheaton was presented, he greeted her in Latin, which was not altogether an affectation. He might easily have spoken Latin to another Cambridge man he had just met.

Wolsey gravely lowered her eyes, but Brewster saw the ends of her lips slightly rise and knew what was coming. He saw that his beloved pupil was amused. She replied to Wheaton in better Latin than his own, not in his scholar's Latin but in the language in which her father, then Brewster, and then the canons at York had for twelve years habitually instructed her and conversed with her. Her Greek and Hebrew were merely more thorough than Wheaton's, but her Latin was a second native language in which she was as much at home as in English.

Wheaton heard this immediately, but could not straight away abandon his Latin. But he did look sharply up in a moment's perplexity, and, as he did so, he saw the tattered hat hanging above her head.

'What,' he asked, 'is that hat left there?'

He was making small talk. Wolsey saw that, too.

'This is the archbishop's palace,' she said. 'One archbishop was a cardinal. When he died, his scarlet cardinal's hat was displayed openly so that everyone would see how soon it fell into tatters, and how soon even a cardinal's glory perishes with his hat, and so, how all the glory of the world soon perishes. That's what it means.'

He said, 'Such marks of the old popish religion have been taken down everywhere else.'

'And would be here, if Scrooby were not so far out of the way. But better let it stay. I suppose the death of human vanity is as much a part of the new religion as of the Pope's, or of King James's in London.'

'So it is,' he replied. 'And much more so.'

'More so,' she said. 'Yes. You disagree with the king's church and want to take us away out of the kingdom, away from it? And that's why you've come here?'

'That is why.'

'And that,' said Wolsey, 'will be enough Latin, don't you think?' – and she said this in the strong northern English of York. 'You'll talk to the people today in English that they'll understand? So we'll speak it too.'

Wheaton assented. When she spoke Latin he had heard only the sense of the words. When she spoke English he heard her voice too. It was a bold contralto, and it shook him.

Wolsey was right about Wheaton's reason for coming. For twenty years, men from Scrooby and the villages around in Nottinghamshire and Yorkshire had been strong Puritans, wanting a purer religion, they said, than that of the king's church, without the trappings. It was true that an English king, ninety years before, had broken away from Rome, set up an English church, and declared himself and not the Pope to be its head. Now the Puritans wanted to separate themselves from the king's religion, thinking it had kept too much of the old. Many had taken themselves off from Scrooby to Holland and lived there, some for as long as twelve years. Brewster had been with them for some of the time. But now the English in Holland saw their children becoming more Dutch than English and wanted to find a new England across the seas in Virginia. About sixty of them from Holland were going to make the terrible voyage and had sent Wheaton to Scrooby to find others to join them. Wheaton's address that afternoon was given to forty-three men and women who came from ten miles around to hear him preach in the palace chapel. There were no seats. Everyone stood. He was God's recruiter. In his innocence, he wanted, with others, to found a plantation in northern Virginia. In his innocence he offered them a promised land, for had not the Lord led the tribe of Israel out of Egypt? And in their innocence, his listeners saw these lands of promise as he spoke of them. In the growing dusk, the church was lit only by flickering rushlights, which illuminated the faces of them all as they looked up at Wheaton.

He assured them that God had sifted the nation to be sure to bring only choice grain into His new land. It would be a new England. But they should not fear a wilderness. The same sun shone there as in England, and they would serve the same God. The Lord had said, 'And I will appoint a place for my people. And I will plant it, that they may dwell in a place of their own, and move no more; neither shall wicked people trouble them any more.'

The people were silent. They had no conception of an Atlantic Ocean to cross. None had ever crossed as far as to Ireland. And if they imagined a wilderness, it could hardly have been harsher than the flat fens in which they had lived their flat lives.

'There are many rivers and fresh springs,' said Wheaton, 'few savages, an abundance of fish, as much fowl as a man wants to shoot, plentiful corn, timber to build ships, and good merchandise to send back in them as cargoes. For beasts – there are some bears, and they say some lions too, but small ones.'

An older man, a forester, said, 'What woods grow there, sir?'

'Oak, elm, beech, tall fir, and others besides.'

'You have been there, sir?'

It was Mr Wheaton's great advantage that he had been there – once, and only briefly at that, but he had been there.

'The temper of the air,' he said, 'is one special thing that commends the place. There is hardly a more healthful place to be found in the world that agrees better with English bodies. A sup of new England's air is better than a whole quart of old England's ale.'

One of the rushlights fizzled out in the gloom. The heads of a few of the congregation turned towards it, and Wheaton seized his chance. 'Now in this new land,' he said, 'candles can be made just from pine trees, with no tallow. From the wood of the pine tree, cloven into little slices which are so full of the moisture of turpentine and resin that they burn as clear as a torch.'

One of the congregation answered him. 'It may be,' said the voice. This was the miller, a strong man, who would not be going, as why should he since he lived so plentifully where he was? 'It may be. But all men cannot be planters. Planting a colony is not work for which every man is fit or strong enough.'

'Nor is it. I won't say you can reap the corn before you have sown the land. The deer won't come when they are called and stand to be shot. The fish won't jump into our nets. But' – and here Wheaton dropped his voice so that his congregation listened the more intently – 'but, the days are bluer, the clouds are whiter, the stars are brighter, the plains are broader, and the forests deeper and more silent. The heavens are infinitely higher.'

He paused.

'In this new country,' he said, 'I have plucked grapes from the boughs of tall trees.' In the chapel he raised his right hand high, stretching up as if to pick grapes from the wooden beams, and held his arm stretched high. When he let it fall there was an exhalation of breath, a believing sigh, from the congregation.

He said a lot more, but the rest was theology. When he had finished, each of the men present came forward and shook his hand. The village women curtsied. Wolsey came up with Brewster. 'And now,' she said, 'you will take supper with us.'

Brewster, Wolsey, and their guest walked from the chapel into the great hall, across the hall, which now appeared all the greater because it was lit only by two flaring torches at the outer door, beyond which stretched the paved courtyard, the fish ponds, the orchards, and the moat. They were to eat at Brewster's house in what had once been the gatehouse. Even though only a gatehouse, it was grander than any other house in Scrooby village.

They stopped at the outer doors of the hall, three figures in the dappling light of the torches, standing for a moment in the welcome freshness of the evening air. They looked upwards into the near-darkness, with the scent of the air and of honeysuckle all around them, and held the moment. Wolsey let her mind stray back over the meeting in the chapel. Wheaton had said nothing she had not heard before, and she had thought him too dramatic. So she was not at all sure why she was so drawn to the man. But his presence was palpable. You could touch it with the senses. And then there were the man's eyes. He had preached infinite heavens with the mildest blue-grey eyes, not at all the piercing, disconcerting eyes of other enthusiasts she had heard. As they stood together in the doorway she could feel his tall presence next to her.

'Mr Wheaton,' she said, 'you preach a long sermon.'

Again he heard that candid northern voice of hers.

'I've been told that before,' he said. 'Men I knew at Cambridge told me I was too conscientious in that way. They said it would be better for everyone if I didn't so ruthlessly feel it my duty to preach on until *all* my congregation eventually awoke.'

Wolsey laughed, a very open laugh for so decorous a girl. Wheaton, facing her in the torchlight, saw her white teeth and the pink inside of her mouth as she laughed.

'But anyone,' she said, 'would have to say you pick grapes well.' And she stretched her hand upwards as he had stretched his, and held her hand there, picking grapes from the dark sky.

Then they both laughed, and he put up his hand and took hers. He could not, at that moment, readily have told his conscience what kind of grapes he was reaching for.

He slowly brought her hand down and released it. She put her hand to her shoulder, and then turned and started across the courtyard.

At supper, in Brewster's house, she said, 'Mr Wheaton, you are a spirit.'

'A spirit?'

'A spirit. They called the man a spirit who was hanged last month at York.'

'Hanged?'

'For spiriting men and women out of the kingdom to serve on a plantation in Virginia, where they died. They were supposed to be hired for seven years, and then to have their freedom and land of their own. But they died, and the spirit had the money.'

'Ah,' said Wheaton, 'but that man was spiriting them away to *sell* them into servitude.'

'And the women into marriage,' she said, 'to become His Majesty's breeders in Virginia.'

'But *selling* them,' said Wheaton. 'I ask no price.'

'Only,' said Wolsey, 'that people who go with you should risk their lives and everything they have.'

'Yes. I ask that price.'

They drank wine. Wine was not forbidden even to the strictest Puritans. As they ate, Wheaton watched Wolsey. If she turned her head, he watched the movement of her dress on her shoulders, and the movement of her hair across her cheek. He saw the shine of the torchlight on her hair. He saw her white teeth again as as she lifted a chicken bone with her fingers to eat. He watched her fingers as she dabbed them on the towel held out by the serving girl. Wheaton had known women at Cambridge. It had excoriated his soul, but he had on four occasions possessed the body of a woman. He remembered with passionate regret but nevertheless with passion all four occasions of his sinning.

Now, watching Wolsey's fingers, slim but short, and watching her mobile hands, he conjectured from their shape the contours of her covered arms, her shoulders, her breasts, and all the shape of the girl.

These were the images in his mind when at one moment she caught his eye. She looked away. And at this the Puritan heart of Wheaton said to him, 'Desire not her beauty in thine heart, neither let her take thee with her eyelids. Can a man take fire into his bosom and his clothes not be burned? Or can a man go upon coals and his feet not be burned? For because of a woman, a man is brought to a morsel of bread.' Wheaton had never in his life been reduced, by a woman or any other cause, to a morsel of bread. He wanted Wolsey badly. His instinct for her was strong. But his certainty that woman was the seducer, that all women were the descendants of Eve and the primal cause of man's fall, was just as strong. It had been bred into his mind. And just as strong, too, was a sense of his own sin. Puritan Calvinism has its piquancies, and Wheaton, as he watched Wolsey, truly walked on coals, and found it good.

And as for Wolsey? In the chapel a few men had shaken their head at the seduction of Wheaton's promises. The rest had been held in fascination. Wolsey had seen the fascination, and felt it herself. She had known it for what it was, known that it was excessive, and yet still allowed it to take hold of her. She had even mocked at his picking grapes out of the air, but it had made no difference. Her clear mind had observed its own seduction, for a promise, but she was not the less wholehearted for all that.

As they talked of this and that after supper, Wolsey sat straight, with her head high. Her eyes, in conversation, were as rapid in movement as her mind. And if she made a point or gave a reply, there was an animation about her hands that was peculiar to Wolsey. She held them lightly poised before her, one above the other, palms downward, and emphasized her speech with a delicate lateral movement of the hands.

But Brewster had become uneasy. It was he who had

asked the young man to Scrooby. He had known what the young man was after – men and women to follow him across the seas to found a colony in the true faith, and a wife. That was why he had brought Wheaton to Scrooby. He liked the young man. He loved Wolsey, and knew she would make a good wife for any man. He had thought Wheaton worthy of her. But there was not only that. If Brewster told himself the truth, and he was a man of conscience who did tell the truth, his first reason for wishing Wolsey to come to America was that he was going himself and could not easily bear to be parted from her. In his heart he knew that there would be much pain in such a parting. And yet now, when he saw that she would very likely come, and that he would not be parted from her, he was uneasy in his mind. He was assailed with doubts, which came to him at that moment because he saw, all at once, how she had allowed herself to fall under the fascination of the man. He had seen her stretch her hand high at the hall door, and seen Wheaton take it. He feared the power of fascination over the mind and heart of his ward. Emigration and marriage required reasons of more substance. He knew that once Wolsey made up her mind she would not lightly change it, and that whatever she put her heart to, she would carry through. She was in his trust and he was uneasy at what he now saw.

Wheaton had been leaning back, watching Wolsey, and at that moment, he asked her, 'Will you come?'

She smiled straight at him. 'To bluer days and infinitely higher heavens?'

'Will you come to be one of our number?' Wheaton reached across the table and let his hand rest on hers.

'Grapes on great trees?' she said.

She was smiling, but Brewster was now more than uneasy. He did not want her to go. She could marry well enough if she stayed at home in England. He rose and said, 'There is tomorrow. It's late.'

Wheaton asked Wolsey again, 'Will you come?'

Brewster called out her name, 'Wolsey.'

She looked up at him, and in a turmoil of mind he put his

own interests aside, faced the dreadful possibility of their parting, did as his honest heart told him, and warned her.

He said, 'I beseech you, never forget, that when you emigrate, you leave home.' Then he held out his hand for her to take, to leave the table and the room.

She smiled but she did not take his hand. She remained sitting.

Wheaton did not ask her again, but waited. His hand still covered hers. Brewster waited too, in an agony of mind. He could not have said, at that moment, what he really wished her answer to be.

Wolsey raised her downcast eyes and looked full at Wheaton.

'I will go,' she said.

2

THE LAST OF ENGLAND

So they came to the port of Plymouth, to set sail. There were one hundred and two of them, and twenty of those were children. To enlarge the party of sixty or so who had come over from Holland, only forty more were found in England. Wheaton talked to hundreds, persuading and promising, but most were too cautious or afraid. The Virginia Company of London, wanting to populate the new continent with Englishmen, if only to ensure that the Dutch did not have a free run of the place, granted the pilgrims a commission to settle by the mouth of the Hudson, in what was then known as north Virginia. Once the pilgrims secured their land, they did a deal with a small group of merchant venturers to supply them with food, necessaries, and some capital in exchange for a share in the profits of fur trading with the Indians and of the fishing which was rich along the coast to which they were bound. The bargain was struck, the merchants made their first payment, and the pilgrims procured supplies as best they could, buying arms and tools in London, and food and drink in the southern counties. For food, they had biscuit, salt pork, and beef. They bought wheat as it stood in the field, saw it reaped and carted to the miller to grind, and then to the baker to bake until it was hard and would keep. They bought cattle and pigs on the hoof, found butchers to slaughter the animals, and paid salters to pickle and preserve the meat in casks. They bought strong ale from the brewer, and found coopers to put it in casks. They took water from springs, and then needed more casks to hold it. Not new casks, which would warp, or old casks, which would rot. Good casks used once in the liquor trade were best. Not wine casks, which would taint water in a week, but brandy casks well scoured, which, with God's help, would keep their water fresh.

Then, because they expected the Indians to be savage, they hired a professional soldier, Myles Standish, to train them in the use of muskets and cannon, and to be their captain if it should ever come to war. He was not a Puritan, but a good soldier.

They did all this. Then, one afternoon in the late August of 1620, a party of four men and two women looked down from the heights of Plymouth Hoe at a vessel lying tranquilly at her moorings in the sparkling waters of the harbour far below.

Five of the six were pilgrims, and the sixth a stranger. The pilgrims were Brewster, Wheaton, Wolsey, William Bradford, who was next year to become governor of the colony, and Bradford's wife, Dorothy May. The stranger was a broad, short, grizzled man who appeared to be going through a ritual of his own, taking four paces to one side, then four paces back, then pausing, standing with his hands clasped behind his back, balancing on the balls of his feet, and rocking to and fro. His walk was that of a man who had for years paced a quarter deck. He was Captain John Smith, known as John Smith of Hungary, and the pilgrims had retained him to survey the vessel in which they were to sail.

While they waited for him to reach his conclusions, Wolsey and Brewster walked apart from the others, gazing across the expanse of Plymouth Sound. The grassy downs of Jennycliffe lay to the east and the wooded headland of Penlee to the west, and between these two points stretched the wide horizon.

'And beyond that,' said Brewster, 'the English Channel, and then open sea.'

'William,' said Wolsey, 'there is something I have wondered about, but not asked you. That night at supper, when

Mr Wheaton came to Scrooby and asked me to go, you were suddenly apprehensive, and you warned me. You said I must never forget that if I emigrated, I should be leaving home, and all that meant.'

'I remember.'

'But you must have known Mr Wheaton would ask me. I think that was the purpose of our meeting.'

'I brought him there. Yes, it was the purpose.'

'But when he asked me, you were alarmed. You seemed alarmed. It was as if you did not wish me to go. If we were to have been separated, you and I, if I had been going alone, it would have been different. I would have understood. But you were going too. You had told me. If I had not come, then we should have been separated, and you could not have wanted that. So, William, why did you warn me? Why did you not want me to go?'

Brewster had feared this question, because he could not give a wholly truthful reply. Wolsey was in his trust, and she of all people ought to have been able to look to him for an honest answer. But he was also bound by his word to her dead father, who had given her in trust to him, and required him not to reveal to Wolsey certain circumstances of the past which it would be useless to her to know, and which in the religious turmoil of the day might do her harm. The same trust which had bound Brewster to silence had been the cause of her extraordinary upbringing, though how extraordinary it was she hardly knew, having taken most of it for granted. It had all seemed a natural progression. When she was five her father had started her instruction in Latin. By the age of eight she could speak that language without effort, and by the age of ten compose tolerable Latin verses. When she had passed into Brewster's care, and then into that of the canons of York cathedral, her instruction in Greek and Hebrew had been rigorous, in the last years more rigorous than it would have been at the universities of Oxford or Cambridge. She was a splendid Biblical scholar. But the canons of York had taught her far more than that. They were men of the widest civilization, and had imparted to her a disinterested love of knowledge. She was a Christian – as how, being a woman of her time, could she not be? – but it was impossible for her to be a zealot. She had read Calvin's *Institutes*, which next to the Bible was the sacred book of any Puritan. But she had also read the works of the humanist Erasmus, a man of tolerance and wit, neither of which were Calvinistic qualities. Erasmus hoped as much from the mind of man as from the will of God, and that to a Puritan was near-heresy. Wolsey also had an easy acquaintance with the classical writers. In Latin she had read for pleasure the urbane comedies of Terence and the odes of Horace, in Greek the lyrics of Sappho and the philosophy of Aristotle. She could besides read Italian and French. Her father had wanted a son, whom he would have educated to be a priest. A daughter could not be a priest, but he had given her all he had to give, which was his learning. Brewster, and then the canons, were delighted by her evident capacities and had continued her father's work. Had she been a man, it would have been the education of a boy destined for the priesthood, and a boy in whom great abilities had been seen early and assiduously cultivated. In a woman, it would have been the education of a princess, to fit her for affairs of state, or at least of an earl's daughter. She was not a princess, or the daughter of an earl, but the daughter of a parish priest, though that again was not quite the whole truth. But anyway, Brewster had hesitated at Scrooby not only because he saw her fascination with Wheaton, which he feared as he would have feared and mistrusted any fascination, but also because he was afraid that by letting her cross an ocean to unknown hardship he would be wasting her accomplishments and failing in his trust. He should have seen all these things before, but they had come to him in their full force only at that moment at supper.

She broke into his thoughts. 'You do not answer me,' she said.

'Why did I warn you? Wolsey, because it might have been simple selfishness in me to want you to come, who are very dear to me. And because you could marry well at home. For you *are* leaving home.'

'Do you think I do not know I am leaving home? Yesterday we sat together in the garden of the house in New Street, where we are staying. You remember?'

He nodded. It was a fine, timbered house, newly built with the spoils of Plymouth privateering in West Indies waters.

'We sat in the sun by a fig tree, and then moved for shade under a palm which they say Drake brought home from a voyage forty years ago. And there was honeysuckle, too. I asked myself when I should see another fig tree, or another garden such as that. And I heard the bustle of the people in the street outside, and knew we were going where there would be no one but ourselves, and nothing but what we took with us. I knew it was the last of so much.'

Brewster put his hand on her shoulder.

'And last night, when I could not sleep, I lay in a carved oak bed, and I do not expect to see the like of it where we are going. At dawn the light came in through those mullioned windows, so much light, and I know that there will be no such wide windows where we are going. But most of all it was the sound of the people. It is the last of that. It is the last of so much. The last of England. And I looked at you in the garden, and I knew those same thoughts were in your head, because I know you.'

'It is true,' said Brewster. He had been abroad before, abroad for years at a time, but only in Holland, which was a day's sailing. Now that he was leaving for a new continent, and leaving irrevocably, his early days at the university, and then his life at court, all long ago left behind, had come crowding back into his mind again.

'And over there,' he said, gesturing behind them. 'Look. It is the last of all that too.' From the Hoe, if they looked southwards and westwards, they had a high view of the sea. If they turned round and looked behind them, inland, they were as high above the lush Devon valleys as they were above the sea. They could see for miles.

'The last of that,' he said.

'And that's a grief,' she said. 'But yesterday I went to the church in the town. The verger told me the people were in that church the day Drake came back from round the world, with his palm tree I suppose, and how all the people rushed down to the barbican when his sails were sighted. And the verger showed me a scratching in the wall of the church, inside. It was the device Drake took for his coat of arms afterwards. The verger said Drake scratched it himself. There is a ship, and a world, and a cord coming from the prow of the ship and encircling the world, and then rising up into what the verger called the hand of Providence. That was a great venture. So is ours a venture, perhaps.'

These words were a consolation to Brewster. He was delighted she was coming, but had still not been certain that was the right course for her. Now he was comforted that she should speak of a great venture, and reassured that she had made the right decision after all, for she was a woman fit for a venture. Her theology, her Latin, her Greek, her Hebrew, her Italian and French, were fine things, granted – at a court. But far above that, it was the spirited mind these things had helped form which was her strength, that and her heart. She had a breadth of sense, will, wit, and pure strong-mindedness which could carry through a great venture. The pilgrims were brave but narrow. Narrowness of purpose would for many years be necessary to their survival. But they also had a narrowness of perception which Brewster, old courtier, saw only too clearly, a narrowness he hoped Wolsey's generosity of mind would help offset. Besides, she was a golden, loving woman. By letting her come to New England, he would be very well carrying out the spirit of her father's trust. She would be one of the strengths of the party.

He knew that another strength would be William Bradford, whom he watched as he and Wolsey moved back to join the others. Bradford was a strong, blunt man of thirty, who had started from nothing, and early left England for Holland, and prospered there, but had thrown his prosperity away to join them here at Plymouth and sail with them. He was with his wife, Dorothy May, a wistful, slight creature, who stood beside him now. They were a strangely assorted couple, but very close. Bradford was given to impatience, though never with his wife. But he was impatient now with Captain Smith who, he thought, had been viewing the ship long enough.

So Bradford spoke up for them all. 'You have seen her now, sir.'

'Seen her and surveyed her,' said the old captain. 'I see her now. It is a custom of mine to want to view a ship from far off, or from a height, to see how she rides in the water. How she holds herself. I've already been on board and surveyed her this morning. Masts, spars, timbers, tackle, spread of sail. I know her master and I've seen her crew.'

'And, sir?' Again it was Bradford who spoke for the pilgrims.

'The vessel is sound, tight, fit. Fit for the passage, though it's a late passage, late in the year.'

'And the men?'

'Most of them good. For the rest, some dive-sweepings among them.'

Bradford raised his eyebrows.

'There always are a few,' said Smith, 'to make up the numbers. I've made six passages to Virginia, with good ships, do you see, but always had to take my share of dive-sweepings. Nothing to fear, sir. A good captain beats them into shape.'

Smith looked down again at the vessel, remembering, regretting, wanting back, vessels of his own that he no longer had. He had spent a life of adventure. He was self-styled Smith of Hungary because he had either subdued Hungary while leading a holy crusade against the Turks, or had taken a Hungarian princess for his mistress, again in the course of a crusade. Neither of these stories was absolutely believed, but he had told both, many times. He had been soldier, sailor, and pirate. His use to the pilgrims was that he had made passages to America. Not six, as he said, but four, and two of those had ended in shipwreck so that he was now a Jonah to whom no one would give a ship to command. But his knowledge of the eastern coast of the new continent was never doubted. He certainly knew Virginia, north and south. Another of his titles was Admiral of New England. And whether or not he was ever really an admiral, he had certainly invented the very name New England, having coined it four years before, in 1616. For his knowledge and reputation, he was often retained by merchants and explorers, to give advice. This was why the pilgrims had gone to him.

'And the provisioning of the vessel?' asked Bradford. 'Are we well victualled? Are the casks sound?'

'You have enough,' said Smith. 'I mean enough for the passage. Whether enough for a plantation I cannot say. I have seen plantations starve.' So he had, and in Virginia, too.

Wheaton spoke up. He had made his one passage to America under Smith and had suggested his name as a man whose advice should be asked. He said, 'We know there will be hardships. But we are God's pilgrims.' As if to say there could be no doubt of *their* success in planting a colony.

'Ha,' said Smith. 'And your faith will keep you whole? But you must eat before you can pray. You have seed corn and barley, but I cannot say what crops you will raise. But any man can fish in those waters. All you need for that is nets, hooks, lines, knives, and salt to preserve what you catch. And take some Irish rugs, coarse clothes, hatchets, glass beads, and such trash, to trade with the savages.'

Smith wanted a last look over the ship, and no doubt a last drink with the captain, so they walked down the steep green slope to the barbican, passing through crowds of pilgrims gathered on the quays, and taking a cutter to the anchored vessel. Most of the emigrants had not yet boarded, but a dozen or so were on deck, gathered round one of their number who had laid on a capstan a large quarto Geneva Bible, the Bible translated in Geneva into English. The book was open at the beginning of the New

Testament, to which the frontispiece was a map of the Holy Land, covering an entire page. In the Mediterranean Sea, four ships in full sail approached a prosperous coast, along which, from west to east, stretched the castled cities of Gaza, Caesarea, Carmel, Tyre, and Sidon. Inland, the River Jordan was depicted with fishing boats on its waters. Near Jericho, which was represented by two towers and a spire, some species of cattle grazed. North of Nazareth and south of Bethlehem, forests flourished, represented by groups of English deciduous trees. In the Arabian desert, two wolves prowled. At Carmel, three men ran to join a crowd assembled near the city – Elijah gathering all the people of Israel to hear him.

The pilgrims' lips moved as they soundlessly formed the names of cities they recognized. A boy traced with his finger the southern course of the Jordan as it flowed into the salt sea. A young woman pointed to fish that swam near the ships. All thought of themselves as new Israelites being led into a new Canaan, and saw in a map of the Holy Land an almost literal promise of their new America.

Smith walked across to the capstan, looked down at the map, up into the earnest faces of those gazing at it, and then down again. He saw that the very longitude and latitude of the towns were marked – Bethlehem 65° 55′ East and 31° 51′ North, Jerusalem 66° 00′ East and 31° 55′ North.

He turned to Wheaton. 'Navigating, they are, the lot of them, setting their course to the coasts of Salvation. And it's a coastline they know better than that of their own country, all of them.'

Wheaton did not reply. Wolsey said, 'Captain Smith is right, though. They *are* navigating towards your Promised Lands, your bluer skies, your infinite heavens.'

Wheaton answered, '*Their* promised lands.'

Smith shrugged. 'Theirs if you like to say so. But that chart there – those concoctions of an engraver's fancy, I mean those ships, those rivers and forests and towns, all drawn with the strokes of an artful pen – that chart is the coastline of their imaginings. When they find the real coast, after they have crossed the sea, I hope they will not think it should have been drawn rockier, and more dangerous.'

Wheaton bowed and turned away. Smith took a glass of rum with Captain Jones, the master who was to take the ship to God's country. They were on easy terms. Jones, knowing the command was his, knowing that Smith would never get another, and knowing too that his vessel was well found, did not grudge old Smith's earning a few guineas prowling round the decks, pressing his thumb into a caulked seam, or sniffing a few barrels of drinking water. Let the old man do that, and write books on his marvellous travels. Let him dedicate them to the Right Honourable and Most Generous Lords of His Majesty King James's Privy Council, as he had; or to the ancient Duchess of Richmond, lady-in-waiting to a long-dead queen. Books were now all that was left to Smith. The generous Lords of the Privy Council gave him nothing for his dedications. The duchess sent twenty guineas. But Jones was still master of a ship; he was what Smith once was and never again would be. So they were on easy terms.

'You see her well found, Admiral?' asked Jones.

'Well found, Captain,' said Smith, and launched into the tale of a grizzly bear long ago overpowered by himself on the Scots island of Benbecula. By Smith's lights, a modest yarn.

Wolsey and Dorothy May were standing on deck, Dorothy gazing in awe at the sailors shinning up the mainmast, seventy feet above them. 'It is a Big Ship,' she said. 'A Big Ship that is to carry us.' But as she said this a slight breeze ruffled the calm waters of the harbour, the ship rolled, and Dorothy caught at Wolsey's arm.

Smith had watched the two women together on the Hoe, as they descended to the quay, and on board. Wolsey was much the younger, and strong. Dorothy was slight. Even walking down the hill she had stumbled once, and the walk had made her breathless. Looking down at the ship from the Hoe, Smith had remembered other ships, his own ships. Watching Wolsey he had remembered other women, his women, and two in special, whose memory lay deep in his affections. Women who had waited for him. Oh, his Mary and his Rachel, long ago.

The ship rolled again, hardly a roll yet, more a shiver of the deck, an almost imperceptible movement, but Dorothy felt it and needed to walk a few paces to steady herself. Smith had seen enough fear in his life, and knew the woman was afraid – of the sea, the ship, the passage, the plantation, the promised lands.

As for Wolsey, she was still gazing around and aloft at the ship, at the high masts and yards whose names she was beginning to learn. The bowsprit and spritsail yard, the foremast and foreyard, the fore-topmast, the main mast, the mizzen mast. As she gazed she saw in her mind's eye the canvas spreading on those masts and yards, clothing the ship. She imagined the foretopgallants filled with a fortunate wind, carrying them to their new land. When she had first heard Wheaton speak at Scrooby, she had smiled at the extravagance of his language. But now, on board ship, she quickened to the spirit of the venture. She looked aft at the master's cabin, and saw above its door the ship's emblem, the white May-flower.

Smith watched Wolsey, and then called gently to her. She heard and came over to him. He had never met her before that day, but he knew her instantly for what she was. He was a creature of habitual resource recognizing the same spirit in another.

'Ma'am,' he said. She met his sailor's blue eyes, and followed his glance to the little group of pilgrims. His glance included not only Dorothy May and the group round the Bible, but also, it seemed to her, Wheaton, even him.

He said, 'The lady, your companion, feels the motion of the ship already.'

She nodded. 'But she says it is a Big Ship.'

'Ah. Ma'am, you will have a hundred souls and more in this vessel. I know that ocean. Your landsman, before he has been a week at sea, is an altered man. I have often seen it. How could it be otherwise? I have never seen it otherwise. The sea can drown a man's spirit. You will see the change.

Don't fear it too greatly, but I am telling you so that you will know, when you see it. Men recover and get their spirit back. Most recover.'

Wolsey thanked him and offered him her hand, and then John Smith of Hungary, Admiral of New England, accepted his fee from Brewster and left the vessel. The pilgrims sailed next day.

3

THE CROWN OF THORNS

Wolsey awoke from a dream of sweet meadows, of the light and warmth of the sun. It was a dream of land, a dream of being on land, a dream sustained through the first few moments of her consciousness until a roll of the ship threw her against the timber sides, and she knew where she was. There was no warm sun, only the chill darkness of the ship. There was no light, only the green gleam of a feeble lantern in the whole 'tween decks. The air was not sweet; one hundred souls lay in the fetor of the 'tween decks, and most were seasick. They had been three weeks at sea, and already it was a long imprisonment. Wolsey raised herself on one elbow, and as she did her cheek brushed against the ship's side. The timbers were running with slime, and outside, through only two inches of timber, was the tormenting Atlantic. She looked down the whole length of the ship, and could dimly make out the rows of figures, lying under sodden, ragged covers of coarse cloth, huddled against each other for warmth.

Another roll threw her against her companion, to her right. It was Dorothy May, who had lain awake all night.

The woman put out a hand and Wolsey took it.

'You slept,' said Dorothy May. 'For two hours. Three. You slept.'

Wolsey said, 'I dreamed of land.'

'If you had known it would come to this, you never would have left land, would you? But you was not afraid, was you

Wolsey? I was afraid. But my fears was small to what it really is.'

Dorothy May lifted her head too, surveying the rows of pilgrims. The men were forward, the women aft. Even the married people were separated. They lay on sodden straw, in shoddy bunks run up by the ship's carpenters out of old planks. Each bunk was six feet by six feet, and four souls lay side by side in each.

Dorothy May said, "Think, Wolsey. We have not more room than we shall have in our coffins. No, not so much. And there's Mr Wheaton, there for'ard, doing what he can for some poor sick man.'

'He would not like to hear talk of coffins.'

'Oh, he would chide me. But it's my way of speaking. It just came to me. I would not say it to him, though it do look like coffins. I would not say it to William neither. William has been very bad with the sea, and Mr Wheaton has been up most of the night with him.'

Wolsey knew this was likely. William Bradford, a sturdy man, had been prostrated by the sea. So had Myles Standish, their chief soldier. So had Brewster. But Wheaton, almost alone of all the men, had not been seasick. Through Wolsey's head had run again and again, in their time on the ocean, Smith's warning to her at Plymouth: 'Before a man has been a week at sea, he is an altered man.' She had seen this was true. And yet Wheaton had resisted the sea, and had not been seasick. She did not know why this surprised her, but it did. She had thought that Captain Smith, when he had uttered those words on the deck of the big ship as she lay tranquilly at Plymouth, had glanced not only at the group of pilgrims so trustfully gathered around the map of the Holy Land, but also at Francis Wheaton. She thought he had included Francis in his glance. But Wheaton had proved strong.

She rose, and walked the length of the ship towards him, treading carefully between huddled pilgrims, pausing now and again to brace herself against the roll and pitch of the vessel.

Wheaton was kneeling by Brewster, encouraging him to take sips of small beer. Wolsey's old mentor glanced up at her weakly, and then Francis Wheaton noticed her and greeted her.

'I am told,' murmured Brewster, 'that the sea is quieter today. I cannot say I feel it to be quieter, but Francis tells me it is.'

'So we shall light a fire today?' asked Wolsey.

Wheaton held out his hands wide. 'That's as God wills it.'

'But you have asked the captain?' she said.

'The captain sleeps well through the worst of it. But before dawn, half an hour ago, I asked the mate. He told us to hope, but not to hope with too great expectation. I told him I would pray. "But neither pray," said he, "with too great expectation." He thinks the sea may get up later.'

Wolsey said nothing. Since they left Plymouth they had never been able to light a fire, because the movement of the ship would scatter the live coals. Without a fire they could not make even soup to cheer stomachs that had eaten no hot food for three weeks. Nor could they dry their drenched clothes and sodden bedcovers. And a fire would purify the air, besides. But they knew there would probably be no fire today.

'How are the women?' asked Wheaton.

'I think better than the men,' she told him.

He nodded. Throughout the passage the women had been better sailors, and the captain and mate, observing this, had said it was generally so.

The mate was right. There was no fire lit that day, but at about noon the sea quietened for a while. The main hatch was unbattened because the day was fair, though the mate said it would be fair only for a while, until squalls overtook them again. As many as could walk or crawl from their bunks gathered to look up through the open hatch. They looked upwards and saw the masts, the rigging, the sails, the clouds, and the sky. They longed for the sky, for a patch of blue. All the time they longed for light. At night there were no candles, only the lantern with its eerie green light, and that often flickered out and failed. And by day there was little more light either, only when the hatch was unbattened, but that was rare. So at noon that day they clustered round to gaze at the high sun, to see the sky and feel the warmth. They no longer looked at themselves at all, filthy wretches, but at the sun. Soon the wind rose, and the sea broke over the bulwarks and spilled into the 'tween decks, and they closed the hatch again. When they did, one man wept aloud for the loss of the sky.

Then again it was Wheaton who comforted them, by making a virtue out of the darkness which oppressed them all. He stood and addressed them, and they listened.

'I share your tears,' he said, 'but that's a confession. It's a confession of a lust of the flesh, the lust of the eyes. The eyes love beautiful shapes, and delight in colours. Light is the prince of colours. Light is Satan, showing us the glories of the earth, to tempt us. Even when for a moment my heart is pure and unsinful, light slides up to me and forces to my consciousness the seduction of shapes, and colours, and rich clothes. For men there is a seduction in the sight of a woman, for women in the sight of a man. But the love of mere things must not seize my soul. It is only for God to do that. I should rejoice not in the *things*, but only that God has created them, and in God Himself.'

The man who had wept said, 'But to lose sight of the sun itself?'

And another man exclaimed, 'Yes, sir, to lose sight even of the sun, which is God's sun?'

To which Wheaton replied, 'The sun is God's indeed, and we should rejoice in that. But to rejoice in the sun itself is sinful, as it was sinful in former days for the pagan to worship it. We should rejoice only that the sun is God's, and that He made it.'

'But how rejoice in darkness?' asked a voice.

'We should rejoice. This is a darkness we must endure. But we should also rejoice because it takes away from us the occasion of sinning. In the dark we cannot be taken unawares by light that slides into our eyes and brings before us objects of lust. You cry because you cannot see the sun. But the sun does not vanish because you cannot see it. It remains there, and it remains the work of God. We may rejoice in this knowledge, and, at the same time, be saved by darkness from the sin of delighting in the sun for itself.'

They believed him and were comforted, and afterwards did not rail against the dark. Wolsey, listening, thought Wheaton's theology dubious, but was glad he comforted the people.

So far their misery had been in fair weather, their dreadful seasickness in what a sailor calls light airs and moderate seas. Then came a storm, but before the storm the hand of God showed itself. This was just as well, since the sailors were beginning to be openly scornful of the pilgrims. When the pilgrims first came on board at Plymouth, and while the vessel remained in harbour before setting sail, services were held on the main deck at which it was made clear that these men and women regarded themselves as God's chosen. They openly called themselves saints. This did not at first excite derision among the crew. The pilgrims' sanctity, or at least their probity, was obvious. They were also the charterers of the vessel, and indirectly paying the crew's wages. And a few of them had evident authority. They had hired Captain John Smith of Hungary, no less, to survey their provisions and the ship, and Smith, though no man would willingly sail under him now, still had a great reputation as a fearless navigator and explorer, and a man who had taken as mistress a princess, or was it queen, of Hungary. And Smith had told the crew, some of whom he knew from old times, that Mr Brewster was none other than Mr Secretary Brewster, a courtier, a man of the court, a gentleman who as a very young man had been sent by the old queen, Elizabeth, to deliver, as Smith had hinted, the death warrant of another queen, who could only have been Mary, Queen of Scots. This unlikely story excited awe, as talk of queens and courtiers and death will among sailors or any other men.

One day, when the weather was fine enough for the

strongest to go on deck, the mate approached Wolsey as she was washing her face in a bucket of salt water.

'Ma'am,' he said, 'I beg your pardon to come on you now, but you know Mr Brewster, I believe.'

She dried the water from her face with a coarse towel, and said she did.

'And it be true, ma'am, that he was Mr Secretary Brewster, in the old queen's time?'

She said it was.

'And took the death warrant for Mary the queen to be beheaded?'

'Mr Mate, you must ask him that yourself, when he is recovered.'

She knew that the story was true, and that her mentor, as a young man down from Cambridge, had served Mr Secretary Davison, who was commanded by Elizabeth to convey Mary's death warrant to the prison governor. She knew too that in disgust Davison had tossed it to his assistant, Brewster, who had delivered it. It had been his duty. He had told Wolsey once and never mentioned it again. To others, he never spoke of it. Whether because he regarded it as disgraceful, no one knew. It had been his duty.

But the mate, hearing Wolsey confirm at least that Brewster had once been Mr Secretary Brewster, took the rest for granted, knuckled his forehead to Wolsey, and retired to convey this important matter to the captain.

The exchange was overheard by several lounging sailors, whose dwindling respect for the pilgrims was thus preserved for a little while longer. But it could not last. The miserable condition of the pilgrims became daily more evident. The sailors were in their element, the sea. The pilgrims were in the 'tween decks, a filthy, vomiting rabble.

'Saints they may be,' said one sailor, 'and among them a fine courtly man like Mr Secretary Brewster. But where's your Mr Secretary now? Spewing up like all the others.'

'And I've not noticed that the saints' slop pails smell sweeter than any others,' said a second.

These were common sailors, decent men without malice,

but men who could now smell very well that there was no scent of the court about the 'tween decks.

But there was a third sailor, called Richard Roberts, who was one of the dive-sweepings signed on at Plymouth to make up the numbers, and he took it on himself to taunt the pilgrims whenever they came up on deck, damning them and God, confident that he was impressing his colleagues with his own boldness.

One day Mary Mullins, a servant girl, brought on deck a canvas sack she was sewing.

'A shroud for a saint,' said Roberts.

The girl did not reply.

'Shall I tell you then,' he said, 'how we wind them up in a shroud, dead men, when they're gone, and weight them with a shot at the tail of the shroud?'

The girl continued sewing.

'Shall I tell you then? A shot at the tail of the sewn canvas, to take you to the depths, nearer the devil? On the deep sea bed? Shall I see you to your bed, Mary Mullins, shall I lay you there? You're a poor thing, Mary. Will that saintly lot press you to a bed? Not you, Mary, even if the men had spirit for it, groaning as they all are. But I'll see you to your bed, Mary, the deep sea bed, sewn tight.'

The girl tried to escape below, but he held her wrist.

'Mary, Mary, I'll see half of this cargo of saints to their rest before we make land, and some of you rotten before you're dead, and the lucky ones dying last. You ask me for why they'll be the luckiest that die last?'

She had not asked. She bowed her head.

'They'll be the luckiest because there aren't shrouds enough for all, so the last ones will be pitched overboard naked, where they will float, not sink, Mary. And they that float will be nearer to heaven.'

For days the sailor baited the woman, until he began to sicken himself. The first day he was subdued, and seasick. The second, he was seized with colic pains. The third, he lay inert, breathing shallowly. The fourth day he died.

Then, while the crew still gaped at the man, and before

the captain could order his burial, Dorothy May took from Mary Mullins the half-sewn canvas sack and came on deck.

'See,' she said, standing over the body, 'see the tints of green and blue and orange creep over his face. That's him that taunted Mary, and see him now. See, his eyes are open yet, but now they're yellow.'

She closed his eyes with her hands, and then, summoning two sailors, directed them to heave the stiffening body into the canvas sack, told them to weight it with lead, and then began to close it, sewing diligently. By then half the crew were watching, and the news had spread among the pilgrims. Bradford and Brewster were still too weak to climb on deck, and when Wheaton was about to go, Wolsey restrained him.

'I know her,' she said, and went herself.

On deck she knelt by Dorothy's side. 'What is it you're doing? Leave it, Dorothy. Leave it to the sailors.'

'Oh no, Wolsey,' said the woman. 'It is only fitting. He taunted Mary, you see, and said it was a shroud. Now it is a shroud for him.'

'Pray for the man, Dorothy, and leave him.'

'I do pray for him. Oh, Wolsey, this is not done as a revenge. You wouldn't think that of me? But I'll sew him up so that he'll be safe in the dark, as Mr Wheaton said. See? A man can see no sin in the dark. He'll be free from sin, all sewed up.'

Dorothy May was nearly finished so Wolsey did not argue with her. The sack was closed as a shroud, the men took the body to the rail, watched by the entire, silent crew. Then, on the down-roll of the ship, they slipped Richard Roberts overboard. Even the captain said it was the hand of God. The saints were afterwards held in fear and respect.

Then the storm came. It took three days to blow up. They thought their passage before had been stormy, but it was nothing to this. Now they could not hear themselves talk for the wind in the rigging, the thunder of the rain on the deck above, the pounding of the seas on the hull, and the straining of the timbers. The last was the greatest terror. The pilgrims had grown used to the sounds of the sea, and had come no longer to hear the creaking of the ship. But now the timbers groaned. The waves, as they pounded against the hull, stunned the pilgrims, making them deaf. Brewster and Bradford sent for Captain Jones.

'Can she stand this wracking?' asked Brewster.

'She has done,' said Jones. 'Many times. Nothing has sprung.'

Nothing had, though that night, with a wrenching crack, a mizzen spar was torn from its mast. Deafened as they were in the 'tween decks, they heard the crash and fall, and thought a mast had gone, but the bitterly cold morning showed the masts still in place, though bare of all sail, and the sailors hacking tangled cording from the deck and throwing overboard the uselessly shattered spar so that it should not thrash around in the gale and smash into the superstructure.

In the great gale, the pilgrims changed. Before, they had feared seasickness and wished for death. Now they feared death and wished for life. The ship stood vertically on her stern, then dived into the succeeding trough. Barrels of salt pork broke loose from the tetherings in the hold, and smashed against each other and the hull, spilling and ruining in one hour what was intended for a month's supply. In the 'tween decks a water cask careered sheer into the mainmast, did not shatter even at this impact, but was then, with a sudden dropping of the vessel, hurled upwards, rising as if of its own will, and crashing against the deck above. The hoops sundered, the staves split, the barrel exploded, and a week's drinking water was lost.

Wolsey, clinging to a stanchion, watched helplessly as the clear water sluiced across the green deck, and then let her head fall. Throughout the passage she had cheered the other women, but now she was near despair. For the first time the utter wretchedness of their condition pressed heavily on her mind. She closed her eyes. Then she felt a strong arm around her shoulders. It was Wheaton. She lifted her eyes and saw it was him.

'Francis,' she said. 'It is too much.'

He said nothing but held her closely to him. She let her head rest on his shoulder. And so they stood, observed by very few, because most of the others were too terrified to be conscious of anything but their own fear. It was the first time she had called him Francis. It was the first time he had embraced her.

Then came the moment that everyone on board remembered; the men and women because they thought their death had come, the children, too innocent to be afraid of death, because of the awesomeness of the moment itself. It was this.

After more than a month of perpetual movement, the ship – as a child was to say fifty years later when he was an old man – the ship just stopped. She rose on the crest of a great wave higher than her mainmast, and then hung still. Had the fury of the storm been less great, had the seas been less violently in motion, she would have stayed there one second longer and broken her back. But the wave that lifted her was instantly gone, and as it went the ship hung still in clean mid-air. It could not have been for more than the fragment of a second, but the ship hung still, quivering, and then fell vertically into the trough. That was what they remembered, the moment of suspension and the quivering. When she fell she was swamped by the following seas, from which she slowly lifted, shaking herself.

Throughout this brief, interminable moment, Wolsey and Wheaton clung together. Both shared, as if their bodies were one, the quiver of the ship, and the long stillness, and the fall. And as the ship lifted, both were drenched as the invading seawater ran down their clasped figures.

The force of the rise, the force of the fall, united them and held them together. They could not have separated had they wished, and they did not wish. Wolsey surrendered herself to the rise, the fall, and to Wheaton's arms, and wept unashamedly.

Then he said, 'Wolsey, Wolsey,' and unclasped her arms from his. She did not smile. A smile could not exist at so awful a moment, but she laughed aloud, and he kissed her forehead and then left her, to go about the saving of the ship, if it could be saved.

There was much to do. The fall had sprung her timbers. She drove helplessly before the wind. The sea gushed in through planks that were no longer caulked, and poured through the deck above.

As the water rushed into their eyes and mouths the pilgrims cried, 'We are drowning.' And they would have drowned, but the wind fell, and the sea abated, and in less than an hour they were almost in a calm. Captain Jones saw the hand of God in that too. And so, before he summoned his own sailors and carpenters, he invited the pilgrim leaders to his cabin and asked them what to do. It was Brewster and Bradford, stunned and ill though they were, who told him to call the carpenter and his mate, to bring with them their nails, clinches, leather, and pitch, to caulk, bream, and staunch the leaks. In her hull, under the waterline, the ship was still strong and firm. From her hold and 'tween decks the water could be pumped, and the crew was put to it. Where the deck timbers were sprung they were caulked afresh. The greatest damage was what no one had seen before. The main beam, which supported the mainmast as it passed through the 'tween decks, was buckled. The carpenters had no timber strong enough to shore it up, but Brewster had an iron screw, four feet long, which he had brought out of Holland with him and stowed in the hold. It was screwed into the beam, which with a timber post under it was then made sure and safe. It was the screw of a printing press. So the ship was saved, but the beginning of printing in New England was put back ten years.

Then it was a more prosperous voyage. It was now very late in the season, and growing colder, but in calmer seas they were able to light fires and cook, and eat their first hot food for six weeks, a stew of salt beef. Seasickness left them. The pilgrims swabbed and holystoned the deck, and dried their clothing. The fire freshened and warmed the air. They would be wet again, and cold, but for the moment they were recovering and able to rest.

Except for Dorothy May. Bradford comforted his wife, but she could not talk to him, and gazed at him in silence. Whenever the hatches were opened, she cringed in the farthest, darkest part of the 'tween decks. She would not warm herself by the fire. Wolsey went to her again.

'You will not come to the fire?'

'Oh, no. See how it flickers.'

'Flickers?'

Dorothy May was sitting hunched, averting her eyes from the direction of the fire. She looked up at Wolsey as if puzzled not to be understood, as if the meaning of her words was evident and plain, and said again, 'Flickers, yes. See how it flickers.'

'Yes?'

'See how it shapes us all.'

The flames were illuminating the faces of the men and women, catching the colours of their clothes, and casting shadows on the timbers. Wolsey thought it was the fantastic shadows of which the woman was afraid. But it was not. Wolsey learned this when the after hatch was opened, almost above them, for a sailor to hand in a bucket of seawater for washing, and Dorothy May recoiled from the light and covered her eyes with both arms.

Wolsey stroked her hair, and the woman spoke calmly.

'See, light is a great prince, but a prince come to tempt us and show us the way to sin. Mr Wheaton, he said so. You remember, Wolsey. You remember. Mr Wheaton said so. And you remember I sewed up the sailor, to save him from the light. Light is the way to sin, and sinning is damnation, and we must rejoice in God's darkness.'

She said this too as if it were the most reasonable thing in the world.

Wolsey tried, saying, 'But Mr Wheaton said that to comfort us in the darkness, when darkness was all we had.'

'Yes,' said the woman, looking Wolsey candidly in the eyes. 'Yes. He did comfort us. We should love the darkness. I do love the darkness. Darkness can't show me sin. No occasion of sin. And, Wolsey, will you pray with me?'

Wolsey and Dorothy May said the Lord's Prayer together. After they said Amen, Dorothy May added one sentence of her own, praising God for the dark. She slept and Wolsey left her.

At daybreak on November 19 they made the landfall. It was Cape Cod. All that could walk came on deck and the few that could not were carried. There was great rejoicing. Not for two months had more than a few ever been on deck in the open air together, and they greeted each other like long lost friends and brothers. But in the captain's cabin there was a matter to be resolved.

Captain Jones spread out on his table the only chart they had of that coast, the one made by Captain John Smith of Hungary on his voyage of four years before. The gift of his map was the second service of John Smith to the pilgrims. As he had mapped the coast, he had given to places, where no town or village or single hut existed, the names of Oxford, London, Falmouth, Bristol, Hull, Ipswich, and Norwich. Near Ipswich he had drawn a prancing panther, to indicate wild beasts. He had embellished the chart with a small representation of the arms of England, and with a large portrait of himself, to indicate the only discoverer of all these lands.

'There,' said the captain, pointing out their landfall on the chart.

'Cape Cod,' said Brewster. 'Then...'

'Then,' said Bradford, 'we are too far north. Our patent is for north Virginia, and our promise was to settle the mouth of the Hudson River.'

'The Hudson is far south,' said Jones, 'and the season too late.'

Wheaton agreed. 'It is too far south to go. The year is far advanced. And this is the coast I have seen and know.'

'But it is not our patent,' said Brewster. '*That* is for the Hudson.'

So they made for the Hudson. All day they beat south, down the length of the Cape, against a headwind. The afternoon found them perilously close to shoals. The pilgrims were muttering and their leaders undecided, but Jones would not risk his ship further. In the late afternoon they turned north and changed the course of history. It was not the mouth of the Hudson they settled. They did not colonize Long Island as they might, or the island known as Manhattan, as they might, but turned north again, and came to anchor for a while in the harbour which is sheltered by the north-east hook of Cape Cod. It had been a passage of sixty-five days and nights.

There had been no contagion, said the captain. No ship's fever.

Bradford agreed. 'But one of your sailors is dead,' he said.

'A profane man,' said the captain. 'The hand of God. That apart, she has been a sweet ship.'

'Sweet!' said Bradford, remembering the stench and effluvia.

'Why, sir, yes, sweet. I told you when we first met, when you chartered her, that she had done the ocean passage before, but had mainly been in the wine trade to Rochelle, in France?'

Bradford said he remembered that.

'Then, sir, she is sweet because the ullage in her bilge is brandy, or was brandy once, which is a marvellous disinfector of your ship, a great sweetener. Sir, it is *proved*. Your people lived.'

And Wheaton said, 'Amen.'

As they lay at anchor, not having decided where to land and make their settlement, everyone came on deck again to see the land. The last to come up was Dorothy May, when the light was almost gone. She barely glanced at the land, which was now no more than a shadowy shore, but saw as if for the first time the ship's emblem, above the entrance to the captain's cabin. It was a flower of five petals, white but dashed over with purple.

She said, 'They grow in the hedges everywhere, great shrubs, the height of a pear tree. I have seen them.'

'And in woods,' said Wolsey. 'Mr Wheaton has told me

they grow not only by the highways at home in England, but in the woods here.'

'To the height of a pear tree,' said Dorothy May, 'and the flowers are of a pleasant sweet smell, but the branches of the tree are cruel, with long, sharp thorns. It is the sign of the Crown of Thorns.'

'The May-flower,' said Wolsey, 'no more.'

'But cruel thorns, of which they made the Crown of Thorns, for Jesus Christ our Lord.'

The two women went below. The men had caught and cooked some fish, the first fresh food for more than two months. The pilgrims were cold, but full of hope for the next day. Dorothy May, eating well, talked about the future into which God would receive them. She would not take from her eyes the scarf she had habitually worn for the previous few weeks to keep the lustful light from her eyes. She explained, to those who asked, that she wore it because the saltiness of the sea on the long passage had affected her eyes. Brewster, who knew some medicine, had examined her, but found no inflammation which could not have been caused by weeping. Wolsey had later gone to Brewster and told him the true cause. He said that was something only time would cure. She told no one else, not Wheaton, not even Dorothy's husband, and Dorothy herself said nothing to anyone but Wolsey.

That night, as they lay at their moorings in the harbour, Dorothy May rose and went on deck. Wolsey heard her go, but did not follow. It was night, and it was not darkness that held any fears for the poor woman.

But it was a moonlit night. Dorothy May raised her scarf. She gazed at the shoreline of the new land showing silver, then across the deck planking, which shone white from the scouring of the seas, and then up at the white emblem of the ship over the captain's door, the white flower dashed with purple, the flower of the Crown of Thorns. She looked out across the sound where the moon streamed over the water. More light. Then she looked straight down from the ship's side where the water, in the shadow of the hull, was black.

Shaking her head to free herself of the scarf, she steadily approached the midships waist-ladder of the vessel, which the men had left over the side when they returned from fishing, and, taking hold of it, let herself slowly down into the welcoming water, and there was not a sound.

Only the scarf was found next morning. It was a terrible blow to Bradford, that the hand of God should have taken his wife, and taken her before she could even set foot on the new country they had travelled so far to reach. Wolsey wept that she had not followed Dorothy May when she heard her go on deck. It was believed to be an accident, and the accident was lamented and the woman mourned, but there was work to do. Taking the ship's boat, the men prospected, skirmished with the Indians, survived the near-wreck of their little shallop, and found a pleasant place which offered spring water, fertile land to grow crops, and a hill to build a fort. On Captain John Smith's map, made four years before, the place already appeared, just south of Oxford, and he had named it Plymouth.

From Plymouth in old England they had come to Plymouth in the new. The evening after they brought the big ship round to that part of the coast, and anchored offshore, Wolsey and Francis Wheaton stood together on deck scanning the land which would be theirs.

'On the ship,' she said, 'in that waste of water, I dreamed of land. It was a dream of sweet, green, light country. Oh, Francis, above all it was a dream of land.'

'There is your land,' he said. 'There is our land.'

She looked at him in the evening light. She had admired his courage during the length of the intolerable passage. She had admired his strength. She was ashamed she had been surprised by it. Above all, now, she admired the man.

'The lands of promise, Francis,' she said, and raised her arm as if to pick grapes from tall trees.

He remembered the time she had raised her hands before, to pluck grapes from the Scrooby sky, and smiled.

'The New England sky *is* bluer,' he said. 'You see it is.'

'But as to the season,' she said, 'it is winter.'

And he replied, 'The spring is not long coming in this country.'

4

THE LANDS OF PROMISE

But it was deep winter, and a long one. The spring did not come soon. They were used to the damp winters of northern England or Holland. In Scrooby it had rarely frozen hard for a week at a time. But here in New England, if the day was still, the cold numbed their faces if they were five minutes outside, and in the first weeks they had to be outside working, for there were no houses until they built them. When the wind came from the north, the chill amazed and exhausted them. They possessed no clothing to keep out such bitter cold. But if they did not build houses they would not live, so all the fit men took their axes into the woods and hewed timber to build a common house.

On their first Christmas Day in the new land the men went into the forest as usual. Of the pilgrim leaders, Brewster and Wheaton went to the ship and stayed there all day negotiating with the captain, urging him to stay at least until the first houses were finished. Bradford had chosen to go into the forest with the others. He was fiercely grieving for his dead wife, and needed to throw himself into the work. The first house was half complete. There were three walls and half a roof. When the open end was closed with a tarpaulin canvas, it made a shelter.

Most of the women had stayed on the ship while there were no houses for them, but a few of the strongest had come ashore. Among them were Wolsey and two of the older women, Susannah Tilley and Jane White, who were cooking a meal for the men's return. Some of the salted pork had not gone rancid, and remained edible. There was fish to boil, and a sort of broth made of scrawny turkey shot in the woods.

'Here they come,' said Susannah.

Wolsey looked up, and saw them straggling in, carrying kindling on their backs and dragging the oak they had felled. It was an hour before sunset, and the western sun fell full on them.

Susannah said, 'Look, see, the frost has glazed the cloth of their coats. The sun makes them shining men.'

'Shining men,' said Wolsey, 'shining men, maybe. But cold men. Mr Brewster has told me, if a man stops a minute to rest, his sweat freezes on him.'

She and the others built the fire higher, and the men huddled round as they came in, silently taking the bowls they were offered, drinking the hot ale spiced with cinnamon, and warming their frozen hands on the bowls as they drank.

Digory Eaton, their only carpenter, said, 'It is a desolate country full of wild woods, wild thickets, wild beasts, and wild men.'

'We have not seen many wild men,' said Bradford, 'and we are lucky there are woods for timber.'

'A wilderness,' said Eaton; 'and if we look behind us, at the ocean we have come across, what is it now but a barrier to keep us from all the civilized world?'

'We have the ship to help us,' said Bradford, but he knew that the ship was helping them very little. The ship's carpenters refused to lift a hand to help build the houses the pilgrims must have, and have soon. The sailors would not even come ashore, for fear of savages. That was why Wheaton and Brewster had gone to the ship that day – to ask for help, any help.

The eyes of all the pilgrims looked out from the shanty at the ship as she rode a mile out in the shallows of Plymouth harbour. They saw lights and heard singing over the water.

'They are celebrating Christmas Day,' said Wolsey.

'Pagans,' Bradford said. 'Idolaters. They turn what they call Christ's day into a rout.' The men around drank more of their steaming ale, and kept their peace. Few of them would not rather have spent the day as the sailors had. In a wilderness, the Christmases of their youths passed through the minds of these longing men. But no true Puritan would celebrate Christmas Day.

After a pause, one of the men broke the silence. 'Well, we have come this far for our faith, and we should keep it whole, so Christmas Day is the same as any other.' But the regret in his voice for the old ways was not hidden.

Bradford heard this tone in the man's voice, and replied. 'It *is* a pagan feast. Besides, as we have been told by Mr Wheaton, no man can rightly know the date of the Nativity. It cannot be worked out. So whoever celebrates Christmas Day only does it on the off-chance that he hits the right day.'

The men did not reply. Nor did Wolsey, though for herself she would have taken the chance of hitting the right day, and celebrated it to raise the spirits of these flagging men.

Then Wheaton and Brewster returned too. Wolsey gave them hot ale, and the men made room for them round the fire. Everyone knew how much depended on the answer these two men brought from the ship, but none dared ask openly.

After a few minutes Bradford stood up, and gestured to Brewster and Wheaton to follow him away from the rest, deeper into the house.

'What of the ship?' he said.

Brewster replied, 'Captain Jones is loudly declaring that he will go, that he will make sail and leave us.'

Bradford said mechanically, 'He will not sail at this season, and he knows he must refit.'

'He could go south to refit. He is talking of Antigua, or of a cargo he could take on at Barbados.'

'A privateer would get him before he got a cargo. Besides, it is his contract to stay with us. And he will keep his word.'

Brewster nodded slowly and then said, 'I hope he will. But it was a contract made in another world, his word given in another place, and he is afraid.'

Bradford stared at Brewster. Wheaton said, 'It is true. We saw that today. Jones is afraid for his ship, and afraid for his crew. The one moment he was declaring, yes, he had given his word; the next, that he would put the women and children off who are still aboard the ship, and leave them with their goods piled on the beach.'

'He will not do that,' said Bradford. 'It would be murder, while we have no houses for them.'

'I do not think he will,' said Brewster, 'but I would not be sure. He is not at heart a God-fearing man. I know he saw the hand of God in it when one of his sailors died on the voyage, but a man tends to fear God when he sees death. Today, when Mr Wheaton reasoned with him, he said bluntly that he feared his crew more than God, and his crew are saying they will for sure not stay until all the food is eaten. They will keep enough to see them home again, and the day they see food running short, they will oust the women and go. But still, I do not think Captain Jones will desert us.'

'The crew are drunken men?' asked Bradford.

Brewster shrugged. 'They say today is Christmas Day, and that they are sailors after a hard passage.'

Bradford said, 'I shall go to them tomorrow.' And so he did, taking the shallop, with two other men they could hardly spare from the work of tree-felling. He set out at dawn, and returned in the early afternoon when only the women were at the house, and a few men who were thatching the roof.

Bradford was cold and deadly tired. He sat against the wall of the house looking fixedly out over the harbour. Wolsey came to him. She did not know him well, as she knew her old master Brewster. But she knew that Bradford was a brave man, one of the pillars of the pilgrims, and that if he crumbled the whole colony would feel the loss, and he was near the end of his tether. Bradford was tall and big-boned, a strong man on land but not one to stand easily the rigours of a long sea voyage. At sea small men are stronger. He was from Scrooby, and had spent all his life thereabouts until he went to Holland with others from the village, ten years before. So Wolsey had known him when she was a little girl, and he was a digger of ditches, having come down in the world. His father was a yeoman farmer who lost his land and died young. Bradford worked as a day labourer. When he joined the separatists in Scrooby and attended their services, his work-mates laughed at him, and his uncles, who had been his guardians since his father's death, were angry. Bradford's leaving Scrooby to go across the water to Holland was a childhood memory of Wolsey's. Her own father was then still alive, and though he had been at heart no separatist, he had wished Bradford well and given him an Old Testament in Hebrew, which the young man had promised he would learn to read. Wolsey did not see him again until the pilgrims assembled at Plymouth to sail for north Virginia. He had become a weaver in the Low Countries, and had a house there which he left. But he brought his books with him. He spoke Dutch of course, after so long a stay, and had taught himself Latin and some Hebrew. On the crossing, Wolsey came to know him through his wife, during the time of her distraction. After Dorothy May disappeared and all the rest said it was an accidental drowning, Bradford did not believe it. He believed she had drowned herself in despair, and so he bore the double blow of her death and his knowledge of its sinfulness. Self-killing was a sin, and he feared for her soul. He did not know that she had gone to her death in the dark not despairing, but rejoicing – an even greater sin. Only Wolsey and Brewster suspected that, and would never tell him.

As Bradford sat on the dirt floor of the unfinished house at the edge of a wilderness, leaning against the wall of newly sawed planks, Wolsey came and knelt by him. He did not see her, but kept gazing out to sea. She put down the cup she had brought him, and took his hands in hers.

'William,' she said.

He recognized her. 'I learned to read your father's book,' he said.

She nodded. 'Will you drink this?'

'I learned, though it took me four years, and then I spelled my way through. I read it to myself, and then to Dorothy, when we were in Holland.'

She held out the cup again, and he took it and sipped.

'Today,' he said, 'I brought my books from the ship. They are with Mr Brewster's and Mr Wheaton's, and I brought the chest of books back in the shallop. It will be a comfort to them. Mr Brewster has a great library. Eighty books and more.'

'And a comfort to you too.'

'When we have time to read, it will be. I still have your father's book that he gave me. Shall I tell you what is happening on the ship?'

'That they will go, and will put the women and our goods ashore?' she asked.

'I do not think so, yet. No, it is this. Yesterday, when they said it was Christmas Day, a man fell from the deck into the hold, after they were drinking, and broke his leg. And they say he lay cursing his wife, saying that but for her being such a harridan he would never have gone to sea again and made that voyage; and cursing the other sailors, saying he had done this and that for some of them, he had spent so much and so much among them, on liquor I suppose, but now that he needed help no one would help him, and they would let him rot. Well, he gave another man, last night, all he had, if he would help him out, and look after him. And this man gave him more ale, and made him a dish of meat.'

Bradford drank more from the cup.

'When I came to the ship this morning the man was still lying in the hold. They had not moved him or covered him, and he was cursing still. And the other man, to whom he had given all he had, and promised all he left if he should die, was swaggering up and down the deck, swearing the hurt man would cheat him by not dying, and should have died sooner. The man called out from the hold for water, and some meat, but the other said he would see him choke before he made him any more. He did not give him anything. While I was there, the man died.'

Bradford, who had not allowed himself to weep when his wife was drowned, wept now, and Wolsey took him in her arms and put his head on her breast.

Two women saw, looked at each other, and then went back to their work.

The thatchers were returning from the shallop carrying what they had been sent to fetch. Bradford recovered himself and stood.

Wolsey, watching them come, said, 'That's more than your books. What did you get?'

It was pork, two salted barrels, and a barrel of ale, and more carpenter's tools, which the captain had lent though the carpenter would not come.

'But the captain said he would desert us,' said Wolsey, 'and now he gives you this?'

'He will not go. He gave his word.' Then Bradford said, and with the ghost of a smile, 'His word given this time in *New* England, which I do not doubt he will keep in New England.'

Wolsey stood squarely in front of Bradford, and smiled. What Brewster, with all his worldliness, and all the former authority of Mr Secretary Brewster, had been unable to get the day before, and what Wheaton with his persuasion had failed to get, Bradford with his bluntness had got. And he was deadly tired. She took him to a corner of the shanty where there was a trestle table and a bench they had made. He sat, and drank the last of the cup she had given him.

'What is it?' he asked.

'Cumfrey, a sovereign herb for a wound, or an inward hurt.'

It was also spiced with opiate. William Bradford put his head in his folded arms on the table, and slept.

In the first days after their landfall, before they even decided on Plymouth as the place of their settlement, they had found Indians, or rather Indians found them as they camped by night. They came unseen. The first to be heard of them was the flight of arrows through the air, the impact of arrowheads burying themselves in a keg of water by the fire, and the alarm of the lookout, who cried, 'Ambush. The savages are on us.' They fired their muskets at an enemy they could not see. At the flash and crack of the muskets, howls came from the surrounding forest. Two men swore that in the flash they saw Indians not ten feet away, armed with hatchets, but in the morning no footprints were found that close. Ten spent arrows were found, two in the cask and the rest lying on the ground. All had iron arrow-heads. The next day Indians were seen walking in single file on the western shore of Cape Cod, and ran when they saw the white men. But after that, the Indians were feared everywhere, no man went unarmed or alone into the woods, and Captain Standish, who had led the expedition that was ambushed, was forever wanting to explore farther, to rout out enemies. Where Standish's rank of captain came from was uncertain, but he was known to have fought many skirmishes in the interminable wars of the Low Countries, for this petty faction or that. He was an able soldier, but he had never seen an Indian except those by the shore, at a distance. But he reasoned that where there were a few, there might be many. He was prepared to trade with the Indians if they would, or, if they would not, to kill them. He knew nothing about Indians except that they were red, adept hunters, treacherous, and liked to kill their captives by slow torture.

While the pilgrims' first houses were still building, no men could be spared to hunt Indians. As soon as three houses were up, enough to shelter them all, Standish went out with a dozen men. A day's march inland, they found cleared land with corn stubble in it. Then they found loose soil which still bore the imprint of the hands which had patted it down. When they dug, they found baskets filled with Indian corn, which they took with them. Then, a mile farther on, they came on what they took at first to be a battle ground. A hundred skeletons, clean to the bone, lay at random on the ground. But their tools and weapons lay beside them. The skeletons were not mutilated, but whole, with no bones broken. The rags of clothing were not stained with blood. The bones of a child still lay in the embrace of the bones of a woman, both skeletons curled together on the ground. The huts and tepees still stood, uncharred, unburned, and intact. Standish and the men looked at each other with nothing but guesses to make. Then one man, who had strayed farther off, called out. He had found the finished graves of a hundred more men, some graves which were dug but not filled, and one grave-hole with the body of a man half-in, half-out.

'Half-in, half-out,' said Standish when they returned to Plymouth the next day to give an account of what they had found. 'As if they were suddenly overtaken by a plague. At first they buried their dead, and then there were not enough left living to bury the dead. They left that man half-way, and then fell down around. Some we found had wandered into the woods and fallen there, but most stayed together.'

What plague it was, the pilgrims never discovered. They assumed smallpox. The question then arose, if it were so, could they still eat the corn, or was that infected? To which Brewster's answer was that the infection was long burned out, since the Indians were not corpses but clean skeletons; that the corn, being already buried in the earth, would not be tainted; and that even if it were, pounding and cooking would make it fit and wholesome.

'And in this,' said Wheaton, 'the wonderful wisdom and love of God is shown, that He sent His Minister, I mean the smallpox, to this place before we came, to sweep away the savages in heaps to make way for us, who are His chosen.'

Most agreed with this. Those who thought that God would not choose to act in so particular a way to aid even His chosen, were reminded of the plagues visited upon Egypt and of the deaths of the first-born. Standish was glad that an enemy had been removed, by whatever means. They all were. But they all still feared other enemies. If there had been one tribe, might there not be another? They still went armed into the woods, still posted sentinels at night, and were never sure they were not watched by savages waiting to destroy them.

It was January, and then the pilgrims themselves began to die. It was not smallpox which killed them, but the exhaustion of the voyage, the bitter and astonishing cold, meagre food, fear of the unknown, the reaching of the end of any ordinary man's endurance, and the bloody flux. In the very hour that Thomas English died, who was the first to succumb, the lookout saw an Indian skulking in the river valley which ran down to the sea at Plymouth. The leaders consulted. While they talked, one of the children died. The pilgrims already had two dead to bury. Others were sick and might die. If Indians were watching, if the man seen in the valley was not a solitary wanderer but a scout belonging to a larger party, then was it expedient to bury the dead in open day, so that an enemy could see the colony diminished by each burial? It was determined that the dead should be buried by night, silently and in darkness, on the hill where the pilgrims planned to build a fort.

So at midnight, on the hill which in daylight overlooked the harbour to the east, and the brook and its valley to the south, and from which England lay three thousand miles east-north-east, the first victims were buried. They carried the corpses there in sacks, with no lanterns, and no sound. The mourners muffled their shoes with sacking. Earth was heaped over the dead not with spades, which might strike a flit or a stone, but by human hands. No words were spoken at the interment.

'*No* words?' asked Wolsey. 'Nothing?' They had all known the dead man and child.

'Nothing,' said Wheaton. 'The great John Calvin himself was buried in Geneva in an unmarked grave, as he asked, and with no words, which was also his wish.'

'That was his affair, Francis. And thousands followed his body, whether he liked that or not.'

'Let the dead bury the dead,' murmured Wheaton, quoting Christ cryptically. He well knew the words could mean any one of three things, or none of those things, but they were his slender authority for the absence of all ceremony. The dozen friends who came darkly and silently, and left as they came, believed Wheaton was right. If they did not understand his text, they sensed that all ceremonies were Papist and therefore abominable. But many of them, still used to the old ways, felt stirrings in their hearts that a man should have a few proper words said over his body. And so, though it was blasphemy to pronounce openly even a *requiescat in pace*, several who left that night prayed in their inner minds for a dead friend, or a dead child.

Throughout January and February the pilgrims died, sometimes two or three in a day. In mid-February, the time of their greatest distress, only six or seven remained fit, among them Captain Standish and, once more, Wheaton. Both were a great encouragement to the others, Standish because of his soldierly common sense, and Wheaton because his own preservation seemed to the poor people a confirmation that his promises would be kept. Standish, a very doubtful Christian during the voyage, and one who had always made it plain he came for the employment and pay and not for faith, became a convinced believer as the trials grew greater. He said he had seen men die often enough, but never with such good heart. Wheaton remarked that the closer they were to dying, the more fervently they grasped at his idea of a Promised Land, which, if it were not to be theirs in New England, would be in another world. Bradford sickened, but after a long week, recovered. Wolsey was delirious for several days, and in her mind was back at Scrooby.

'Vines again today,' said a woman who nursed her. 'Vines and grapes, and she touches her back as if the vines were there, and the grapes.'

'It was not at her back she was reaching for grapes yesterday,' said another. 'She was trying to pluck them down from above her, but always fell back. And spoke in tongues.'

'Perhaps it be Hebrew.' Hebrew was a sacred language to the pilgrims and they regarded the ability to construe a bit of it as a sure sign of sanctity. But it was not Hebrew. It was a line of Greek which Wolsey had learned long ago from her father. He had not taught it to her. It was something she read in a book he left open on a table in his library, and it was distinctly secular. When he asked, he had laughed, and said she would very well know the meaning one day. It was a simple line, which had stuck in her mind ever since. It said, being translated: 'God give me more such afternoons as these.'

Wheaton, visiting her, heard her say the words and was puzzled. When the women told him she had reached for grapes, he remembered well, and it touched him. He prayed with her. When on his third visit she recognized him he was overjoyed.

The pilgrims were heroic, fetching wood and food, making beds, and washing loathsome clothes, until many of those who at first acted as nurses, themselves fell foul of the disease and died of it. By March the infection left them, but half of all those who had crossed the Atlantic were dead, silently interred on Burial Hill at dead of night. Only fifty were left.

They were lucky that the first weeks of March were fair. The first Sunday they assembled for a meeting since the sickness was a day of the clearest blue, promising a spring which would not come for another six weeks, but still promising. To cheer them, Wheaton preached on Death.

'If a man tells you that you shall die, then reply to him that life is only a pilgrimage. And if *you* say to me, "You shall die," I shall reply, "I thought you meant you had some *news* for me." And if you tell me that I shall die in a strange country, as many of our husbands, and wives, and children, and friends have died in a strange country, then I shall reply that the way to death is in every place. Death has a thousand different doors. There is no earth that is foreign to a man or woman who dies. So I shall die in a strange country? And if I do? Sleep is no more grievous abroad than at home and no less sweet.' That is how he comforted them; and for the most part they *were* comforted.

He comforted them too in another strange way. Even on the coldest day, he never wore his heavy coat, but walked around more lightly dressed than in an English winter. It was as if he was denying the cold, to them and to himself. It was as if he said to himself that, in spite of all the evidence of his senses – numbed ears, numbed fingers, and chilled limbs – this was still the New England that he had visited once, in the fall, when the skies were blue, and higher, and the climate always temperate. It was stubborn of him. It was foolish. It was proud. But he wore no coat, and did not fall ill, and they were encouraged.

For a month there had been no more deaths. April was coming soon, and the pilgrims were recovering in body and spirit. They brought ashore from the ship two more cannons which were theirs. Now they had four, which commanded the country in all directions from the hill. They began to build a palisade to enclose the fort on the hill and the houses which ran towards the shore. What furniture they had stowed in the hold, they took from the ship to their houses. No longer did they fear from day to day for their very existence. They took courage from the everlasting blue skies of the new spring, the skies of Wheaton's promised lands, and felt anew that they were pilgrims. When the Big Ship left in early April, not one of the saints wished to leave with her. In the long evenings they gathered round their hearths as passages from the Bible were read aloud. They read about the Canaan to which the Israelites had come, and thought of themselves as the new Israelites, and of New England as their New Canaan. It was their land. They, and their children, and their children's children, would live and prosper there. They exalted. Only a few of them, Bradford and the other elders, knew in their darker moments how frail the colony still was, and how it depended on the crop sown that spring. If that should fail, the next winter would see them in no better a state than the one they had just survived.

April nights are cold, and the dark falls early. It happened one night that Wolsey, walking in darkness from the common storehouse to Brewster's house where she stayed with him and two others, skirted the uncompleted palisade, and came upon a figure squatting by the ashes of a fire over which the pilgrims had roasted a goose. It was a clear night with enough moonlight for her to see first that a figure was there, and then that it was an Indian. She stopped. They were ten feet apart. The eyes of the savage were upon her face. Her instinct was to cry out and raise the alarm. She did not know why she did not. She knew the man must have seen her before she saw him, for his eyes were certainly already upon her when she saw him. He did nothing, but remained squatting by the ashes. She saw that his hands were in the ashes, and that he did not move them. She saw that he was a boy, the size of an English boy of twelve. Then it came to her that he had been searching for scraps, the skin and entrails of the goose which lay in the ashes. His left hand held a scrap of skin. She saw that he was as afraid as she was, and that he was shivering. She moved two paces toward him, and still he did not attempt to run at her, or away. Never taking her eyes from him, she broke off part of the bread she was carrying, and placed it on the ground. She stepped back. The boy moved cautiously and fearfully toward the bread, took it, and backed away, all the time keeping his eyes on Wolsey until he slipped behind the palisade and into the forest.

The chill thought did not strike her until afterwards that he might be suffering from the same disease which had killed the tribe whose skeletons had been found forty miles away. As soon as she reached Brewster's house and told him, he was at first struck by the same fear, but then reasoned that the tribe of skeletons had died long before, and that even if the boy did come from them, he must have escaped the disease. But an Indian had come unnoticed into their village at night, unseen by the guards. Brewster and ten armed men made quiet rounds of the camp, but the Indian was gone. They were more vigilant after that. Bradford told Wolsey he was glad it had passed off quietly, without a general alarm, but (and this he put to her rather

THE LANDS OF PROMISE 67

gruffly) he would rather she fed no more savages.

Only four days later another Indian came, this time striding boldly into the village in plain day, and greeting them in English. 'Welcome, Englishmen.' It was broken English, but astonishing. He said his name was Samoset, and that he was from Maine, having been brought from there by English fishermen. He had observed the English at Plymouth since their arrival, and, having seen how they entertained a young brave some days before, had come to offer his services. The entertainment he spoke about was Wolsey's chunk of bread, torn off the loaf she was carrying, and taken by the boy. The bold Indian said he could do the English great service. When he was given ale to drink, he told them what this service was. He could bring to them another Indian, called Squanto, whose English was more fluent than his, and who was moreover from these parts. On his promise to bring Squanto they gave him a green coat, and he did return with the man. Then there was a strange story told in the wilderness. Squanto had been taken by a Captain Hunt six years before on this same coast, who seized him to sell as a slave in Spain. But he got away from Spain and worked for a merchant in London, who later employed him in Newfoundland. From there he came to New England with an explorer, also an Englishman, called Dermer, and had jumped ship at Patuxet to find his own tribe again.

'Patuxet?' asked Bradford.

Squanto explained that they were all sitting at Patuxet.

And what did that name mean?

'The place of the little waterfalls,' he said. And so it was. The little falls, never more than a few feet in height, originated at the town brook as it flowed down to the sea, where its fresh waters trickled across the beach at low tide.

The tribe that had lived in this place was called the Patuxet, said Squanto, and he was the last of them. He had gone back to the planting grounds of his tribe, and found only a tribe of skeletons.

'Some buried, some unburied?' asked Standish, remembering the field of death he had found.

Squanto said that was so.

'One man half-in, half-out, of his grave-hole?'

Squanto had seen that too. Now, said Squanto, he, the last of the Patuxets, came to welcome the new Englishmen.

What of the boy who had come to the village a few nights before? Squanto said he had seen this, but the boy was not of his former tribe but from the north, from a people whose custom it was to test a boy, before he became a man, by sending him into the forest all winter long. If he returned in the spring he was a man, and could have a tepee and wives. But Squanto said that was of no account. He proposed that he should help the English. He could interpret for them with the tribe in the north, which was numerous. He could show them where to catch fish. And, he said, he had already watched the English plant seed, which would come to nothing.

Bradford, whose father was a farmer and who had himself worked on the land, feared this was very likely true. He said, 'It will do well enough. A thriving harvest.'

Squanto gravely said the ground was old, used by his tribe for generations. Nothing would come of the crop they had planted. But he could show them how.

The pilgrims listened. Squanto showed them how to catch herrings in the brook, and then how to plant the Indian corn, which they had taken from his people, with fish around it to manure it. Then it would grow.

Wheaton declared, in the meeting that following Sunday, that this savage was a special Minister sent by God, beyond their deserving or expectation. He had said the same only a few weeks before of the plague which had killed all that man's tribe, sweeping the savages away in heaps, clearing the land for His chosen.

Bradford gave Squanto a riding coat, and he stayed with them. The winds changed to the south. Spring gave way rapidly to summer, spring being a shorter season and much more suddenly over in New England than in the old country. And the birds sang in the woods most pleasantly.

5

THANKSGIVING BECOMETH SAINTS

After the long imprisonment of the Atlantic passage, and the long ordeal of the dying-time during the winter at Plymouth, none of them would ever be the same again. From the time they left Plymouth in England, until the spring days of March, for more than six months, they had lived in daily fear of their deaths. But they revived with the summer, and thrived in it. Winter had been bitter beyond their imaginings, colder than the sea, colder than their dreams of icy death. None of the pilgrims, before he came over, had ever suffered a chill of the spirit – from the death of a father, or of a beloved child – that could compare with the chill of the body that a New England winter brought daily to his flesh. But when the New England summer came, that was beyond their expectations of delight. They had never known the like of it. The days *were* bluer, the few clouds whiter, the stars brighter. The heavens *were* infinitely higher.

Of course, their minds were likely to believe this. They felt more than ever that they were pilgrims. Their survival assured them that they, perhaps more than those who had died, were the chosen. To express this thought would have been a prideful sin. No one did express it, and many thrust the serpent-thought from their hearts. But they were in a state most susceptible to exaltation, and they did exalt in the summer.

For six days of the week they laboured, all without exception working in the fields or gardens, or fishing, or completing the houses, or making furniture. They were already trading with the Indians to the north, through Squanto, who was successfully exchanging English glass beads for beaver. He brought back beaver skins which had plainly been sewn together as coats, and when asked where he got them, said he had bought them off the very backs of Indian women, who had then covered their nakedness with birch boughs. 'In which,' said Wheaton, 'they are more modest than some of our English women.' Wolsey laughed at the extravagance of this. But it would have been true to say that, in the marvellously clear New England light, young men, now that the ever-present fear of death was gone and their vigour returned, looked longingly at the young women, and had their glances returned. The seduction of light abounded.

Six days they worked, and on the seventh spent most of the day listening to Mr Wheaton. Occasionally Brewster or Bradford would take the prayer meeting and give shorter sermons, but Wheaton spoke most often and at greatest length. But then the Sabbath afternoon was free. Games were forbidden, but so was work and it was held no *great* sin to take a modest pleasure in walking on the shore, wondering at the goodness of God. It could be even less of a sin to wonder at the goodness of God in the company of Mr Wheaton, as Wolsey often was. One soft evening in September, when the air was still as warm as on the finest English afternoon in high summer, they walked together across the beach. Wheaton wore the heavy work-boots which were the only ones he had. Wolsey slipped off her light shoes, and was barefoot. They came to the point where the town brook, having come a hundred yards inland to the last of its little waterfalls, meandered over the sands to the sea. Wolsey walked at first on the hot sand, and then, with a soft 'ah,' felt the cool waters of the brook running beneath the soles of her feet. Wheaton, watching her, felt vicariously the sensations of hot sand and cool water which showed themselves in her face and in her exclamation. Seeing her face and hearing her soft cry, he felt the texture and heat of the sand, and the running coolness of the water, as if he were barefoot himself. Wolsey saw what he felt, and he turned his eyes away. She bent down, all suppleness, caught the fresh water in her cupped hands, and drank. She held her palms to her temples to cool her forehead, then stooped again, filled her cupped hands, and offered them to Wheaton to drink from, holding her hands up to him. He bent his head down as if to drink, bringing his face so close that the scent of her hair came to him, and he could sense the coolness of the water she held up to him. But then he raised his head and could not drink, fearing the pleasure. Wolsey stood with the water cupped in her palms until he shook his head. Then, parting her fingers, she let the water fall back into the brook, keeping her eyes on him.

It was as open an invitation as she could have made. Nothing goes unnoticed in a community of fifty. The women talked. Only the younger ones were surprised, but they were innocent. The older women, particularly those who had been fortunate in their lives, saw nothing that surprised them.

'I do suppose she be the only one for a man of his learning,' said a girl of eighteen to her mother.

''Tis not his learning she wants,' said the mother, 'but the man.'

'Ah,' said the girl, who was slow, 'I suppose she has enough learning of her own, then?'

The older woman sighed that her girl should understand so little.

Wolsey and Wheaton walked together the next Sunday afternoon, and met two other young couples, who greeted them respectfully.

Wheaton returned the salutation and observed to Wolsey, 'There will be marriages soon.'

'I think so,' she said.

'And it's as well, for the increase of the commonwealth.'

'Indeed,' she said.

They walked on.

Then it was Wolsey who took the initiative. Since their

first meeting at Scrooby she had felt the magnetic pull of the man. Since the moment on the ship, when they embraced in what they feared would be their last moment, and stood clasped as one creature as they were drenched by the invading seawater, their intimacy had been strong. His attraction to her was obvious as hers to him. But he could not easily admit this.

Wolsey could be plainer. When they came to the brook again she looked down at the rippling water, and up at him. She did not repeat her gesture of the week before, but could see that it was in his mind.

'Francis, you have said there will be marriages.'
'I have said so.'
'You are the pastor,' she said. 'Let yours be the first.'

Brewster was not surprised when Wheaton came formally to ask for Wolsey as his wife. He had at first feared the fascination that Wheaton held for Wolsey, but he had come to see that, fascination or no, the real sexual power was hers. He did not think she knew that, and in this he was right. They had a power over each other, but hers was the greater. As for Wheaton, Brewster could have wished the man was not so narrow in his religion, but had rejoiced at his strength and courage on board ship and in the first, bad months on land.

Wheaton said, 'You are hesitating?'

Brewster came out of his reverie and stood.

'No,' he said. 'Dear Francis, forgive me. You may ask her, and I know what her answer will be.'

The next meeting of the elders happened to be in Brewster's house. With him were Bradford, Wheaton, and Standish. Wolsey also was in the room, and because she happened to live in Brewster's house, and was now also Mr Wheaton's betrothed, there was no objection to her presence. She sat by the door sewing while the men got down to the business they had to attend to. They were, between them, the judges and parliament of the colony. The law was theirs to administer or make, provided only – according to their patent – that it was conformable to the laws of England. To assist them they had two books. The first was a small octavo entitled *The Offices of the Justice of the Peace*, badly out of date because published in London in 1592, twenty-nine years before. It bore on its cover the arms of Lord Burghley, first minister to Queen Elizabeth, and had been given by Burghley to Davison, and by Davison to Brewster, which was how it came to Plymouth. This book adjured the magistrates to do their work, 'So help you God, and by the contents of this book.' It set out elaborate laws for the impounding of cattle, useless in a colony where there were no cattle, and for the regulation of dress, again of little use where no man present possessed more than two suits of decent clothes and was unlikely to offend by wearing silk, not being at least of knight's rank, or the heir of a knight. The other and larger book was a Bible, from a few sentences of which the pilgrim elders derived for themselves more powers than a thousand statutes could have given. Did not Peter say, 'Be subject to every ordinance of man for the Lord's sake?' Did not *Romans* say that there was no power that did not come from God, that the powers that be were ordained by God, and that whoever resisted them would receive damnation? The elders were the powers that be, and in so God-ridden a state the voice of the pastor was paramount, and would rarely be overruled. Wolsey was about to become the wife of a man of great power.

To their business. There was Squanto. The fur trade was flourishing, and without him it would not have flourished. The harvest of Indian corn had gone well, and without him they would not have known how to plant it. And he had brought Massasoit, chief of the northern Indians, to them, when, outside the palisade, they had made him presents of beads and mirrors, and concluded a treaty of trade and peace. Massasoit was chief of the tribe fifty miles to the north. Squanto had gone farther north than that in his trading, into the lands of the Narragansetts. This tribe was now complaining that he had come among them boasting he had the plague hidden in the ground, the same plague that had killed all his own people, and that he could release it on whomever he chose, and whenever. This boast had been made to induce them to trade at better rates. The Narragansetts demanded that Squanto should be delivered to them. The elders returned a politic reply: that they would vouch that Squanto should have no power to turn the plague on any Indian friendly to the English, but that he should remain.

Then there was the request of many younger saints that since the harvest was almost gathered in, and was good, a festival day should be appointed in celebration. This was a matter of the greatest moment, touching the consciences of all the elders.

'The harvest,' said Standish, '*is* good, and it has saved us.'

'That is God's grace,' said Wheaton. 'But it is God's stated will that there shall be no festivals, which are idolatrous. Mr Bradford has already determined that point in the colony at Christmas, when the ship's sailors drunkenly caroused, and were condemned in the minds of us all.'

Governor Bradford said, 'It *was* idolatrous on the Yule day, which is itself pagan and papistical.'

Brewster said Christmas was Christmas. This was not Christmas, nor were the pilgrims drunken sailors. He knew Mr Wheaton's opinion, but would like to hear his authorities.

Wheaton said, 'The observance of all holy days, save only the Lord's Sabbath, is condemned. Then how much more culpable and sinful would it not be to celebrate a day in no way, even formerly, held to be holy? For all banqueting, playing, feasting, and other such vanities are condemned.' Wheaton was in full flight about superstition and idolatry when Standish interrupted him to ask:

'Condemned by whom?'

Condemned, it seemed, by the most weighty authority, by no less than an assembly of ministers learned in the scriptures, at Perth in Scotland, only two years before.

'Particularly,' said Wheaton, 'the singing of carols and setting of bonfires were reckoned among the corruptions to be amended.'

Brewster inclined to allow a festival, but knew that the deliberations of the ministers at Perth had been very weighty indeed. He did not wish to hear them recited, but Wheaton was there before him.

'Reason,' said Wheaton, 'either the words, "Six days shalt thou labour" are a commandment, in which case keep the commandment. Or they are a permission to work for six days, in which case no riot should be allowed to spoil the liberty of a man to work on those days. No craftsman can be commanded by men such as us to lay aside his tools and pass his time in roistering.'

'I do not think,' said Standish, 'that we should be spoiling the liberty of any man to work. They do not want to work. They say so. They want a festival.'

'And there *are* reasons to grant it,' said Bradford. 'Yet I fear it might become an annual transgression.'

If Wheaton had said no more, there would very likely have been no festival, but he had taken the Bible from the table and was hunting after further authorities.

They waited for him, as he turned the pages of the heavy, leather-bound book. At last he found it.

'*Ephesians*,' he said, 'Chapter Five. Where it is said that the followers of God, His dear children, for whom he gave His son as an offering and a sacrifice, shall suffer no uncleanness among them, as it becometh saints. Neither shall there be foolish talking, nor jesting, which are not comely things, but rather the giving of thanks.'

'Rather,' said Wolsey from her place by the door, 'the giving of thanks. Yes.'

Brewster turned toward her and half held up his hand, to tell her she had no part in this, learned though she might be.

But they all knew their Bibles, and that Wheaton had overstepped himself, because the passage he had quoted was to do with fornication and covetousness. Brewster and Bradford knew this. Even Standish knew it. Wolsey knew it, and she was not inclined to be silent.

'The giving of thanks then,' she said. 'Thanksgiving becometh saints.'

'The word of God is against all festivals,' said Wheaton.

Wolsey replied, 'Say what you like of festivals. Let it not be a *festival*. Call it what you like. But a day of thanksgiving is proper. Let it be called Thanksgiving.'

They could not officially hear Wolsey. Being a woman, and no elder, she had no right to speak. But her words echoed the inclinations of Brewster and Standish, and gave Bradford who was wavering, a reason which satisfied his doubts.

Wheaton was overruled. He fired one parting shot. 'But it shall *not* be a Harvest Home in the old way.'

Bradford received this objection with gravity, and appointed a day of Thanksgiving for late October.

6

THE WEDDING OVER THE BROOK

But before Thanksgiving, the day set for the wedding arrived. It was to be in the open air, by the town brook, in view of all the people of the colony. As Wolsey lay in bed the night before, the last night she would sleep in Brewster's house, she heard incessant rain beating on the roof above her. She lay awake for hours, and was lulled asleep by the sound of the rain still falling. But in the morning, the rain had ceased, the wind was gone, and the forest, which the night before had thrashed around in the wind, was still.

It was an article of Puritan faith that a marriage was without ceremony, and it was expected that the whole wedding day itself would be without ceremony, too. But this was a strictness that the older women were unable to observe wholly. They were strong in their faith, and knew very well that unnecessary trappings were the foistings of Satan himself, or of his servant the Pope, upon the purity of their own conscience and beliefs. But they did not forget their own weddings, or other weddings seen in their youth. So Susannah Tilly and Jane White came to dress the bride. Wolsey had said she would wear what she had brought from England with her, but the women liked Wolsey and had made her a new dress. A wedding dress was not white. Nor was it a dress for a woman to wear once and then put away. It was meant to be worn often afterwards, and to wear well. Many a wedding dress lasted a marriage through. Susannah Tilly and Jane White were both more than twice her age, Jane with her husband still alive, Susannah having lost hers in the great winter sickness. As they dressed her they were seeing themselves as girls again, dressing for a lover. The skirt they had made was of red wool, the rich red of the darkest sandstone of northern England, and heavy and full. They fastened it at the waist and Wolsey stood wearing that alone, while they stepped back to admire and praise her.

'Will you turn, Wolsey?' said Susannah. There was supposed to be no ceremony on a wedding day, and the women knew, and Wolsey knew, that it was an old and unchristian superstition for the bride to turn full circle as she dressed, to bring her good fortune.

'To show us the lay of the skirt,' said Jane.

'No it isn't either,' said Susannah. 'We can see how that lies now; don't you listen to her, Wolsey. And on her wedding day it's proper for a girl that more than her skirt lies well on her. But turn, Wolsey. Turn to the four corners of the room, and keep in your mind the four corners of the earth beyond the room, and the world will be good to you. There's no harm ever came of that, and I've known the world be good to some.'

Wolsey turned, to face the four corners of the world that were hers, keeping her hands clasped loosely before her as she did. It was a grave turn, no frivolity, but the skirt was heavy and swung of its own weight, so she let it take her and swung round again, and the second time not so gravely, and with her arms outstretched.

'Now that's *eight* corners of the earth,' said Susannah. 'And God be with me, I never saw a girl fitter for a man.' Wolsey returned her steady gaze with an open smile.

'And now the coat,' said Jane, bringing it forward.

'Wait,' said Wolsey. She opened a small leather box and took from it a gold chain, which she fastened round her neck. The two women gazed fascinatedly at her, with their eyes on the ring suspended from the chain. The ring lay between her bare breasts, and was inlaid with a scarlet design.

'It will not count for decoration,' said Wolsey.

'But 'tis,' said the women, both together.

'It will not count for decoration because it will not be seen, or known of, any more than my turning will be known.'

'No, true, my dear,' said Jane, 'your turning shan't be talked of, but *that* will be *seen*.'

'No,' said Wolsey. 'Because it will be under the coat.'

The coat was more a bodice, made of heavy grey linen. Wolsey held out her arms for the coat to be eased over them, and over her shoulders. Then the fastening. The coat was fastened by laces to the waist of the skirt, and by laces down the back from neck to waist. The long sleeves covered her arms entirely, coming down to the wrist. The neckline was high, and nothing of the chain could be seen.

Then the shoes, grey leather, but, as she stood, hidden by the length of the skirt.

'Now the bonnet,' said Susannah.

Wolsey tossed her dark hair away from her face. 'There's God's plenty,' said Jane. 'Some might say a sin to show it, and some might say a sin to hide it.' But there was no doubt it had to be hidden today. The two women gathered up her long, shining hair, pinning it up at the back so that it was wholly covered by the white linen coif, which tied at the nape of the neck.

The women regarded her, and then said, 'Now go to your man,' words that were spoken to them when they were brides.

She went out to be given to Wheaton, first meeting Brewster, who was waiting for her at the door. She was most plainly dressed, and yet she was glorious with it. When Brewster turned to greet her, her eyes shone. She went to him and kissed his hand, saying, 'You have been my father.'

'Then I have been fortunate,' he said.

'And I have been a most fortunate daughter.'

Brewster grieved to his heart to lose her from his house, but he hid it, gave her his arm, and they walked to the place set for the wedding, by the town brook.

They stepped out into a fine day, warmed by the sun, and walked across the meadow to where all the people were gathered. Wheaton was waiting for her, having come from the other side of the brook where a new house had been built for him and his bride. Bradford was there, who as governor and magistrate would marry them. There was no other minister but Wheaton, but, even had there been, Puritans held that marriage was a civil matter, and that it was nowhere in the Scriptures set down as part of a minister's duties to perform marriages. There was no music, no singing even, for fear that the congregation might take more delight in the sweet sound of the singing than in the meaning of the words sung, even were it a hymn.

When Brewster and Wolsey came to the brook, they saw that it was flooded with the night's rain. It had not burst its banks, or flooded the ground around, but it had risen so that it was seven feet across.

The men present were speculating whether Wheaton would go to Wolsey, or Wolsey come to him. There were steppingstones, but they were submerged, and in going to him she would soak the hem of her skirt. But was it for the minister to go to her, wading through the brook, letting water into his boots? Three men, who had been murmuring to each other, proposed to go and get a great plank to make a bridge, but Wheaton thanked them and shook his head, and appeared quite unruffled. Wheaton and Wolsey faced each other across the brook, seven feet apart, unable to meet each other, certainly unable to join hands. Wheaton stood there all in black, except for white cuffs; Wolsey, opposite, in her red skirt which the high sun shot with crimson. She had so far stood with eyes downcast and her hands clasped before her, as she had on the walk from Brewster's house. Now she looked down at the brook, looked up at Wheaton, and opened her hands wide. She said nothing, but her widespread hands asked eloquently just what he proposed to do. Bradford, by Wheaton's side, turned towards him too. It seemed to Bradford there was no help for it but to get a bolt of timber, throw it over the brook, and then climb over it to

Wolsey's side. But that, he thought, would be a pretty scramble. Either that, or everyone would have to walk down to the beach where the brook ended in a trickle, and then walk all the way back up the other side, which could, he supposed, be done in some sort of proper procession.

He was about to suggest this when Wheaton spoke.

'Governor Bradford, we have done away with all Popish ceremonies which have crept in, or been foisted in. Priests, vestments, incense, music, fanfares, the wearing of veils, the lifting of veils, and the giving of rings. What do these things matter in God's eyes? Nothing. Now, we have a brook between us. What does that matter in God's eyes? Nothing. It is for you to perform the marriage, but I can say that my understanding of the scriptures is that we have everything here necessary for a lawful marriage – the man, the woman, the magistrate, and the congregation. The man and woman to state to each other and in the face of the congregation that they take each other, and the magistrate to perform and record the wedding.'

Bradford said, 'You cannot take your bride's hand, man.'

'I do not have to. Nowhere in the Scriptures is that said to be necessary.'

It was true. He was right.

So Bradford then said the few words of a Puritan wedding, that marriage was commended by St Paul to be honourable, and was not by any one to be taken in hand unadvisedly, lightly, or wantonly to satisfy men's carnal lusts like brute beasts; but reverently, discreetly, advisedly, soberly, for the procreation of children, as a remedy against fornication, and for the mutual society, help, and comfort of man and wife. Francis Wheaton stated that he took Wolsey Lowell to be his wife, after God's holy ordinance, and Wolsey Lowell that she took Francis Wheaton to be her husband. In the sight, hearing, and witness of the congregation – and watched by one lone Indian who stood motionless throughout, two hundred yards away on the edge of the forest – they made these brief promises. It was the bare bones of the English wedding service that all the older women knew. The husband gave the wife no ring, for that was idolatry too.

Then came the adjuration, and Bradford chose, as he had often heard Puritan ministers choose in the Low Countries, to take his theme from the Song of Solomon. 'My well-beloved is mine and I am his: he feedeth among the lilies: our bed is green and the beams of our house like cedars.' A learned minister in Holland had written no fewer than fifteen sermons rightly explaining the true meaning of what might otherwise seem a wanton poem, and a volume containing these sermons was the frequent gift of magistrates to couples they married. In his address, Bradford spoke what he could remember of these sermons.

'In this book of the Bible,' he said, 'which is the Most Excellent Song that is Solomon's, the bride and groom *do* highly extol and praise each other. They *do* unfold the vehement passions of their love, each with a most fervent desire to be most nearly joined to the other. Think of kings, empires, princes, coronations – and all these things are trash if you compare them with the glory and pleasure the bride and bridegroom take in each other. So here are two people, in the poem, who are lovers, betrothed to each other. This is so clear and evident from the words that no one can deny it. It is, without controversy, a song between a bridegroom and his bride.'

The young pilgrims, who had attentively read the Song which was Solomon's, but had never heard a magistrate publicly state what it most evidently was, were listening intently.

'But,' said Bradford, 'the bride and groom are not *named*. So it is also out of controversy, and as clear as the sun, who they are. For the bridegroom is described as a king, of such glory and majesty as no mortal possesses. So of necessity it follows that the bridegroom is Jesus Christ the Redeemer and Saviour of the World, and the bride is his Church. These are the two reverent lovers which are meant here, and by the bed is meant the temple which Solomon made.'

Then, when it was over, the two parties each side of the

brook did walk down to the beach and meet there, and Wheaton offered his hand to his bride. She went to take it, but then checked herself. Wheaton and Wolsey stood there, and the whole of the wedding party watched them.

'Why do she not take his hand, then?' said Jane White to Susannah Tilly.

'She's smiling,' said Susannah. 'Smiling broad, very broad.'

So she was. Wolsey was smiling, and gazing down at the stream which had separated them higher up, but was now no more than a rivulet running between her and her new husband across the sands.

'This is the place we came before,' she said, 'when we came to the beach.'

'It is. Shall we move on?'

'And I offered you water to drink in my hands, but you would not drink.'

'We were not married then,' he said softly, so that the others should not hear, though some did.

Wolsey stooped, let the fresh water of the rivulet flow into her cupped hands, and held it out to Wheaton.

'We are married now,' she said, and that was heard by everyone. Hers was a bolder voice than his.

He looked down at her hands.

'Drink,' she said.

Conscious of being watched by the whole colony, Wheaton hesitated.

'Drink, Francis,' she said, raising her hands to his lips, and then he did lean forward, take her cupped hands in his, and drink the cool water. Then he raised his head. She let her hands fall, and the fresh water remaining in her hands splashed onto the dark red of her wedding skirt. A soft 'Ah' came from the women who watched, and Wolsey laughed, looked round at the assembled congregation, took her husband's hand, and ran towards the settlement, drawing Francis with her.

It was a colony that rose with the sun and went to bed with

the sun. After sundown that evening, Susannah Tilly and Jane White stayed up, talking about the events of the great day. They had been friends for thirty years, had seen each other's weddings, and known Wolsey at Scrooby when she was a girl.

'Did you see that savage,' said Susannah, 'by the forest edge? He stood still as a statue through the whole thing, even through Mr Bradford's sermon, though he can't have heard a word at that distance. When we went down to the beach afterwards, I looked back, and he was still there.'

'It was a show for him,' said Jane.

'Wolsey was beautiful today. Seeing her today, I called her father to mind. I remembered him. I knew him.'

'And I,' said Jane.

Susannah stared into the fire. 'I thought you did,' she said. 'I always thought you did. But he never said.'

'No,' said Jane. 'He never said.'

'And you never said neither, Jane, not till this day. Not even to me.'

'No,' said Jane, 'especially not to you, we being friends. He was a good man, and it was after his poor wife, Wolsey's mother, died, when Wolsey was a little girl. And you knew him too, about that time.'

'I did.'

The two women sat by the fire and smiled over summer days in years gone by, and things never talked of between them till that day.

Susannah said, after a time, 'You have seen the ring before, then, that Wolsey wore today, under the dress?'

'I have. On him.'

Susannah said, 'Yes. On him. He was a fine man. I daresay he was good to both of us. You knowing him, was that why you helped dress her today?'

'As it was with you, I suppose?'

'Yes,' said Susannah, 'yes. He was a fine man, in many things, and there's a lot of him in Wolsey.'

'I see there is. And I pray that Mr Wheaton is as fine a man to her as *he* was to me when he lived.'

Susannah said, 'Amen to that.'

As the old women talked, Wolsey lay in Francis Wheaton's bed, and in his arms, and the silence of the house and of the forest enclosed them.

7

HARVEST HOME

'Wild men,' whispered the children. 'The wild men are coming.'

The sentinels had already seen that Indians were coming, and more than they had ever seen together before. A boy ran to the house of Captain Standish to warn him, and he came up to the palisade still buckling on his breastplate.

'Ten of them, Captain,' said James Cleary.

Standish shook his head. 'An alarm, Cleary?' he said. 'When you see them coming in daylight, in procession, two by two, and slowly, and there behind those ten men is the chief, and only two men with him for an escort? But send for Mr Bradford and bring Squanto.'

The Indians approached to within twenty feet of the closed gateway in the now completed palisade, and waited.

Bradford came up. By now all the men and women of the settlement had come from their work and were clustered near the gate.

Standish addressed Bradford. 'Indians,' he said. 'Bringing gifts by the look of it. Now, I shall send four men to go quietly and mount the cannons, and then we'll receive them with courtesy. And where is that Squanto?'

'With them, Captain,' said Cleary. 'The chief has squatted down behind his savages and one of his warriors is standing by him, but the second man we saw with him is running up and down all busy, and he's Squanto, wearing the green coat we gave him.'

So it was. The gates were opened, and Bradford and Standish, both in breastplates and helmets, and attended by two men with muskets at the port, walked solemnly out. Indians stood two and two together, each pair carrying, slung on a pole over their shoulders, a fine red deer. Behind them stood the chief.

'Venison,' said Bradford.

At a slow and stately pace the four Englishmen walked down the line of Indians towards the chief, who bowed as they approached. It was Massasoit, with whom they had concluded their treaty. Standish, always a man for a military flourish, saluted with his sword. Bradford and Massasoit bowed to each other with gravity. The chief spoke, with Squanto translating. He had seen that the governor had sent four men out into the woods to shoot turkey. He had seen cooking fires of the white men burning now for two days. He wished to make this offering for the white men's feast. He made them a gift of five deer – the flesh for their feast and the pelts to warm them in their houses.

The giving and accepting of the deer having required at least forty minutes of elaborately exchanged courtesies, and the chief having been invited to return to share in the Thanksgiving, which was the next day, the deer were carried into the village and laid on trestles by the Indians, and then Massasoit and his men departed, Squanto remaining.

For two days, four of the pilgrims' best hunters had shot turkey in the woods, and other fowl in the marshes, and killed enough to last for a week. The women had baked cakes in their oven. New ale brewed from the August crop of barley, a poor harvest but enough for beer to last a month, was waiting in cask. But venison was a marvellous thing to them. The pilgrims had caught glimpses of red deer in the green forest, but never come near to taking one. Plainly the Indians were better hunters, even without firearms. But there was more than that to it. Venison was truly the food of a Promised Land. Mr Wheaton's grapes that grew on trees had long been a symbol to them, since he had reached up for them in the church at Scrooby. It was a gesture he had repeated often enough to other congregations, when he went recruiting in England. Every one of the pilgrims at Plymouth had seen it. It had certainly been a symbol and a promise, but now it was less miraculous because they had all seen the truth of it, and all done it. Near Plymouth, particularly in the sandy, gravelly soil near the beaches, vines did cluster round the trunks of trees, and that fall they had all reached up and plucked grapes from trees. Blue grapes with a bloom, too sweet to be good wine grapes, but good to eat. Mr Wheaton's marvel had become commonplace, but venison was a miracle. It was not a food for common men in England.

'Venison,' said the women wonderingly, as they gathered round the deer. 'Well, I never did.'

It was beyond the dignity of Bradford's office as governor to say publicly that he never had either, but he did say so in his house, to Brewster. 'In England, it was not for us,' he said. 'It was meat for the bishops, when there were bishops at Scrooby, at the palace. But the bishops were never at Scrooby in my day. They stayed at York, and the forests around had been hunted clean until no creatures were left but foxes, and the woods mostly felled for timber by the squire, for money, and by people, for kindling.'

'I never saw a deer there in my day, either,' said Brewster.

'But my father did,' said Bradford. 'He died young, when I was too young to remember him; but what I do remember is that he once took a deer, though we never got to taste it. The squire heard of it, and sent his keepers, and when they found it hanging in the barn, they took the deer and my father too, to the squire's house. And he said he would have the deer, that the meat was not fit for the likes of my father, that it was meat for those of good birth, such as him the squire, and the squire's betters. He would not bring an indictment against my father, because it was capital to take a deer and he would not hang a man for that, and besides, as he could see, my father was ailing. He died that winter. I don't remember him, but I do remember that deer, and how we never got to taste it, or any part of it.'

'But you,' he said, after a pause, to Brewster, 'you've eaten venison?'

Brewster smiled. 'Long ago, and does a taste stay in the memory? At Hampton Court I've eaten it, and the old palace at Greenwich, at court in the days of the old queen.'

'Does taste stay in the memory?' asked Bradford. 'After salt-horse for a year, which we've called salt-beef, do I still recall the taste of fresh roast beef – beef that's not horse, and beef that doesn't carry the tang of salt and the rotting timbers of rotting casks?'

'Venison,' said Brewster, 'is sweeter than beef, and stronger. Bad, it was like marinated mutton, but when it was good it was sweet. But, Bradford, that's all thirty years ago....'

'You shall have it again tomorrow.'

When the next day came, it was the finest they could have had, a warm, blue-skied day in late October, a day of Indian summer. And there was plenty. Their own barley, it was true, had produced a moderate crop, and their own wheat brought from England had shrivelled in the ground. But the twenty acres of Indian corn that Squanto had shown them how to manure with fish had flourished. They would not be hungry that coming winter. And for the day, there was more than plenty. Apart from venison, the royal crown of it all, they had turkey and geese and duck, cakes and ale, and rich frumenty. With the women's help the butcher skinned and gutted two deer to roast whole, and with the aid of the blacksmith rigged up two spits to roast them on. The other deer were butchered into joints, and would last them for a month, but they were thinking only of the day.

The Indians came early, Massasoit and five warriors. While the feast was cooking, there was the show of arms. It was traditional in England, and besides it would be good for the Indians to see the white men's force. 'And first,' said

Captain Standish, standing before the wooden fort, 'the drum.' The drummer, eager to be heard, was as good as starting out by himself and had already got as far as the first taps, but Standish restrained him, placing a hand on the drum to muffle it. 'First,' he said, addressing all the men, women, and children of the settlement who had assembled to watch, 'first it must be explained what your drum *is*. Your drum is the voice of the commander above the noise of battle. The drum is my voice. The drum is the spirit of the valiant, the heart of the coward, and by it you must receive your instructions over the roaring of the cannon and the clashing of arms. For battle is a confusion of noises.' So the drummer, instructed by Standish, went through his calls. First, the troop to 'stand ready,' a rattling call. Then a 'preparation,' a firmer, louder drumming. Then a march. Then a 'battle,' a slow, strong pounding of the drum, as loud as the drumskin would stand. Then a 'retreat,' a scurrying kind of call. And then, so as not to end on a retreat, the march again, all spirit.

Then the men formed the Diamond Battle. This was a figure that twenty men could perform, and they were down to twenty men. It was also a tactic that would be of most use to them if they ever had to defend their settlement from a general attack of Indians from all sides. At each corner of the diamond, protected by the pikemen, and firing out in each direction, were the musketeers. The pikemen ported, comported, and ordered their muskets. The Indians watched, intent and silent. Standish let the silence endure, and then, with a downward flash of his sword, gave the awaited order, and the musketeers, all eight of them, fired high into the air. The whipcrack of the explosion echoed and reechoed through the surrounding forests.

Then the people prayed, all standing, the men with their hats still on, and all with closed eyes, not kneeling, not with heads uncovered, and not with eyes open as in the old English church. 'For,' said Jane White, who had already taken a quart of the strong ale, 'for us to pray with our eyes shut do show we can see our way to Heaven better that way than other folks can with theirs open.' Wolsey standing at her side, touched Jane's shoulder and shushed her. On another day, these words were enough to be counted prideful and blasphemous.

They sat to eat. First the squirrels, which the children had caught, were served roasted, quartered, seasoned with pepper, garnished with parsley, and very tender. Then the fowl, of which the geese were best, the turkey being scraggy.

'A goose done,' said Jane, who had cooked the geese, 'as a goose should be done, is done like this goose here. Sear the outside of your goose quickly, the natural skin – and 'tis as if you sugared it outside and coated it with caramel; and then, inside this sugared coat, the goose do cook in its own juice. But mind it don't burn. Mine don't burn.'

All the while the two deer were still turning on their spits, and after the goose the pilgrims rested from eating and watched the cook give the spit its last few turns before he announced it done. At this the table gave a cheer, and cook and butcher began to dismember the first deer and carve it.

This was the first time the pilgrims had really feasted for two years. It was not their custom to feast at Christmas, at the time of the previous harvest feast they had been at sea, and so the last time was the harvest supper of two years before, when some had been in Holland, some in England. They watched as the venison was carved, watched as it was served first to Bradford, Brewster, Wheaton, and Standish at the head of the table, and waited their turn as they sat on benches running the length of the long table. The children ate theirs sitting on stumps of trees felled to clear the ground for the village.

Then the frumenty, a rich creamy mess of corn meal boiled for two days, fortified with duck's eggs, spiced with cinnamon and honey, and laced with the last of the brandy from the ship.

Then corn cakes, for those that could still eat, and more ale. They sat in the open air under the clear sky of their newfound Canaan, with the scent of wood fires and roasted meat all round them, sated with the best of food and happy with the rich ale, and the brandy of the frumenty, and forgot, many of them for the first time, that they were three thousand miles from any place they had previously called home. At the head of the table, Brewster was conceding to Bradford that he had not at all remembered the taste of venison, not at all remembered how tender and rich it was; only that it was sweet, which it was. Captain Standish had left the table and was demonstrating to Massasoit and his braves the speared tip and many hacking points of his iron-frilled halberd, partly out of natural soldierly pride in the weapon, partly to demonstrate clearly its daunting superiority over an Indian spear, and a little out of the fellow feeling of one fighting man for another. But in Standish's mind there was very little of the last. He believed a savage was a savage. Wheaton did not join in the conversation of Brewster and Bradford, but sat looking down the table at his new wife, half in pride at her beauty, half in irritation that she was so animatedly absorbed by her own companions that she did not see him. Then she did look up, and glowed at him.

Wolsey was sitting next to Jane White, and across from Susannah Tilly, who caught Wolsey's glance at her husband and asked, 'How is it then, dear, to be a wife of two weeks? How does it go?'

Wolsey said, 'You *know* how it is, for a wife of two weeks. Or I think you do, Susannah.'

'*Knew,*' said Susannah; 'oh, I knew. Oh, that I were in my bed, and he in my arms again.'

'Which *he* would that be?' asked Jane. There was no envy in this, no jealousy, only friendly feeling, and Susannah never for a moment took it any other way.

'Whichever *he*, whether the *he* you'd say the same for, Jane, or whether another, all that's left of him is here,' and she touched her forehead, 'in my remembrance of him, or,' leaning over to place a hand on Jane's head, 'or there maybe, in your remembrance.'

'And his soul in Heaven, God grant that.'

'God grant. But we can know something about Heaven,

leastway by hearsay, by what the minister says, but up there *he* can't know of us, because there never was this country while he was living, nor no white women in it. And he never knew of this country, or thought we would come here when he was living. So he don't know of us, Jane, do he?'

Wolsey had slipped away to Wheaton at the head of the table. She put an arm on his shoulder as he sat, and nuzzled her face into his shoulder.

'No, no,' he said quietly, wanting her to stay but unable as minister to let himself be seen to be held in such open affection, even by his wife. He raised her so that their heads were not together, but she still leaned on him, and he held her with an arm around her waist. They were in this attitude when the ceremony of lord and lady was performed.

The Lord of the Harvest, the youngest man over full age who had helped bring in the harvest, sat opposite the Lady of the Harvest, a woman of his choice, a girl of fifteen, whose name was Grace. All the women had made a crown, a circlet of woven herbs – Southernwood for faith, Thyme for courage, Lady's Mantle for hope. They presented this crown to the Lady of the Harvest, putting it into her hands, and she stood, moved right round the table until she stood behind her Lord, and placed it on his head. 'And a bit of boxwood as well,' said Grace, taking a sprig from her neckerchief and twining it into the boy's hair. 'A bit of boxwood as well, for strength, to make a lord strong for his lady.'

All the table laughed.

Then the people sang the old songs of the harvest – 'Lavender blue, dilly dilly, lavender green, you be my lord, dilly dilly, I be your queen.' All the people took it up. The crowning, and the singing, were as pagan an offering and invitation as any in old England. During the ceremony, Wheaton took his arm from Wolsey's waist. She felt his shoulders stiffen, and saw that he would not look up at her.

In a final exercise of arms and show of strength, the four cannons of the fort were fired off, one after the other, one to the north, one to the east, one to the south, the last to the west, where the sun had died an hour before. The early dark of late October had come. The flames from the cannons' mouths vividly lit the whole company. In the hush after the crashing and reverberating noise, Bradford led a brief prayer, Wheaton having motioned him to do so. The Indians melted into the forest, the nightly guards were mounted at the stockade, and the people of the settlement went to their houses.

Wolsey walked with her husband of two weeks to their house. The fire was still burning in the hearth, as it had been kept burning all day.

He opened the door, and they stood in the open doorway together.

'It was a Harvest Home,' she said, lifting her eyes to his. 'It was a *proper* Harvest Home.' She was spirited and delighted.

'Wolsey,' he replied, 'that is just what it was. A Harvest Home, in the old way.'

His voice was cold. She heard that he was angry.

'It was a thanksgiving,' she said.

'A thanksgiving?' He was now angrier than she could have imagined, and the angrier he grew the more quietly he spoke. She had never seen him like this before. 'Wolsey, you have just *called* it a Harvest Home, a proper Harvest Home you said, and it was. You saw. And you stood by me throughout that performance of the lord and lady. It could have been any pagan Popish village in England.'

She dropped her hands to her sides, and said, 'Francis, and what if it was a Harvest Home? It *was* also a thanksgiving, you know. And you can see that too, if you look. It may not be altogether what you would have wished. You cannot change these people altogether. Leave them some of the old ways.'

'Leave them *that?*'

'Leave them that.'

Then he said what had been on his mind for weeks, since before their marriage. 'Wolsey, why did you oppose me when it came to the matter of the festival day, in the council? Why did you oppose me? Why?'

'I did not oppose *you*. I said what I thought was right, and the others thought it right too.'

'You *did* oppose me.'

'I opposed your opinion.'

'That was not yours to do. It was not up to you. And you opposed me.'

'I have said I did not.' She was angry now too.

'But why?' he said softly and insistently. 'Why?'

She flared at him, 'Because you were wrong.'

Her eyes were furious.

They stood for a minute in great anger, and then they were both miserable. They had felt the presence of each other all day. They were warm with feasting and drinking, and now it all came to this.

Neither would take back a word, and each knew that. But though Wolsey would not take back a word, she had the sense not to let a few moments destroy the day.

So she did not take back a single word, but tried to turn the quarrel away. It was a fragile moment. If he had continued, she would have given better than she got. But while he stood silent she said, 'Oh, Francis, Francis,' and took him in her arms.

He drew deep breath. She put up a hand to his face. Still his pride would not let him unbend.

She drew back gently, and said, 'Let me show you.'

In the firelight he could see that she had decked the house with leafy branches of white birch, over the door and by the one small window. On the rough table she had placed a wooden bowl of distilled rose water and on its surface floated the vivid leaves of the wild, red rose of New England.

She took his hand, and now he held it.

They stood looking around the house of one room which was theirs, which Francis had built with the other men, as he had helped them build theirs. It was a scented house, and made fragrant not only by the delicate scent of the rose water, and not only by the sharp woodsmoke of the pinewood fire. The structure of the house had a scent. It was that of the new oak planks sawn only three months ago for its walls, roof, and beams. That was the scent of the forest. Then there was a tang of the sea, which came from the salty, dried seaweed lining the east wall, to keep that side the warmest, because the bed was there. On that side the wall planking was double, and the hollow between was stuffed with seaweed from the shore.

As his mind became alive to this salt scent, Francis's eyes went to the wall against which the bed lay in the flickering shadows. He moved to the fire, lit a taper, held it up, and saw that Wolsey had decked their bed too. Above its head she had arched two more birch branches. And in the centre of the bed she had placed a green garland of meadowsweet, three long fragile stalks with their many little clustering flowers of white.

All this time the outside door had stayed open. Francis shut it, and came to Wolsey where she was standing. Their anger was forgotten. Neither said a word. Keeping her eyes down, she loosened the laces of her bodice at the back. He watched. When all the laces were undone she looked up, held out her arms, and he took the garment and eased it off her shoulders. She let it slip down her arms until it fell to the floor. Then he saw that she was wearing a golden chain, and the glint of the ring suspended from it. It was the chain she wore on her wedding day. He took the ring between his fingers, and turned it round.

'I have not seen this before,' he said. He had not. On her wedding night she took it off before she went to him, and had not worn it since. The chain and ring were for wedding days, high days, festival days. She wore it on her wedding day because it was an heirloom, and meant the world to her. But she had taken care he should not see it because she knew that any sort of wedding ring would offend his beliefs, and she did not want to offend him. But a harvest festival, even if it were called a thanksgiving, was a high day, a festival day, another thing altogether. She had worn the ring because it was the right day for it, and proper, and she simply had not thought to conceal it from him.

'A ring,' he said. 'Wolsey, there are those who say that a

ring, a bishop's ring, or a ring used idolatrously as a wedding ring, or as an adornment, is a ring for the devil to dance in.'

'It is a ring I had from my father, and he from his, and he from his, and so on back. I wear it in remembrance of them. It is the only thing I have of theirs. And the devil no more dances in that ring than he dances in me.'

He let it drop back on to her breast. 'Now,' she said. She took his hands and led them behind her to the fastening of her skirt – the skirt of russet Piedmont silk she had worn for Thanksgiving because it was the best she had, the only piece of silk she had brought with her from England. He unlaced the skirt and it fell rustling to the floor. Then she stood only in a cotton petticoat, and guided him to the unfastening of that too. She helped his hands, and then shook herself so that the white cotton fell on to the russet-coloured silk to make a circular heap of her clothes, out of which she had to step as he led her to the bed. There she stayed standing as he undressed. When he had done this he touched her on the shoulder, and she lay down on the high bed.

They were lucky, fortunate lovers. He was gentle and she was generous. 'Do not let me hurt you,' he said on their wedding night, after he had hurt her for a sharp moment. 'Do not ever let me hurt you.' Since the first days he never had, and never would, because she was a silky woman, easy to enter. But still he said to her that night as he entered her, 'I do not hurt you?' and she smiled with her lips, because her eyes were closed as they always were in any embrace, and held his shoulders close in an invitation to enter her deeply.

Francis knew that Wolsey was a delight to him and a gift. He did not know how great a gift. She was the rarest, and most delicate, and yet most bold of women, and he was a fortunate man. As he lay inside her she held his shoulders, then his back, then his waist, then his head, with the lightest touch of her hands. It was a light touch, sometimes of her palms, sometimes of her fingers, but one that said plainly that she was his and that she adored him. There was already, after so short a time, a rhythm of understanding between them. They would lie still for a moment, he inside her and she enclosing him, and hold hands, entwining the fingers. Holding hands was a more intimate caress to them than any kiss. They sometimes kissed in affection, never when they lay together. Except that sometimes there was not what could be called a kiss, but a moment when she parted his lips with hers, and they lay so that they breathed together, breathing the same breath. After they had lain still together, perhaps even while they were lying without movement, an imperceptible change in the touch of her fingers, an imperception he had learned to perceive, would tell him that she was beyond herself, and about to travel further beyond herself. That was what happened on the night of the Harvest Home. He was too close to her to be able to see distinctly anything but the long eyelashes dark against the closed eyelids, but her face was transfigured. He held her more closely, went more deeply into her, and moved and moved, and then held her head, not caressing her but holding her head still, so that he could feel the pulse in her temple. She said softly, 'Oh,' and then, with other soft exhalations, and then cries, came so that her whole body shook.

He said her name again and again, 'Wolsey, Wolsey.' She was quite beyond any ability to say anything. She was transfixed. She came with her heart. But when she recovered the ability to speak, she opened her eyes and said to him, 'Come,' and encouraged him, and then caressed him, stroked him, spoke to him, and drove him into her until he splashed quite helplessly into her and buried his face in her hair.

They lay for minutes like this. Wolsey lay feeling his weight on her and wishing to keep his weight. Above his head she could see the birch branches with which she had decked their bed. Francis, coming to himself again, saw, in the centre of the room, in the fire-shine, the circular pool of white petticoat and russet silk skirt lying where they had fallen from Wolsey. Then he caught, beyond the scent of Wolsey beneath him, another scent. It was the meadowsweet she had placed on the bed, which in their absorption they had lain on. He reached down, plucked one of the white flowers and give it to her. She cupped it in her hands, felt its texture, and realized what it was.

She laughed, and held it in her cupped hands.

'Do you remember,' she said, 'the day we walked by the brook, and I held up my hands full of water for you to drink from, and you wouldn't?'

'I would drink it now,' he said.

'We were not married then,' she said.

He laughed.

She raised herself on her elbows, and swished her hair so that it caressed his chest, and he reached out and took her by the waist again. As she arched over him, he could see the dull glint of the fire on the gold ring. As she swished her hair to and fro, so the ring swung to and fro, to and fro.

And what was in the mind of Francis Wheaton? In the deepest of moments, the sharpest forebodings may come to such a man, and even as he had splashed into his beloved wife the grotesque Old Testament warning came to him, that a woman would hunt for the precious life of a man, and draw the precious life out of him. Wolsey was his beloved wife. He held her and gave thanks for her. And yet in his heart he was troubled that he had made a carnal compromise with the devil, who might indeed, as he believed, dance within the sweet body of a woman.

8
THE CHILD AND THE UNICORN

In its first years the colony quietly prospered. More settlers came from England, and a few from old Virginia in the south, until the fifty survivors from 1621 grew after five years to one hundred and thirty. Good clapboard houses were laid out on two streets which intersected at right angles to form a cross. The Indians had kept their promise of peace, though Squanto was dead, poisoned, it was rumoured, by the Narragansetts whom he had threatened with the plague he kept hidden in the ground. The only Indian who still lived with the pilgrims was Samoset, the man who first walked into their camp and greeted them in broken English. But they no longer needed the Indians to show them how to plant corn. Crops were good, and cattle were brought out from England, so there was fresh milk and butter. The pigs multiplied, so that there was abundant pork and even, on special days, the delicacy of roasted suckling pig. Thanksgiving had remaind an annual transgression, the high day of the year. Wolsey bore a son, and bore him, as the women said banteringly, nine months to the day after her wedding night. At which Wolsey smiled, and said if that were true, then what could have made her happier? The boy was called Robert, after her father, and was the joy of her life. Mr Wheaton loved the boy, too, as he loved his congregation and his faith.

After six years the pilgrims still owed the merchants money. Ships' masters who visited Plymouth had taken back various tales – good and bad – from which the merchants, not having made what they thought a sufficient profit, selected all the bad. Then they sent a letter to Bradford questioning everything – the diligence of the settlers, the suitability of the site, everything. The letter had come by the supply ship *Mary Jane*. She still lay in the harbour, and Bradford wished to send his reply back by her. He was also wondering whether to send back the ungodly pack of women sent out on the *Mary Jane* as settlers.

He was composing his reply, and Wolsey was acting as his amanuensis.

'What does it say again, Wolsey?' he asked. He had read it, but now had to reply point by point. 'What's it about?'

'Objections,' she said. 'It is headed "Objections."'

'Well?'

'First, Neglect of the Lord's Day in the colony.'

Bradford raised his eyes to Heaven. 'Deny it. No, write down that it is ridiculous. And say, we wish they in London had a better example to set us.'

Wolsey wrote.

'What next?' he asked.

'The water is not wholesome.'

'If they mean,' said Bradford, 'not as wholesome as the beer and wine of London, which they so dearly love, then right. But as water, the water here is as good as anywhere in the world. What more?'

'No grass,' said Wolsey.

'Ah,' said Bradford, 'the country barren and no grass, yes. Well, it's like any other country, some places better, some worse. Tell them to look at their own English woods, and see if they find such rich grass there as in their meadows and fields. Tell them the cattle here find enough grass. Tell them we have grass for one hundred times as many cattle, if only they would send the beasts. What else?'

'Fish,' said Wolsey. 'No fish.'

'A thing very likely to be true, along a coast where so many ships come from as far as England and Spain, every year, to fish.'

And so the list of objections went on. That the country was annoyed with foxes. 'Would they like us,' said Bradford, 'to dress up in red and hunt them with hounds?' That the people were much annoyed with mosquitoes. 'Anyone,' retorted Bradford, 'who cannot stand a mosquito bite is too delicate to come to a colony, and had better stay home till he is mosquito-proof. And what more?'

Wolsey said, 'Twelfthly and lastly, that the Dutch have settled near the mouth of the Hudson, and will take a lion's share of trade.'

'Tell them,' said Bradford, 'explain to them in short and simple words, that the Dutch are likely to come, and the French too, if those in England are too timid to come out for fear of a mosquito.'

Wolsey wrote, and then gave him the parchment for his signature and seal. Bradford liked Wolsey to write his letters for him. She had a fair clerk's hand, more elegant than his own. Brewster had at first done this work, but his fingers had grown stiff with a sort of rheumatism, which caused him much pain. Besides, Brewster, with his instinctive diplomacy, had sometimes softened Bradford's tart replies, while Wolsey was amused at his directness, and approved it.

He put the signed letter aside.

'How is the dictionary?' he asked.

This was Wheaton's dictionary of the Indian tongues, which he was composing not out of any desire to convert them by talking to them in their own language, because he was certain all savages were irredeemably damned, but rather to support a thesis of his that American Indians were the degraded remnants of the destroyed Greek and Roman civilizations who had migrated to America centuries before. This thesis was based on a similarity of some words in the classical languages to those spoken by the Indians.

Wolsey said, 'Francis still works on it. It is a large work now. He wishes that the screw from Mr Brewster's printing press, the one that was brought from Holland, had not been used to shore up the Big Ship's timbers after that storm. If he had a press, he says he would print his dictionary, after he had first printed tracts for the children.'

'So the work still goes on,' said Bradford, who knew enough Greek to have his doubts. Wolsey doubted too, but would never say so even to Bradford.

'It goes on. But today Francis is more concerned with unicorns.'

'Ah,' said Bradford. 'It is true that the Indians have said...'

'He is walking in the woods this afternoon,' said Wolsey. 'He took Robert with him.'

Bradford glanced out of the one glazed window of his house. It was a still, cold day, unusually cold for October. 'In the woods,' he said. 'Yes.'

It was certainly too cold for Wheaton to be walking with his five-year-old son in the woods. But his custom of walking out into the cold without his coat had lasted. In the first year it had served its purpose, to encourage the others. It was a show of defiance, and a pleasantry. The pilgrims had smiled at it and taken courage. Now it no longer served any purpose except to keep Wheaton cold, but he persisted in it. His persistence distressed Wolsey. It was very much in her mind as she said good-bye to Bradford and stepped out into the air. It was bitingly cold. If the wind got up it would be bitter, but still she knew Francis would refuse to wear a coat. All the settlers noticed. Some shrugged their shoulders and thought him a fool, but a hardy fool. Others thought it an eccentricity in the man, but they were the kinder sort. Some thought it fanatical. If another man had acted as Wheaton did, he would have been thought a bit touched in the head, but in theocratic Plymouth it was impossible for a minister of God to be thought a bit touched. It was certainly impossible to say so. No man would dare say so, though boys whispered it among themselves at the back of the meeting house on church days.

Those who knew him intimately kept their fears to themselves. Bradford would simply look out of the window, and say pensively, 'In the woods. Yes.' Brewster would see, but say nothing. As for Wolsey, she could talk about it to no one, not even to Brewster. It would have been disloyal to Francis. Anyway, it would have been no help to him. She saw clearly what she hoped no one else did, that Wheaton was coming close to believing his own confidently reiterated statements, which he always made in the most quiet, matter-of-fact tone of voice, that there were no extremes of temperature in New England. She thought that he was on the edge of self-delusion. She had tried gently to reason with him, but he smiled, and said she must not bother herself. Short of telling him plainly what she feared, there was nothing she could do. So she gave up trying to change him and only insisted that if he took Robert with him, as he frequently did, the child should be warmly clothed.

That afternoon, Wheaton walked in the forest with his head slightly bowed and his hands clasped behind his back, and Robert adopted the same posture. Walking together like this, father and son looked strikingly alike; but the boy's hair was darker, and his green eyes were Wolsey's.

'Samoset the Indian has told me about the unicorn too,' the boy was saying. 'But we shall have to go far inland, a day's march. They have seen the beast there, and brought back a skin. I never saw it, but Samoset said he saw it, and that there were whole herds.'

'Herds are unlikely, Robert,' said his father. 'We are told it is a rare beast.'

'Samoset says there are very many, if not herds.'

'But,' said Wheaton, 'we must not rely on the words of savages alone. There is Biblical authority.'

The boy nodded wisely. Ever since he could understand, his father had taught him Bible stories. Wolsey told him nursery stories and children's tales, but his father instructed him entirely from the Bible. And since the boy had learned to read, when he was three, his only reading was the Bible. His father had promised that on his sixth birthday he would begin his instruction in Hebrew, to which the boy looked forward as if it were a magic language.

The Biblical authority for the existence of the unicorn was

that it was mentioned briefly eight times. Wheaton and his son had skirted the woods until they reached the town brook, but they were far enough from the beach, and near enough to its source, for it to be called a river there. Wheaton stopped and surveyed the terrain.

'Robert,' he said, 'it is written in the book of *Numbers* that when God brought the Israelites out of Egypt, he promised they should be as strong as unicorns. And in the same passage, in the next verse, it says – I will give you the words – "Where the valleys are stretched out, as the gardens lie by the riverside." Now, the valley is stretched out here before us, and down by the mouth of the brook there are gardens. And just as the Lord brought the Israelites out of Egypt, so he surely brought us out of England, and to this land.'

'And so,' said the boy, who had rapidly learned the language of argument and demonstration expected of a Puritan, 'and so the unicorn is a special sign for us.'

Wheaton was pleased with this reply.

'And we pray,' he said, 'that this sign may be shown to us.'

That night the foreshore was rowdy with the drinking and singing of sailors and sailors' women. This happened whenever a supply ship put into Plymouth, and was universally decried by the inhabitants of the town, or by almost all of them. Bradford, in his bed, determined to get shot of them as soon as he mercifully could. They had already taken the cargo of beavers on board, but he knew they had not yet shipped enough water or salted fish for the passage back to England. He would hurry that up. He was also determined that, besides his letter to the London merchants, the *Mary Jane* should carry back the half-dozen women the merchants had sent with her to add to the colony's breeding stock. He had seen them, and made his intention plain to the ship's master. They were all Londoners, these women, not a Christian among them, therefore probably dissolute, and must anyway have been desperate to make the passage without faith. They would pollute the colony. He would ship them back. For the moment, he sent the town constable and three armed men to drive the sailors and the women back on board their ship for the night, and this was done.

The next day was a busy one for Plymouth. At dawn the hunting party moved off into the woods, looking for unicorns and for a sign. The party was composed of four Indians, who swore they knew the way, four pilgrims, who hoped to shoot at least a deer or two and hoped for nothing more, and Wheaton. As they left, the town was already up and preparing for its work. The crew and women on board the *Mary Jane* were still drunk asleep, anchored far out in the harbour.

It was noon when another sail was sighted. A brig of two hundred tons, under topsails in the light breezes, made her way round the hook of Plymouth beach and moved slowly into mid-harbour, where she stood off, furled all canvas, and fired a salute of nine guns. All Plymouth lined the shore to watch her come in. She was the largest vessel they had seen for many years, larger than their own Big Ship, and three times the tonnage of the *Mary Jane,* who also lay at her moorings. The newcomer flew at her mainmast, as a courtesy to the sovereign whose port she was entering, the Red Cross of England, and at her stern the ensign of the States General of Holland.

Bradford and Brewster went down to the shore to greet their visitor. Standish assembled his militia in ranks, to do the ship full courtesies. Plainly she came in peace. England and Holland did not love each other, but, so far as Plymouth knew, the two nations were not at war. If it had been war, they could not have resisted so large a ship, armed as she must be. Whether she came as friend or enemy, it would have to be courtesies. So the settlement's cannon returned the Dutchmen's salute, and the elders waited at the quayside while the ship's cutter brought her officers ashore.

The Dutch and the English made their introductions. The principal Dutchman was Isaak de Razieres, trading agent of the New Netherlands and secretary to the governor of Manhattan Island. Bradford, who was fluent in the language from his long years in Holland, greeted him in

Dutch, at which the second Dutchman, who turned out not to be Dutch at all, said with vigour, 'And thank the Lord for that, Mr Governor. My name's Harry O'Brien, of Cork, sailing master of that States vessel. And Mr Razieres brought me ashore, an Irishman, thinking that an Irishman could translate his respects into the English. I told him the style was different, sir, if not the mere words, and besides that, my Dutch was a bit Irish, too. So I rejoice to hear you have the language well, sir.'

After some ceremonial shooting off of muskets, and before they all went back to the governor's house to talk, Bradford turned to Wolsey, who was standing behind him. 'It seems,' he said, 'that the Dutch are here sooner than our masters in London thought, and will be wanting a share of the Plymouth trade, too,'

'You must write again,' she said, 'and tell them there's a Dutch alliance with the Irish too, to which they can take another objection.'

Razieres had gone ahead with Brewster and Standish, but O'Brien heard this exchange, and bowed to Wolsey and to her son, who stood holding her hand.

O'Brien was a big man, with broad hands, broad shoulders, plentiful curly hair, which was red, and eyes as green as Wolsey's.

'He is a very loud man,' said the boy.

'He is an Irishman,' she said.

O'Brien could hardly help hearing this either, grinned widely, and was about to answer her when the trumpeters the Dutch brought with them struck up a fine brassy noise as Razieres and the Englishmen, attended by English musketeers, walked two by two to Bradford's house. There was no speaking over that noise, but O'Brien was a man of resource. He leaned down to Robert, holding out his great hands, and offered by gestures to carry him. And before Wolsey could say yes or no, or anything, the big Irishman hoisted the boy on his shoulders and carried him in state as far as Bradford's house. Wolsey had no choice but to follow. At the governor's door he lifted the child down, nodded to

Wolsey, and said, 'I give you back your fine boy, ma'am.'

She gave him the coolest of looks.

'And I hope,' he said, 'to make his acquaintance again. But now, in for the horse trading.' He entered the house.

Horse trading it was, but with ceremony.

'Noble, wise, prudent, and worshipful governor,' began Razieres, in Dutch, bowing to Bradford. 'Powerful councilors, dear friends,' he continued, bowing to Brewster and Standish. Then he went on to remark that their native countries lay not far apart, that they were united in their opposition to the Catholic king of Spain and to his pretended monarchy over all Christendom, which God forbid, and that they of the New Netherlands would be happy to trade cloth for beaver and tobacco, and were in any case delighted to offer a few small gifts. Two Dutch sailors then presented the council with a barrel of white sugar and two Holland cheeses.

After which they all waited.

'Sir,' said Bradford, 'thank you, though you give us too high titles.' Puritan plainness and Dutch courtliness then traded Dutch cloths of three colours for Plymouth beaver and otter skins. The courtliness led into dinner, and to an invitation for the Dutchmen to stay and rest for a few days before they returned.

Two mornings later, the unicorn hunters returned. In the distance, as they approached, they were seen to be carrying two creatures slung on poles, but the creatures were not white. One of the Indians was carrying, slung over his shoulders, an animal which appeared to be white. But it could not have been a large animal, for one man to carry it on his shoulder. The gates were thrown open and the hunters welcomed. The town was buzzing. Razieres and O'Brien, who were watching with the rest, thought it a great fuss to make for two red deer, which was what the hunters were carrying. They hardly noticed the white pelt the Indian was carrying, which had appeared from far off to be a third creature.

There was some cause for celebration in the colony.

Venison was still a rare delicacy. And though one of the deer had been stalked and killed by an Indian, the other was shot by an Englishman, and was the first an Englishman had ever killed in the forest. But most of the people gathered round the white skin which might be that of a unicorn. It was brought to the square by the governor's house, and laid on the ground. It was not the skin of a whole animal. The hunting party had got it from some Indians they met. These Indians had caught the beast two years ago, and swore it had only one horn. They had cut the pelt into parts, to make coats for the winter. What they had traded the pilgrims for strings of beads was a part of the pelt that did include the head. There was no horn, but there was a hole through which a horn might have grown. It was inconclusive. The sign for which Wheaton had hoped had not been given to them, at least not wholly.

In the two days before the hunters returned, Robert had taken a liking to O'Brien, who was a sailor, with a sailor's stories to tell, of passages to Malta by way of Gibraltar, of the sea to China which some men said lay west of southern Virginia, of the French who lived in the frozen north in a city called Québec, a city built on the side of a steep hill that was almost a cliff. O'Brien liked the boy. And through the boy he came at least to say a few words to Wolsey. He soon learned that she was the minister's wife. He did not even try to banter with her, knowing that if he did she would be pretty short with him. But even her brief presence warmed him. In two days he had four times had occasion to return Robert to her. Her simple words, 'Thank you, Mr O'Brien,' – and she could hardly have said less – pleased him. She was a handsome woman, and his day was the better for seeing her.

That evening the governor was giving a farewell supper for the Dutchmen, who were leaving the next morning. The white skin, whatever it was, had been hung against the inside wall of the room where they ate.

They drank a lot of the strong Plymouth ale, which was always plentiful at this time of year. Bradford, Standish, and Razieres were engaged in deep politics. O'Brien found himself being entertained by Brewster and Wheaton, and the talk turned to Wheaton's idea of the classical Greek origins of American Indians.

'It would,' said Brewster, 'be very gratifying if it could be shown to be so. Some are very striking men, tall and dark.'

'The Greeks I have seen,' said O'Brien, remembering the Greek sailors of the Mediterranean, 'have mostly been short and dark.'

'But in ancient Greece,' said Brewster, 'it is known they were taller.'

'And the language,' said Wheaton, 'does bear uncanny similarities.'

O'Brien drank. 'No Indian I've known,' he said, 'and I've known them in the plantations in south Virginia, and in New Netherland, and now I've seen a few here, ever had a written language at all. They cannot write. They have signs.'

'But their speech, when properly transcribed,' said Wheaton, 'does produce words of a classical sound. I am compiling a dictionary which compares the classical and the savage languages.'

'Ah,' said O'Brien, 'Greek-Indian. For sure now.'

Wheaton said, 'The Indians hereabouts, when they cry out for help, utter the *Wananumau*.'

'I never heard an Indian call for help,' said O'Brien. 'But,' he pursued, with his mind on the glorious girl he had seen, who was the minister's wife, 'may I ask, does your wife, whom I've seen with your son, help with the work of making the dictionary?'

Wheaton was surprised. 'Her Greek *is* excellent, Mr O'Brien, yes, and she has helped copy out some parts of the work.'

Ah, thought O'Brien, the Greek could go hang; but what a delightful creature to be a minister's wife.

'But the *word* for help,' Wheaton continued, 'the word in Greek is *anunime*.'

'Close,' said O'Brien, finding difficulty in maintaining

his gravity, and yet sorry for this man and his obsession.

'Close indeed,' said Wheaton. 'Very close.'

O'Brien considered this.

'And now,' said Wheaton, 'when the Indians mean a gorger, a man who gorges his food – as they do gorge themselves when there is food, since they may then have to go days without anything – they say *pascopan*. Now, *pasco* in Latin is to eat. *Pan* in Greek means everything. *Pasco-pan*. To eat everything.'

'And there are other European connections,' said Wheaton. 'The Indians live in mud huts very like the wild Irish.' He stopped. He had forgotten O'Brien was Irish, a difficult thing to forget, an error possible only to a man in the full flight of an enthusiasm. He had not wished to offend O'Brien.

O'Brien carefully took no offence. 'Ah,' he said. '*Pascopan*. No doubt. Very like. But that's for men more learned than I am. But I see that skin which hangs on the wall, and while you were away hunting it, your fine boy Robert told me why you were hunting it, and how it was a sign.'

'A sign of the Promised Land, yes.'

'Well, and we have them too in Ireland.'

'The unicorn?'

'The unicorn. And there's no miracle in that, since Ireland is as holy a land, excepting yours here in New England, excepting that, as exists on this earth.'

Wheaton did not remark that Ireland was Papist, which showed restraint on his part.

'And I have a fine song about the unicorn, which I learned at my mother's feet. On the floor of me mother's mud hut, as 'twere.'

Wheaton began as if to apologize, but O'Brien stopped him, 'No, no, I'll just give you the song.'

And he did, interrupting the early course of commerce between New England and New Netherlands with this verse:

> *Oh, the unicorn is sovereign*
> *In the forests that are deep,*

> *And no mere men can trap him*
> *For the unicorn is fleet.*
> *And he laughs at spears and arrows*
> *And at men and hounds who seek,*
> *And only a woman's mystery*
> *Shall betray the noble beast.*

They were all merry enough to listen to this, even Wheaton, who had first to suspend his disbelief that so auspicious an animal as a unicorn could inhabit Ireland.

'Only an old song,' said O'Brien, 'and not sung well, and I have some of the rhymes wrong, as you will have heard. And there are more verses, which I will not sing, only tell you the gist of, which is that try as the men will, they never catch the beast, but a woman – a virgin is needed, they say – can approach the beast unharmed, and stroke the beast, and lull and subdue him, and then the dogs and men kill him, having crept up suddenly.'

The supper broke up. Razieres and Bradford had come to an understanding, and there would be trade. Then O'Brien said, 'One thing. This is back to the unicorn. Now, that skin on your wall is white. And your authority for the beast, you say, Mr Wheaton, is Indian talk and Bible reading. I have heard the Bible read, in the church, back home, and heard the unicorn pieces read, but nowhere does it say that a unicorn is *white*. Only your Indian beast, and your Irish beast, but not your Bible beast, is white.'

Wheaton reflected that this was true, but did not answer. He was downcast. He would have to return to the texts in the original Hebrew, to try to detect some hint of whiteness in the scriptures.

The meeting ended. Dutch sailors with torches, who had been waiting outside, rose to escort Razieres and O'Brien back to their cutter to row to the ship. Wheaton and Brewster went to their houses.

O'Brien watched as the door of Wheaton's house opened, and glimpsed Wolsey in the lighted doorway as she greeted her husband.

The Dutch party began to walk down hill to the shore. In Razieres's mind were two thoughts. That the strange English were most diligent in hunting unicorn, which he would report to his superiors. And that Bradford had gently warned him that, though trade would be welcome, the Dutch had been on Manhattan for only two years, and that the island lay in waters which Elizabeth of England, the old queen, had been navigating and colonizing for the past forty years. He would report that too, as he would that Bradford had told him that two Indians had recently been seen hunting with muskets, which they certainly had not got from the English, and which, in Captain Standish's opinion, they must have had from the Dutch. Razieres knew nothing of this. He had told Bradford that he would not, as a Christian, have traded muskets with savages, and Bradford had taken his word for it.

O'Brien's mind was on Wolsey, whom he would almost certainly never see again. She was already as lost as a hundred women seen by him once, in passing, and then passed by, some remembered for a day, some for months. It was a regret to him.

Down by the shore a girl came timidly out of the darkness. She was one of the women from the English supply ship, who had inveigled her way ashore. She approached the Dutch party, silently offering herself. One of the sailors pushed her aside. O'Brien stopped, and she came up to him. She could not have been more than sixteen. She was dark, and thin.

'You are from the settlement?' he asked, knowing she hardly could be. Both virtue and well-being shone from the pilgrims, and this girl had neither.

'From the English ship, sir.'

O'Brien had seen the other ship at anchor, a sloppy bark.

'And they will send me back to London, sir.' O'Brien had heard talk of this.

'What is your name?' he said.

'Anne, sir.'

O'Brien was a sailor. Besides the women seen, never

known, but remembered, there had been many girls, like this one, had for the night, and not remembered.

'Then, Anne, come with me,' he said. They hurried to catch up with the others at the cutter, and O'Brien took dark, thin Anne back to his cabin aboard the Dutch ship that night.

9

TO CHERISH AND MAINTAIN ENTIRE

It was by unhappy chance that, only a few months after such a friendly visit, a Dutch vessel out of Manhattan bound for Amsterdam was blown off course and forced to take shelter at Plymouth. By then, two more Indians had been seen hunting with muskets. Where, Standish demanded again, did the muskets come from? And where did the savages get their powder and shot? Bradford replied that he had put all this to Razieres, and believed him when he said no Dutchman would trade firearms with Indians as a matter of simple survival; no Dutchman would do that. Standish retorted that Bradford had taken Razieres's word too easily. It was all very well for Bradford, having lived for many years in Holland, when Holland was at peace, to take a Dutchman's word. But he, Standish, had fought many skirmishes against the Dutch, and knew they could be as bloody as any men living. To which Bradford replied, that Standish had hardly been fighting against soldiers of the States General of Holland, but against Dutch mercenaries, who might very well be no better than they ought, and might be bloody men. And as far as Dutch mercenaries went, said Bradford, Standish had no doubt in his time, hiring his services out to different masters, fought alongside some of them. Hadn't he? Standish growled that he had too, but that only enabled him to see at closer quarters that they *were* bloody men.

When the Dutch ship was blown off course and struggled

into Plymouth harbour, Standish much exceeded his authority, boarding her and demanding to search the vessel. The captain refused, whereupon Standish, referring to nobody, searched her by force. The captain complained bitterly in the name of Their High Mightinesses the Lords of the States General. Bradford and Brewster interceded, but not before the Dutch captain had got a shallop off to Manhattan stating that his vessel was seized. Manhattan relayed the protest to Amsterdam, and Amsterdam to its ambassador in London. By that time the ship had been long released, reparations made, the whole ship's company entertained for three days at vast expense by the town of Plymouth while sails were mended and rigging repaired, and Standish made to feel small. But none of this was known in Amsterdam or London, only the seizure of the ship.

'Manhattan, Manhattan?' repeated Albert Joachimi, ambassador of Their High Mightinesses to the Court at Whitehall. 'Manhattan?'

His secretaries could not find it on any map they had, but explained to him the cause of complaint. They summarized for him the letters from the governor of Manhattan to Their High Mightinesses, and of Their High Mightinesses to His Excellency the ambassador in London. They agreed with his Excellency that it was hardly a jewel of the Dutch seaborne empire.

Joachimi made the most formal request for an audience of His Majesty Charles I, of England and her dominions beyond the seas King, Defender of the Faith, and so on. He was told that the king was at Newmarket races, where he would remain for several days. Reminded by his secretaries that Their High Mightinesses considered the matter as one of the greatest urgency, Joachimi reluctantly set off on the journey of seventy miles, on wretched roads, to present himself to the king. He later complained bitterly to his wife that in order to get to the king he had to present himself at a race course and jostle with stable boys, jockeys, bookmakers and underlings of no rank whatever.

But when Joachimi was eventually admitted into the

royal presence, on the verandah of a pavilion at Newmarket races, Charles was all urbanity.

'Your Grace,' began Joachimi, making many flourishes with his hat, and, taking a paper from his pocket, putting himself in a dignified stance to read it. At which the king waved a serving man to pour the ambassador a glass of decent wine, saying, 'Do sit down, Joachimi. Sit down, man.'

The ambassador, having taken the gilt chair held out for him by a young aide, began afresh, or was about to begin, when the king, reaching out for his own glass, compelled Joachimi, out of courtesy and necessary deference, to pick up his glass too. The king sipped. Joachimi sipped.

It was often said by his contemporaries, in his early days, that Charles, had he been born not the son of a king but the son of a peasant, would have raised himself by his own grace and abilities to be the king's first minister. He was a natural diplomat.

So, having put himself at ease, the king leaned back and waited.

'My dear Joachimi,' he invited.

The ambassador began his recital of the outrage, setting out the heads of complaint which his secretaries had so carefully prepared for him. The ship. The storm. The seizure. The indignity. The natural hurt felt by Their High Mightinesses at a slight least expected from so gracious a king.

Charles listened, even once nodding in sympathy.

The ambassador reached the point where he stated that the ship had been outward bound from the island of Manhattan, in the West Indies, and was continuing when the king said, 'Ah.'

'Your Grace?'

'Surely Your Excellency means the Manaddos, at the mouth of the Hudson's river, in our colony of northern Virginia.'

'Manhattan, Your Grace, in the West Indies.'

'Hyperion,' exclaimed the king with animation, suddenly standing.

'Hyperion, sir?' asked Joachimi, scrambling to his feet.

Charles waved toward the paddock where six splendid animals were being led round by stable lads, before their jockeys mounted for the next race.

'The bay,' said the king.

Joachimi inclined his head, and wondered dismally at this English passion for racing horses when they could better have been put to work, though, as he later told his wife, the beasts had been bred so fine they would be incapable of pulling a dog cart. Hyperion was a bay gelding, the most handsome two-year-old of the season, who had not lost a race. The king watched the ensuing race, which Hyperion won by five lengths. This delighted the king, because the horse was from his stables, and he received and congratulated the jockey, the steward of the royal stables, and two other horsey gentlemen of no rank whatever, before he resumed his seat and turned back to the ambassador.

'The Manaddos,' said the king. 'You were saying?'

Between races, which demanded the king's whole attention, Charles listened languidly to Joachimi's representations, which included the statement that the island of which they spoke – Manhattan in the West Indies – had been purchased by the Dutch governor there, and paid for.

'Purchased?' the king inquired.

'Indeed, Your Grace.'

'Ah,' said the king. The ambassador would of course be certain that at the time of the supposed sale the savages were in possession of the island in good faith, in good Christian faith? He assumed the savages were Christians? And that the Indian chiefs, supposing they possessed the land, had unanimously agreed to the sale? And if all this were so, then those chiefs could of course be produced by the ambassador to swear, as Christians, to the fact of the sale?

The ambassador kept silence.

'And what,' asked the king, 'was the price paid, or said to have been paid, by Their High Mightinesses for this island?'

The ambassador gave a list of goods, remembering what

his secretaries had told him. 'Wampum, looking glasses, beads, and other valuables.'

'Wampum, Joachimi, wampum?'

'A species of shells, Your Grace, exceedingly rare, which the Indians esteem highly and use as currency.'

'Whelk shells,' put in the young aide who had been standing quietly at the king's side, and who had prepared him for this audience as the ambassador's secretaries had prepared him.

'Whelks, ambassador? That is so?'

Joachimi said miserably that he did not know.

'I too am at a disadvantage, ambassador. I have never seen a whelk. But other valuables, you said. Other valuables also. To the undoubted value of what?'

'Sixty guilders, Your Grace.'

'In English money, today's exchange, say six guineas, ambassador? Seven, then?'

Seven being agreed, the king begged the ambassador to accept, as a token of His Majesty's good faith, the trifling sum of seven guineas, to be wagered on a horse of his choice in the next race.

Joachimi demurred. 'Your Grace...?'

'You will not refuse me, Joachimi?'

Joachimi *could* not refuse him. He would have to treat with the king again, and with his ministers, on matters of more importance than this unheard-of island. He had to retain the king's goodwill.

Horses were once more paraded in the paddock before them, and, as the mortified ambassador later told his wife, a fellow was summoned who made his living taking wagers, seven guineas were counted out into the fellow's hand by the king's aide, and the fellow given to understand that this sum was paid on behalf of His Excellency the ambassador of Their High Mightinesses.

'Take Titania,' said the king, pointing out a magnificent beast which, even to the ambassador's eye, did stand out from the others. 'Can't lose. She's mine, I'll vouch for her.'

The wretched ambassador agreed, the bookmaking

fellow departed with backward bows to the king and a leer at Joachimi, and the horse then inexplicably came in last in a field of nine, even though ridden by the king's own jockey.

The king was decently sympathetic.

'Enough of matters of state then, ambassador, what? Come to dinner, man. Your ship shall be released. But as to the Manaddos in northern Virginia, it is a colony which I have always taken occasion to cherish and maintain entire, and shall do so.'

10

THE SNOW NEVER COLD

The pilgrims' children took to the country more quickly than their parents had done, because the children had known no other country. Wolsey's son Robert was, at ten years old, an adept trapper of squirrels and snarer of foxes, and knew the forest trails round the settlement as well as the Indians. He could fish with ease, knowing when the herring were running. He could not remember how he had learned that the trumpet honeysuckle stopped the itching of insect bites if its leaves were chewed and placed over the bite, or that the liquor of the horsetail fern would soothe a burn, but he did know these things. He knew where the water was sweet to drink and which berries were safe to eat. He was too young to be encouraged by the blacksmith to turn his hand to making tools, but he knew, from hanging round the smithy, how metal was heated, hammered, shaped, tempered, and cooled. He had observed the making of barrels and the shrinking-on of hoops to hold the staves together. He knew what rushes were good to strew on a floor, and which were strong enough to cover a roof. He had seen houses in the building, and knew the use of bevels, squares, levels, chisels, augers, and draw knives. He and his friends of the same age could have survived in the wilderness, which was no wilderness to them because it was so familiar. Robert was a tall boy for his age, with his mother's sense and sturdiness, and her eyes. His father had taught him the gentlemanly and scholarly accomplishments of Hebrew and

Greek, which he could already read. Wolsey could very well have taught him that as well, but by tacit agreement between husband and wife that had been left entirely to Mr Wheaton. Hebrew and Greek would enable Robert to read the Old and New Testaments in their originals. He was on his way to being a complete pilgrim. As a pilgrim should, he loved and honoured his parents. He was easier with his mother, who sometimes knew his mind before he spoke it, or knew when he was unwell before he did himself. But for almost the last two years he had spent more time with his father. This was principally because Wolsey had new children to look after, twin daughters born to her eighteen months before.

It had not been an easy pregnancy. She had not discovered why until Susannah, who acted as midwife in the settlement, told her, as late as the eighth month, that she was bearing twins.

'They fight inside the mother,' said Susannah. 'That's the way of it. They always do. The stronger fights to be the first to be born and see the light. If there are twins, one is always stronger than the other.'

The first child was born half an hour before the second. When she saw the first was a girl, Susannah mumbled to Wheaton that it would be better if the second were a girl too.

'Better than that it should be born a boy, see. Better, seeing the first is a girl.'

Wheaton, wanting another son, and half distracted by Wolsey's cries as she lay in labour, snapped at the woman to be quiet and get about her work.

She took no notice.

'See, sir,' she said. 'The first is always the stronger, and if the first be a girl, and the second a boy, then the odds are it will be a boy that is too weak for a boy.'

But the second child was a girl too. 'Better,' said Susannah. 'Better. It's no odds if one *girl* is frailer than the other. Now, if it'd been a son, sir....'

Wheaton cut her short, and told her to babble her superstitions elsewhere.

He took the twin daughters, when they were washed, and went to Wolsey.

She held first one and then the other, and then Wheaton took the children and laid them one each side of Wolsey in bed. She was exhausted and weak. The children were born at dawn. At noon she drank some broth, and she and Francis named them Rebekah and Ruth. Rebekah, the firstborn, was a pound heavier, and had more copious and darker hair

It was midsummer, and exceptionally hot even for New England, the hottest summer they had known so far. On windless days the heat was insufferable. Men who should have worked the fields rested in the shade bare to the waist. Only Wheaton strode round the town at high noon, fully dressed, remarking to all who would listen that it was temperate. The people thought him queer, and no longer disguised their feelings.

Brewster, visiting Wolsey a few days after the birth, was astonished to be asked by her, 'How do you think Francis is?'

Even to Brewster, her mentor, her surrogate father, and her oldest friend, she had never before, in all the years of her marriage, talked about her husband.

Brewster waited, looked her in the eyes, and nodded. He had never seen her afraid before. He said, 'Wolsey, my dear, I believe I think as you do. But new children can give a man new life.'

'I hope so,' she said. But in her heart she knew Francis's delusion was complete.

Brewster sat down again. He was helpless to say anything to reassure her.

'He no longer even reads,' she said.

This had been true for nearly a year. Except to teach Robert, Wheaton never opened a book. He never even read the Bible, only referring to it now and again when he needed a point for a sermon.

His dictionary was quite abandoned. Wheaton had compiled a rudimentary lexicon, but the more he learned the more clearly he saw that his thesis was untenable. There were certainly a hundred or so examples of words which sounded much the same in Greek and in the Latin. But since there were dozens of Indian dialects, and several separate Indian languages, this was hardly surprising. If American Indians were the remnants of classical Greeks and Romans, there was nothing in their languages to prove it. The manuscript had grown to several hundred pages, but had lain neglected for two years.

'He feels his exile,' said Brewster.

This was a deep, unspoken truth in Plymouth. It was true of many people. In the first months they had been conscious of misery, but the struggle for life fully occupied their minds. When the Big Ship returned to England in April, no one returned with her because those that desperately longed for home and safety could not face another Atlantic crossing. Later there was loneliness, not the loneliness of a man alone, because there were fifty of them, but the loneliness of a village in a continent. They knew their nearest neighbours were in the far north at Québec, or in the farther south at Charleston in south Virginia. The later visit of the Dutch, and the pilgrims' knowledge that New Holland and Manhattan were a few days' sailing, eased this loneliness. It was then that they began to know they were exiles, exiles from the country of their birth, from their families, their friends, and from the familiar customs and seasons of their native country.

Not all felt this. Those who had previously been in Holland hardly felt it. Those who had been hardy enough to stand many years in Holland had proved themselves immune to the malaise. And not all who came from England felt it. The labourer who had never left his own village in England was not desolate when he came to another place he never left, and where, besides, the living was better. But those who had travelled in England often felt it bitterly. It was certainly a self-imposed exile. They could have returned, on the supply ships which came once or twice a year, but few had. They were pilgrims. To return would have been to admit defeat. It was this pride which kept Wheaton in New England. He had recruited them all. He had *told* them they were pilgrims. He had spoken about Promised Lands. He was their spiritual leader, but his own spirit sickened. He had known London and Cambridge. He missed his native country, the society of his companions, and the society of learning, which had all sustained him. He now knew, and had known for many years, that he was one of those men who are not fit to plant a colony. But he of all men could not admit this and leave. All he could do was convince himself that the Promised Lands were as he had promised, so that he could convince the others.

So it fell on Wolsey to support him. But he had not told even her, as how could he tell anyone, when he would not begin to admit his fears and agonies even to himself?

He did take new life from the new children. He carried them about and was proud of them. He talked about them. He gave sermons on the blessing of children, and his congregation was pleased at what seemed a return to plain sense.

He delighted in Wolsey, too.

Not that he had ever ceased to do so. A man supremely conscious of sin is likely to be sensitive to the delights which are occasions of sin. So, though the imagined sin of it at times tormented him, he was his wife's gentle lover – various and subtle. In another place and at another time Wheaton could have been a subtle libertine. So the society of Wolsey had always meant a great deal to him, and in the months after the twins' birth he did gain new life, and recovered a boldness which had faded. Wolsey in return was as ardent as a girl.

The events of one afternoon in particular would have surprised his brother elders. The village was preoccupied with the last gathering of the harvest. Robert was with the harvesters, and Rebekah and Ruth with Leah, Susannah's daughter, who had come as nurse and maid. Wolsey went into the woods to look for saffron, as seasoning for a cake. Wheaton saw her go, and followed. She was leaning down pulling flowers out of the ground when he came up to her.

She knew it was him by his tread and did not turn. He held her by the waist, and slid his hands up under her warm bodice to her warm breasts.

'What are you looking for?' he asked.

'Saffron,' she said, 'saffron, Francis.' But she did not move. He touched the tips of her breasts with the palms of his cupped hands, and she moved herself against his hands.

'Give me a flower,' he said, and she handed a saffron flower back to him.

'The leaves are like the white lily,' he said, easing the bodice upward until her back and breasts were bare, and he caressed her breasts with the leaves, until she laughed and raised herself, arching her back against him. Then she turned, encircling him with her arms, and drew him down to the forest floor.

Afterward she lay in splendid disarray with a tangle of skirts round her waist, and her petticoats full of leaves.

'I cannot breathe,' she laughed. 'Oh, too much.' And more laughter.

They both lay back and looked up at the sun through the trees. Wolsey said the line of Greek which she remembered from a book in her father's study long ago, a secular book. She remembered that her father, when she asked what it meant, said he hoped she would know very well one day. The line said, 'God give me more such afternoons as these,' and at that moment, lying on leaves, she did know very well what it meant.

She spoke it aloud. 'Too much, too much,' she laughed.

But to Wheaton it was only a line he had heard her speak when she was delirious in the sickness of the first winter. And that night it was he who was delirious, not only in body but in soul.

He would not eat supper. He sat in the dark until Wolsey lit a rushlight. He sent Robert to bed, saying there would be no Hebrew that night. The boy was puzzled, and looked at Wolsey for an explanation. She had none to give him, and just said, 'It will be all right tomorrow.' The boy did as he was told, and said good night. Leah saw the two babies to bed, cleaned away supper, and was then sent to bed herself.

When they were alone, Wheaton began to speak.

There was little privacy in the house. Since it was first built with one big room, two more had been added. The children slept in one, and Leah in the other. The inside walls were no more than thin sawn planks. Any substantial privacy was impossible. Conversation in an ordinary voice was heard all over the house.

But Wheaton spoke with a soft intensity, so softly that Wolsey had to strain to hear him.

'To be man and wife is honourable,' he said.

She waited.

'But it ought not to be a *provocation* to lust. I have said, in the church, that no married person should think *all* things are permitted to him. Each man should possess his own wife soberly.'

'Hush, Francis,' said Wolsey. 'You torment yourself.'

Wheaton took no notice. 'And each wife should possess her husband soberly.'

'But not sadly,' she said.

'Marriage contracted before the Lord,' he replied, 'should preserve modesty and measure and not become lewdness.'

Wolsey denied the accusation of lewdness with all her heart, but knew it was useless to reply.

'The man,' said Wheaton, 'who has no regard for shame or honour in his own marriage, is an adulterer – towards his own wife.'

Wolsey stayed by him for several minutes, but he said nothing more. She went to bed. She was still awake when he came to bed an hour later. He did not touch her or say anything to her. She watched all night as he slept a disordered and broken sleep. He tossed his head restlessly. When she put out a hand to smooth the pillow beneath his head, she felt that it was soaked with sweat.

The next Sunday, he preached in the church on the same theme with the same intensity, and with many biblical illustrations. Wolsey sat very straight as she listened, next to her son Robert. She did not know whether her son felt the gaze of the congregation upon them, as she did. At the end, Brewster came over to her and offered her his arm, and the two of them left together, with Robert.

The winter that followed was bitter. Snow fell early and deep. When it lay three feet deep on the ground, and the trees were shrouded with ice, Wheaton announced, while his breath froze in the air as he spoke, that to a true believer it was never cold. Even while cutting winds penetrated the timbers of the meeting house, he remarked that, as they would have observed, trees and shrubs in New England never bent before the wind, and then remained crouched and stunted, as they did in even the mildest parts of the old country. He was heard in silence.

Most men could hardly have failed to hear the pointed silence of the congregation. Wheaton was so self-absorbed that he did not notice. But it was not quite true to say that his absorption was with himself. It appeared to be, but he was really absorbed by the confident belief that his knowledge of God was becoming daily greater, that he was growing nearer to God, and understanding His will more clearly. Wheaton, who could not tell even Wolsey about his fears and terrors, did tell her that he believed a closer knowledge of the divine will was being opened up to him. He was careful to say that this was because of no virtue in himself, but was a gift of grace to him, utterly undeserved.

The evening of the same Sunday that he was received in church with silence, he talked earnestly of the will of God, and His blessings, and then played with his daughters, whom he counted among the greatest of these blessings.

'They sang today, Mr Wheaton,' said Leah. 'Both little darlings sang.'

'Sang?' said Wolsey.

'Bekah sang first, and then Ruth,' said Leah, kneeling down by the twins, and coaxing them: 'Now sing for Daddy.' They would not.

Leah hummed four notes herself, 'La-la, la-la,' to encourage them, but they would not follow her.

Wheaton knelt on the floor, and Wolsey came and sat by him, to be closer to the twins.

'They did sing, ma'am,' Leah insisted. 'Not a song with words, but la-la, la-la, a tune. Bekah first, and then Ruth.'

It was always in that order. At twelve months Rebekah had shaken her head and Ruth had copied instantly. At thirteen months Rebekah crawled, and, after two days of struggling, Ruth crawled too.

They were handsome children, much admired in the town. Both had Wolsey's dark hair, even darker than hers. But the eyes of both were deep brown, in which they resembled neither of their parents. Wheaton's eyes were as blue as Wolsey's were green. Wheaton said he could remember a grandmother with brown eyes, who also had the almost olive skin of the twins. He secretly felt that there was more in them of himself, or of his side of the family, than of Wolsey.

'Sing,' he said, coaxing the twins himself. 'La-la, la-la?'

They would not, but sat and gazed at him, holding hands.

'Well,' said Wolsey, 'they'll sing again if they've sung once. And I'm glad they have. They're late with speaking.'

The two had been later learning to talk than other children.

'That's only natural,' said Leah, reassuring the parents. 'They're so much alike and so close they don't need to speak, knowing what the other thinks without any words needed.' Leah spoke with all the experience of a girl of sixteen, but what she had observed was true. The twins did, without words, look at each other and begin to cry together, demanding food. Or they did look at each other and then straight away begin making a din with metal spoons banged on the table.

But they could speak very few words, and Ruth not even her name.

''Twill come,' said Leah. 'Soon enough we'll not be able to stop them talking, all day.'

Wheaton brought out a metal looking glass and held it

up. Rebekah reached for it, looked at her reflection, and said, 'Bekah.'

Ruth held out her hand for the looking glass, and her sister gave it to her. They hardly ever fought for a toy, but passed it from one to the other.

Ruth looked at her reflection in the mirror.

'Ruth,' prompted Wolsey. 'Ruth.'

Ruth did not look up at her mother, or let her eyes leave the mirror. Still gazing intently at the reflection of her own face, she said, 'Other Bekah,' and was pleased when they laughed.

Father, mother, and the two babies played for another half an hour in the firelight. Then Leah took the twins, fed them, and put them to bed. Robert came in from the smithy where he had been watching the blacksmith fashion a shovel, heating the metal until it was white, shaping it on the anvil, and then thrusting the glowing red-hot metal into a trough to cool it, so that the hissing steam rose.

When he came in, Robert's boots were sodden.

'Snow's deep,' he said as Leah fussed round him, taking his boots to warm by the fire. 'Snowed all day.'

'Snow indeed,' said Wheaton, 'but not so wet or cold as English snow. Winters are crisper here, but the snow never so cold. And the wind has died.'

It was already dark. Wheaton, Wolsey, Robert, and the serving girl ate supper, and then went to bed. Inside, the only light was from the fire, which was kept slowly burning all night. Outside, the only human light came from the small, narrow windows of the other houses. The bright snow reflected these glimmerings, but the reflections grew fewer as house after house closed its wooden shutters for the night. By nine o'clock the town was asleep. The night was dark and still, with a waning moon.

At midnight Wolsey was roused by Leah shaking her. First she felt a chill cold, and then heard the girl's frightened voice telling her, 'They are gone, ma'am.'

Wolsey sat up.

'All of them gone,' said the girl wildly.

Francis was gone from their bed. Running into the other room, Wolsey saw that Robert's bed was empty too, and that the twins were gone from theirs. She came back into the big room where Leah huddled shivering by the fire. Wolsey shook her by the shoulders.

'Where are they?'

'I woke with the cold, ma'am, and they were gone, the babies, and Robert, and the door was open, and I came to you.'

The outer door was wide open. In spite of the fire, the house was bitter cold. Wolsey ran to the door and looked out into the night. The only fire in the township flickered from the watch-tower on the hill. There was little moon, but it was a night of clearest star-shine. Wolsey looked out to sea, where the horizon was visible only because it was a line above which the stars began. It was so clear a night that rising or setting stars were cut in two by the horizon. She looked into the forest, where she could make out the hills only because their shape was a darkness made visible where it blocked out the stars. She looked across the snow, and the wan moonlight, and the light of a million stars, reflected by the snow, was just enough for her to perceive two sets of footprints.

Behind her, Leah was crying.

'Dress, girl,' said Wolsey, rapidly pulling on all the clothes she had.

The girl was still shivering and sobbing.

'Dress,' said Wolsey, pushing her towards her room.

Wolsey pulled on her boots. She saw Francis's coat hanging by the door. He had left that. She pulled it over her own shoulders. Leah appeared, having dressed. Wolsey stooped down, stripped the covers from her bed, and thrust them into the girl's arms.

'Carry them. Come with me.'

Wolsey knew the next house was Susannah's and her husband's, twenty yards away. She must go there, raise the alarm, and raise the town. She started for the door, and then stopped. In the light of her own hearth fire, she could see a figure standing before her.

Leah stifled a scream, and then began a low wailing.

Wolsey saw the figure was that of an Indian. He covered his face with his hands, bowed to her, and gestured her to follow.

'I cannot, I cannot,' sobbed Leah. Wolsey slapped the girl sharply. She recoiled, but then came after, still weeping.

They walked through the northern gate in the palisade, which lay open, followed the man on to a forest track where the snow fell from low branches as they passed, and powdered Wolsey's hair.

'Why are we going?' moaned Leah. 'I will not go into the dark.'

She would not have gone farther, but at that moment, the Indian motioned them to a stop. He squatted down, brushed a frost of snow from a figure lying by the path, and showed it to Wolsey. She saw that it was Robert, and knew her son was dead. She knelt in terror, by the stiff, crouched figure of the boy. She heard the voice of Leah, saying repeatedly, 'God help me, God help me, God help me.'

The Indian wanted Wolsey to go farther, but she could not move, and knelt as rigidly as her son lay.

The Indian raised her face slowly, so that she looked into his face. He had no English, but he was impelling her to come with him.

'My babies?' she said. 'My babies?'

He led on and she followed him desperately. Leah followed too, because her fear of the darkness behind, and of being alone with the dead boy, was greater than her fear of going on. She stumbled into a drift of snow, recovered her balance, and scrambled on, but left the bedclothes where she had dropped them in her fall: red blankets in the snow.

The trail widened, the forest thinned, and Wolsey could see now they were following the footsteps of a man who had worn boots, leading north. They came to a clearing, and there, at the foot of a tree, Wolsey's daughters lay in the snow. She fell to her knees, with her face and hair in the snow, weeping hopelessly. The Indian then uttered the only word she heard him speak. It was a word she did not understand, but it was imperious. She looked up. He unwound the skins in which Rebekah and Ruth were bound up. They were lying together on their faces, entwined together, breathing and alive. She felt them with her hands. They were warm, and alive. The man covered them again, wrapping them in the fur pelt of a deer, and lifted them into Wolsey's arms.

She stood holding the children, but looking at the line of footprints receding into the forest. She took two steps in that direction, but the Indian checked her. She obeyed him, and she and Leah followed him back the way they had come, past where Robert lay. The Indian picked the boy up and carried him over one shoulder.

They passed through the open gate of the settlement, and entered Wolsey's house by the door she had left open. The Indian placed Robert on the table, inclined his head to Wolsey where she stood hugging her two daughters in her arms, and slipped away into the night.

Leah turned wildly to Wolsey, who did not see her but continued blindly rocking the babies. Leah went to the frozen boy on the table. She saw the boy's open, green eyes staring back at her. Then the spell broke. Leah ran screaming from the house, hurled herself at the next neighbour's door, which was her mother's, and the town was raised.

Unknown arms took Rebekah and Ruth from Wolsey and warmed the children by the revived and roaring fire. Later, Brewster examined the skin in which they had been wrapped and agreed it was Indian. Robert was dead beyond any trying to revive him. Susannah closed his staring eyes and the women took him to lay out. The twins were put into a warmed bed, watched over, and soothed. Leah was put to bed in her mother's house. There was no sign of Wheaton.

Wolsey recognized no one, and shook off all attempts to put her to bed or even bring her nearer the fire. She stood on the dirt floor of the house, no longer knowing herself, rocking back and forth in grief, seeing in her mind only her dead son, footprints leading farther into the forest, and her two daughters lying entwined on the forest floor.

Outside, a heavy snow began to fall.

PART TWO

11

THE WOMAN APART

Wolsey continued to live in the settlement, but she was a woman apart. She was not alone. She brought up her infant daughters. Brewster visited her and read with her. Susannah, who had nursed her in the fever of the first weeks after the catastrophe, remained her faithful friend. Susannah's daughter Leah stayed with Wolsey to help look after the twins. So she was not alone, but she was apart from the rest of the townspeople, who regarded her with pity, and then awe, and then fear. They shunned her as people do shun someone who has suffered a calamity, wishing to keep themselves away from the contagion of it, fearing something of the sort may happen to them.

The isolation of her grief kept her at first away from the life of the town. Robert's death and the manner of it were hard enough to bear, but a peculiar circumstance made it harder. He had died in the middle of a hard winter, the hardest they ever had. Those who had died in previous winters had been buried the day after their death. But at the time of Robert's death the ground was so iron-hard that no tools could dig a grave, and the body lay for three weeks in a low shed by the northern palisade, where the bitter cold preserved the crystal corpse. After three weeks the ground was still too hard to break, but Brewster, seeing that Wolsey's thoughts never left the boy while his frozen likeness was still above ground, went and paid three men to light fires on the ground to melt the frost and enable them to dig. Even after a day's fires, they could dig only a shallow grave, and the earth they hacked out froze solid again within fifteen minutes of their shovelling it aside. So Robert was buried under two feet, at the most, of frozen clay, which resisted all their efforts to compact it. They sealed the cracks in the broken and frozen earth with sand brought from the beach, and then heaped boulders on the grave.

But still, that was not all. The death itself was a mystery, and so was the disappearance of Mr Wheaton.

The night of the disappearance, snow fell again heavily, and by morning all footprints had gone. For what had happened, they only had Leah's hysterical account, and Wolsey's. But they had neither of these accounts at first hand. They heard Leah's only through her mother, and Wolsey's through Brewster, and neither Wolsey nor the girl would ever after talk about that night. What were the members of Wheaton's congregation to believe? The boy was dead: that was incontrovertible. Wheaton had disappeared: that was certain. They knew that Wheaton – whether out of courage, folly, stubbornness, or madness they could only guess – had often walked out in the iron coldness denying that it was any colder than in old England. They knew he had often taken his son with him into the forest. From all this they surmised that Wheaton had walked out with Robert that night, that they had become separated, and that Wheaton in search of his son had gone farther and farther into the woods and become lost. How it was that an Indian had come to tell Wolsey that her husband was lost and her son dead, they did not know. The Indian had been seen by no one but Wolsey and Leah, and never afterwards reappeared. They did not know why the town watch, even on such a dark night, had not seen the comings and goings across the snow. This was because the town watchmen were asleep, and they were unlikely to confess this. The members of the congregation suspected strongly they had not been told everything, and they were right. When Leah at last ran hysterically to her mother's house and raised the alarm, the whole town woke. But the first to arrive at Wolsey's house were Susannah and Brewster. They had listened to Leah's incomprehensible story, seen Wolsey was distracted, and closed the door. It was Susannah's arms that took the twins from Wolsey, and warmed the children. She and Brewster formed a rapid idea of what had happened, and agreed not to disclose it. By the time other neighbours roused themselves, dressed, and came to the house, they saw that Robert was dead, Wolsey distraught, Leah hysterical, and Wheaton gone. It was natural that Brewster should be attempting to console Wolsey, and natural that Susannah should be looking after the twins, who were lustily crying. Other women took the babies and nursed them so that Susannah could take Leah back to her own house to put her to bed. No one was told that the twins too had been taken into the forest and found there. For a day Wolsey was incapable of saying anything, and then would not. Brewster and Susannah said nothing more. That left only Leah who knew and could tell. Next morning Susannah threatened her with everlasting hellfire if she did. These threats were uttered while Mr Brewster stood by. He said nothing, and made no threats, but his presence added force and authority to Susannah's.

At their next meeting the elders found themselves confronted with a difficult situation. Brewster did not tell even them all he knew. It troubled his conscience that he did not, but he did not. The elders – Bradford, Brewster, and Standish – had three choices. They could record a decision that Wheaton, for many years their pastor and himself an elder, had knowingly walked into the forest with his son, intending not to return; but that would be suicide, and perhaps even murder and suicide. Or they could say that both Wheaton and the boy were accidentally lost, and that Wheaton's body had not yet been found. Or they could say that, for want of more information, they could come to no conclusion at all. They took the third course.

They did not foresee that most of the congregation would stubbornly wish to believe Mr Wheaton was not dead at all, but still alive. The congregation, encouraged by the lack of any statement by the elders that Mr Wheaton was dead, did proceed to believe he was alive. This belief was lent some colour by the accidental discovery by Governor Bradford that Wheaton's manuscript dictionary was also missing. Bradford drew no conclusion from this except that the manuscript might be lying beside Wheaton's body under many feet of forest snow, but the congregation took it as an indication that Mr Wheaton, having taken with him his work of many years, had done so rationally, and was the more likely to be still alive.

The state of Wheaton's mind in his last hours was known only to Wolsey, and, in part, to Brewster and Susannah. But they said nothing, and Leah, in fear of hellfire, said not a word to suggest that the babies, too, had been taken into the forest that night.

Then a new light came among them. To take Mr Wheaton's place until he should return, the Reverend Wrestling Shepard came down from the new Massachusetts Bay Colony, to ensure that the souls of the pilgrims were in good keeping. With him, to ensure that he was himself in good keeping, he brought his sister, to keep house for him. Her name was Humility.

Mr Shepard was small, utterly assured, neatly dressed, and as precise in his beliefs as in his dress. His coat was black and his cuffs were white, and there were no greys. Humility starched his cuffs. At the first meeting on his first Sunday, he announced his holy intentions with a pleasantry.

'And now,' Bradford said to the congregation, having concluded a few remarks as to the learning and beneficence of the gentleman he was presenting to them, 'here is Mr Shepard.'

At which Mr Shepard, in his very first words, hoped that he might prove, with God's help, a true shepherd to them all. He then gave an unbending sermon, to do with the Grace of God. Afterwards he left the church in procession, after the governor and before Mr Brewster, and with his sister Humility walking beside him. Wheaton had never paraded like this. It was plain from her stern appearance that Mr Shepard's sister was likely to be as unbending as his sermons.

'Humility,' said Susannah. 'Yes. It is humility with which Mr Wrestling Shepard will need all his strength to wrestle. She is mighty proud that she is so humble.'

With Mr Shepard's arrival the saints became more saintly, and yet, at the same time, it was remarkable to observe that, with his coming, wickedness did seem to break forth. One man stole his neighbour's goods. He was placed in the stocks. Another man broke into his neighbour's house at night, which was burglary, and was branded with a Roman B on his hand. Adulteries were detected. These were grave offences, but the elders let them go unpunished except by the shame of public proclamation, and this in spite of Mr Shepard's protests that the will of God should be done, at least partly, by public whipping. But this was not done. Neither Bradford nor Brewster would have it. But the will of God, as expressed through Mr Shepard, became daily more powerful.

One Sunday he said his memorable sentence: 'We be the Lord's great chosen few, the rest of you are damned.'

This was unexceptionable. If Wheaton had been questioned when he was pastor, he would have had to agree that this was plain Puritan theology. It was the revealed truth. But he had never stated it in as many words.

The pilgrims had always accepted that they were chosen, and that the rest of the world was not.

But now Mr Shepard was urging on his flock that not all of them were chosen either. Those among them who *were* chosen, had been chosen before birth. The rest had been damned, also before birth, and no good deeds could save them. It was all predestined. God could save whom he chose, and for a man to question this power was to show that Satan was at work within him. God had saved the tribe of Israel, showing that he could save a whole people if he chose. He had likewise damned whole other nations. In his mercy he *had* chosen the pilgrims, but was not the iniquity breaking forth among them – as theft, burglary, and other uncleannesses he would not mention – evidence that He had not chosen all?

Over the weeks, as the power of Mr Shepard's theology grew, the proportion of the saved, even among the pilgrims, dwindled. After two months he was telling them the chosen were only a remnant, a slight portion. There were murmurings at this, not in church, which would not have been seemly, but in the houses. But these doubtings came to the ears of Wrestling and Humility, and on a spring Sunday the congregation was called to account for its murmurings. Was it not written that man was wholly sinful, and worthy of damnation? And if so, was it not the pure Grace of God that some of them, however few, were saved?

A brave soul, if not a saved one, did rise at this, and ask, was it not also written that Jesus said, let a man repent from his wickedness and live? No one had ever interrupted Mr Shepard before, but his reply was all sweet reason. That was so. But surely repentance was predestined too. If a man repented, then his sins were forgiven. True. But a clear reading of the Scriptures showed that only they could repent who were chosen to repent: only those men were capable of repentance whom God invited to repent. And this choice too was made, and this preordained repentance foreseen, allowed, and invited, before the conception of a man, before he was as much as a child in his mother's womb.

At this a murmur arose even in church, so that Mr Shepard replied in anger, 'Do you carp, rail, bark, or scoff? Do you bark? Do you bark? For it was in the power of God to have created you dogs, but He made you men. And is not this a great evidence of His great power, *and* His great mercy? That you are *not* dogs?'

Brewster was for sending the Reverend Mr Shepard back to Massachusetts colony with an honorarium. Governor Bradford demurred at this, saying that wickedness certainly had been breaking forth and required narrowly looking into. Standish was preoccupied with the Indians, who had shown signs of insolence and acquired a few more muskets. He shrugged at Mr Shepard, who was allowed to continue with *his* preoccupations.

It fell out that one of those narrowly looked into was Wolsey.

Humility had called on Wolsey and, expressing fulsome condolences, was received with what she took as insulting coolness. Wolsey did not mean to be cool, but did not like the woman or her enthusiastic piety. She also found condolences from a stranger painful and impertinent. Humility attempted to play with the twins, who would not play with her. Humility warmly invited Wolsey to attend the meetings of townswomen convened by her to look more narrowly into the wickednesses now sundry and prevalent among the pilgrims. It would be fitting if Wolsey, as Mr Wheaton's wife, the spouse of a man celebrated for his godliness, should assist them. Wolsey could not bear to hear the woman speak of Francis. Tears stung her eyes, she declined the invitation, and rose. She was sure, she said, that Miss Shepard would find her presence only a hindrance. The two women parted on terms of cold civility.

All the women except Wolsey did attend Humility Shepard's meeting, which was held in her brother's house while he was at a meeting of the elders.

'I did ask Mrs Wheaton,' Humility began, 'but she did not wish to assist us.'

'Wolsey's still grieving,' said Susannah. 'Poor lady. To my mind, only the babies have kept her heart-whole.'

'The Lord's will be done,' said Humility.

'She loved the boy,' said Susannah. 'The Lord's will be done, but the Lord's will is sometimes hard, and I pray He may have better things stored in His will for you.'

'You are friends with Mrs Wheaton?'

'I knew her when she was a girl, and her father before her, a priest of the parish, an honest man...'

'Her father a *priest?*' asked Humility, and all the horror of Papism was in her voice.

'Of the English church he was brought up to. No man can

do more than that. He was a good man.'

'Were his eyes green, her father's eyes?' asked Humility, who did not forget the green eyes of Wolsey on her, dismissing her.

'His eyes? Her father's eyes?' replied Susannah, amazed that Miss Shepard should be interested in anything so merely human, and therefore of so little account, and so little to do with her, as the colour of a man's eyes.

'The little girls' eyes, the twins, are very dark,' said Humility. 'They are dark children. Mr Wheaton's eyes were dark? His eyes were dark too?'

Susannah did not answer this question of Humility's. What was it to the woman? She would not answer.

It was timid Juliet Shore who volunteered an answer, a girl eager to please authority. 'Please ma'am,' she said, 'Mr Wheaton's eyes were blue.'

'The eyes of the children are dark,' said Humility. 'Very dark. And their complexion dark.'

That was all. Then they passed on to the more profitable investigation of profane swearing, the wearing of masks for unlawful and lascivious ends and purposes, the naming of notorious drunkards, and the unlawful and malicious supplying of savages with strong waters. The meetings continued with success. No fewer than fourteen transgressors – all profane swearers and drunks – were turned over to the civil power in the first four months of Miss Humility's enquiries.

Brewster did not like it. 'This woman,' he said to Standish one evening as they were smoking together, 'is uncovering petty things we should be wise to turn a blind eye to. Even Bradford, who is a reasonable man, is becoming convinced that there is so much uncleanness here that the devil must have a greater spite against puritans than against other churches, when all that's happening is that this woman is nosing out what we never bothered to look for. A few men are now whipped for drinking, when before they were left alone. They are whipped, and then comfort themselves for the whipping by drinking themselves daft, and then are whipped again. Because of his sister's vigilance, Mr Shepard is now considering whether Satan does not possess more power in this heathen continent than he does in Europe. He tells me that's what he's considering. A fine way to put heart into the people in a strange land. It encourages them to see Satan in everything. If they look for him, they'll find him, and it will be his sister's doing. The woman's a curse.'

'Except,' said Standish, 'that she now seems to have found a woman who has been giving strong water to the savages.'

If this was so, it was justification enough for Humility. Strong waters were brandy. Standish did not want drunken Indians prowling round his palisades, and nor did any pilgrim.

'Indians?' cried the timid Juliet Shore, when at the next women's meeting she was accused of trading one pint of brandy for beaver skins to make a coat. 'I'm not the one that has close dealings with Indians. Ask Mrs Wheaton about truck with the savages, her who gave food to Indians, her who had a savage at her wedding, her who's been with Indians in the forest, her who – '

But this was too much for Susannah, who leaped at the woman, scratching her face and pulling at her hair, shouting, 'You liar. Worthless, wanton liar, Jezebel...'

This did no good. Susannah was restrained, and Juliet Shore exculpated herself by blackening Wolsey, repeating scurrilous scrapings of envious gossip.

Humility Shepard gravely considered, and told herself that it was her duty to listen, so that the truth might be brought out of darkness into the Lord's bright day.

It was remembered from years before that Wolsey had given bread to an Indian in the first winter. It was remembered that one single Indian stood on the edge of the forest watching her wedding to Wheaton.

'And,' said Juliet Shore, 'a savage came to her the night Mr Wheaton left her, and she went with him to the forest.'

Leah, Wolsey's maid, who had been there and seen it all,

started to speak, but then lapsed into silence.

'What is it?' asked Humility. 'You must say what you know. God wishes it.'

But Leah restrained herself from saying a word, fearing that if she said anything about that night, she might say more than she should, and talk about the little girls in the forest. And besides, Susannah had threatened her with hellfire if she ever did say.

Wheaton's last sermon, concerning adultery in marriage, was remembered. And what, Humility asked herself, could be the the only plain meaning of that? Was he not calling his wife an adulteress?

'She is a man-pleaser,' howled Juliet Shore.

Susannah again leaped at her, but was again held back by the many women who now wanted to hear this calumny through.

Then Jane White, Jane White who was growing old, Jane White who was now tired all the time, Jane White who had helped Susannah dress Wolsey for her wedding, summoned all her strength and courage, and cried out, 'Shame, shame, and shame. Wolsey is a sweet woman, and this is lie upon wanton, wicked lie.' She stood quaveringly, glaring at Juliet Shore, who then laughed wildly and, raising an accusing arm, said madly, 'Shame is it? Shame? You *saw* it, Jane White, you saw it. You saw *her*. You tell us what you saw in the forest.'

Jane White sat down, fainting. One evening, having drunk too much of Juliet Shore's brandy, she had told her what she once saw in the forest.

'I will not,' she said.

But she did. She did not mean to tell. She fought not to tell. But she was old and weak, and the fear of the devil and of the damnation the new preacher promised for most of them, and the holy hectoring of Humility Shepard, finally broke her down, and she said what she had seen. It was mostly what she had heard. It was Wolsey's laugh, and Wolsey's voice, and Wolsey's cries. It was the time when Wolsey went into the woods for saffron and Wheaton followed her. They were close enough to the village for anyone standing by the palisade to hear dimly. Jane had heard, and known it was Wolsey's voice, which was distinctive enough. She had heard Wolsey's laugh, and the unmistakable cries. But she had not heard Wheaton's voice, which was lower.

'What did you *see?*' Humility demanded. 'On your immortal soul, what did you see?'

'Nothing,' she said, 'nothing.'

'As you wish to be saved from perdition, what did you see?'

'Nothing.'

Jane had seen very little, but she did, when her strength quite failed her, tell them what. A flash of skirts and petticoats, the entwining legs.

'It was Mrs Wheaton?'

'It was Wolsey.'

When the old woman said this, she wept.

'And look at the children,' said Juliet Shore. 'Look at the twins. Indian children. Black eyes. Olive skins. Indian children.'

It was true they were dark.

'It was an Indian she was with?' Humility asked Jane White, and she sobbed and said No.

But she had said she did not see the man clearly. It was an Indian then?

'No,' she said, 'no, no, no, no, no.'

Susannah said, 'And no. And no. And that day was *after* the twins were born. They were babies. It was months after they were born. No.'

Then, Humility concluded, if that were so, though they could not be sure of the date, seeing the state of mind of Jane White, who had seen it, then might it only have been one of other encounters, many encounters?

'No,' said Jane White. 'Never.'

Susannah spoke again, and this time nothing could stop her.

'Won't any of you speak up against this? None of you? You liked her. She never harmed you. She has lost her man and her son. Many of you've grieved in your time. Now, none of you will speak up for her? Not a word? No one? Not one of you?'

There was some unhappy shifting among the women, but not a word.

'Then,' said Susannah, 'think of *your* immortal souls.'

Susannah sat down, and suffered Humility's rebuke for speaking lightly of the soul, which was God's gift. She bowed her head in fury.

With her only defender put down, it was then remembered against Wolsey that she had worn silk, russet silk, at the first Thanksgiving, when, according to the laws of England, with which the laws of the colony were conformable, no one below the rank of knight's lady, which she was not, could do so.

It was then remembered that Jane White had helped dress Wolsey on her wedding day.

'And so did I,' cried Susannah, 'and it was honest and plain enough. Wool.'

'Wool,' said Humility, 'but was there silk underneath, and the more insidious to be beneath?'

'There was no silk,' Susannah said, and then burst out, 'and it is your heart, Humility, that is insidious beneath.'

'Jane White,' said Humility, 'Jane White, you dressed her too. Was there silk beneath?'

Jane White was in agony. There was no silk beneath, but now she remembered, in anguish of heart, that Wolsey had worn a ring concealed on her wedding day, a ring beneath. And in a ring, she had heard men say, a devil might dance. Wolsey had worn a ring. Dazed, bewildered, exhausted, and ashamed as she was, Jane White began to doubt. She began to ask herself in her mind whether it had been a savage with Wolsey that day in the forest.

Broken and weeping, she denied the silk beneath, but admitted the ring. On her wedding day, Wolsey had worn a ring beneath.

Humility stood erect, silent, and in triumph.

The only sound was that of Jane White's weeping, until

the near-silence was broken by Juliet Shore, who cried in ecstasy, 'Man-pleaser, man-pleaser. A ring for Wolsey, man-pleaser.'

12

A GOD-DRUNKEN PEOPLE

When the intoxication of the meeting left them, they were all ashamed. It was not Humility Shepard who brought to God's daylight any account of this riot of Satanic calumny. Susannah Tilly and Jane White, both weeping, went that night to Mr Brewster and told him what had passed. Brewster called in Bradford, Standish, and Wrestling Shepard, and, in the presence of Susannah and Jane, repeated what they had told him.

Both women were trembling, and Jane weeping.

When Brewster had finished, Susannah said, 'You must not blame Jane, sir. She was made to and she could not help it. It was not her wickedness.'

Bradford said, 'We do not blame her,' and sent them away.

Juliet Shore and Humility Shepard were brought together before the elders, reminded by Bradford of the earthly penalties for Bearing False Witness, Slander, and Calumny, and then by Wrestling Shepard of the eternal penalties prescribed in God's Holy Scriptures for such offences. Both were told, and the other women later given to understand, that it would go hard with them if any of these slanders came to Wolsey's ears. They would have come to her ears, of course. It was too small a settlement for them not to, but as it happened, there was not time.

The turn of events was strange.

After Humility and Juliet Shore were dismissed, the

elders remained together for a while.

'Less Satan-sniffing now,' remarked Brewster, with the humbled Humility in mind. The Reverend Mr Shepard made no reply, but pursed his lips.

Standish was outspoken. 'But I would whip that bloody woman Juliet Shore.'

'We cannot,' said Bradford. 'If we whip her for slandering, the reason will have to be known.'

'No, not that,' said Standish. 'Whip her for trading with the savages. Strong waters for the savages. I'd whip her.'

'But we do not *know*,' said Bradford. 'Oh, we may know, but we have no witnesses.'

They had not. But Standish swore he would have the constable watch her day and night, and this was agreed. She was watched, and only three days later was detected not in trade with savages but in what the constable called an unclean act with a common sailor from a Dutch ship which had put into Plymouth to trade cloth for tobacco.

The constable, carrying his black staff tipped with brass, and accompanied by his assistant, brought the woman to the elders. The man had slipped away and returned to his ship in the harbour.

Juliet Shore denied any wrongdoing, and said the constable was lying.

The constable retorted that both he and an assistant had seen the act. Juliet Shore had been observed hanging around idly, waiting for sailors. Moreover, to induce her to perform the act, the sailor gave her a scarf, of which the constable had taken possession, and which he produced in court.

'What did you see?' asked Bradford.

'An act of uncleanness, sir.'

'What?'

It turned out to be a very small transgression, but still horrifying in its nature to Wrestling Shepard. Even though there had been no penetration, he said, *contactus et fricatio usque ad seminis effusionem* was a grave offence.

'She pleasured him with her hand, and that is all?' asked

Brewster. 'Is that what you're saying? Is that all?'

But, said Shepard, in his view there had been no penetration only because the encounter had been in open day, when quick concealment might be necessary. Besides, the transgression was on the Sabbath, which compounded it. And besides, the woman, in denying what had been seen and attested to by two witnesses, had forsworn herself.

'Had she any strong waters with her?' asked Standish. The constable said she had not, and Brewster said really that was nothing to the present case. But this question revealed to Juliet Shore what she was really to be punished for, and thereupon she changed her story and confessed the lesser offence of which she stood accused.

But Shepard would not let it go at a confession, and insisted that she was the more guilty since it was one thing to do an act of uncleanness by sudden temptation, and quite another and graver thing to lie in wait for it, as this woman had. She had lain in wait for sailors.

She was sentenced to be whipped in the marketplace.

At noon a crowd gathered as the wretched Juliet Shore was led out and tied by her wrists to a tall post. At first she was defiant, and glared round at the faces of women who only a few nights before had joined her in denouncing and blackening another. Now they had come to see her suffer, and she saw no pity in their eyes, only curiosity. Now she was the one to be condemned and mocked. Susannah had not come to see the punishment. Nor had Jane White, who had hardly stirred out of doors since her trembling appearance before the elders.

Humility was there. She had steeled her tender sensibilities, feeling it her overriding duty to see God's will done.

The elders were present, and Wrestling Shepard stepped forth from among them to state her offence publicly and then comfort her with the words that, though her iniquity was great and the punishment sharp, yet she should embrace the chastisement in the knowledge that the pain of her body would bring her closer to an understanding of the infinite mercy of God.

Hearing Shepard's voice, Wolsey came out into the marketplace. All eyes were suddenly not on the girl at the stake, but on Wolsey's figure, as she stood, apart from the rest, with her eyes on Mr Shepard as he intoned his words of comfort.

Wolsey looked at the girl, and what did she see? A girl she hardly knew, a girl of nineteen, a girl who stood with her hands bound in front of a post so that she could not escape the birch rod which the constable held in both his hands, while he waited to do his duty. Still Mr Shepard continued his disquisition on mercy. Juliet Shore no longer looked round but let her head drop forward and rested her forehead on the post.

Wolsey had no idea that here was a girl who had lasciviously slandered her, nor that most of the women standing in the marketplace had joined in her calumnies. Mr Shepard at last concluded, and stood back. The constable came forward, holding the birch rod up high, demonstrating it first to all the people, and then, in a final gesture, to the assembled elders, awaiting their sign to do his work.

An unseen voice from the crowd whispered, 'Man-pleaser,' and was quickly shushed.

Wolsey did not know the words were meant for her. She thought they were intended for the girl at the post, and that they were mocking and horrible.

'Prepare her,' said Standish.

The constable's assistant tried to unlace the girl's dress at the back, but then tore it, so that her back and shoulders were exposed. How thin she was. Her backbone showed, and her lower ribs were plain beneath the skin as she breathed rapidly in fear. In the extremity of her fear she was shaken by a shiver, which rippled across the slight back. Even at that moment she moved her shoulders so as to stop the remains of her dress from slipping right off her shoulders.

'Sirs?' the constable addressed himself to the elders, still awaiting their sign to begin.

Bradford sighed deeply. 'Put down your rod,' he said.

Then he said to the girl: 'Juliet Shore, there are those who feel that we are too tender, but we remit the rest of your punishment. You shall not be whipped. But you shall stand at the post for an hour, so that all shall see you, as an example.'

A groan came from the people. Most had wanted a whipping.

It was this groan which, of all that had occurred in the marketplace, most revolted Wolsey. She burst through the crowd to the girl at the post, covered her back, and then turned on the crowd, and on the elders.

'Haven't you shamed her enough? And for what? You have kept her here tied to a post, seen by everyone. She is a girl, and you rip her clothes and make a show of her half naked. You keep her in fear of the pain of whipping, and then, when in your mercy, as you say, you remit that, you say she shall still stand here for another hour?'

Wolsey was tearing at the rope binding the girl's wrists, until it was loosened.

Brewster came towards Wolsey, but she turned on him with a ferocity that stopped him.

'You?' she exclaimed. 'You, and you others' – this was to Bradford, Standish, and Shepard – 'have the power to govern, but not to torment. She shall not stay here.'

She turned to the girl who, though untied, was still cowering by the post.

'Go. Go home.'

Juliet Shore stared wildly at her, and then ran, holding her torn dress around her.

The people involuntarily made way for her, but then turned back to Wolsey.

'Man-pleaser,' a voice called out, and there was laughter. Still Wolsey did not know this was for her. Only the shaming of the girl was in her mind, and her disgust at the elders, who had inflicted such a punishment, and at the crowd, who clearly wished it to have been greater, and to have seen the girl flogged.

She stood there, astonished eyes all round her. 'Did we

come into this wilderness for this?' she said. 'Is this God's mercy? You have become God-drunken. You are a God-drunken people.'

She strode back to her house, and the people recoiled from her blasphemy.

'That she should have done such a thing,' said Susannah, 'in the face of the preacher and the elders. And all for the sake of *that* worthless, wanton girl. It is strange.'

'Fortunate for that Juliet,' said her daughter.

'Cruel unfortunate for Wolsey. Cruel for her she should say what she did. And do it for Juliet Shore. But if she'd known Juliet's wickedness, she might still have done it. It was the shaming of the girl, and the way of it, that she thought shamed us all.'

'And it did shame us all,' said Leah. 'But the elders *were* merciful.'

The elders had been merciful. It was certainly mercy that Bradford and Brewster intended to show. They had been very much swayed, when first deciding the punishment, by the vehemence of Wrestling Shepard, who was all for condign severity. It was only when they came to the market-place that Bradford, seeing the girl at the post shivering, told himself in his heart that a whipping would shame them all, and was too severe. He knew Shepard's stern mind thought the commerce with the sailor an abomination. He knew Standish wanted an exemplary whipping, not for the matter of the sailor, which he thought trivial, but to remind Juliet Shore what she could expect if she were ever caught trading brandy with the savages. He knew Brewster was for mercy. At the last moment, consulting no one, Bradford exercised his right as governor, and stopped the whipping. To be condemned by Wolsey for his leniency was irritating, and he heartily wished she had kept away.

The calumnies of the previous week against her had been baseless, but he knew the taint of them would stick. He also knew that, threaten as he might, someone would in the end take care to ensure that everything said against Wolsey should come to her ears. And now there was Wolsey's flagrant blasphemy, which was unpardonable.

'Rash woman' said Standish sadly.

'Blasphemer,' railed Mr Shepard. 'Presumptuous and high-handed blasphemer.'

Bradford did not like Shepard, but he knew that Wolsey's outburst would be regarded by all strict believers as blasphemy. 'She must recant,' he said.

'Or soften what she said.' This was sensible Standish.

'Soften?' cried Shepard. 'How soften sin? She must recant, and in the face of the congregation, in the public square, and do penance.'

Brewster asked quietly, 'You would treat her as Juliet Shore was treated today?'

'I would,' replied Shepard. 'And perhaps it is God's will that she should answer for more than blasphemy. Perhaps we were too sudden and ill-considered to censure Humility in her looking-out of sins. That matter, too, of Mrs Wheaton's wantonness, should be looked into by the elders. After her outburst today, can any sin be beyond her?'

Brewster rapped out, 'Nonsense. She is as innocent of that as any woman could be. It's you who slander her by saying what you do. You do not know her. I have known her all her life.'

Shepard was about to reply, with heat, when Bradford stopped the talk. 'Enough of that. But she must recant.'

He glanced at Brewster, who said, 'Then I will go and reason with her. I see she must take back her words.'

'And in the face of the congregation,' Shepard insisted.

Brewster did not reply to this, but repeated, 'I will go to her. Tomorrow.'

But Wolsey had a visitor that evening, who knocked on her door at dusk. Leah, who answered, returned to her mistress and said there was a great, strange-speaking man asking for her.

Wolsey asked him in, and he stood in front of her where she sat by the fire.

'You will not remember me, perhaps?' he said. 'I have

changed?'

She remembered him well. Broad shoulders, broad hands, curly red hair, and bold eyes. She motioned him to take the chair the other side of the hearth. 'I have changed more than you,' she said.

'No,' he replied, but it was true. When they last met she was still a girl, a girl who had endured the first pilgrim winter, but a girl untouched by close sorrow.

'You carried Robert on your shoulders,' she said.

'He was a fine boy. And I am sorry. For that, and for...'

She nodded. He would have heard of Robert and Francis. No one could stay an hour in Plymouth without hearing the tale of the boy's death and the preacher's disappearance in the winter snow.

'But I have two daughters,' she said.

So he had heard. And he had already heard whisperings that they were half Indian. The day before, he had knocked down the sailor who slyly told him this.

'Captain O'Brien,' said Wolsey, 'it must be six years since we met?'

'Six,' he said. 'Seven. Seven years. When I came with the governor from Manhattan.'

'Are you from Manhattan again?'

'I am. Master of the Dutch vessel in the harbour. I've stayed in the Dutch service.'

She offered him ale, which he accepted. He caught her eye across the flickering fire. She was a handsome woman now, not so slender as the darting girl, but handsome. It was difficult for O'Brien to conceal anything he felt, and she knew what he was thinking. He lowered his eyes, warmed his ale by the fire, and reminded himself that his business tonight was to be diffident.

He spoke, gazing into the fire. 'I was in the market square today.'

'Then you saw it.'

He had seen it, and thought that though they might call him Wild O'Brien, she was wilder, and for Plymouth dangerously wild.

'Shall I be telling you something?' said O'Brien. 'Something in my own history. I was a Roman, a Catholic, as coming from Cork in Ireland I am likely to be. I say "I was." I am. Once a Catholic, always a Catholic. Now, as a boy in Cork I was encouraged by the monks of the seminary. But it was soon clear to me that my vocation lay in other places than a seminary, and I was encouraged to go to sea. Sent to sea. But my time in the seminary taught me one thing I never forgot. I know the geography of a mind on the lookout for sin. My boy's sins were looked out. I know the channels and shoals of such a mind. And the Roman church is easier with sin than yours, being more accustomed to it, having got more the measure of it, and jogging along with it, not being afraid of it. On easier terms, do you see? To be brief, ma'am, a God-drunken people – people who become easily drunk because they are not much used to drink and are drinking new wine, do you see? – will not be much at ease with a creature that tells them to their faces that they *are* drunken.'

Wolsey watched O'Brien, but said nothing.

He put down his empty mug. 'I've foisted myself on your house, and I beg your pardon for it. But if you should want to leave this colony, ma'am, and bring your children, and one or two others, I have a ship in the harbour and can give you a passage to Manhattan, and find you proper lodgings there. It is not Dublin, or Cork, but it is a fine country. They are not a God-drunken people. They get drunk, but only on wine.'

She thanked him candidly.

O'Brien nodded. 'I see you don't refuse. And I pray you may accept.'

Next morning, before Brewster could come to her, Wolsey went to him and, standing before him, told him of O'Brien's visit. 'It is an honest offer,' she said, 'but I shall not go.'

Brewster looked slowly up at her. 'It is an honest offer, and you must go.'

Wolsey was astonished.

'Sit down,' said Brewster. 'Wolsey, dear woman, you do not know what danger you are in?' Then he told her. He did not reveal the calumnies of Humility Shepard, which her reverend brother wished looked into, but he made it plain that he could see no way in which she would not be forced to recant, and very likely in the square.

'Like that poor girl yesterday?' she said. Her eyes were all defiance.

'It might be so.'

'Then I shall face them, and will not recant.'

'Then no one could help you. I will not see you shamed. If you will recant, then that *may* be done quietly, before the elders. If you will not, then at the least you will stand in the marketplace for an hour, and Mr Shepard in his mercy will hang around your neck a card bearing the word "Blasphemer." It would be that. And I will not see you suffer that. So, as you love me, you will go.'

She refused. 'I will not run from these people.'

'If you stay you will bring public disgrace on yourself, and dissension into the colony. There are some that love you, but more who envy you.'

'I will face them all.'

Brewster got up and stared out of the one small window at the town square.

'Think of your children then,' he said. 'If you will not recant, you will be an outcast from the congregation. Not from me, not from Bradford, not from Standish, though it would be their duty to shame you if you did not recant. Not from Susannah. Not from some others. But in the eyes of most, you would be an outcast, living among us, and so would your children; they would take the taint from you. Think of them. It would be horrible.'

Then Wolsey broke and gave way. For herself, she would have defied the whole colony. But at such a cost to her children, she could not. She would go to Manhattan.

Wolsey asked Susannah and Leah to come with her, and they agreed. She asked Jane White to come, at which the old woman was overcome with tears of shame. She said, when she recovered herself, that she could not, that she was an old woman. She did look an old woman, though she was no older than Susannah, who was a vigorous fifty. Jane said she could not stand another emigration. Then she astonished Wolsey by falling on her knees and asking forgiveness. Wolsey looked at her wonderingly, not understanding, seeing only the woman's distress. She went on her knees too, raised Jane White's head in her hands, and kissed her, saying that she, of all people, could have nothing to ask forgiveness for. Jane allowed herself to appear consoled, but was not. After Wolsey left her house she collapsed in racking sobs, for she believed that if it had not been for her weakness, and if she had kept her tongue, Wolsey would never have left. Which was in part the truth.

After dark, Wolsey and the children went down to the beach, where Brewster took a solemn leave of them. Susannah and Leah arrived separately ten minutes later. None of them carried more than a few clothes. They were leaving their whole world behind them.

Brewster too was losing a large part of his world. Wolsey knew this, and at the last she hesitated. She turned to Brewster, who had so bravely said good-bye to her, and went back to him as he stood desolately on the wet sand. The others waited. He looked at her in silent distress.

'Go, my dear,' he said. 'Quickly.' He could not stop his tears and turned away from her, throwing his hands high above his head. It was not a prayer. It was an involuntary lamentation.

'William, I am leaving you like this?' She folded him in her arms. He could no longer hide his grief, and the tears ran down his face. If she had been going alone, she could not have gone on. But there were the children. She could not go back. He summoned all his courage and said, 'You are right to go. I told you that you were right to go.'

His thoughts were not for himself. He was tormentedly asking himself, again, if he had been right to bring her in the first place. He still thought he had, but the cost to her had been terrible. Had he been right to marry her to Wheaton? When he had first hesitated at Scrooby, when he first saw her fascination for the man and warned her, had he dimly foreseen the nature and madness of the man? He did not know. Chance had treated her cruelly, but he had put her in the way of that cruel chance. He blamed himself. Now she was leaving Plymouth, and he knew that wherever she went she would be a gift and a strength to those around her. Only then did it come to him, bleakly, that he would see her no more and that his shining pupil, his daughter, would be gone, and that his days would be deserts without her. No, that was blasphemy, he told himself, more blasphemous than Wolsey's calling the pilgrims God-drunken people, which he knew in his heart had only too much truth in it. The settlement would remain to him, and the church, but Wolsey would be gone, and he knew the pain would be aching and deep.

The Dutch ship's cutter slipped in under muffled oars, and he put Wolsey gently away from him, saying, 'God be with you.'

Then they were gone. Brewster waited on the beach for half an hour in the cold night, pacing back and forth in his agony, running his hands through his hair and then again throwing them upwards with the palms stretched wide, as if to fend away the grief.

At last he walked slowly back to the settlement. The ship sailed half an hour before dawn the next morning, before the pilgrims discovered that Wolsey, her children, and the two others, were gone.

13

MANHATTAN ISLAND

They sailed south in calm seas, and at ten o'clock on the morning of the second day, in sparkling daylight, rounded Sandy Hook and, with a fortunate wind, began the last few miles of their passage to Manhattan Island.

Wolsey stood on deck, lifting her head to breathe in the air of a fresh day in early September. She was warmed by the sun and cooled by the breeze, which shaped her dress to her figure. That morning, as for the last many years in Plymouth, she had completed her dressing by putting on the white bonnet which laced at the nape of the neck. Now, on the deck of the Dutch ship, feeling the wind in her face, she unlaced the bonnet, and her dark abundant hair streamed out behind her, and, as she leaned forward into the wind, was tossed and ruffled by the breeze. Three seamen for'ard stopped work and watched her. She did not notice them. She was looking west, towards the distant land.

O'Brien appeared from the door of his cabin, behind her. She did not hear or see him, but the men did and got on with their work. O'Brien took in the sight of her, and then approached.

'Leaning into those airs,' he said, 'you look like a figurehead.'

She turned her head so that the breeze took her hair across her face, and she had to brush it away, and hold it back with her raised hand.

'And what is your ship's name?' she asked.

'*Vliegende Hert.*'

'And what is that?'

'Flying Deer,' he said.

'It is a fine name,' she said, smiling. It was the first time he had seen her smile since she was a girl with a young son he had picked up and carried on his shoulders. She had not smiled when he met her for the second time at Plymouth. Now she did.

'Now, ma'am,' he said briskly, 'how are the little girls? And your other people?'

'Well,' she said, 'very well. All curious about what they shall see today.'

'Ah. Well, let me tell you what you are seeing now,' he said. 'It is different from your first landfall on this continent?'

'That was winter,' she said, 'and cold, and stormy, and uncertain.'

'Well, let me show you now. All night we gave a wide berth to the Long Island, over there, to starboard. I am wary of Long Island. Reefs, ma'am. Reefs the length of it, a hundred miles of reefs. Now, the ocean astern is the last of the Atlantic. We are steering west. And do you see those beaches to starboard?'

'Very white beaches,' she said.

'The last we shall see of the Long Island I told you about.'

'How much longer shall we be?'

'We shall be at anchor this afternoon.'

The ship's first mate came up to O'Brien, looked enquiringly, and was told, 'You take her in.'

'Now,' said O'Brien to Wolsey again, 'we shall go about as soon as we round that point you see, which is called Conyne Island, though it is no proper island, just a sandbank jutting out from the land.'

Within ten minutes the mate brought her about, with a running of seamen about the decks, and a hauling on ropes to trim the sails, and a creaking of timbers as the vessel changed course and put her head north-north-east.

'Now, see those two high points ahead, and a channel

between? We are making for that channel.'

'Then we shall be up to Manhattan?'

'Not quite.'

O'Brien gestured to his right. 'That point there, the right of the two points, is still part of Long Island.'

He gestured to his left. 'And that is Staten Island, where a Dutchman has a farm. And the channel between those two points is what I call the Narrows, but which the Dutch give a different name.'

'If it is narrow, it is a difficult entrance?' Wolsey asked.

'No, no, no, no. Twelve fathoms at half tide. A cannon shot across, two thousand yards. And when we are up to it, and through the Narrows, then you shall see what you shall see.'

The crew had all made this passage twenty times, in all weathers. On a fine, clear, summer's day these waters were as easy for them to navigate as the streets where they lived.

The *Vliegende Hert* cruised through the Narrows, and there ahead of them lay such a stretch of water, and such a vista, as Wolsey had never seen.

O'Brien had waited to see her pleasure at it, and laughed aloud with delight to see her exhilaration. 'There,' he said, 'is the finest harbour in the world, the finest I have ever seen, or any man I ever sailed with.'

'The children must see it,' she said, and went to the cabin to bring them on deck, with Susannah and Leah. Holding Rebekah and Ruth one on each arm, Wolsey gazed round at the six miles of safe harbour, at the wooded country on all sides, and towards the roofs of the town she could see in the near distance.

The children were becoming too heavy for her to hold both at once, so she gave Ruth to Susannah.

'That before you,' said O'Brien, 'is the city of New Amsterdam, and the rocky island on which it is built is Manhattan.'

They were now sliding up to the southernmost point of the island, making for their mooring by the fort. 'This river, here, in which we lie,' said O'Brien, 'is the North River, because it comes from the far northern country inland, though the English call it the Hudson. And the other side of the island is a narrow river they call the East River. Two fine rivers. A fine island.'

'The Hudson?' said Wolsey. 'Mr Brewster, whom you have met, told me that when we first came over as pilgrims in the Big Ship, we had a patent to settle the mouth of the Hudson, but that we settled farther north, where we did, because the winds were contrary and the season too cold to sail further. This is it?'

'This is the mouth of the Hudson.'

Susannah took both children, and she and Leah set about preparing to disembark. O'Brien left Wolsey to go about the ship's business. She still stood gazing at the grandeur of the country all around her – harbour, forests, and the rocky island called Manhattan. She was in a reverie when a sailor touched her elbow, and held out to her the white bonnet which she must have left fall when she took the children in her arms. She accepted it, looked at the thin worn fabric and the constricting laces at the neck, and then let it drop over the side of the *Vliegende Hert* into the waters of the Hudson.

The turning tide caught it and took it out again towards the Atlantic.

It was a bewildering afternoon for Wolsey. A woman who could remember York cathedral was unlikely to be awed by the governor's house at New Amsterdam, but it seemed very grand to her. It was built of stone, and was not the only house on Manhattan to be stone-built. There were six others. O'Brien's own house was made of good brick, and had many rooms. Wolsey had not seen a stone-built house, or one built of bricks, since she left England – for thirteen years. The decaying palace of the archbishops at Scrooby was far more splendid than anything in New Amsterdam. But York cathedral and Scrooby palace were three thousand miles away, and a world away in time as well as distance. On the new continent she had seen no house that was not made of timber, and no house with more than three rooms. Bradford's house at Plymouth had three rooms, and he was governor.

Then she was struck by the space all around her. As much of an unknown and unexplored continent lay behind Plymouth as behind New Amsterdam. New Amsterdam was as much in a wilderness as Plymouth. But in her new home the wilderness was not so oppressively close. At Plymouth the wilderness began at the fringe of the woods, half a mile away to the south, and to the north only twenty feet beyond the palisade. At New Amsterdam the wilderness was farther off. She stood at the southern tip of the town and saw vistas before her. She saw the splendour of the enclosed water of the harbour. She saw the splendour of the wilderness to the west on the far shore of the Hudson, but it did not threaten her because the river put an end to the wilderness and was a barrier to it. She saw the wooded slopes of Breuckelen to the east, again the frontier of a wilderness, but a wilderness whose shores at least could be commanded by cannon from ships in the East River. And then Manhattan Island itself was safer because it was an island, and more secure because from it you could quarry stone to build stone houses.

But most of all she was uplifted by the spirit of the place, which she felt but could not express. She had not thought of York for many years, but now on Manhattan she remembered the numenism of the cathedral there. Manhattan had no soaring pillars of stone, but the air had a magical aspiration in it.

As a city, New Amsterdam would in Europe have been counted a small town, but to her it was a metropolis. Apart from the stone houses, there were another eighty made of timber. Besides the fort and the church there were two alehouses. The streets were rough and dirty, but they were used. The town was a permanent market. She saw fruit, meat, fish, furs, and cloth openly sold and bartered in the streets.

The town was full of sailors. Six vessels lay moored near O'Brien's in the North River – from Amsterdam, Québec,

Curaçao, and Brazil. In her first afternoon she heard five languages spoken – Dutch, English, French, Spanish, and German. O'Brien identified the German and Spanish for her, which she had never heard before. There was disorder, and thirteen years in Puritan New England had cultivated in her an instinct for order. She saw negro slaves, and had never before seen either a black or an unfree man. There was dirt and garbage in the streets, which she had never seen before: Plymouth was neat. There was a rowdy life which had been stifled and whipped out of New England. The dirt and noise were alien, but the essential spirit of the place lifted her.

She went early to bed. She had at first insisted on finding lodgings elsewhere in the town, and O'Brien had said he would find some for her if she wished, but she was welcome to two rooms in his house, where there were a dozen to choose from. His servants would assist Susannah and Leah. Wolsey accepted, and went early to bed, lying in a large room with the two children in a wide truckle bed at the foot of hers.

Her windows – and glazed windows of many panes, the first she had seen since the house in Old Plymouth, in England, were a wonder to her after years of dark houses – opened to the street from the second storey. From an alehouse twenty yards away, on the opposite side of a busy street, she heard quarrels in three languages. She heard O'Brien's voice put an end to one which threatened to become a brawl.

'Bloody Dutch, insolent Dutch,' yelled an English sailor. 'Domineering everywhere, calling themselves kings of the seven seas, and the Indian seas, and – '

'And understanding what you're saying quite well enough to knock your head in,' said O'Brien, who threw him out. She heard the man led grumbling off down the street by a less-drunken friend.

When she was almost asleep she heard a woman's voice singing. Again it came from the alehouse, again it was English, and the singer was merry if not yet quite drunk.

She was singing, to the accompaniment of a fiddle.

> *I want a dozen pairs of sheets, I don't intend to plank it,*
> *I want a bedstead and a bed, two pairs of Yorkshire blankets.*
> *If I find a man who's to my mind, with pleasure I'll bewilder him,*
> *For I want a husband who can get me half a dozen children.*

Where did this woman come from? Did she live in New Amsterdam? Or was she a woman who had come ashore from one of the ships in the river, and would sail away? Where would she go?

Wolsey drifted into sleep.

14

THE SUMMER GARDEN

After eight months the twins were utterly confident in New Amsterdam. The streets and wharves were a never-ending entertainment to them. They were not yet four years old, and to a child of that age eight months in a new place is a new lifetime, which quite erases the old life and its daily habits. They now habitually behaved with a boldness that was not encouraged in children at Plymouth. They saw their first horses, for there had been none at Plymouth, and in a week were unafraid of horses. They were also unafraid of the strangers, black slaves, tottering sailors, soldiers, merchants, and other rogues who made up the population of the town. They were drawn to the wharves. To the incoming and outgoing ships. To the sailors eager for land after months at sea, and swearing they would never go to sea again; to the same men a month later, having gambled and drunk all they had, cursing their way back on board for a last, always a last, voyage. They were drawn to the goods and merchandise in bales, barrels, sacks, and sea chests. They watched linen and canvas and holland cloth brought ashore from vessels out of Amsterdam; sheafs of tobacco and barrels of fruit from the holds of ships out of Charleston; barrels of rum from barques out of Curaçao; brandy from French carracks out of La Rochelle, by way of Québec or Martinique. They were drawn to the fragrances – the sharpness of tar from the maritime fringes of New France in the north, the zest of spices from East Indiamen out of Java, the sweetness of molasses brought by vessels of doubtful flags and no fixed allegiance from West Indian islands.

Only English ships were a rarity in the port which King Charles of England had sworn to be his royal colony, which he would always take care to cherish and maintain entire. But Charles, being in difficulties with his own Parliament at home, had forgotten his colony for the moment. He was irked that the Dutch possessed four ships to his one, but as to Manhattan, he had forgotten even where it was on the map. So the Dutch flourished there, barely attempting to govern what was an open port for merchant and privateers of any nationality, but exacting duties on all goods, pirated or honestly bought, flowing in or out.

On the wharves Rebekah and Ruth were made much of because their twinness was distinctive. It was a distinction they took pains to emphasize. They always held hands. Neither Wolsey nor Susannah deliberately dressed them alike, but the twins insisted. If one wore a blue ribbon, the other demanded and got a blue ribbon for herself. It was one of the sailors' amusements to toss them oranges, two oranges at a time, and then watch. They never quarrelled over the oranges, never fought because one orange was bigger than the other. They shared the fruit, peeling first one and eating it together, and then the other, and dividing and eating that. The sailors thought this droll, and taught the little girls a good deal of bawdy Dutch, which they innocently repeated at home. Their Dutch was now as fluent as their English.

It happened one afternoon that Leah took the twins to see a French vessel newly arrived. The Frenchmen, lounging curiously round the quays of a town unknown to them, saw Leah and were very gallant to her, in the hope of luring the girl on board, or into the back room of a tavern. Leah's head was turned by their eager attentions, and the twins slipped away to a rushy meadow, only a hundred yards from the wharves, where a group of Indians, hangers-on in the town, were passing an afternoon playing Seneca.

This was a game played with the round stalks of feather-headed rushes. The stalks were cut into different lengths and shuffled with such rapidity of the hand that the eye could not follow. It was like a game of cards in that the value of a particular piece or stalk was determined not only by its length but by the number of notches cut into it, and by its colour. It was also like a game of cards in its object, which was for one player to acquire as much as he could of everything the others possessed.

The twins sat and watched in the long grass. The Indians were so absorbed that they hardly gave them a glance, and took no notice.

There were seven Indians. Each wore a string of Dutch beads, which they called *machampe*, and a string of wampum, seashell money collected and shaped by themselves. The Dutch beads were trash and evidently recognized to be trash, because they were the first that a man gave up to an opponent. Then the wampum was lost and won, a single shell at a time. When a man lost all his beads and all the wampum he carried with him, he began to shed his clothes. One tall young Indian wore a coat of turkey feathers knitted together with small threads. It was this man who first lost all the wampum he had. Then the game became animated.

The rushes were shuffled more furiously. The Indians, who had previously been impassive, talked rapidly, and laughed at each hand. Only the tall young Indian remained quiet, and he was losing rapidly. As he lost, he detached the feathers, one at a time, from his intricate coat. Half a coat was still left him when a woman approached. She was European, small, and dark-haired. The men glanced up at her, but immediately went back to their game. The woman sat by the twins.

'You're missed,' she said. 'They're looking for you.'

Rebekah replied mischievously in Dutch, and Ruth laughed.

'No, my dears, you're missed, and you're as English as I am, so no more of that talk, and I'll see you home.'

Rebekah shook her head very decidedly.

'Yes I will, miss, and take you back to your mother, who's been told you're lost and is down asking sailors after you. So come on with you.'

But they would not.

'Want to watch,' said Rebekah.

The woman saw she could not drag them both away screaming, and gave in.

'Ten more minutes then, but no more, mind.'

It was the disappearing coat of feathers which fascinated the children. Feather by feather it diminished as it was won from its owner by two of his more adroit opponents.

What had been a coat of feathers was down to no more than a circlet around the man's neck when Wolsey and Susannah came up behind the children and the strange woman in the long grass. They were heard and seen by the twins, who commanded them by gestures to stay still and not interfere. They obeyed, half in amusement at such authority in tiny children, and in part seeing the twins were spectators of a ritual which was about to come to an end.

It soon did. The Indians had taken no notice at all of the women's approach. At last one of the dexterous Indians won the last hand and gave a low, exultant cry, at which the handsome young Indian slowly nodded his head, rose, and took first from his neck the circlet of feathers, and then from his waist the lappet which was the only other garment he wore. He tossed them both at the feet of the winner, and stood, naked.

The other Indians stood up too. The game was finished. They gathered up the rushes, and then one looked directly at the spectators of their game. The twins and the strange woman were sitting six feet away from the players, and Wolsey and Susannah stood a few feet behind them.

The one Indian who was staring directly at the twins gave a cry of excitement. The others, following his eyes and seeing what he saw, gazed intently at Rebekah and Ruth. Susannah ran to the children, but they were the only ones not alarmed. Still staring at the twins, the Indians carefully picked up their beads and wampum, and began to back away. Then the Indian who had looked first in the children's direction said something in a low voice to the others, who agreed. The one Indian took from the man who had won them with such intensity the dismembered remains of the feather coat, gathered them in his hands, approached slowly and with deference, and placed the feathers at the feet of the twins. Then they all went, first walking and then running away from the group of white women and children. The children smiled calmly after the retreating figures.

'I found the little ones,' said the strange, dark woman, speaking to Wolsey, 'and was going to bring them back, only they would not come until the Indians' game was finished.'

Wolsey nodded.

'And what was all that about?' she said, indicating the fast disappearing Indians.

'Some superstition of theirs, I daresay.'

'And these?' said Wolsey, picking up one of the feathers.

'There's no knowing.' The woman picked up the circlet, and a handful of the feathers. 'They were playing for these as if their souls depended on it, and now they give them to the children. Well, there's no knowing. But he was a fine man who lost these feathers.'

'Yes, he was,' said Wolsey. He had indeed been a fine man who had stood in front of them quite naked.

The children went ahead with Susannah, carrying their feathers. Only Wolsey and the dark woman remained.

'I'm Anne,' she said. 'And I know who you are.'

Wolsey smiled. 'Yes?'

'That *was* a fine man,' said Anne. 'But no finer than yours.'

'Mine?'

'He was good to me. He brought me here, and I've lived here since. He brought me here when they were going to send me back to England again. It was from the English colony, who were pure people and did not want us. Captain O'Brien brought me here.'

Wolsey nodded.

'See, I work at the tavern, the Swan, near the captain's brick house,' said Anne, and it suddenly came to Wolsey that here was the girl whose voice she had heard singing a ballad on her first night in Manhattan, just as she was falling asleep.

'He's a fine man, ma'am,' said Anne. 'And you'll keep him, you see.'

This was said with such wistful candidness that Wolsey could not take offence. The two women walked back to the town together – thin, dark Anne, whom O'Brien had used kindly for a day or a week or so and then found a place at the Swan, and Wolsey, who, living in his big, brick house, was assumed to be his mistress.

At the time, O'Brien was away on a voyage to the West Indies on behalf of the governor. O'Brien was not the governor's man. He took no pay from the Dutch. He was his own man. He made his own bargains. He was a born speculator, and had soon come to an understanding with the governor that if the Dutch cared to furnish him with holland cloth and Dutch guilders, he would trade in the islands at a profit, half for the Dutch, half for himself. These were hard terms for the Dutch, particularly since the vessel was theirs and the crew paid with their Dutch guilders, but O'Brien had such a way of talking himself into a profit that half of what he made was more advantageous to the Dutch than the whole cargoes that their own ships' masters brought back after longer voyages. So the Dutch accepted O'Brien's hard bargain, and did very well from it. So did O'Brien. The brick house was his. The ship was not his, but he was her master, and, besides, with his profits from voyage to voyage, he was buying an increasing share in her too. At the time of Wolsey's meeting with Anne, in early summer, he was cruising in the southern Antilles, in the warm waters between Antigua and Barbados. He had high hopes of Barbados.

In the six months Wolsey had stayed at O'Brien's house, he had been five months away at sea, returning to Manhattan only for two periods of fourteen days. She had early on proposed an agreement, saying she certainly could not and would not stay in his house for nothing. If he was to be away, she would at least look after the house and manage the servants. That was all she could offer, and she thought it little enough. He happily agreed, and the house was better run for it. But even when he was at home, he spent little time in the house. Much of the day, he was out bargaining with the merchants and with the governor for cargoes and commissions. Many of his evenings he spent at the Swan, always returning after Wolsey was in bed. She often heard his laugh and his voice as it carried from the alehouse. Once he sang the old song of the unicorn which she had heard him sing the very first time they met, at Plymouth.

> *And he laughs at spears and arrows*
> *And at men and hounds who seek,*
> *And only a woman's mystery*
> *Shall betray the noble beast.*

When he was at home, he sometimes played with the children, carrying them around one under each arm. Towards Wolsey he was gruffly affectionate. On the occasion of his second return, he gave her a silver medallion he had bought in Curaçao, which he said came originally from Mexico, or so he would think, and he would be pleased if she would accept it. It was inlaid with some blue stone in the likeness of a snake, or dragon. She thought that for an Irishman he was very diffident in offering it. She accepted it warmly, and he was pleased, and very pleased when she wore it the next day, though he affected not to notice. Once, when she was coming from her room on the upper floor, along the passage to the staircase, she saw him in his library through the open door, and he, hearing her, stood and said, 'My land cabin, you see,' and showed her the celestial and terrestrial globes, and spun them with his hands.

Now, in his absences, Wolsey explored his house as she never had before. She went into the room where he slept, at the far end of the house from her bedroom, and flung open the shutters and the windows. The floor was carpeted with deerskins, a wolf's skin, and the great grey pelt of what she took to be a bear. The bed was vast, larger than her own, which was wide enough. It was a high bed, with steps to climb into it, and six feet wide. The bedstead was in dark, satiny wood. She ran her hand along the smooth wood but could not recognize it. The sun streamed onto the bed in shafts of light, making the green silk-embroidered cover shimmer. Then she closed the shutters and stood in the darkened room, felt for the bedposts, and ran her fingers over the silk wood again. She went to O'Brien's land cabin, sat in his high-backed leather chair, too high in the back for her, and too deep. She stretched her head against the carved back of the chair, and tried to be tall enough for it, pressing her shoulders against the back and reaching up with her head, tilting her chin back. But still the chair was too big for her. She opened his chart drawer and found the chart she wanted, and carried it into the garden.

O'Brien's was a splendid brick house, but the garden was its beauty. It was walled with red brick, which trapped the sun. It was a formal garden, a hundred feet long, with paths the length of each side, and another running up the middle. The paths were bordered by box hedges. In the flowerbeds tulips flourished, white flowers dashed with red; and tall red peonies, a much darker red, with thick stalks, growing near the walls; and, in the borders, tufts of Ladies Cushion, with small, tender, naked stalks growing six inches high, with no leaves, but little flowers on top, in soft purple.

Wolsey sat on a bench by the south-facing wall and opened the chart on her lap. The chart was only ten years old, but was too recent to show Manhattan marked on it, though she could see the shape of Long Island, and make out the mouth of the Hudson. She traced the course of O'Brien's voyage, south across the Atlantic to Hispaniola, and then farther south into the Caribbean, to St Christopher, Gaudaloupe, Barbados, and then Grenada. She was suffused with the warmth of the sun, and let herself drift into the warmth and into a dream of fruition.

She sat until the sun went, and then took the chart upstairs, but to her own room.

Three days later, a scouting privateer put in from the south with letters of marque from the Venetian Republic. The privateer had good Spanish and French wine on board, taken from a Spanish bark off Hispaniola, and brought news of O'Brien. The privateer, using its shark's licence to prey on whatever ship it could, would have taken O'Brien, too, but did not care to tangle with a ship so well armed and manned, though slower. So when the Venetian master, no real Venetian but a capable scoundrel out of Genoa, had sighted O'Brien off Cape Charles, the two captains exchanged wary courtesies and then, after a bottle of the good French wine, sailors' confidences. The Genoan's wine-warmed confidences were mostly of successful pillage. O'Brien talked about Barbados. As the Genoan told an audience at the Swan the night he put in, O'Brien had spent a most pleasant time on that island.

'There they lay,' said the Italian, 'the ship at anchorage at Bridgetown, and Captain O'Brien and his black girl at leisure under a palm tree. I have it from his own mouth. He told me, and I remember his words, "Signore, there we lay, under the stars, on the beach, on the fringe of the water, at the point where the Caribbean meets the south Atlantic, my sweet girl and I. I remember her scent, I remember her fragrance, I remember her voice, I remember her name."'

Thin, dark Anne, at the Swan, could not hear this without a pang, refused to sing that night, and slipped off.

When she met Wolsey the next day she said nothing of the spot where the Caribbean and the Atlantic met, only that O'Brien had been sighted, and would very likely be home in two days. This was something the whole town knew by then. The Italian, with nothing to lose by doing so, had delivered a letter entrusted to him by O'Brien for the governor. It was brief, telling the governor simply that it was 'full Maytime.' The privateer had discovered this when he carefully separated the seal without breaking it, and then resealed it. It meant nothing to him. But full Maytime meant to the governor a most prosperous voyage, so prosperous that a feast was prepared to greet O'Brien on his return, which was indeed within two days. He was spotted approaching the Narrows, and a small party waited on the shore to welcome him. Among them were the governor, and Wolsey. It was the first time she had gone to meet him.

O'Brien, coming ashore, leaped from his cutter, accepted the governor's hand, and then looked past him at Wolsey, whom he had seen from the ship in the North River. He saw that she wore his medallion. He took a pace toward her and held out his arms. She stood still. He let his arms fall, walked slowly up to her, and said, 'Wolsey, dear woman, I have the *Vliegende Hert*. Now the ship is mine.'

'I have waited for you,' she said. 'I am glad.'

He seized her hand, took it in both his, and turned to face the ship as she lay at moorings, with the men still clearing her decks, and a host of small boats scurrying about her to take off the cargo.

'I have the ship, Wolsey,' he said. 'She's mine.'

15

THE SEVENTH OF THE SEVEN SEAS

The governor was after all the representative in the new continent of Their High Mightinesses the Lords of the States General of Holland, and so that night the flaring torches in the streets, and the meat, the wine, the strident trumpets, the show of lace and silk, and the sounding speeches at the banquet were such as would have done honour to a monarch. And that was only the fair deserts of Captain the Honourable Haraldus O'Brien, as he was described by His Excellency the Governor. 'Honourable' was a complimentary title for the evening. 'Haraldus' was because the Dutch liked to dignify a name into Latin on memorial stones and in encomiums. O'Brien, said the governor, was a man stalwart in the service of the States General, a man to whom Their High Mightinesses were much beholden. In their name, the governor offered this banquet as a small remembrance of their gratitude.

At the moment of the ceremonial toast, the governor raised his glass to O'Brien, and the governor's wife hers, as etiquette demanded, to the woman O'Brien had brought to the feast. The governor's wife had demurred at this, but the governor, a tolerant man who had expected better things than New Amsterdam and still hoped he might rise to be ambassador to some German principality, if nothing better, diplomatically and firmly told her to do as he said. The preparations for the banquet had been a whirl. When O'Brien told Wolsey she was coming with him, she too had demurred, but he swept her protests aside. That did not mean she took any notice of him. So O'Brien, seeing her divided between a stubborn pride that touched him and a desire to please him that also touched him, said gruffly that if she would come, he would be very happy, and she had.

After the feast, the dance. Wolsey had not danced since she was a girl of fifteen. It did not matter. It was a kind of formal square dance unknown to either of them and to most of those present, but in the light of a hundred candles reflected from two great crystal chandeliers, and in the glow induced by good wine acquired from the Genoan privateer, they managed well enough. Wolsey and O'Brien met only at points in the dance, which was one that required a constant change of partner. Whenever they met she had some question for him. 'What did you bring back to deserve all this, Mr O'Brien?'

'Those,' he said, glancing upwards.

The music parted them.

'What?' she said, 'what?' when they came together again in the figure.

'Chandeliers,' he said. 'Wax candles. Chandeliers. Look up. See.'

And it was true. He had in Barbados bought from a pirate, who had stripped a Portuguese merchantman, two chandeliers and a barrel of wax candles intended for the palace of some South American grandee. O'Brien got them for two hundred guilders. They were the first wax candles seen in Manhattan, and the governor had been so delighted with the chandeliers and candles that he had the whole lot erected and put in place in the hour after O'Brien docked, commandeering the service of every builder and carpenter his men could find.

'Chandeliers?' Wolsey laughed. 'Chandeliers? Is that all?'

'Oh, no, Wolsey me dear, that's just the brilliant part of it. The rest is dark enough, but very welcome.'

'What?'

They were again parted by the music of trumpets, fiddles, and light drums.

'Blacks,' he said, the next time round. 'One hundred fine, healthy blacks.'

'Slaves?'

'Slaves, Wolsey, but rather ours than let them go to the Spaniards. Which is where they were bound for.'

O'Brien had done a little privateering on his own, and taken the blacks from a waterlogged Spanish ship drifting off Hispaniola with both masts lost in a storm.

'Woman,' he said, 'if I had not taken them, they would have gone down in chains with that hulk, or else have made land and been flogged to death by now.'

She knew. And each slave was worth, say, two hundred guilders, each worth three times what the Dutch had paid the Indians, in goods of undoubted value, for the whole of Manhattan.

They were lighted home by the governor's escort, bearing torches.

At the door the escort saluted, and Wolsey and O'Brien were alone in the hall of the house. The only light came from two rushlights left burning, and a small oil lamp. 'Harry,' she laughed, with her hands on her hips, 'chandeliers!'

In her room, Susannah heard their entrance and their laughter. She glanced at the twins, whom she had taken in with her that night, but they slept on.

'My cabin?' O'Brien asked, taking up one of the rushlights.

They went up the stairs and into the room. She went in first and stood by the terrestrial globe, with her fingers on the chased silver arch inside which the globe swung. He stayed by the door, holding the light.

'Harry, you said the ship was yours.'

'Ah well now,' he said, placing the torch in the wall bracket and sitting in his high-backed chair, 'ah well now, in a manner of speaking, she is. In fact, she half is. Which means she is. She's mine.'

'Ah,' said Wolsey.

'It was agreed I should take a full half share, when I could buy it. The governor agreed. And I said I would have it by the full Maytime. "Tell me then," said the governor, "when the full Maytime comes, even supposing it should fall out to be the Christmas after next." But I fell in with the Spanish hulk, and the blacks, and half the profit of them is mine. Half the sale price is mine, and that's enough and more to buy my half share in the ship. So I've half, and if I've half of her, then she's mine, Wolsey. The governor himself only has an eighth share, and the rest is owned in Holland, a spar here, a bit of tackle there, down to thirty-seconds and sixty-fourths. She's mine.'

He splashed brandy from a decanter into crystal glasses and held one out to her. She shook her head, but he still held the glass out, and she took it, twirling the stem between her fingers.

'Plunder, Harry?'

'Honest plunder,' he said, 'under the commission of Their High Mightinesses.' Susannah, at the end of the corridor, again heard their laughter.

'Brandy, decanter, glasses, all taken from the Spanish?'

'Ah,' said Harry, holding the glass up to the light. 'French, this one.'

As he watched, she put down her glass, and put her palms flat against the wall behind her, and leaned on the wall. All the time she looked at him, and he saw her face change. He put down his own glass, walked across to her, and folded her in his arms. She drew a long, deep breath, and then clung to him. Her hands were upon his back and caressing his back. She drew his head down and found his mouth, and kissed with an open, eating kiss, as she had never before kissed anyone. He bent and kissed her throat, but she raised his mouth to hers again, exploring him with an inquisitive tongue. When she drew away breathless, he took her hair in both his hands and then let his hands follow her shape, her neck, her shoulders, breasts, waist, hips.

'Figurehead,' he said. 'When I first saw you on the deck, you were like this, and I saw you as a figurehead. But when I said I saw you as a figurehead, in my mind I held you like this.'

Wolsey gave an answering laugh, and with both her hands held his waist and then slid down from his waist, caressing him with light fingers.

The door was still open. He took her hand to pull her towards his bedroom. She pulled back for a second, and he saw she was reaching out to take the rushlight from its bracket, to light them.

He stopped her hand.

'We shan't need light,' he said. 'Come on. Come on.'

He threw open the door to his bedroom, led her to the high bed, picked her up, held her up, and laid her down across it. She lay sprawled half-on, half-off the bed, smiling, marvellously dishevelled, and held out her arms to him, but he stood and threw off his clothes, and she lay and admired him. When his clothes were thrown all round the room, he knelt on the floor, held her ankles, then with one movement swept her wide skirts up to her waist and laid his tangled head on her warm belly, and brushed his hair between her strong legs, parting them wide, caressing her with his head and hands, and breathing in her musky fragrances. Then he stood, leaning towards her, and she put out one hand and slowly ran light fingers along the length of his prick, and then held her arms out to him again.

'Come into me,' she said, 'Harry.'

He took her by the hips and, drawing her closer to him, entered her still standing.

She lay with her head thrown back, and her hands by her head. He bent to kiss her lips, and the separate fingers of her spread hands, and moved into her.

'Oh, you fill me,' she exclaimed. 'You fill me.'

'You are my *Vliegende Hert*,' cried Wild O'Brien, Irish O'Brien, 'my *Vliegende Hert*, sweet ship, on the Seventh of the Seven Seas.'

'*Vliegende Hert?*' she murmured. 'Because you have me too?'

She reached out and tried to find his mouth with her fingers, but he was too far to reach. He took her hand and went more deeply into her until she called out his name again and again, Harry Harry Harry, as if it were a litany, and then she came with broken, ascending cries. He leaned down and stroked her hair, and kissed it, and then kissed her hands, her eyes, and her forehead.

When they disentwined, he knelt by the bed with his head resting in her lap, encircling her with his arms, and they slept for half an hour like that.

She woke first, stirred, and raised his head. Then he woke too, and shook himself.

Wolsey thought he looked vastly pleased. She sat up on the bed, looked down at herself, and kicked up both legs.

'And my shoes still on,' she said, and laughed, her open, contralto laugh.

He stroked her ankles. Then, as she raised each leg high for him, he took her shoes off.

'*Vliegende Hert*,' she said. 'Seven Seas. Oh, Harry, it was wanton.'

At which both shook with laughter.

'Wanton,' he said sternly. 'Wanton wantonness, Wolsey my love. A lovely thing to have, and you're lucky to have it, to have for yourself and to give me.'

Her dress was still round her waist, so he undressed her and she stroked his head while he did. It was only then that they noticed in the dim light that the door to the room was open, as they had left it when they came in. They would have been heard by anyone in the house who was still awake.

'Should you...?' asked Harry, glancing towards the door and the corridor beyond. She shook her head. It had been wanton, and they were drunk with wine and with each other. But it was honest, and wholehearted, and Wolsey refused to slip back to her own room as if it had all been a casual night frolic.

He closed the door, and looked at her, and laughed at his good luck.

It was two in the morning.

He put on a coat and roused his own oldest servant, who fifteen minutes later brought them hot water to bathe in, and warm towels, and cool water and coffee to drink. Then they slept.

Next day O'Brien went about his business with a contented gravity, which the merchants he bargained with put down to his acquisition of the *Vliegende Hert*. One said as much to him, and he answered with a broad smile, 'Oh, yes yes. You have it there. Yes.' Wolsey read in the walled garden, and Susannah, bringing her tea, saw she was a changed woman, and knew perfectly well why.

'Your face is softer, ma'am,' she said. 'It has a bloom on it.'

'I think it has,' said Wolsey, drawing her fingers up her cheek. 'I think it may have.' Susannah met her eyes and smiled.

For an hour at a time, Wolsey put down her book and dreamed in turn of wanton connections and of calm satiety.

But if Wolsey and Harry O'Brien had been man and wife, it would have been not the night before, but the one to follow that would have been their wedding night.

When they went to bed, she preceded him, and he discovered her waiting in a nightgown of white linen. When he lay beside her, they said not a word, and he took her head and gently kissed her forehead, and eyelashes, and lips, and gently parted her legs, and slipped easily into her. When she came it was at first with little cries that pleased his man's vanity and made her the dearer to him, but then something happened that astonished him. Tears came to her eyes, and she wept most bitterly as if in the deepest grief. She wept aloud, without restraint, racked with shaking sobs, and he was alarmed because he had never seen this before in any woman.

'Why?' he said. 'What is it?'

For many weeks she could not tell him why. But she was weeping for Francis Wheaton, for all that moment had meant to her with him, when he came inside her: it had never been a flimsy thing, and sometimes she had felt as exalted as by an invasion of Grace. She was weeping for her lost son Robert as she saw him lying dead in the snow. She was weeping for her daughters as she had seen them entwined on the forest floor: they were alive and her joy, but she wept for the terror of the night they were taken. She was weeping for the moment of coming itself, because it was all there was on earth, and the deepest that there was, but so fleeting and fragile. And she was weeping for another reason, which was all of a piece with the others, and part of them, so that she was telling the truth when she told Wild Harry O'Brien all she could bring herself to say that night, as he held her and tried to comfort her.

'Why?' he said. 'Why?'

And she replied, 'Because you touch my heart.'

16
FIRES QUENCHED BY BLOOD

'Pequot,' said Standish, cursing. His two companions in the small boat sat stock-still. 'Now, easy, ship your oars. Softly.' David Dempsey and John Flanagan did as they were told, and then reached just as softly for their muskets. The boat drifted on the gentle current of the Connecticut river. The only sounds were the drip, drip, drip of water from the shipped oars on to the boat's bottom planking, and the lapping of the river against the sides.

All three men gazed at the spectacle before them. At a bend in the river, suspended from two trees, were the two maimed torsos of what had once been men, left there so that anyone moving on the river would be bound to see them. The heads were off. The arms were gone, hacked off at the shoulders. The legs were gone, hacked off at middle thigh. And the whole chest of each hanging creature was split through, and the ribcage torn open, so that daylight showed through from front to back. The bloody carcasses were new, or the crows would have cleaned the bones.

The silent boats drifted past the slaughtered bodies.

Standish said, 'Easy, boys. But those that did it are gone, or they would have taken us by now. So we'll get on quietly.'

Dempsey and Flanagan took up their oars, trembling, and at evening found the trading post they were looking for, ten miles upriver from their own, which they had left that morning.

It was a plank hut belonging to the Massachusetts Bay Company. Their approach was narrowly watched until it was plain who they were. Then the four white traders inside lowered their muskets and opened the door.

Standish was known.

'Are you all here?' he asked.

'Two more of us trading downriver, back any day. Looking for beaver, from the Nipmuks.'

Standish paused.

'We saw your men,' he said. 'They found Pequots and not Nipmuks.' And he recounted what they had seen, or rather that there were two men hanging dead. There was no need for any more. The atrocity of the men's deaths and display would be understood and expected.

One of the Massachusetts men wept with rage, because he had known the carcasses. The other three remained grim and silent.

This was the early winter of 1636, when murder and atrocity were nothing new to the Massachusetts colonizers. Plymouth plantation had long since been overtaken in population by new colonists from England who had preferred to go farther north to Massachusetts Bay, and had founded the towns of Boston, Dorchester, and Salem. Plymouth had a trading post on the Connecticut, but Massachusetts had five, and had built a fort and whole settlements there.

'I will tell you,' said Richardson, the Massachusetts man who had wept with rage, 'I'll tell what happened at Saybrook fort when I was there. They were two men from Dorchester you saw by the river today. They were at Saybrook too. And at Saybrook, while we stayed inside the fort, because we could not go out against an army of savages, they burned the ricks in our sight, and slaughtered the cattle, and took three men who were returning, not knowing the savages were there. They took these men. We knew them. In the night, we heard them crying out to us, but could do nothing. Next day, the savages dressed in the clothes of these men, and came up just out of musket shot, and writhed and howled, mimicking these men and the way they had tortured them.'

Standish passed the man a flask of brandy, from which he drank.

'And then they somehow took two women by stealth, and we never saw them again, only savages in their skirts. It is in their nature. When they were outside the fort, they took one of their own number, who was not a Pequot but from some other tribe, and put ropes to his arms and legs, and put twenty men on each rope, and pulled, and tore him into two, and even then he was not dead, and they put live coals on his eyes. And all in our sight, so that we could see it from the fort.'

'I have seen it,' said Standish. 'They were always bloody among themselves.'

'When *you* were at Plymouth first,' said a Massachusetts man, 'before we came to our towns, why were they never bloody? Why did they never attack? They did not attack you. But they were always bloody men in Virginia.'

'The tribe that had been there, the Lord had removed with a plague. We found their village, where they had died in piles, unburied. There was one who came back. He was called Squanto, and showed us how to plant corn, but he died. And we were always friendly with the Narragansetts, and with others, who came to our first Thanksgiving, and have come since. The Pequots used to be far to the south, but now they are moving north for new land, and they are bloody. They are Grey Foxes, that is their name in English, and they murder men like chickens. And I am sorry for it, but the land they most want is what you have settled.'

Richardson laughed a weird laugh. 'Captain,' he said, 'do you think they can tell you, who are a captain, from me, who was a labouring man in England and am little more in this new land? Do you think they can tell that I am from the Massachusetts colony, and you from Plymouth? When I saw the Pequots drag one of their own kind in two, with ropes, did I know that he was not a Pequot, but a wanderer they had taken from another village, and was not a Pequot?

I did not know that. Nor will they tell you from me, and they will kill us all, if they can, unless we kill them first.'

When the Plymouth men left the next day to continue their journey home, carrying the prosperous load of beaver pelts they had brought from their own trading post, Dempsey kept on all day, arguing that the Massachusetts man was right and that the white settlers should all strike together. 'Those two men we saw yesterday,' he said, 'those two butchers' scarecrows, they could have been us if we had passed a day sooner.'

'And then,' said Standish, 'there would have been three dead men hanging there, not two. But if we fight, in a fight that is not ours, more than three of us will die. I have been a soldier twenty years. I daresay I shall fight again, and in the thick of it I am as good a killer as the next man. Better. But I shall not look for a war. Never again do I want to walk across a battlefield an hour after, or a day after, and see what you saw yesterday, only one-hundred-fold. You trembled at what you saw yesterday, and a battle would be one-hundred-fold.'

Dempsey was stubbornly silent.

'Think, boy. All those limbs, and men's brains out. Brains out is bad, but that's your *art* of war, a man killed quick. But here are savages who press hot coals in a man's eyes. That is slow. That's your savages.'

At Plymouth there was news. The Narragansetts, said Bradford, had offered a treaty to fight with the English against the Pequots, if that tribe should attack either.

And furthermore the Pequots, hearing of this alliance, had sent a messenger with a written letter.

'Offering alliance too?' asked Standish.

'Offering threats,' said Bradford.

Standish took the letter. It was on parchment which he guessed had come from a Dutch settlement. And it was written in English, which he guessed had been learned by an Indian who had picked up bits of the language by hanging round the wharves at New Amsterdam, and then come north with the Pequots. It demanded tribute from the white men, and ended:

Els we shl pile yr dead cattel high as howses and no man shal stir out of his howse to piss but he shal be siezed and made to howl

'And what else?' said Standish.

'An appeal,' said Bradford, 'from the Massachusetts Bay Colony for fifty men of ours to join with theirs and strike at the Pequots before they strike at us.'

But before the elders could meet to consider this appeal, David Dempsey and John Flanagan slipped away on a coasting shallop to Boston, where they offered their services to one Captain Mason, against the Pequots.

'We must write with all ceremony,' said Mason, 'and thank our brothers in God at Plymouth for *two* men.' But he took them and armed them, and trained them through the spring, and they were at the Mistic massacre.

It was a two days' march in hot sun for Mason's ninety Englishmen, wearing iron breastplates and carrying heavy muskets, before they met the five hundred Narragansetts whom their chief had promised. Together they approached the Pequot camp after dark, and waited and listened. A noisy celebration continued inside the Pequot camp until the small hours of the morning. The English waited, within twenty yards of the camp, and the Narragansetts waited behind the English. At the first light the English saw what they had to storm. It was a palisaded village of twenty acres, crowded with wigwams, with gates at east and west. The attackers approached silently, and not until they were at the palisade did a sentinel cry out a warning. But the English were upon them, bursting down both gates, hacking with heavy swords, bursting into wigwams and killing all inside with musketfire. The brave Pequots fought back, but then they did an act which was to kill their people. Seeing so many Englishmen coming at them, and thinking in their bewilderment that seventy men were a thousand, the Pequots resolved to fight them with fire, and, running back into their wigwams, fetched torches which they flung in the white men's faces. But the fire caught their own huts, a rising wind carried the leaping flames from hut to hut, and a firestorm swept in one minute through the twenty acres of crowded wigwams, which were very dry with the hot summer. The Pequots then were very brave, and ran back into the fire to rescue their women and children, but were burned with them. The English withdrew to the palisade and fired into the flames. Those Indians who did escape from their burning huts, found the heat outside so great that first their bowstrings were burned with the heat and snapped, and then their skin was seared, and they were roasted in their own fire.

The Narragansetts did not enter the stockade with the English, but waited outside, encircling the camp and hacking to death any Pequots who did run from the fire. Only two were seen to escape into the forest. Only seven women were captured. When the fires died down, those English who had a stomach for it went into the ruins and counted seven hundred men, women, and children dead in the red-hot ashes.

'It was complete,' said David Dempsey, when he returned to Plymouth and gave an account to the elders.

Flanagan said, 'The Narragansetts, outside, when they saw the Pequots dancing in the fire, called them a word in their own language, deriding them. "*Brave* Pequots. Oh brave Pequots," they were saying, and they exalted.'

'And victory was a sweet sacrifice,' said the Reverend Wrestling Shepard. 'Leviticus. Let us praise God for enclosing our enemy in our hands, and for the wind that rose when it did, by His will.'

Standish turned away so as not to let Shepard see the disgust in his face.

Young Dempsey did not turn away, but faced Shepard. 'Sir, it was a *terrible* thing to see them frying in the fire, and only the streams of their blood quenching the fire, and the stink and scent were horrible.'

Standish turned and caught the boy's eye, and Dempsey

met his gaze, and said, 'It burned their bowstrings. Not *flames* licking at the bowstrings, but just the bowstrings catching fire from the searing heat of the air. It was fearful, and I wish I had not seen it.'

Standish put a hand on the boy's shoulder. Bradford looked at the two of them, Standish and Dempsey, and slowly nodded. Shepard was about to speak, but Brewster said, 'Enough, man,' and silenced even him.

'And we have this, sir,' said Dempsey, 'which was found in the village. Mr Downing said he would explain it to you.' He put down a charred parcel that he had been holding in his arms.

George Downing, who had been standing by the elders throughout, bowed like a courtier. He was a young man, only eighteen, only recently come from England, a scholar at the new Harvard College, who had been sent from Boston to Plymouth with Dempsey and Flanagan to convey the grateful thanks of Massachusetts to Plymouth for its magnanimity in sending these two men. The Massachusetts governor saw Downing for what he was, and thought he was a man who could very well convey the flavour of such thanks. He was the only man present who had remained impassive throughout Dempsey's and Flanagan's account of death by fire. Mr Shepard may have praised God, but Downing was the one man untouched in any way by the story of the Mistic massacre.

'But first a word to you, Mr Downing,' said Bradford.

Downing listened deferentially as Bradford explained that the Plymouth elders had decided, three weeks before, to send fifty men to Massachusetts in response to the governor's letter.

'But that,' said Downing, 'will not now be necessary.'

'No,' said Bradford.

'But I am to thank you for the two, sir.'

Brewster broke the silence. 'Mr Downing, if you please, tell us what it is you are to explain to us.'

'A trifle, sir, but a strange trifle.' He indicated the charred parcel on the floor. 'Those are several hundred written sheets, which a Massachusetts soldier found in a parcel in the burned Mistic village. They were in a hut near the palisade. I have looked into them, and they are partly in the classical languages, and partly in savage tongues, which the man who found the sheets understood better than I did when I read out the sounds to him. It was recalled at Harvard College that a man who was once minister here attempted such work. The governor, thinking it the property of Massachusetts colony – having considered how it was found – offered it to the Harvard library, but the gift was declined, and so I am happy to return it to you.'

Bradford motioned Dempsey to pick up the parcel and place it on the table before him. It was wrapped round with a leather covering, inside which the sheets were loose. Brewster turned back the covering and took one sheet. It crumbled in his hand, and fell in dry fragments. At the bottom he found pages which were still whole, less scorched by the fire. He and Bradford exchanged glances. There was no doubt that the sheets were in Wheaton's hand, and in Wolsey's where she had copied in entries for him, and that this was the remains of Wheaton's lexicon.

Bradford turned to Dempsey and Flanagan. 'Was the body of any white man found in the Pequot village after the fire?'

'We lost seven soldiers, sir,' said Flanagan.

'No, no,' said Brewster, 'apart from the soldiers, was any other white man seen during the battle, or after?'

Neither Dempsey nor Flanagan had seen any other white man, or heard of one. And as he replied, Dempsey was swaying on his feet.

Bradford looked sharply at him. 'What is it? You look green.'

Dempsey said, 'It is when you open the papers, sir. They bring with them the stink of the burned village, and all the burned men.'

Downing produced a fragrant linen handkerchief which he held with two fingers and fanned in front of his nose, to ward off the stench.

Standish growled, 'You did not need your scented handkerchief before, Downing.'

But Standish and all of them now recognized the sweet stench for what Dempsey said it was. They let the two young men go.

'And now, Mr Downing,' said Bradford, 'did *you* hear any tale of a white man who may have visited that village?'

'I did not. It was in the hut of an Indian, who lay dead. We assumed an Indian brought it there.'

'But you were not there, Mr Downing,' said Standish. 'You cannot say this of your own knowledge.'

'You do not think me to have been *there*, gentlemen. They were soldiers that did it. But I have spoken with Captain Mason, and know what he told me, and what he surmised. It was a small matter, gentlemen, and we did not enquire closely into it.' And then he took his leave of them, saying that with their permission he would rest for a day before continuing his journey, which would take him on a mission to the Dutch at Manhattan, and that if he could be of any conceivable service to them, he begged them to require it of him. He declared himself Their Excellencies' servant, and withdrew with a flourish.

Standish broke the silence. 'Butterfly,' he said.

The charred lexicon lay on the table before them as a reminder of a past incident they had wished to forget. They would never know how it came to be in the Indian camp, any more than they would ever know why Wheaton had walked into the forest, and it was futile debating these matters. Most likely an Indian had found the lexicon with Wheaton's body, and taken it out of curiosity. In the four years since that night, Wheaton had been assumed to be still alive. Mr Shepard was still minister only until Wheaton should return. Previously, Wheaton could not be declared dead, since the law of England, to which their laws had to conform, required a man to have disappeared for seven years, seen by no one, before he could be assumed dead. But now the finding of the dictionary, and its finding at Mistic, where no man had survived the fire and most were burned to charred bones, gave them an occasion to consider Wheaton dead.

'And a *proper* occasion,' said Bradford. 'It is plain sense that the poor man is dead.'

It was sense. Then they could carry out the terms of Wheaton's will, which he had made a year before his disappearance, and which the elders held as trustees.

'The will is very much to the church's benefit,' said Brewster, 'but we ought to send to Mr Wheaton's wife, at Manhattan, the things which are hers.'

'But what,' said Wrestling Shepard, 'is owed to a woman who lives in a foreign land, and in a state of manifest sin?'

Bradford mused. 'She fled our jurisdiction, and does live in the Dutch colony, and, it appears, in a state of sin. But if her husband is dead, it is a sin she could mend by marriage.'

Brewster said wearily, 'Since she is out of our jurisdiction, it is not for us to decide what her state may be. And in any case, the state of her soul is for her Maker to decide. What she is owed is to receive what is hers, and we should send it.'

'She was a pupil of yours,' said Shepard with severity, 'and you were always tender to her, and still are. You must confess that.'

'She was my beloved pupil, and almost a daughter to me. I do not confess that, Mr Shepard, I assert it. But that apart, and that is not the point, we should send her what is hers.'

Standish settled it. 'The Butterfly,' he said, 'is going on to New Amsterdam, when he is rested. He is Our Excellencies' servant, gentlemen, so let's use the fellow and send Wolsey's stuff with him.'

It was done. The congregation, who had so stubbornly thought Wheaton alive, was now as immovably convinced that he had died at Mistic with his lexicon, and had all these years been attempting, however misguidedly, to bring the savages to Christ. At any rate, he was now dead. And Downing found himself encumbered by Their Excellencies the elders with a large chest to be delivered to a woman in

Manhattan. He left reflecting that he must not in future allow his too great courtesy to lumber him so, and ought to be on guard against his better nature.

Downing was prompt, as he always was in all his dealings. His instinct was to please, and he had cultivated such attributes as he knew would please. Promptness was such an attribute, and had become so nearly an instinct with him that he was prompt even where he did not need to please. So on his first day in New Amsterdam he sent to O'Brien's house the letter Brewster had given him for Wolsey, with a note of his own saying he would attend Mrs Wheaton that afternoon to deliver a trunk he had for her, as soon as it was brought up from the hold of his vessel.

O'Brien was away. Wolsey took the letter into his land cabin to read.

'My dearest Wolsey,' she read, and heard Brewster's old voice in her mind. He told her about the lexicon found at Mistic. He enclosed a copy of Francis Wheaton's will. Wheaton left to the church his house and garden, value ten pounds, and two cows and a calf, value forty-one pounds. He left to Wolsey his beloved wife one feather bed, one bolster, and three pillows, value three pounds ten shillings, which Brewster enquired whether she would wish to be sent to her.

'There is also,' wrote Brewster, 'a trunk of clothes which are left to you, and an inventory found with the will, which I have placed with the clothes. The man who brings this letter and these things is Mr Downing, of Massachusetts, whom Captain Standish calls a butterfly, but who is very serviceable to us in bringing these things to you. In my earlier days I saw many such men about the court, and though there are few courts here, such as there are he will find out and thrive in. But you must deal with him as you find him.'

Wolsey smiled and then went on. The letter ended:

And so, dearest Wolsey, though this letter's news may be no news to you, who thought him dead, yet it must give you pain to be remembered of Francis, who was a good man, and I pray that the pain may be softened by my love, which I send with these poor words. Let me have better news of you than I send with this.

She had barely finished the letter, and sat looking out from the window into the garden, when Mr Downing was announced.

She descended the stairs to the hall, where the trunk stood on the polished black and white stones of the floor, and Downing bowed, and trusted she had received the letter sent earlier.

'And I thank you for it,' she said, 'and for all your trouble.'

'Though I fear it is no good news, ma'am?'

She looked at him. He was scarcely taller than she was, neatly made, very civil, and as finely dressed as a puritan could be without transgression. A boy, a courtly boy.

'It is good of you to come so promptly, Mr Downing,' she said.

She went across to the trunk, on which someone had written in chalk, 'Old lumber and things forgotten.' It was a trunk Wheaton had brought from England. She stooped to open it, but Downing got there before her.

'You permit?' he said, producing a large iron key and opening the trunk, throwing the lid up. She saw that it contained her own faded clothes that she was unable to bring with her in her haste when she left Plymouth. On top of the packed clothes was a sheet of paper. It was an inventory, in Wheaton's own hand, of all the clothes she had possessed:

> 2 little pieces of bunched taffetay ... 1 shilling
> 1 red petticoat ... 16 shillings
> 1 violet-coloured petticoat ... 5 shillings
> 1 mingled-coloured petticoat ... 3 shillings
> 1 russet-coloured skirt of Piedmont silk ... 16 shillings
> 1 pair white Irish stockings ... 1 shilling & sixpence
> 1 pair skye-coloured kid gloves ... sixpence

And so on. All her clothes were itemized.

She stood with the inventory in her hand. Francis had

written this. When had he written it? And why placed it with his will?

Downing, as if to assist, leaned down and ruffled among the clothes, drew out the skirt of russet silk and held it up before her.

Mr Downing's diplomacy had been practised among men. He knew nothing of women. Holding the skirt as if to exhibit it, he smiled his ingratiating smile.

Wolsey was astonished at the insensibility of the boy.

Then she saw that the skirt he held in his hands was the russet silk she had worn the night of the first Thanksgiving, and fiercely turned on him.

'Put that down.'

He was amazed by the break in her voice, and stood still holding the silk in his hands. He did not understand how he had offended.

'Put it down. Leave it. Go.'

He met her angry eyes, replaced the skirt, bowed his courtier's bow, took two paces back, bowed again, and then left. He had never been so brushed away, and he would never forget her.

Left alone, Wolsey felt slow tears roll down her cheeks – tears for the russet skirt, and other old things forgotten, and for Francis.

Her husband's will had been made a year before his death, but the inventory of her clothing, could not have been made until a week before his disappearance, because it was only then that he had given her the skye-coloured kid gloves, value sixpence.

And now she was made certain in her mind by this itemizing of everything – not just sure in her heart as she had been before – that Wheaton died the night he walked out into the snows. Not meaning to kill himself or his children, which would have been a deadly sin, but following, as he imagined, God's will, and walking out, taking his children with him, into the blessings of his last great promised land.

17

GONE TO BREUCKELEN

Six months after the messenger came from Plymouth, Wolsey sat in the sun in the garden, and Harry O'Brien stood before her, feet apart, hands clasped behind his back.

'A man,' he began, and stopped short.

'A man?' she said.

'A man ought, perhaps, to take a wife.'

'A man living alone,' she said, 'ought perhaps to take a wife. Perhaps so.'

'Wolsey,' he said, 'I'm not a man living alone. If you take my meaning.'

'Harry, you're shy. You always were. Six months I lived in this house, with you in my mind, before you lifted me up, as you ought to have lifted me up long before, and put me down on your bed, where you ought to have put me down long before. And then you talked about figureheads, how you'd seen me as a figurehead the first day we sailed into the bay, and straight away wanted me in your bed. And then you boldly took six months about it. No one would credit it to look at you, but you're a shy man.'

'Ah, so I did take six months, mostly in a ferment about you. And maybe I am a shy man, though no one I know would credit that either. Maybe I'm shy. But, Wolsey, what do you say? I want a wife, and what's your answer?'

'I'm not wife enough to you already?'

'You're a fine woman, and it's a fine prideful thing for a man, such as myself, to have the loveliest creature in New

Amsterdam in his house and in his bed, and for all New Amsterdam to know he has her, and a fine thing for him to be seen with her in the town, and a fine thing for him to wake up to her in the morning, and for her to be the first sight that man sees. But that man wants a wife.'

'He'd be less admired for having me as a wife than as a mistress, Harry, and that's a fact.'

O'Brien took a few paces up and down, then stopped in front of her, ruffled her hair, and said, 'And if that's true, which I grant you it may be, then I'll have you as mistress and wife, both. Do you think you'll be less a mistress for being a wife? If you change your name, will it change your nature?'

'I'd not be less a mistress to you for being your wife, but to the world I'd be no mistress at all to you, being your wife.'

'Then the world can go hang.'

They were married by the governor. And if Wild Harry O'Brien did appear a bit less wild when he had Wolsey no longer unlawfully in his house and his bed, he was proud of his new wife, and proud that Wolsey was now Wolsey O'Brien.

He told her so.

'Naked pride,' she said, proudly.

Nothing did change. It was a serene and happy marriage, and very wild for the first few days after he returned from each voyage. Then they hunted each other through the large house, and in the garden. Once, at a grand dinner to celebrate some unusually successful piece of piracy by a Dutch privateer, in which New Amsterdam took its share, O'Brien and Wolsey were seen by the assembled aristocracy of New Amsterdam to slip away between the roast and the pudding, before the speeches and the dancing. And the governor, to whom O'Brien made his brief apologies, waved them amiably away.

'Better things to do than dance, O'Brien?' he said.

So it was a happy marriage in its own good way. They fought now and again, once when Wolsey overheard, as she was meant to overhear, some tale of Wild O'Brien's Barbados woman, whose scent, fragrance, and name he remembered.

It was not a new story to her, but it came at a bad moment. Leah, who had once or twice before stayed out overnight with a Portuguese sailor, had stayed out again, this time swearing she would leave and marry the man, and had only just been persuaded back by Susannah and Wolsey. Wolsey was anyway worried because O'Brien was more than a week overdue, and the voyage from which he was late returning was to Barbados.

'So what is her fragrance?' demanded Wolsey, when he did return. He did not know what she was talking about.

'"I remember her scent, I remember her fragrance, I remember her name,"' repeated Wolsey, who, when she was angry, still spoke in the bold, direct tones of her native York. 'Well, what is her name, your Barbados woman? What is her fragrance?'

'Ah, Wolsey, Wolsey,' he said, and tried to stroke her hair, but she knocked his hand away and swept away to her own sitting room, determined to sleep there. O'Brien, for his part, slammed out of the house to the Swan, sang one or two of his old songs, and stayed very late, though he drank less than usual. After midnight he went home, found Wolsey asleep on a sofa, and coaxed her back to their bed. Next day neither said a word more, and thereafter both had the sense never to mention his island women.

It was a happy marriage, but they had no children, though, as Wolsey remarked, you'd have thought they'd have got a dozen. It was saddening, but it made the twins more dear to them. Rebekah and Ruth now slept in the room which had been Wolsey's when she first came to the house. They slept together in the large bed that had been hers. Late at night, Wolsey and O'Brien would go in to look at them asleep. They were striking children, very winning, received everywhere with pleasure, made much of because they were twins, and liking and cultivating this attention. Only Wolsey, O'Brien, and Susannah could readily tell them apart. At ten years of age it was plain that they were going to be taller than Wolsey. Rebekah was half an inch taller than Ruth, but this was the only thing that distinguished them physically. Both walked in the same way, and sat in the same posture. Their voices were so alike that even Wolsey could be deceived which it was calling to her from another room. A single word spoken by them – which could be something as simple as Yes or No – was distinctive in its tone, and nuance of inflection. The word could have been spoken by no other child. But even Wolsey could not say *which* of the two it was. They needed the same sleep. She had seen them fall asleep at the same time and at the same moment, and wake at the same time and stretch in the same way. They slept in the same position, each on her back with the right arm covering the eyes. Their hair fell over their faces. It was longer than Wolsey's, darker, and finer in texture.

They were strong, wilful children.

One night, as Wolsey and O'Brien stood looking down at them from the doorway, she said, 'Harry, they really take to you more easily than to me, don't they?'

'Good God, woman, no,' he said, denying what she said the more vehemently because he suspected it might be true. 'What on earth should make you dream of that?'

But it was true. When they were smaller, O'Brien had carried them about with him, one on each shoulder. Now they were older, they liked to accompany him to the ship. They scrambled over every inch of the *Vliegende Hert*, and he had given his men strict orders that they were never, never again to be allowed in the rigging. His heart had stood still one morning to see them both climbing the foretopmast with the litheness and a fearlessness that many sailors lacked.

'What on earth should make me think that?' replied Wolsey when O'Brien made his too vehement denial. 'What I have seen, that's what. They can be sweet children, and I've never found them less, but they're easier with you.'

'Because,' he said gently, 'I am a man. They are sweet children. They are children still. But soon they will not be children any more. They'll be women. It does not mean they think the less of you. And it is not true that they are *easier* with me, but just that they flirt with me. It's almost flirting. That's what it is. To all intents I'm their father, but they still flirt with me, because I'm not a woman. I'm a man, and a sailor besides, and so they try to please me, and to be with me. But you must never think, because of that, that they do not love you. They do.'

And this was true too, so far as it went. O'Brien was right that with him they were learning to flirt. He was right to say that they loved their mother. But more than they loved her, they were absorbed in, and loved, each other. It was the natural condition of twins.

Wolsey accepted Harry's explanations, or let him think she did. They closed the children's door quietly, and went to bed.

Next morning they were woken by a pounding at the door, and by the lamentations of Susannah and Leah.

'They are gone, ma'am,' wept Susannah. 'They are quite gone. And I don't know where. No one knows where.'

Wolsey was standing by the bed in her nightdress. O'Brien was still in bed, raising himself from the pillows. To Susannah he appeared a tangle of red hair and a brush of red beard.

'Come here,' said O'Brien to the two women. 'Now, what's gone?'

'The children, sir, both of them, and no sign of them anywhere,' said Susannah. 'Leah went to wake them, and there was only the empty bed, and it never happened before. She always woke them. They have always been asleep when she went in.'

'They never went off before,' said Leah. 'Never, and now they're gone.'

'Then look in the kitchens, and the garden,' said Wolsey. 'Both of you.'

The two women looked at each other dismally. 'We already have, ma'am. And none of the Dutch servants saw them either, only the front door was unbolted and left open.'

'And there was only this,' said Susannah, holding up a paper, 'left by the bed.'

'Well?' said O'Brien.

'I cannot read it, sir.'

Wolsey snatched the paper from Susannah's hand, and then gave it to O'Brien. On it was written the message:

>Gone to Breuckelen
>Gone to Breuckelen

The hands were almost identical, but Wolsey knew the first line was written by Rebekah and the second by Ruth.

It was still only past five on a fine June day. Wolsey sent her two women to search the house again. O'Brien sent one man to ask in the streets and another to go down to Jacob Colaar's farm, which was the nearest point to Breuckelen on Manhattan Island.

No one in the street had seen them, though the town was by now well awake and people were going about their business. Jacob Colaar had not seen them. Susannah and Leah were crying, and Wolsey was on the edge of tears herself.

O'Brien looked at her. 'Now,' he said, 'they have often enough been gone for hours during the day. This time they've gone early. They cannot have gone to Breuckelen unless they swam, or have a boat. Keep looking here. I'm going to the ship. They may have gone there.' But on the *Vliegende Hert*, the mate and two men left aboard while she lay anchored in the river had not seen or heard of the children. O'Brien sent the mate to rouse a dozen of his crew from their dives and doss-houses in the city, and set them searching. He went himself to the Swan, where half a dozen other members of his crew stayed when they were in port.

Two hours' search produced nothing.

From her window, Wolsey could see O'Brien standing with three of his men outside the Swan. They were shaking their heads. Then she was seized with an idea and ran from the house across to her husband.

'There is a woman called Anne,' she said, 'who lives at the Swan. I have seen her before with the children.'

'I know her,' said O'Brien.

Thin, dark Anne was sent for. She curtsied first to Wolsey and then to O'Brien.

'Now Anne,' said O'Brien, 'you know the twins are missing?'

The woman nodded.

'You have been with them before,' said Wolsey. 'Have you seen them?'

The woman was terrified, thinking she was being accused.

Wolsey took her by the shoulders and shook her. Anne was now white in the face.

'No, no, no,' said O'Brien, gently, drawing Wolsey away. 'Now, Anne, we are old, old acquaintants, you and I. Is there anything about the children that you know?'

She shook her head miserably.

'Anne, they left a note saying they have gone to Breuckelen.'

'Oh, God, sir,' said Anne, 'not Breuckelen?'

Breuckelen, only a quarter of a mile across the East River from Manhattan, was Indian territory. They all knew that. They were all afraid. And yet something in Anne's voice told O'Brien that it was not only fear in her voice.

He took her by the shoulders, but gently, and lifted her chin so that she looked him in the eye.

'Now, Anne, help me. When did you last see the children?'

'Yesterday, sir. And you were good to me, and – '

'The children,' said O'Brien, 'the children.'

'It was yesterday, sir, in the afternoon, and they were playing white deer.'

Wolsey looked up fiercely. 'Playing white deer?'

'We often played,' said Anne. 'You remember, ma'am, years ago, when the children ran away, when they were small, and I found them with the Indians.'

O'Brien looked at Wolsey, and she nodded. He had been

away and she had not told him about the meeting or about the Indians. But now she nodded. Yes, it had happened.

'Well, yesterday,' said Anne, 'they were playing deer. They often played deer. The Indians say there are white deer and black deer, besides the ordinary kind.'

'What Indians?' said O'Brien.

'The Indians that told Rebekah and Ruth, sir. By the wharves there are always Indians.'

O'Brien glanced at his mate, who nodded, and set off with three men to look for Indians on the wharves.

'Well,' said Anne, 'the Indians say the white deer, which are very few, are honoured and looked up to by the other deer, who bring them food and groom them. And there are black deer, who are scorned by the others, and are turned away from the herd.'

Anne was in tears again.

'Yes,' said O'Brien, 'now all right, easy. What is this game of deer?'

'Rebekah and Ruth play with the other children, and the other children are always ordinary deer, and your two children, ma'am, are always the white deer. And the others bring them sweets. And they play that they are going hunting, and the white deer are never caught, but always catch the others.'

'And the black deer?' said O'Brien.

'If a child is naughty, sir, he is made black deer until someone else is bad. The black deer cannot play, and is out of the game. But Rebekah and Ruth were always white deer.'

'Well,' said O'Brien, 'and what then?'

'Sir, the Indians say that the white deer live over the water, in Breuckelen and further into Long Island. And yesterday, when one of the children was made a black deer, and they would not let her back into the game, she said there were no white deer, and it was only a story. And Rebekah and Ruth laughed, and...'

'And what?' said O'Brien, but the woman had fallen to her knees. 'What?'

'What?' cried Wolsey, seizing Anne by the hair. 'Now you tell me what, or . . .'

Anne sobbed. 'Rebekah and Ruth laughed, and said they would show them all. They would go and fetch a white deer from over the water.'

The woman looked beseechingly up at O'Brien. 'I couldn't have known, sir.'

'All right, Anne,' he said. 'All right.' The woman walked away in tears. She too loved the twins.

Wolsey faced O'Brien. 'And I suppose they've heard your unicorn song?'

'Often enough,' he said. 'And I suppose we've both told them about unicorn hunts in Plymouth.'

At that moment two Indians, rather cuffed about, were brought up by the mate. They had told him no more than they all knew from Anne already, but kept insisting that the girls would be safe on Breuckelen.

'Which they might well say,' spat the mate, 'seeing what will happen to them if your daughters ain't safe.'

Twenty militiamen were raised and armed, and they and O'Brien's crew were embarking in cutters for Breuckelen before it was learned for sure that this was where Rebekah and Ruth had really gone. A ferryman found on the wharves said he had taken the two children over from the jetty near Jacob Colaar's farm and landed them on the other side of the water near Gegeorgysn's plantation.

'When?' said O'Brien.

'First light.'

'You took two little girls there, at that hour, alone?' said O'Brien, very angry. 'You did that?'

But the ferryman protested that they had not been alone. They had crossed with two men, who the ferryman knew were going to the plantation because he took them every day, and that was where the children said they were going, too. And after they left his boat, he watched them all the way up to the house.

'And saw them go in?' asked O'Brien.

'No, sir. I couldn't. The door is away from the water, the

other side. But they went up to the house, and then I came away.'

Three cutters were sent, one to the plantation, and the others to land a mile east and west of that spot. O'Brien himself commanded the first cutter, for the plantation. He ordered his mate to take the *Vliegende Hert* into the East River and anchor in plain sight of the plantation. He did not know what use she could be, but from there her four cannon could command the shoreline. Wolsey insisted upon coming. O'Brien insisted she should not.

'I will not obey you,' she said. 'They are my daughters.'

'Wolsey, my love,' he said, 'and they are mine. But I cannot *make* you obey, can I?'

'Because all your men are with you, and you have no one to hold me back and keep me here?' She managed a smile.

'That's why.' He took her in his arms and rocked her back and forth, hugging her.

'Then I'll stay and wait, Harry. But find them.'

At Gegeorgysn's plantation the two foresters who went over on the ferry certainly remembered the children, who said they were going to the same plantation house. And they did walk up to the same house, but then, when the men's backs were turned, just walked off. By the time O'Brien found the men, at eleven o'clock, they were about to raise the alarm themselves.

'You know the Indians?' asked O'Brien.

'They're your little girls, aren't they?' said the forester.

'Yes.'

'Well,' said the man, not looking at O'Brien, 'if they walked north along the shore, there's Claes Norman's plantation, and if he saw them he'll have taken them in. If they missed that, and went further north, there's still nothing much there, except forest, and I've seen no Indians there for months. Years.'

'And if they went south?' said O'Brien.

'Wick Quawanck,' said the man. 'Techonic. Indian country.'

'Carnarsie?' asked O'Brien.

'That's the tribe. *Have* been peaceful enough. They're not Mohicans, Captain O'Brien, not the river tribes, and that's a mercy. The Carnarsie are in terror of the Mohicans, who send a raiding party now and again, twice a year, for slaughter and for pleasure. But I've heard of no Mohicans lately.'

'Inland,' said O'Brien. 'Suppose they went east, inland? Into Long Island?'

The foresters shook their heads. They had never been inland.

All day the men searched. Claes Norman had not seen the children. The Indians to the south, surprised in their villages by twenty armed militiamen, swore they had seen nothing. That evening, the governor of Manhattan sent another twenty armed men, and the captains of other ships sent two more cutters filled with their own men to help.

In the evening, at sunset, O'Brien sat five miles inland in the village where Penhawitz lived, the chief of the Carnarsies, and explained interminably what he wanted. In Indian country, Indian courtesies had to be observed. Etiquette demanded the eating of a feast and the presentation of many beads before direct questions could be asked. To betray anxiety would not be prudent. The one-eyed Penhawitz smoked his long pipe, and nodded and nodded, and knew nothing. But he promised to send trackers to help.

O'Brien withdrew, leaving more gifts, and returned to the northern shore. Flares were lit on board the *Vliegende Hert*, and in the three camps of the searchers, stretching five miles along the coast. Wolsey could see them from the East River shoreline. Most of Manhattan could see them.

It was a slow night. At four o'clock in the morning, O'Brien woke his ship's mate.

'Those Indians you rousted out on the wharves this morning, and brought to the Swan. What tribe were they?'

The mate, like O'Brien, could not tell one Indian from another, but they found a Dutch soldier who could. He had seen the men and knew them. They were harmless, he said, as far as savages could be harmless. Indians who lived for years on Manhattan, away from their tribe; they were pretty well outcasts.

'But what tribe?' asked O'Brien.

'Mohican,' said the soldier.

Then O'Brien remembered telling Wolsey, years before, at Plymouth, that he had been a Catholic, and then corrected himself by saying, 'Once a Catholic, always a Catholic.' Now the question ran through his mind, 'Once a Mohican, always a Mohican?'

At dawn the searchers spread farther out, and went farther inland. The soldiers knew the country better than O'Brien, and he watched them closely. They became more silent as the day went on.

They worked farther inland, and found nothing. The trackers Penhawitz had promised did not appear. A Dutch military officer appeared and touched O'Brien on the shoulder.

'Now we'll work our way farther in, but it's better for you to go back to the shore, captain. My men know this territory, and you don't, and we know the Carnarsie, and you don't. And if we all go on, we'll run out of food twice as fast.'

O'Brien saw the sense of this, and took his party back, leaving their supplies. It was a sad, dispirited return, and would have been more dispirited if the Dutch officer had told O'Brien what he knew, which was that a raiding party of Mohicans had silently come upon a white settlement on Long Island the night before, and left two men and a woman dead.

But O'Brien, not knowing this, was still hardening himself for the worst news, and hardening himself to break it to Wolsey. He was within a quarter of a mile of the shore when a cannon crashed out, from the *Vliegende Hert*. Then a second, then a third. It was the signal to return to the spot where they had all first landed. Hardly allowing himself to hope, O'Brien pushed on with his men, and then they came in sight of the shore, by Jacob Colaar's plantation. Soldiers were lying exhausted on the sandy beach. Sailors from his own ship's crew were standing in an amazed circle, and there, in the centre of them all, were the slight figures of Rebekah and Ruth. On a lead they had a small, white fawn.

When they landed on the Manhattan shore, half the town was there to meet them. The governor himself was there. O'Brien stepped out of the cutter first, and then handed out Rebekah and Ruth, who were calm amid the excitement. Wolsey ran to her children and embraced them, but she was in tears, not they. The fawn was then handed up, and the children stood, both holding the lead, waiting as if expecting praise. After greeting their mother, they had turned back to the fawn straight away. As this was noticed, a strange quiet fell over the spectators. O'Brien took Wolsey to one side.

'They *are* all right,' he said. 'And fresher than any of us.'

Wolsey looked at him. He was haggard and deep-eyed. The soldiers, as they landed, were plainly exhausted.

O'Brien went up to the governor and thanked him. The governor clapped him on the back, and then asked what had happened and how.

'I do not know, sir,' said O'Brien. 'They will not say.'

'They are well?' asked the governor. 'They look well.'

'They are fit, and well, and fresh.'

'Yes,' said the governor thoughtfully. He approached the children, and they curtsied to him together.

'Well,' said the governor. 'Who gave the fawn to you? Will you tell me?'

'He just came up to us. This morning. After we slept in the woods,' said Rebekah.

'And his lead?' said the governor.

'He had it with him,' said Rebekah.

'With him?' asked the governor, turning to Ruth. 'His lead already round his neck?'

Ruth looked at Rebekah and said, 'Oh yes.'

The governor beckoned to an officer who was his chief Indian adviser, and indicated the lead.

The man took it between his fingers, and turned it over. It was made of three strands of plaited leather.

'Mohican, sir.'

The governor turned to the children. 'But you must have bought him, surely? Didn't you buy the little deer?'

'Oh no, sir. We put down our feathers, that we have had for years, to help bring a white deer to us, and he came up to us. We left the feathers, and he came up to us.'

Wolsey told the governor what the feathers were. The governor glanced at his officer.

'If they were turkey feathers, Mohican, sir.'

'You did not trade the feathers, perhaps, for the deer? It would have been a good trade, wouldn't it?'

'He came up to us,' and both the twins said this together, looking the governor candidly in the face as they did so.

The governor said to O'Brien, 'They're more tired than they look, O'Brien. Home to bed with them.'

The town's children had gathered, too, and Rebekah and Ruth were proudly demonstrating to them the proof that white deer did exist, and could be caught. Two children came up to pat the fawn, but Rebekah stopped them. 'He's *our* deer,' she said. 'Ours.'

O'Brien turned to the dead-beat soldiers and sailors who were standing around. He saw that dark Anne had come down to meet the boats, too. He said, 'It's a better end than we could have expected, and I thank you, as I'll thank the others of you who are still on Long Island. Harry O'Brien does not forget, and when we've had two days to sleep this off, there'll be a mighty feast for you all.'

'Which'll take us another two days to sleep off?' called a soldier.

'Three,' said O'Brien. 'Three at least. Set aside three. And be sure I thank you with all my heart, as my wife does. You're brave men, and I thank you.'

The feast was given, and was for many years remembered as the finest proof of O'Brien's generous heart. But as to the white fawn, and how they came by it, there was not getting any other story out of Rebekah and Ruth. It had just walked up to them. If that was not the truth, there was no getting any other truth out of them. It was a week before they would let any other child touch it, exclaiming that it was their deer, *theirs*. The wilful strength of her daughters, which Wolsey had for some time suspected, was vividly brought home to her.

18

ANOTHER COUNTRY

The next two years were prosperous, and were marred for Wolsey only by Susannah's distress at the final departure of her daughter, who defiantly went off with her Portuguese sailor, to live near Lisbon. Leah did not want to leave her mother, or Manhattan, but she did want the man.

'Couldn't he settle in Manhattan?' asked Wolsey, but he could not. He said men of his region always retired from the sea when they married, and went home to settle on the family farm and raise children. He resolutely declined to raise children in the new world. His family had never done it before.

Wolsey reasoned with the girl. Susannah went about the house tearful after many fruitless arguments.

'You came across the sea yourself,' said Leah, 'and left all *your* folk behind,' and there was no answer to this.

'He will never marry you,' said Susannah. 'He will take you away and then leave you, and never marry you.' But this objection was removed when Leah and the sailor married quietly in the city hall in New Amsterdam, and came to Susannah to say the thing was done. The parting was bitter for both mother and daughter, but Leah left. Susannah cried wildly that she would never see her daughter again, which Wolsey tried to deny, though he knew it was only too likely. And in fact Susannah never did see her daughter again.

Leah was one of only three people who knew what had

really happened on the night Wheaton walked out into the snow. Now only Susannah and Brewster remained, and Brewster was soon to go too. A month after Leah's departure, Wolsey received a letter brought by a coastal bark which had called at Plymouth the week before. Her name was written on the outside in a hand which was familiar but which she could not quite place. She stared at the inscription and turned the letter over in her hand before she broke the seal. It was from Bradford, and told her that William Brewster was lying very ill, and wished to see her before he died. He could not write himself, being too weak, but had something he particularly wished to tell her, which he felt it his duty to impart.

Her mind leapt to Brewster, to her childhood, to Scrooby, to her young womanhood when Brewster brought Francis Wheaton to her in the archbishop's palace, to her first marriage, to the night of Wheaton's disappearance and her son's death, and to Brewster's grief when she left to come to Manhattan.

Bradford's letter brought back two worlds to her: England, when she was a girl, and Plymouth colony, in its hard first years. New Amsterdam was remote from both. Now she was living in great prosperity as the wife of the richest sea captain and merchant in New Netherlands, running not only his house but his business while he was away. The *Vliegende Hert* was now entirely his, and he owned large shares in three other vessels. In Europe he would have been considered prosperous. In the new world, he was a merchant prince. In his absence, Wolsey habitually struck bargains on his behalf, and pledged his word. Ships' masters and merchants in Amsterdam, Québec, London, Brazil, and the Caribbean ports recognized her signature and accepted her orders and drafts without question. Her word was Harry O'Brien's, and Harry O'Brien's was as good as his bond.

She dropped Bradford's letter in her lap, and looked down at her skirts, which were of the richest purple silk. The rings she wore – sapphire and rich ruby – could have bought half a share in any ship in port. They were the gift of O'Brien. The wild Irishman from the poverty of Cork had taken easily to the trappings of great wealth. And so, she reflected, had she. She had been at home in the faded splendours of old Scrooby palace. She had fallen in naturally with the austerity of Plymouth plantation. Now she had just as easily become Mevrouw O'Brien, and had risen naturally to the increasing sumptuousness that O'Brien's strength, worldliness, and good fortune had brought. The only material possessions of her old lives that she still had were the ring and gold chain that had been her father's and grandfather's and great-grandfather's. Since she was no longer obliged to conceal the ring, she had removed it from the chain and wore it on the third finger of her left hand, the same finger on which she wore Harry's wedding ring.

And now this letter brought back England, and Plymouth, and her dear tutor William Brewster, who was dying. She recalled with shame that she had written to him only twice in the last four years, once to tell him of her marriage to O'Brien, and once to tell him that she flourished, that her two daughters were fast becoming young women, and that she still read to herself the books they had first read together. She kept his replies. He had felicitated her on her marriage, and sent his love to the children, though he doubted if they would remember him. In his letters – and his last had been only six months before – his hand had been as firm as ever, and his mind as acute. But now Bradford wrote that he was dying.

O'Brien had just returned from Antigua. She asked for one of his smaller vessels to take her north, but he would have none of that. He would take her himself, in the *Vliegende Hert*. He would get the cargo out of her hold that afternoon. They would sail with the morning tide. Next morning he was up before her, seeing to the ship. When he returned to the house for breakfast he was surprised to see how she was dressed. She wore no silk, no lace, no brocade, just a plain red woollen skirt, and a grey wool coat.

'I do not want to offend them at Plymouth,' she said.

'That's a right thought,' he said. 'But it was not that I was thinking. It was more than that. Dressed like that, you are as I first saw you. Except for a bonnet. I never knew the colour of your hair until you let it loose on the ship.'

'I will not hide my hair in a bonnet now,' she said. 'I have no bonnet.' But she had carefully put it up behind her, so as not to offend Plymouth with the immodesty of her too luxuriant hair.

'And Harry,' she said, 'I have left off all your rings, except the wedding ring.'

'Dear woman,' he said, 'since when have you thought you had to explain yourself to me?'

'And I am wearing my own old ring,' she said, 'because Mr Brewster knows it.'

'Wolsey, Wolsey, you are not accountable to me. You are your own woman.'

'Not quite, Harry,' she said. 'Not quite, I hope.'

He touched her shoulder. 'And that,' he said, 'is as sweet a thing as a man could hope to hear a woman tell him.'

It was a cold voyage, on grey seas. She saw the Atlantic beaches of Cape Cod and remembered her first sight of them when she was seventeen, and then the coastline of the colony, and the entrance to the Plymouth harbour, and the town, larger but essentially unchanged. *There* were the fort and the meeting house beneath, and the two cross streets, and the hill where they buried those who died the first winter, and the town brook over which she was first married. And the everlasting forests behind. It was a homecoming to her young womanhood.

A ship flying the Dutch flag was no longer a rarity at Plymouth, and this ship was well-known. As they anchored, at midday, half the town was there to watch. The neatness, silence, and simplicity of it all struck Wolsey after the chaos and busy commerce of New Amsterdam. She saw that Plymouth now had a new, long jetty at which the cutter could tie up. On the jetty to welcome them stood two men. The older was in the dress of a minister, whom she did not recognize. The other was a man she recognized very well, and had hoped not to see again.

When they landed, the minister came forward, welcomed them to Plymouth, and proposed a prayer, to which Wolsey consented. Harry stood to one side, not concealing his impatience.

'And where,' said Wolsey when the praying was over, 'is the Reverend Mr Shepard? I thought he was still with you.'

'The Lord,' cut in the second, younger man, 'has been pleased to take Mr Shepard to Boston where all manner of wickedness has lately broken forth. But I beg your pardon, ma'am. You will not remember me, and I must present myself again. I am George Downing.'

'I remember you well,' she said. She thought that after their last meeting he would have gone out of his way to avoid her, but there he was.

'Now, gentlemen,' she said, 'where is Mr Brewster?'

The smooth young man said that Governor Bradford would like to see them first. They walked towards the governor's house, a road she remembered well. The street was lined with men and women, but she knew none of them. The young ones would have been children when she left, and the older ones had so changed that she could not remember their faces. Wolsey did not know that she was a legend to them – the wife of the first minister, who had walked into the forest with their son. A woman who had lain with Indians in the forest, a woman whose two daughters were dark as Indians. A woman who was a man-pleaser. All this was legend, a scurrilous legend sharply repressed whenever it came to the elders' ears, but a tale that persisted. She was a woman who had fled the colony, and now lived with the Dutch in the house of a barbarian Papist Irishman with a red beard.

Wolsey was conscious of none of this as she walked between the rows of townspeople. Her only thought was that, surely, they could not all have changed, or changed that much? Not changed so that she could not recognize them? It was only when she saw Bradford that she fully understood how much they *had* changed. She took the hand of an old man whom she knew to be Bradford, but whom she would not have recognized if she had not expected it to be him. She had first seen him as a strong young weaver of eighteen, but that was when she was an infant. Then she had known him as a broad man of thirty, who had become the colony's governor. Then, just before she left, he was still a strong, vigorous man. Now he looked old. Bradford had always read Wolsey's face well. He saw what she thought, and smiled.

'It *is* nine years,' he said. Then he offered O'Brien his hand, and the contrast between the two men touched Wolsey. Of course Harry was younger, but he appeared almost a different kind of creature. His hair was abundant, his beard jaunty, his eyes clear, and he was broad and straight. Bradford was aged with care, and bowed, and yet he could only be a year or two over fifty.

'Mrs O'Brien,' said Bradford, and then stopped himself. 'No. Shall I say Wolsey? You were Wolsey to me.'

'And am.'

'Wolsey, then. Well, in God's Grace we have flourished. We have increased. We have lived long. God has allowed us longevity, you see, though His work has sometimes been hard, and this shows in His servants. You see it in me. But there are many aged people among the pilgrims. I will take you to Mr Brewster. He is eighty. I think he is eighty. He bore the winter well, but the spring has nipped him. Wolsey, he's dying. He knows this, and his first wish when he did know was to see you. He has never ceased to ask for you.'

Brewster, when Wolsey first saw him, was lying fumbling at the sheets. Downing, who had conducted Wolsey and O'Brien to the house, crossed to the bed to help him sit up. Wolsey saw Brewster look with puzzlement in his eyes at the hand that lifted him, and then she went straight to him, took his head in her own arms, and lifted him up onto a bolster, and kissed his forehead. The very old man called out, 'Wolsey? You have come? I did not expect it.'

'I am here, William.'

Brewster raised his head, looked at the two other figures in the room, and said, 'Who...?'

Wolsey said quietly, 'Mr Downing, leave us.'

'If I can be of any service,' Downing replied, 'then I should – '

'No,' she said evenly.

'I'll see you out,' said O'Brien, seizing the man's shoulder in the sort of amiable grip that many drunken sailors had felt in their time. 'Show me the town. Show me anything.' He guided Downing through the door, and Wolsey and Brewster were left alone.

Brewster gazed at her intently and said, 'It is you. You are a girl, Wolsey. I am fourscore years, or almost, if not all out fourscore.'

'Yes,' said Wolsey, 'yes.' She did not know whether this man, who had been so much to her, would be at all able to tell her what he wanted to say. So she took out the locket her daughters had given her for him just before she left. 'This is from Rebekah and Ruth,' she said. 'It is for you. They have put locks of their hair inside.' She opened it and showed him. The two locks were identical. 'One lock from each,' she said. 'The hair is so much the same I cannot tell one lock from the other. But they said that would not matter, and that I was to say it was something from both of them.'

Brewster took the locket. His fingers, which she had thought could only fumble, delicately separated the strands of hair, and he said, 'Your children. That is part of what I have to tell you.'

She realized that he was now quite suddenly lucid.

'That,' he repeated, 'is part of what I shall tell you, because you must know.'

She sat down beside the bed.

'Wolsey, you remember the archbishop's palace at Scrooby. The great hall?'

'Yes, William. Though it seems a whole lifetime away.'

'And your father?'

'I remember it was you who told me he was dead. I remember he gave Mr Bradford an Old Testament when he first went into the Low Countries. I was only eight when he died. I do not know how much I remember myself, and how much I know from what other people have told me. Susannah has sometimes talked to me about him. Susannah Tilly, who came with me to Manhattan.'

'Susannah Tilly. She did know him well. That was after your mother died.'

'I cannot remember my mother at all. Or only once, when she was worried that my father would go out in all weathers. He went out one night to a man who was sick. It was winter, and stormy. I can remember her saying it was winter and he would catch his death. But she died before him.'

'You were only five or six then,' said Brewster.

'Yes. I cannot remember. Or, all I can remember is being taken away from the house when she died, and taken into other houses, and looked after. And when my father died, I remember one woman took me in. She always cut a loaf of bread towards her. She held it up to her apron, and cut it with the knife blade towards her. I remember that. I never saw anyone else cut a loaf that way.'

'And later, do you remember that you came to my house, and I taught you, and we read together?'

'How could I forget that? We read Greek and Latin. I can still see the very books in my mind.'

'Your father asked me to teach you, as he had taught you, and I promised. That was when he knew he was failing. And I promised.'

Wolsey said, 'Yes. One day he told me that you would soon teach me instead of him. I asked him why, because I did not understand, and he did not answer me, but told me I should expect it. I could not have known he was ill. I could not have noticed.'

'Children do not. But now, you remember our reading, and then, when I went away...' He hesitated. He had lost the thread of his story.

'Then there were the canons at York,' she said. 'You took me to York. The canons brought me up. On Manhattan I have often thought of the cathedral church at York. I do not know why, but I never thought of it here.'

'And when I came back from Holland, you must have been seventeen...?'

'Seventeen.'

'The canons said you were as good a scholar as any of them. A better scholar than I.'

'William, *you* taught me.'

'No, better. You were better. At court, in the old days, I spoke Latin with the old queen, Elizabeth, when she was in the mood for it, which was once a week or so, and then she'd conduct the morning's business in Latin, for no reason. Or she would speak Latin to the French ambassador because he could hardly stammer along in it. But that was years before.' Brewster gave a dry laugh that was half a cough. 'She wouldn't have loved you, Wolsey. As soon as anyone answered her in the language as fluently as she spoke it, she would glare at him and cut straight back into English. I've heard her do that a dozen times.'

He coughed again. Wolsey picked up a cup of honeyed ale which was standing on the table, and held it while he drank.

'Did you ever ask yourself,' he continued, 'if there was a reason behind it all? Your father teaching you, and then me, and then the canons at York?'

'At the time, no. I learned what I was taught. I thought it was natural.'

He nodded.

'But afterwards, of course,' she said, 'I wondered afterwards.'

Well then, said Brewster, she would know of Cardinal Wolsey, Lord Chancellor of England, who was disgraced by Henry VIII over the affair of Anne Boleyn, when the cardinal could not procure the king a divorce from his earlier and still living wife? Well, it was to Scrooby that the broken cardinal had retired, with charges of treason hanging over him, but still archbishop of York. He did not go to York, but to Scrooby, fulfilling the office of parish priest there. And when he had died, on a visit to Leicester, he had directed that his cardinal's hat should hang in the old palace at Scrooby.

Wolsey nodded. She had known that. She knew the hat, which hung in the great hall at Scrooby.

Brewster went on. 'In his last months at Scrooby, the cardinal got a village girl with child. And because he loved the girl, he provided for her, and for the proper education of the child, and of that child's children, and so on forever. Those are the words of the trust he created, which I have seen.'

Wolsey sat very straight and said nothing.

'The old cardinal died before the child was born. It was a boy and was brought up to be a priest. That man married late in life – by then a priest of the English church could marry – and he too had a son. That son was also brought up in the church, and was parish priest at Scrooby. He married and had a child. Wolsey, that child was a daughter, and that daughter was you.'

Brewster lay back. There was a long silence in the room. Wolsey rose, took the cup of ale to the fire, mulled it by dipping a hot poker into the ale until it sizzled, and then raised Brewster's head while he sipped it.

'You knew?' he said.

She nodded. 'It would have been extraordinary for me not to guess a great deal of that, though no one till now has ever told me, and I have asked nothing and said nothing. You know, Francis never guessed it at all. But my name alone, with everything else, you see? How could I not have guessed at something? Why should I have been given the upbringing of a priest, though I could never become one? And there is this.'

She held out her left hand to Brewster. And there on the third finger was her father's ring.

'My father gave me this. I remember he gave it to me just before I went to stay with the woman who cut a loaf of bread towards her. It must have been very soon before his death. He told me to cherish the ring. It is all of his that I have. He said I must remember that it had been his, and his grandfather's, and his great-grandfather's. I often wore it, not as a ring, but on a chain around my neck, under my dress. Otherwise it would have been forbidden as a decoration, even in those last days in England.'

Brewster smiled. 'I remember a ring of your father's,' he said, 'but did not know you had it.'

'Here it is,' she said.

He took her hand, and drew it close to his face. His eyes were dim, and he could hardly make it out, but he helped his sight with his fingers, touching the engraved pattern in the ring. The pattern was two crossed keys, in scarlet, with a regal crown between them.

He recognized the arms of an archbishop of York.

'It is not the archbishop's ring of office,' said Wolsey. 'Not his grand ring. But those are his arms. I do not know, but perhaps he had it made for the girl in Scrooby in his last months, and gave it to her. I do not know. But those are the arms. So you see, with everything, how could I not have guessed something?'

Brewster nodded, and then said after a pause, 'The trust still exists, vested in the canons of York, for the benefit of your children if you wish it, and for their children.'

'William, that is in another country. I do not remember much of my father, but I do not forget him either. I do not forget my past. How could I? But we are not in England now. We are here. This is a new country. I shall not tell my children. They must start again for themselves. All their past, everything they know, is American, and that is enough. They were born here.'

'Dear Wolsey, that is wise. For myself, you see, I must confess that I have at times pined in this wilderness. And I know I am dying in a wilderness. I do not regret that I came here, but I cannot help seeing it as a wilderness still.'

She denied that he was dying. He gently waved her words away. 'But,' he said, 'it will not be a wilderness to your children. They will not think of it as a wilderness.'

'They *do* not,' she said, remembering her daughters' fearless venture into Breuckelen.

'And they will not think of an old country and pine for it,' he said. 'And that is good.'

When he had said this, he let his head sink back on to the bolster. She thought he was too tired to talk any more, and, as he lay still, with his mind wandering through its own inward thoughts, Wolsey looked round the bare room, at the bare landscape outside, and let her own mind look back over her own years in this new continent. A wilderness? Yes, it had been a wilderness to her. Not at first, when to survive those first winters had taken all her force. And not when her son was young. But as Francis had become increasingly deranged, it had indeed become a wilderness to her, and to leave for Manhattan had been a release. Manhattan, with its commerce of ships and sailors and many languages had been less a wilderness, though, even there, the wilderness was close, as close as the mainland across the Hudson, or as close as Breuckelen.

But she had been fortunate. Because she had come young to the new continent, she had never felt the wilderness as Brewster had. Because she was strong in mind, and could set herself to a purpose, and carry through that purpose in so single-minded a way as to exclude all other things from her mind, and because she was cheerful, she had never felt the bitter exile that had so oppressed Francis. She had felt the terror of the deep winter forests. Not to have felt that, a man or woman would have been insensate. She never forgot the terror of the night her son was taken into the forest. She never forgot, as how could she, the terror of finding her son dead on the forest floor. But the gnawing ache of exile that had been endured by so many, that she had been spared. The *terror* of exile that had deranged Francis, or hastened his derangement, she had never suffered.

'I have been fortunate,' she said.

She thought she spoke to herself, but she had spoken aloud, and Brewster heard and came out of his reverie. He said nothing for a moment, but his eyes were brighter. It revived him to see her again. He wanted to go on talking. And although he had not recognized Downing when he first entered, he now talked with spirit about the man whom, he was sorry to say, he rather disliked. He was sad to say so, but he did not like him at all.

'Nor do I, and I am not sorry to say it,' said Wolsey. 'He is an impudent boy. You told me, when you wrote to me with the trunk that he brought to Manhattan, that Captain Standish called him a butterfly.'

'Butterfly,' said Brewster. 'Yes, Standish called him that. But rather a moth, I'd say, a moth about the bright candles of any court that attracts him. And a moth who will take good care not to be burned, and will not be burned. I have seen many such moths. They do not get burned. They flourish where better men fail.'

'I shudder when the man comes near.'

'But he can please. He can be pleasing. I am sorry he met you today. Bradford will not admit it, but he feels the cold bitterly now and hardly goes out of doors. Standish is away in the forests for two days, training new men. The minister is good for praying, but little else. So there was the Moth. He has been at Harvard. He was given a fellowship at Harvard. But he is said to be off to the Caribbean, where I suspect his austere principles will still permit him to make a fortune out of slaves and sugar. He will flit around courts and power all his life, like a moth to a flame. And will not be burned.'

Wolsey saw that Brewster was deeply tired again. He looked dully at her, with an effort, but did not want to let her go.

'Standish still flourishes, then?' she asked. 'Still training new men.'

'He flourishes,' said Brewster. 'A flourishing man, but greying.'

Wolsey asked after Jane White.

Brewster seemed to summon up all his powers of recollection, and then said, 'I have been straining to remember, because I have not seen her. But now I remember why I have not seen her. She is dead these two years. I was with her when she died. She talked of your father when she died.

I had forgotten her.'

'She dressed me for my wedding day,' said Wolsey.

'Ah,' he said, 'O'Brien is a fine man. A fine strong man for you, my dear. A fit man for you.'

Wolsey looked at him and tears came to her eyes, because she saw he was wandering, and had forgotten Francis Wheaton, Francis whom he had first brought to her so many years before, Francis for whom Jane White had helped dress her. Brewster had forgotten her first husband and the father of her children.

She embraced him, hiding her head in his shoulder so that he should not see her tears. She felt the frailty of the old man, and the bone beneath the skin, and knew the smell of death. Here was the courtier, the scholar, the man first in all adventures, her beloved mentor.

He roused himself when she lifted her head.

'Wolsey, your children. Remember me to your children.'

William Brewster was asleep and breathing peacefully when, ten minutes later, Wolsey rose and said her last goodbyes.

PART THREE

19

THE REEF

For three days Harry O'Brien had waited at Martinique to take on a cargo of molasses and rum, and each day he had seen the same tall, slight figure of a man standing on the beach gazing out at the Atlantic, never moving, never turning his head. On the third day, when O'Brien at last chivvied his half-caste agent into a firm promise that the cargo would be ready to take on board the next day, he accepted the agent's offer of a glass of wine and talked island talk.

'Who,' asked O'Brien, 'is the man who stands each day on the beach in the same spot?'

'See the French ship in the bay?' said the agent. 'He's out of her, and impatient to go. More impatient than you, Mr. O'Brien, and that I would have said was impossible.'

'Impatient? The man never moves. Just stands there.'

'He was impatient enough the first week he was here, captain, pacing up and down, and the second week he roamed the island incessantly, but then he gave up the ghost and stared at the ocean. He'll be staring at it a while yet, to judge from the state of that French vessel. Look at her.'

'Her?' said O'Brien. 'I've seen her. And hardly seen the likes of her before. Bow near stove in. Bowsprit gone. Beakhead near carried away. Foretopmost clean gone. The whole ship flayed of paint. Not a lick of paint left on her.'

'She crawled in a month ago, in tatters. Half her men gone, swept overboard, half her canvas gone, carried away altogether,' said the half-caste. 'When she hove in sight, she could not make her mooring. She was helpless. The commander here sent out his own men to bring her in, and there she lies.'

'And nothing done to refit her?' asked O'Brien. 'In a month?'

'She's a French king's ship, captain, and must take her turn in the king's dockyard. And there are two others before her. She's likely to be there another month, and by that time the crew, what's left of them, will have recovered, and seen the island, and had the sense to desert. They're still recovering their wits. Give them time, captain, to recover their wits, and then, their wits recovered, and their senses recovered, they'll come ashore and take island women for a week, and then desert inland for a month, and then stagger back and sign on again, on the next ship that offers that's not French. The French would hang them for having deserted. So, any ship that's not French.'

'And he,' said O'Brien, looking towards the man gazing out at the Atlantic, 'he's her captain?'

'That's not my understanding, sir. If he were her captain, he'd have done better by her. The captain's still on board, with his lieutenants. That man's a high-born Frenchman who was a passenger. A passenger I know he is, though from the way he talked to me, the first few days she was here, I'd have said he was more than that. The captain was drunk and his lieutenants sick, and it was that man who came to me and bargained for stores, and the way he did it, I'd have sworn he knew the sea.'

'What, knocked you down to a fair price, did he?' said O'Brien.

'Ah, sir,' said the half-caste, spreading his arms wide. 'As if I have ever asked you more than a fair price.'

O'Brien and the half-caste were old acquaintances. Jacques Ibert, ship's chandler, merchant, and more or less honest rogue, never pressed for an outrageous price when he saw that a man had wits enough not to pay it.

O'Brien walked over to the figure standing on the beach.

A dozen yards behind the man he stopped. The man was not gazing out at the Atlantic, as O'Brien had expected. He was gazing at the reef. Fifty yards from the beach lay a sandbar, and the man was watching the surf break, break, break, on this reef, never taking his eyes from it. This was something O'Brien had seen before. He had seen good men go mad watching the reef on some tropical island. A man slept at night with the breakers in his sleep, and then woke in the morning, and watched the breakers, and drank, and watched the breakers, and then ate a little, and watched the breakers, and then drank, and at sunset he was still watching the breakers and the reef. And after sundown he drank, looking out to the reef, not seeing it, but hearing the sea break on it, and then he fell into a light sleep haunted by breakers, and woke in the morning to the sight of breakers. O'Brien had seen men of resource and spirit broken like that. He had seen men haunted by the reef-stare.

And yet, as O'Brien could see him, the man was not going to pieces. His shirt was clean. His shoulders were straight, and his head held high. He was standing, not lying in the helpless posture of a man who had surrendered his will to the eternal breaking of the sea on the reef. But all the same, O'Brien had seen the man looking out to sea for three days.

He approached. Even on the soft sand the man must have heard him by now, but he did not show that he heard, and did not turn until O'Brien touched him on the shoulder.

When the Frenchman turned, O'Brien saw only half what he expected. The man's face was tanned copper by the sun and wind, and there were flecks of grey in his brown hair. So much O'Brien had expected – a man only in his middle twenties, but made older by the sea, which was hard on a man. But the man's grey eyes were alive, and O'Brien could have sworn they were amused. He was a man not so lost in his thoughts, or so far gone in the reef-stare, that he did not have all his wits about him. He must perfectly well have heard O'Brien approach, and allowed him to do so. He was not at all taken by surprise, and amused that O'Brien should have thought that his approach was unnoticed.

'Ah, now, sir,' said O'Brien. 'Good morning, sir.'

The Frenchman bowed.

Ah, thought O'Brien, the poor man has no English. So he said slowly in his Irish French, 'I have seen your ship in the bay, sir.'

The Frenchman nodded at the ragged vesssel with the smashed-in prow, and then at the *Vliegende Hert*, as she lay anchored very trim, and then replied, in excellent English, 'And I've seen yours, captain, and very fine she is.'

'Well,' said O'Brien, now having suffered two surprises. But, magnanimous in spite of it, as an Irishman should be magnanimous, he presented himself to the Frenchman, and proposed a bottle of wine together.

The grey eyes smiled. 'And my name is La Tour, Pierre La Tour, and I am honoured, Mr O'Brien, to take a glass with you.'

They drank for an hour. In that hour, O'Brien had talked of Ireland, and New Amsterdam, and the islands, and his ship. In return, he had learned that the Frenchman was indeed not the captain of the French king's ship, nor highborn either, but only a passenger aboard her, bound for Québec. But he had certainly once been a sailor, and, although La Tour had not said a word to suggest it, not a single explicit word, O'Brien was certain in his mind that had this man been captain of the French ship, she would certainly have been refitted by now and on her way north. But La Tour would say nothing about the ship's officers, except that in his few years at sea he had never seen such a hurricane as they had passed through, and that it was no wonder the captain was half dead with it, and in no shape to insist that he should be rapidly refitted.

'And no doubt he won't mind staying here a while,' said O'Brien. 'This is a softer place than Québec. It would be a natural thing for the poor man to see things that way.'

La Tour replied, with courtesy, that he had no idea what was in the mind of the French captain.

'No, no, for sure you would not,' said O'Brien. He admired La Tour's loyalty in declining to say a word about the way the French ship had been handled, or why she was delayed so long. His mind went to Wolsey, in whose loyalty he had an absolute trust, who would not reveal to her closest friend the slightest thing that passed between her and her husband, and he smiled.

'You smile?' said the Frenchman.

At which Wild O'Brien said he was smiling at the thought of his wife.

'*À propos?*' said the Frenchman.

'Oh, a man's wife need not come into his mind *à propos*. A man's wife does come into a man's mind, by good fortune, from time to time, *à propos* of nothing, other than herself.'

At this the Frenchman looked downcast, and for the moment lost his spirits, and again gazed out to sea, at the reef.

O'Brien followed his stare, and the two men sat silent for a long minute before O'Brien carried them off on another track.

'Québec,' he said. 'I am often at Québec. It is a fine city, but a city rather at the end of things.'

It was La Tour's turn to smile. 'But,' he said, 'it is not at all the end of things for me, you see, captain. Rather the beginning.'

'A beginning?' said O'Brien. 'Then where are you bound after Québec?'

'After Québec,' said La Tour, 'exploration.'

O'Brien, who was holding a glass in his great hand, took a long draught of the burgundy and then held the glass up in front of him, looking at La Tour over the rim.

'Exploration?'

'The Saint Lawrence, the lakes, and then west to the great Vermilion Sea, and Cathay.'

'Then God go with you,' said O'Brien. 'Others have tried before you.'

'Others,' said La Tour, 'will try after me,' and called for more wine.

They became warmed in spirit, and by degrees more convivial and confidential, until, after another hour, when the sun was well into the subtropical afternoon, each knew the other man's history. La Tour knew O'Brien's. O'Brien knew that La Tour was from Bayeux, in Normandy, had started in his father's wine trade, had first sailed at twelve years old, in his father's ships, had learned his English in English ports, and then, when Louis XIII wanted men in the interminable wars with Spain, entered the king's service at first in coasting vessels, and then as a lieutenant in ships of the line. By twenty-three he was a veteran.

O'Brien nodded. It was a familiar story. 'And your English learned, no doubt, not only from English ports, but from women in English ports? No better way to learn a language.'

'No better way,' said La Tour.

They drank to that.

And then, said La Tour, in his last year with a king's ship, he had been in the Caribbean.

'Ah,' said O'Brien, 'so you know the likes of this island, and the sharks on it, and that is why you could deal with Jacques Ibert on something like equal terms? So you know this island, too?'

'No. But Guadeloupe, and St Vincent, and others. And other beaches. Beaches like these.'

O'Brien nodded.

'And other reefs,' said La Tour, looking out to sea, 'other reefs like that one.'

'Ah, yes,' said O'Brien. 'Reefs, yes.'

La Tour considered O'Brien. Their eyes met. La Tour said, 'I've seen men gaze at reefs, gaze all day at a reef.'

O'Brien said nothing.

'After two months at sea, and with a ship in that state,' – La Tour gestured at the French ship – 'after two months at sea, I've seen men gaze at a reef, as you thought you found me gazing this morning, I think?'

'Not at all, now, not at all, sir,' said O'Brien.

'But you would have been right to think that,' said La Tour. 'You would have been right, and wrong. Both, I was not gazing at the desolation of the sea. I was not broken by that passage from Le Havre, as some men were in the storm that treated her like that, and left her a floating wreck like that, as you see her lying there. So you would have been wrong if you had been thinking that I was a man gazing at a reef in that sense. But in another sense, you were right, very right.'

O'Brien was much the older and much the bigger man, and much the more sober of the two. He remembered the moment when he had spoken of his own good fortune, and his own wife, earlier in the day, and La Tour's moment of silence, and he said, 'In whatever sense I was thinking, man, I beg your pardon.'

La Tour looked sideways at the sun, which was half an hour from setting, and at its rays streaming over the calm water, and up at the sky, which was unbroken blue, and said, 'It is strange, but I do not think it has rained since that day.'

'What day?'

'Six months ago.'

'Man,' said O'Brien, 'you came through a hurricane a month ago. You told me so. And not that you needed to *tell* me. A glance at your ship tells me that.'

'Yes,' said La Tour. 'That is true. But I have forgotten that. That was at sea. It was in the way of happenings at sea. But I do not think it has rained when I have been on land, since that day.'

La Tour poured himself more wine. 'Do you know Gisors, the country round Gisors, in that northern part of France? Narrow lanes, stone walls, flinty fields, very like some parts of England?'

'It is too far inland for me to know. I have put in at Caen, and Le Havre. Gisors is too far inland.'

'It is not far. And it is very English, the countryside, and would be familiar to you.'

'But I am an Irishman.'

La Tour did not hear him, but burst out, 'She was from Gisors, and she meant the world to me.' He was suddenly a distressed and distracted man.

'Oh, man,' said O'Brien, leaning forward and touching

La Tour's shoulder. 'Do not torment yourself.'

But La Tour was not looking at O'Brien, but at the reef again, and he kept his gaze there all the time he told his story.

'It started at Le Havre. You know Le Havre. He was commandant of the port at Le Havre. It was an appointment of honour, nothing to do, everything done by a pensioned-off captain, but he was commandant there when I returned from my last commission, that had taken me to the Antilles. Guadaloupe. There was the formality of giving the king's ship back into the commandant's care, and a ball. Great ceremony. One delivers up one's ship. The captain and all his officers deliver up the ship, and one receives one's prize money, but we had taken no prizes. That was unusual, but that voyage we had been nine months out and taken no prizes. The only ships we took, Spaniards, fought till they were hulks, and then burned, so we had no prizes. And so, one hands over one's ship, and then there is a great ball, and trumpets and the firing of cannons, and then one is on half pay until the next commission. That was no hardship for me. I could go back to my father's house. It was no hardship for any of the officers. All the rest were noble, of a small sort, younger sons, but all nobility, and I the only commoner among them. That was when he was commandant, you see.'

O'Brien asked, 'Who is *he*?'

'*He* was André Barthélème d'Aubusson-Ferney, duc de Gisors. The duke of Gisors. No less. With all his powers, honours, authorities, prerogatives, franchises, rights, fruits, profits, revenues, and lands, and his wife. Whom I should never have met, had he not been commandant of the port. But at the ball, we met.'

O'Brien waited.

'Amadée Yvette Clotilde d'Aubusson-Ferney, duchesse de Gisors.'

'Amadée?' said O'Brien.

'Amadée. When I saw her, she went straight to my heart, you know. She was older than her husband, the duke. She was slight. She was beautiful. And that would have been all

– I mean I should have seen her, and no more. We should never have met again. But because the duke was commandant, we were thrown together. And when we were thrown together, at the dance, I did one of those strange, blurting things one does, I asked her, because I was tongue-tied, what her first name meant, that I had heard when she and her father were announced when they first entered the ballroom at the castle. And she laughed, and said Amadée was an old family name, and meant 'Beloved of God.' The first thing I asked her was the first thing you have asked me. I never called her Amadée. When I came to know her, she was always Yvette.'

'You came to know her?'

'The duke needed an aide for his week's ceremonial duty at Le Havre. I was the junior lieutenant, but none of the others wanted it. They wanted to be off. I was his aide for a week, two weeks it stretched out to, but I suppose in those two weeks I attended him two or three times, no more. He really did have nothing to do. But I was kept hanging around in anterooms at the castle, and so was his duchess. The duke was hardly ever there. I do not think he ever saw her. She was always with her women, and I gathered that the duke was always with his. So we would wait together all day in those antechambers, the duchess and her women, and me. After a few days she no longer brought her women, only a maid. I am not sure that in those two weeks the duke ever saw her except on the two or three occasions when there was some ceremony that required them to be together. They were never together, except ceremonially, except formally. He did not give a hang for her, and she was lonely.'

'But it was only for two weeks that you knew her?'

'At the end of the two weeks, when we had done with Le Havre, it was he who told me to escort her to Gisors. I don't think he noticed me any more than he noticed her. He called me in one day and just said, "Take her to Gisors. I shall be a month in Caen. Take the duchess to Gisors. Keep her amused." He told me to keep her occupied. "See she's amused," he said.'

'So you took her to Gisors, and that is why you remember Gisors, and the countryside around?'

'I shall never forget it. Oh, we were possessed with each other. And it was impossible.'

'Oh, it would be difficult, even in Ireland. Gentleman and duchess is a cruel division. Footman and duchess is more possible.'

La Tour put his head in his hands. 'But it *was* possible, you see.'

'Then, had I been there, I should have rejoiced for you, and been sorry for you. Rejoiced because you had her, and been sorry because you must lose her, and no help for it.'

'All things were possible,' said La Tour, 'and because of it she died.'

'How did she die?'

La Tour said to the reef. 'How do women die?'

'As men do.'

'No. The duke did not stay a month in Caen. He was two months. Near the end of the second month, she knew she was with child.'

Wild Harry O'Brien, taken back to the faith of his Catholic youth, put down his glass and his lips moved in prayer.

'She was with child, and it could not have been the duke's. He had not so much as seen her for two months. I was afraid. There were wild schemes to escape, but we should have been hunted across France.'

'Or out of France,' said O'Brien.

'You are saying I should then be no worse off than I am now?'

O'Brien shook his head. 'I do not know.'

'Some things are impossible. To see a duchess is possible, and to love her, and to be her lover, and to be the father of a child that she is carrying. All those things were brought about, you might say, or helped, by the duke himself. "Take her to Gisors. See she's occupied." But escape with her? That is another thing. But we had our schemes, wild schemes. We were in the middle of making our wild schemes when the duke returned. And then, the wildest of our wild schemes would have been less wild than what we did. With nothing planned, nothing foreseen, we escaped, flying across France, three days of coaches, and post horses, and fear of pursuit. On the second night we stopped, and were looked at very curiously. Shabby hired carriage, dead-beat horses, no more baggage than would have done for a poor sailor making his way to the coast and his ship, but her in a brocaded gown that had cost more than the inn we stayed in that night would have fetched at auction. A gown fit for a duchess is fit for nothing else. It will not do for travelling. And a gown fit for a duchess, with mud on it, is a great betrayer. People say, 'The dress is not hers. She has stolen it.' And they are suspicious. Or they say, 'The dress is hers and she is a duchess, and so that man must have stolen her.' Well, we were up early the next morning, and got on. We did not mean to stop that night, but had to. Yvette was exhausted. Then everything was quick, so deadly quick. She could not eat. She could hardly drink. The girl who showed us to our miserable room at Honfleur looked at us as if she would never forget us, and she has not, I suppose. It was summer, but we ordered a fire lit. Yvette shivered, and did not sleep, and in the small hours she miscarried. The last hand she held was not even mine, but the chambermaid's, who stayed with her while I raised the house and scoured the town for a doctor, but there was no doctor at Honfleur. When I came back she had died. That is how women die. And the girl told me that the child would have been a boy.'

By the beach on Martinique it was now quite dark, except for the flickering light of a torch that the half-caste had brought out to them, with more wine. But neither O'Brien nor La Tour touched the wine any more.

La Tour continued his story. 'The duke's men came only four hours after she died. They saw her body, and then left her for the day while they got a coach – I don't know where from – grand enough for the body of a duchess, and then they took her back to Gisors. They did not seize me. They did not speak to me. The duke only wanted his escaping duchess. I was known. It was all known. It was all plain. But for the honour of his family, it was necessary that the escape should not have taken place. For the sake of his honour, it must appear that she had not run away, had not been with child, and had not miscarried. Her death must appear a natural death, as of course in a way it was. For the sake of her honour, I must not exist. So I was left alone and not seized. She was buried a week later, in the great family vault of the d'Aubusson-Ferneys, at Gisors. It was all done with as much pomp as if she had been his beloved wife. I shall never forget the day. I told you it rained. It was the last day I saw it rain. The duke was there. The plumes of his hat dripped with rain. His brother, the marquis, was there, and all the gentry of the duke's estates, fifty grandees, and their tenants besides. Seven prelates, and two bishops to say the words over her coffin. I stood aside, on a slope, under a plane tree. I remember the smooth bark of that plane tree. Everyone knew I was there. I still did not know whether they would seize me. Everyone knew I was there, and why, and some turned and looked, but most did not. The duke never once stirred, and never once looked in my direction. They swung incense over the bier and you could smell its scent even in the rain, incense and wet earth. Then, as they were finished, and as the men were about to lay the coffin in the vault and seal it up, the duke lifted his hand in thanks to the bishops – it was as casual as that – and then turned and walked towards me. I was twenty yards away. Everyone was waiting to go, to move off after the duke, but now all their eyes were on him, and to a man they believed it was magnanimous of him as he walked up to me, and spoke a few words to me, which they could not hear. I was told afterward that everyone thought it was magnanimous. It did *look* magnanimous.'

'What did he say?' asked O'Brien.

'He said, "La Tour, is it proper for you to grieve more than I do? After all, I shall marry again, a younger wife this time, and let us hope stronger. And perhaps you will console yourself with her?"'

*

The two men sat saying nothing in the dusky warm dark. Then the night breeze rose, and they sat on, cooling themselves from the day's humid heat. Towards the end of La Tour's story they had grown more sober, though both had been drinking for hours. By the time the tale was finished, both men lay back, almost spent. La Tour slept for a while. He did not know whether it was five minutes or an hour. He woke to find O'Brien shaking him, and offering him a cup of spring water, which he drank dry, and then another.

La Tour said, 'I am sorry to impose like that on a new friend. I have told you what I never told anyone.'

'I've been fortunate, d'you see,' replied O'Brien, 'never having had such a tale to tell. It is not much to ask of a man, to listen. You have my word it shall go no further.'

'That's more than I could ask.'

'No. Granted, a man cannot be held to account if his companion chooses to *begin* such a story. The beginning is thrust on his ears. But if he lets the other continue, and continues to listen, he makes a tacit bargain that he will keep the other man's confidences. Or that is the way I see it.'

La Tour inclined his head.

'But one thing. I'll ask you this. How did you get from there to here? What brought you from that funeral at Gisors to this beach?'

'Luck. Chance. Goodwill. What had happened was known all over the region. And there I was, grieving; and on half-pay, which I had forgotten. It was the business of that old pensioned-off captain at Le Havre to see that I got my half-pay. Well, it was really my business to collect it, but he made it his business to see that I knew it was there for the collecting, and to remind me. We had hardly met before. It is strange how, in great distress, it is sometimes men you hardly know who do the greatest things for you. He wrote to tell me the pay was mine, and asked me to do him the honour of taking a glass of wine with him, and to collect the pay, as it were, with the wine. He said, when I went, that my old ship was paid off, and there was no other king's ship looking for officers, but that he knew Mazarin was looking for a man, a competent navigator to go to New France, Québec. He knew so from a cousin of a cousin, who knew Mazarin.'

'Mazarin? The Regent of France?'

'I said so. I said, "Mazarin himself? Mazarin is Regent of France, and I am a half-pay lieutenant." But the captain said, "Go to St Germain." So I did. At St Germain the Regent saw me. "You know New France?" he said. I could only say I knew Guadaloupe, but he cut me short, as if the two were the same, or Guadaloupe, no further from Montréal than St Germain from Le Havre. After that I did not interrupt him. He gave me a commission, if you please, to make the savages of New France live in Christian accord with each other, which I undertook, and to descend the rivers from the great lakes, which I also undertook, and to find the great Vermilion Sea and the western route to China, to which I did not reply at all. But he still gave me a parchment, to present to the governor at Québec, and another piece of parchment to get me a passage to Montréal from Le Havre. I bowed my way out. Back at Le Havre, I found my old benefactor, the pensioned-off captain, who got me a passage to Québec, though by way of Martinique, because that was the next ship. I took it and thanked that kind man. I hope someone does as much for him.'

'But that wreck,' said O'Brien, gesturing out into the darkness, 'that poor ship that brought you here, will take months to refit for Montréal.'

'And so I shall spend months gazing at that reef.'

'Or you should come with me. I am bound for Manhattan first, but then Québec. I shall be gone from here in two days. And so, as your old captain at Le Havre said, if you would do me the honour to take a last drink with me, and to accept my offer of a passage to Manhattan, and then Québec, I should be pleased.'

At which they both laughed, and were suddenly rather drunk again, and merry, and La Tour's eyes were amused again, and his spirits in part restored.

20

THE DISCOVERY

Peter Stuyvesant rather enjoyed the occasions on which he took tea with Wolsey in O'Brien's walled garden. He liked the wild Irishman. He liked the wild Irishman's wife. He got on altogether better with the foreign residents of New Amsterdam than with the Dutch, who constantly grumbled that they were overtaxed. The English, or French, or even the Irish who lived on Manhattan stayed because they prospered, and prosperous people tended not to complain.

So one afternoon, when Stuyvesant had been governor for rather more than a year, and when O'Brien was adding to his prosperity by the voyage to Martinique on which he met La Tour, Stuyvesant sat with Wolsey in the sunny garden, irascibly waving a printed broadsheet.

'Yes,' she said, 'I have seen it. The expression on the face is caught rather well.'

One of the reasons Stuyvesant felt at ease with Wolsey was that she treated him with no airs, as an equal. This was something he could allow to a handsome woman. He felt they were much of an age in their tastes. Stuyvesant was thirty-eight, in fact a bit younger, but much more beaten about and worn by the world than she was.

'Catches my expression?' said Stuyvesant. The broadsheet was decorated with a crude woodcut showing the governor holding back penniless New Amsterdam farmers while his soldiers ruthlessly sheared the farmers' sheep of all their wool and stuffed it into a bag marked 'Peacock's Loot.'

He waved the pamphlet. 'It says, "You cannot shear a lamb until the wool is grown." It says I'm taking the food out of the farmers' mouths, and out of their children's mouths, and out of their sheep's mouths, and unless the sheep eat they will grow no wool, and so on.'

'I have read it,' said Wolsey.

'Ah. Well then, *mevrouw*, do you think me a tyrant? It calls me a tyrant.'

'You can sound mighty imperious.'

'I hope so. The city battlements, at the fort, are so neglected that cows graze on the grass that sprouts out of them. I chased a cow from off the battlements only last week.'

Wolsey smiled. She had heard of this. Everyone in Manhattan had heard the story of the irate governor driving the cow before him, kicking the beast with his wooden leg.

'Am I a peacock? It says I am a peacock.'

'You are mostly black,' she said. 'Black coat, black hat. There *are* silver buttons, though.'

'And my silver leg, I suppose,' he said, raising it. Stuyvesant's right leg, having been shot off some years before in a Caribbean skirmish by a Spanish cannonball, had been replaced by one made of wood, not silver, but it was encircled by a silver band where it met the stump of his own leg. 'They mean the leg. Listen. It says here, "Peacocking around with the arms of his family inscribed on his leg." Droll. Very droll. It is not my family arms, though, only the motto.' Stuyvesant indicated the words engraved round the silver band.

Then, since Wolsey did not ask him what they were, he told her. '"Trust in God, not in Man," it says. Which is good advice for a governor of this place. Just look at the men. But does that make me a peacock?'

Wolsey said, 'There *is* the rosette on your shoe.'

'From my old days,' said Stuyvesant. 'From my university days. I have worn it ever since. I have not told you, I think, but I was not meant for the university. I was meant for better things. After a year I departed. Was asked to depart. To my eternal credit, Wolsey. There can be no greater compliment to a man's wits than being asked to leave a seat of learning. It means he already has wit enough for himself. Well, when I left, the professor, who was a fool –

spoke Greek because fewer people would know him a fool in Greek – drew a gallows by my name in the university register. Whenever I've wanted to hang a man, I've thought, "Better not," because of that recollection. Unless the man was an absolute rogue, of course.'

Stuyvesant rose. 'Well. How is your husband?'

'Back in a few days, I hope. I am coming to miss him more, when he is away.'

'Yes,' said Stuyvesant. 'But you have not told him so?'

'No. And did not mean to tell you. It was just said. It came out.'

'Ah. And the girls?'

'Nearly women.'

As Wolsey saw Stuyvesant out through the hall, they caught sight of Rebekah and Ruth sitting together reading. The girls saw Stuyvesant, and rose and curtsied to the governor.

Stuyvesant nodded to them, and said to Wolsey, 'More alike every time I see them. Two of them, where you might think there was only one, they're so alike. And as for me,' glancing down at his one good leg. 'only one, where you might expect there to be two. What?'

He had made this joke before. Wolsey stood with her hands on her hips, and said good-bye to him with a half-smile. Stuyvesant raised his hat, and stamped away to resume his government of the colony.

While Wolsey and the governor were talking in the garden, O'Brien and La Tour were making an easy passage north from Martinique leaving behind the tropical heat of the Caribbean.

Since the afternoon and evening of their conversation on the beach, neither man had said another word on the matter. But it had created an intimacy which had made them old friends in the space of a week. O'Brien shared his large cabin with La Tour, they took their meals together, and talked a great deal – travellers' tales, or just chat.

When they were two days out of Martinique, La Tour

said, 'Those islands have a heat and a languor about them which soon teaches a man to walk slowly.'

'And to think slowly, and do anything slowly,' said O'Brien. 'And to do nothing he does not *have* to do. I've spent much of my life in and out of those islands. Sailing towards them out of Manhattan, sailing in warmer waters and warmer winds each day, I always look forward to the islands – but only for a few days, and then only if there's a breeze. When the breeze drops, there's a torpor, a sort of heat-torpor, that overcomes the mind. After a week or so I'm always happy to get away. Always.'

'We are northerners,' said La Tour.

'Well, and are we now? Are we northerners – an Irishman and a Frenchman? My wife is a northerner, from the northern parts of England. Even she says that when she first came out she could scarcely credit the cold, but she bears it better than I do. The climate of the French ports I knew was always like that of the Irish ports I knew. Never too hot, never too cold, the skies grey often enough, but the grass greener. In Manhattan now the grass will be brown, in September. It has not the mildness of an Irish summer. But the winters are hard. Winter in Manhattan is a climate that teaches a man to walk quickly, to stop from freezing. But it's more than that. It's an exhilaration in the air. There's energy. At times there's too much energy, for an Irishman, who has an instinct to do things in God's good time.'

In the next few days, O'Brien watched La Tour and knew, from the way the man walked the decks, from the way he glanced at a coiled rope, from the way he sniffed at the wind, and glanced at the sky and saw a squall coming before the mate did, that he was a natural sailor. O'Brien took out what charts he had of New France, but they scarcely went upriver from Montréal. The interior of the continent was empty.

'Along with your commission, were you given charts?' asked O'Brien.

La Tour smiled. 'I was given some Bibles, in French, for the improvement of the savages, who I suppose are neither Christian nor able to read French. These Bibles crossed the

Atlantic with me to Martinique. I'm ashamed to say I left them there in the hold of the ship. The Jesuits will be disappointed, and I'm sorry for that. I was told the Jesuits at Montréal would be grateful if I were able to spare some of the Bibles for them, for their savages I suppose. As for charts, we are back to Jesuits again. I was told they would have charts, because they have been indefatigable explorers of the lakes, in search of beaver and profits, to the greater glory of the church. But beyond the lakes, then, as for charts, I am there to make them.'

When the *Vliegende Hert* came within three hours' sailing of New Netherlands, on so clear a day and in so light and steady a wind that a dozen of the common sailors could safely have brought her in with no order spoken, O'Brien gave her over to his mate, with instructions to call him only when they were within a mile of the Narrows. Then he retired to his cabin with La Tour, where they cracked a bottle of the good burgundy to celebrate their arrival.

La Tour sat back and sipped his wine, while the Irishman told him how he first met Wolsey and brought her to Manhattan. It was convivial, cheerful talk. O'Brien said nothing about Wolsey's dead son, not wishing to remind La Tour of the son that had nearly been his. He talked about Wolsey with such animation that La Tour congratulated him.

'Congratulate me?' said O'Brien.

'On your wife. You talk about her with such admiration.'

'I do admire and love the woman,' said Wild O'Brien. 'A man should have a wife.'

'Not every man,' said La Tour.

'Even an explorer should have a wife.'

When they were into a second bottle, O'Brien turned to Rebekah and Ruth. He told the tale of their Breuckelen escapade, and of their return with the white deer.

'And they still say it came up to them of its own accord?'

'They have never said any differently. They were children then. Children believe their own fantasies. Or, for all I know, it was true. They are fine daughters, as fine as any I ever saw outside Ireland. I say they are my daughters. I am their stepfather. But I call them mine, and think of them as my own, and everyone thinks of them as mine. Fine girls, seventeen years old, splendid girls who will make splendid wives. You must see them.'

'I should like to see them.'

'You will. You will.'

They passed through the Narrows at dusk. In the harbour the wind fell and the *Vliegende Hert* was eventually towed to her North River anchorage by her own long boats. By then it was dark. The sweating sailors, climbing aboard after the long row of a mile to their berth, were rewarded with grog, in which they toasted O'Brien and O'Brien toasted them.

'Now,' said O'Brien, 'home.' La Tour must of course come to stay, and of course meet his wife and daughters. As they left the ship together both men were amiably drunk.

They crossed the town and entered O'Brien's house, where Wolsey and the servants were already asleep, and so were Rebekah and Ruth.

'Must see them,' said O'Brien. 'Fine daughters.'

He took a taper, and led the way up the stairs and then down the passage to his daughters' room.

He fumbled for the latch, and threw open the door.

'There,' he said, 'over there. Show you, I'll take a light to show you. Your first discovery on the way to China.'

O'Brien took three paces towards the great bed, which emerged from the darkness as his taper advanced. He stopped. On the feather bed Rebekah and Ruth were lying uncovered in the warm night. They were sleeping on their backs, with their long black hair covering their shoulders. Each had her right arm thrown across the eyes. In the moment that the taper revealed the bed and the girls, La Tour saw their smooth waists, and their legs slightly parted with the maidenhair between. His senses were invaded by their musky-scentedness, by their warmth, and by the apprehension of olive limbs on white sheets illuminated by the flickering taper.

Then La Tour was suddenly very sober, and drew back, and at that moment the girls awoke. They stirred, a splen-

THE DISCOVERY

did slow stretching, and then, seeing the light and perceiving the figures behind it, lay still, for one infinitely still second, and then instinctively turned over for modesty's sake on to their fronts. Each, as if to protect the other, put out a slim arm across the other's back. Their hair lay disarrayed across their faces and across the white down pillows.

'Well now,' said O'Brien, 'now you've seen them both, both ways.'

Then O'Brien himself became sober, too, because another light was approaching behind them. He turned with La Tour, to see Wolsey standing in her nightdress in the doorway. Her eyes went to the men, then to her daughters, and then back to the men again.

La Tour met her eyes while O'Brien was still trying to find words. The Frenchman held out his arms wide in apology, and bowed his head. At that moment one of the girls on the bed slowly raised her head, took in the scene at a glance, and let her eyes rest on La Tour who, sensing it, lifted his eyes to meet hers.

Wolsey hardly slept that night. O'Brien who loved and honoured her, said what he could to redeem himself and comfort her.

'Wolsey, simply I was drunk, and proud of the girls, and wanted to see them and show them.' She did not reply.

'I thought of them as children, and did not know.'

She still did not reply.

'I did not know what I was doing. I have never thought of them as I saw them then.'

She turned to look at him.

He could not bear her reproach, and only said again, 'I did not know.'

At last O'Brien went to sleep. But all night Wolsey lay with two images in her mind and eyes. She saw her two daughters entwined on the white featherbed, as she had seen them once entwined in the forest snow. And she saw Rebekah as the girl raised her eyes from the bed to seek, and then hold, the gaze of La Tour.

21

THE CARESS

La Tour was woken the next morning from a deep sleep by the touch of a woman's hand on his hair, and sat bolt upright. The woman was a servant. La Tour stared at her, and then round the dingy room.

'You don't rightly know where you are, sir, do you?'

'I remember now,' he said.

'You were all of a sweat, sir. You didn't wake when I knocked, nor even when I came in. And I saw you were all of a sweat, and when I felt your hair it was damp through. And the pillows. You were dreaming deep. A troubled dream, was it?'

He did not answer, so she said, 'Well, there's water and towels that I've brought you. And there's a bell, sir, to ring when you're finished, and I'll bring your breakfast.'

When she left, La Tour looked round the room again and the events of the previous night came back to him. After Wolsey had appeared and he had made his unspoken apology to her, he had rapidly said to O'Brien, 'I must go,' and, giving him no time to reply, had left the room and run down the stairs into the street, where he had seen the sign of the Swan.

Now La Tour got stiffly out of bed, and washed and dressed. When the chambermaid came back, she said, 'That's better, then. And here's some ale and bread and beef.'

He began to eat. She did not go, but stood watching him.

'You're the gentleman that came in very late last night? Knocked up the house, they say.'

'It was late.'

She regarded him again and then said, 'I'm called Anne, sir. If you want anything, you ask for me.'

Still she did not go.

'Did you come in with Captain O'Brien's ship, sir? She anchored late, I heard.'

La Tour nodded and continued eating.

'I came here in his ship, too, sir. Not his ship that he has now, but when it was a smaller one he had.'

La Tour glanced at her. This was dark, thin Anne – still thin but with hair no longer dark but streaked with grey.

'I've known Captain O'Brien these twenty years, sir. A fine man, good to me.'

The Frenchman set about eating the last of the meat.

'And a fine wife he has, and beautiful daughters, sir. But you won't have seen them yet?'

'No.'

'When I first came here, sir, I used to sing in the evenings. They gave me my keep to sing for the sailors. But now I don't sing, not to be paid for it anyway. I'm a chambermaid, as you see me.'

La Tour took a small coin from his pocket and gave it to her.

'Thank you, sir. Though I wasn't meaning to ask, sir, by staying.'

La Tour, who had however meant to get rid of her with the coin, crossed to the street window and opened it.

'The song I used to sing best, sir, I remember it because it was what I wanted, you could say. I used to sing I wanted two dozen pairs of sheets, and a bedstead and a bed, and Yorkshire blankets, and a husband. I used to sing how when I got a man, with pleasure I'd bewilder him. Those were the words. "With pleasure I'll bewilder him." I never did find a husband though, did I, sir? Now, I can see you're looking at Captain O'Brien's house. His two fine daughters, they'll get men, you see, and bewilder 'em. They're twins, sir. I've known them since they were babies, and I can't tell them one from the other. No one can. Did you ever hear that song, sir? My song?'

'No,' said La Tour, indicating that she should take the breakfast things away.

'No, you wouldn't, seeing you're not English. But you're not Dutch either, are you, sir?'

'French.'

'That's why you don't speak much, sir, then, is it? That'll be it, won't it?'

When she went at last, La Tour walked down to the wharves, towards O'Brien's anchorage. He could not call at the house, not wishing to embarrass Wolsey or her daughters more than he already had. But he had at least to find O'Brien and thank him for the passage from Martinique. And though he had no idea what he could say, he knew that a few words had to be spoken to put things right after the disaster of the night before.

O'Brien was not on the wharf, and not aboard the ship. A man suggested La Tour should try the rum store, where the kegs had been taken from the ship. He went there, and as soon as he entered saw the girl. She was standing by the counter with her back to him. He saw the shining dark hair. He saw how the grey silk dress revealed the line of her back and waist, and fell in folds from her hips. He saw one hand, which she raised to push back her hair from her eyes. She was leaning forward, reading something which lay on the counter. He knew instantly who she was. She was one of O'Brien's daughters. He could only see her back, but he knew who she was. They were twins who could not be told apart by people who had known them all their lives, but La Tour knew at once that she was *not* the girl who had turned from the pillow and caught and held his eye the night before.

He was right. When the girl turned, it was Ruth. She recognized him. He bowed. She lost her composure for the most fleeting moment, but then acknowledged him with a nod, and slipped out past him.

The moment La Tour knew for certain that this was *not* the girl, he realized clearly that the power of her sister over him would be very great. Hers was a power that drew him even in her absence.

He was standing with this realization and conviction in his mind when O'Brien clapped him on the shoulder.

'La Tour,' he cried, 'your mind's a thousand miles away.'

'No,' said La Tour; and this was true. It was not. 'But I was looking for you.'

'And I for you.' He grinned widely. 'What a fine quandary that was I got us into. I wish you hadn't gone, but I can see you were driven out. What a quandary I landed you in.'

'I'm sorry for my part in it,' said La Tour.

'*Your* part? It was all my doing. Wolsey has very well convinced me of that. And she asks you to come and stay with us, as was intended. You can't stay at the Swan, where I gather you slept last night.'

'It is generous of your wife. But your daughters?'

'None the worse for it. And overheard laughing between themselves early this morning, and since.'

So La Tour went to O'Brien's house, where Wolsey received him as if nothing out of the ordinary had happened. Then the twins were found in the garden, and La Tour presented to them.

'Now,' said O'Brien to his new friend, 'other things notwithstanding,' at which Wolsey threw her husband a sharp glance, 'you will not know their names. You will not know which is which. This is Ruth.'

The girl he had seen in the store that morning smiled at La Tour.

'And this is Rebekah.'

La Tour looked into Rebekah's eyes for the second time, and was already as good as hers.

In the ensuing days, La Tour turned the moment of this second meeting over and over in his mind. He was not surprised. He had known it would be so. It was only a confirmation of what he had already felt the night before. And in his dreams afterward, he had slept all night with great waters in his mind – broad lakes, wide rivers, endless seas, and roaring cataracts between lakes and rivers and between the last river and the ultimate sea. They were dreams of discovery. Rebekah did not appear in them, but over the roaring of the waters he heard the voice of O'Brien saying, 'There. I'll take a light to show you your first discovery on the way to China.'

In those days Yvette also came into his mind, and he realized for the first time that she had all along been helpless. Amadée Yvette Clotilde, duchesse de Gisors, had been helpless even when he first met her at the ball at Le Havre – helpless in all her rank and splendour. She had gone nowhere of her own will. She was sent. The duke brought her to Le Havre. The duke sent her back to Gisors with La Tour. Her loneliness let her slide into La Tour's fragile protection. Her grateful love for him made her his mistress and conceived the child. By then of course she was already lost, but it was another chance, the early return of her husband, which sent her hopelessly flying to her helpless death. La Tour had never seen these events in this light before. He had always thought of her as powerful. But the real power had been the duke's, and his, and chance. Yvette had been helpless. He saw this now because it was made dazzlingly clear to him by the real power and will of Rebekah, a girl he had seen only twice.

It is all very well to cry out against chance and the pain of the world. La Tour had railed against the world that took Yvette from him, but, after all, he had been grieving not so much for her as for his own pain and loss. But it was Yvette who had died. He felt this acutely now that he saw it clearly. It would be unjust to say he did not. But if the power of Rebekah showed him the helplessness of Yvette, the same power now revived him.

Rebekah did not say to herself, 'I shall have him,' but her instinct made her want him and take him for hers. Which she did. He did not exactly know what was happening. He knew she could do what she liked with him. But he did not see that it was her settled, instinctive, persistent course to pursue him. He even thought that he was the pursuer. If she was sitting in the garden, he would follow her there, but she had gone there in order to be followed. If she walked by the North River, near the moorings of the *Vliegende Hert,* she did so to be found there. In short, she led him. Only Wolsey saw it, but what could she, or should she, do about it? Or did Ruth see it too? Wolsey was not sure of that.

Rebekah would not have needed chance to assist her, but it did. O'Brien's cargo for Québec was delayed two weeks. Cargoes had been delayed often enough before. But then the season closed in that year very rapidly. It had been late September by the time O'Brien returned to New Amsterdam with La Tour. A passage north early in October, as he intended, would have been easy. But the delay made this mid-October, and by then it was unusually cold. That was the year the leaves only *began* to turn red in New Amsterdam. There was never time for the full show of russets and reds because a storm of two days stripped the trees not only of their leaves but of some of their weaker branches. The captains of fishing vessels who struggled into port after the storm reported early snow in Maine. Harry O'Brien watched all this, and listened. Then for the first time in their married life Wolsey said to him, 'Harry, I do not want you to make this voyage. It will be too late for the St Lawrence.'

This was not likely. Harry O'Brien knew it was unlikely. He knew he could make the passage, though it might be a hard one. He knew the chances of his being caught by the winter at Québec, and frozen in, were small. Given all the bad luck in the world, the chances were small. But he too was beginning to be tired of constant voyaging and constant separation. He wanted the peace of Wolsey's company and of his house. But he told her he had promised to take La Tour. She liked La Tour, but said, reasonably, that the French ship was still reported to be stranded at Martinique, would certainly not make the passage north that Fall, and would have to wait until spring, so that La Tour would have lost no time by coming ahead with O'Brien as far as Manhattan.

O'Brien put this openly to La Tour, who said he would take his chance. If another vessel sailed for Québec, he would go with it. If not, he would winter in Manhattan.

It did not need the winter. That very Sunday, Rebekah claimed La Tour in the church. The O'Briens did not go to the Dutch church, and only went that day because the governor asked them. More pamphlets had appeared, describing Stuyvesant this time as 'grand duke of Muscovy.' This decided him that the time had come for a resounding sermon on the loyalty owed to a ruler by his subjects, and he had suborned the minister into preaching it. Caricatures of Stuyvesant as a monster devouring children, said Stuyvesant, were too much, and the minister, who relied on the governor for the certainty of his tenure, promised the necessary sermon. Stuyvesant then called upon the greatest merchants and sea captains in New Netherlands to give authority to the occasion by their attendance at the Dutch church. Few ever went. They were surprised by the request, but happy to please the governor.

Harry O'Brien said, 'But I am a Catholic, and so is La Tour here.'

'You will not be excluded for that,' said Stuyvesant. 'No one shall bar the door to you for that.'

The Dutch church was Calvinist, but without all of its rigour and most of its force. So the whole O'Brien household went to the Dutch church, and, together with other merchant families, mightily impressed the hoi polloi who stood crowded together at the back. All endured an admonitory sermon in Dutch.

La Tour sat next to Rebekah. She had seen to that. It was a sermon that lasted an hour, of which he could not understand ten words. The presence of the girl next to him, the rustling of her silk dress, the substance of the girl as she arranged and shifted herself, the touch of her silk skirts on his boots, the rise and fall of her breasts as she breathed, the contiguity of the woman, the brush of her shoulders, seduced a man who needed no seducing. As nearly as a man and a woman can be, who are dutifully sitting through a cold sermon in a cold church, they abandoned themselves to each other, she as much as him, and without betraying any sign of their abandonment in a glance or a movement or a flicker of the eyes.

When the service was over, and the great ones left the church first, she took his arm as they walked to the door. When they stood outside in the daylight, all the grand and prosperous standing round the governor as an exhibition to the people, as they were meant to be, she took her hand from his arm, so that he looked at her questioningly, and then, in the sight of all New Amsterdam, Rebekah passed the light fingers of her gloved hand across La Tour's cheek. The caress was as overt a claim as could have been made.

Three weeks afterwards, La Tour came to ask O'Brien for Rebekah. O'Brien paced back and forth in his land cabin, nodded and nodded, and then placed one hand on the terrestrial globe and spun it, almost absently, until his index finger rested on the eastern coastline of New France.

Still looking intently at the globe as if consulting it, he covered a whole section of the world with the palm of his hand, and then raised his hand, and looked down again at the globe. La Tour saw that the territory O'Brien's great hand had covered was the unknown expanse west and southwest of Québec, an expanse where any marks on the globe – rivers, mountains, distant coasts – were conjectural. It was the expanse La Tour would have to chart.

O'Brien said, 'Rebekah is Wolsey's daughter, you see. I'm a father to her, I think she can remember no one else as father, but she is not mine. She is Wolsey's daughter. We must ask her.'

So Wolsey came in, and listened as La Tour put his request again.

'If you were to marry,' she asked, 'you would still go on?'

La Tour said he would. It was his duty to carry out his commission. It was now clear that no ship would be sailing from Manhattan for Québec that fall, but he would have to continue in the spring.

'So you would go on – bound for Québec, and then exploration?' said Wolsey.

La Tour assented.

'But what would you do with a wife in the wilderness?'

'She could stay at Québec while I was away,' said La Tour, 'but I do not think she would.'

'I *know* she would not,' said Wolsey.

'Ma'am,' said La Tour, 'I believe you first came to a wilderness yourself.'

'That,' she said, 'is why I ask. I remember that wilderness.'

La Tour had no reply.

Wolsey said, 'You have known her what, five weeks?'

'But those five weeks have been very full,' said the Frenchman.

'I have seen that.'

O'Brien went to his wife where she was sitting, and put a hand on her shoulder. 'I did say to La Tour, very early on, when we were aboard the ship, before we arrived here, that even an explorer should take a wife.'

'But five weeks, even very full weeks?' said Wolsey. 'And then, in the spring, a wilderness, and a worse wilderness, I think, than the one I came to.'

'I do not know that,' said La Tour, 'but it is very possible. A wilderness is a wilderness. I cannot deny it is a wilderness. As to its being only five weeks that we have known each other, that is so, but we should not marry until March. That would be almost six months.'

'Six months,' said Wolsey. 'Six months.'

'Yes,' said O'Brien. He too had been recalling his own six-month courtship of Wolsey, mostly in his absence, a courtship which until its last evening had been entirely oblique. But he had not been proposing to take her to a wilderness.

Wolsey sat in an agony of mind. O'Brien was slowly turning the globe.

'Then, Harry,' she said at last, 'will you ask Rebekah what she wishes?'

'I will ask her.'

'Not,' said Wolsey, rising, 'that you need to ask, because we know what she will say.'

Rebekah and La Tour married in February. Rebekah was glorious, her wedding gown splendid with gold thread, the wedding feast magnificent. Stuyvesant himself, as chief magistrate, conducted the ceremony. All the vessels in the river saluted with cannonshot. When the last cannon was fired, and the last toast drunk, and the last guest gone, La Tour came to Wolsey before he went to his bride.

'We shall return,' he said. 'It is not forever that I am taking your daughter away.'

To lose a daughter cut Wolsey to the heart. She wished the feast could have seemed more of a thanksgiving to her. But La Tour was a good man for a son, and she was moved that he had come and said what he had. She embraced him, and sent him off to his bride, whom Ruth, as bridesmaid, was at that moment preparing for the wedding night.

La Tour, ascending the staircase, heard their low laughter from the bedroom. They were still laughing when he entered. Ruth embraced her sister, lightly kissed La Tour, and glided off, leaving Rebekah waiting alone for her husband in the great bed where he had first seen both sisters together.

Wolsey sat on in her room downstairs. Then she went to the street door, and looked west across the North River, into the forests of the continent. Rebekah would leave her. It was not easy to bear. But there would be children, she told herself, and that would be cause for thanksgiving.

22

THE MANDARIN'S ROBE

Next spring found La Tour in Québec, and in the presence of Monsieur le comte de Villeneuve, governor of New France. The count kept La Tour standing while he read slowly through the sealed letter La Tour had received a year before at the hands of Mazarin. Then he looked up, as if surprised to find La Tour still standing there, and said, 'La Tour, the question is, what am I to be? Governor of China? Admiral of the South Seas? Or governor of this place?'

'Sir?'

'Governor of what? Admiral of where? Sit down. Or governor of this place? I said sit down. Do sit. Mazarin says in this that you are the best man he could have picked.'

La Tour thanked the governor.

'He said the same of the last two. But the question is, as I have said, of what am I to be governor?' He tossed the letter on the table before him, heavy parchment sealed with a heavy seal. 'It recites your commission, which you'll already be familiar with. It's word for word I should think. It generally is. Then it commends you, as it always does. And I am left with the same question, as I always am. Governor of what? Now, you have seen the city?'

La Tour said he had.

'I know you have. It is a city dominated by the seminary. Priests. Jesuit priests. And next in importance is the church. More priests. Then there is this poorhouse they call my palace, and a barracks for the men they call my soldiers. The garrison. But beyond the city, out in that wilderness, as

I have constantly been informed, lies a route to a great sea which leads to China or Japan. Now it may be a short route or a long route, an easy route or a hazardous route. I don't know. It is all new to me, La Tour, though I daresay not to you. I hope it is plain to you. But to me? In my early days, if you wanted to get to China, you sailed east from France. To get here, I have sailed far west. So have you. And now if we go farther west, we shall end up where we would have got by going east in the first place. I can see it on a globe, if I am to trust myself to a globe. Against all reason, though?'

La Tour demurred gently, and suggested that it was very probable that a route west did lead to China.

'Well then, suppose I make that large leap that you ask me to make, and suppose I believe, against all experience, that China's west of here, then if you go far enough west you'll find China. But the question still is, does any route from here lead west? I happen to hope it does, but then I would, wouldn't I?'

'Sir?'

'If there is a route, and it is short and easy, and you find it, and it is a route west, and it is a route to China, then I shall be governor of China, I suppose, being the nearest. Though I must admit I should be governor of China with all of two hundred troops at my command. No doubt they would then strengthen the garrison. But if you don't find China, or if the route is long and hazardous and you die on the way, as they all die on the way, then I shall remain governor of this place. Governor of a seminary and a fur market. But not, La Tour, even that really. This place is not yet so much as a royal colony. I've asked often enough for it to be made one. My predecessors asked too. What happens? The Jesuits oppose it. The traders in furs oppose it. Mazarin sends complimentary letters to me, and an explorer every now and again, also with complimentary letters, but that's all. And I remain governor with two hundred troops who are here as a last resort, and the traders do what they like, and the seminary does what it likes, only requiring my signature now and again, which I have no option but to give them. Sign, sign, sign, La Tour. That's what I do. But make me governor of China if you can. That would be better.'

'Sir, I have heard this sea to the west also called the Vermilion Sea.'

'The Winnebagos, who are a tribe of savages, call it that. The Sioux, who are a tribe of savages, call it the Messipi. The seminary, which is a tribe of priests, call it the Great Sea. And *there* lies another difficulty.'

'How, sir?'

'The savages' views are traditional, and remain constant. The views of the priests change, they being informed men whose views change with new information. They say by new information. By new rumours, I say. At the moment they are adhering to the Mexican proposition, which I don't see at all. Mexico would never do.'

'Mexico?'

'Mexico. Highly unlikely. They say, the priests now say, that the rivers and lakes may lead to a great sea, but that it will be the sea of Mexico. They don't *know*, of course. But that is the way their views are tending. Now, I put it this way. I reason this way. China is to the west, agreed. Very well. How far west this land stretches we do not know, but is it likely to be more than a thousand miles? It is not. Is this land likely to be broader than the whole country of France? It may be, but is it likely or unlikely? Unlikely, I'd say. So if we say it's as much as a thousand miles, east to west, then a great river *might* flow across it to a great sea. Do you follow me? A thousand miles is not too much for a river to flow. But if this great river is to flow to Mexico, well, man, that's south. Mexico is south. But if a river is to run south, what then? We know it is two thousand miles from here to Mexico. That we know. Is a river likely to run for two thousand miles, from the seminary gates here, to Mexico? Not reasonable. Not at all.'

'No, sir, unlikely.'

'Yes. It has the further disadvantage for me that I cannot be governor of Mexico, do you see? Mexico already has a governor, and a Spaniard at that.'

'Sir, as for supplies and men?'

'I had a priest come to me last year, talking of lions, leopards, and tigers which were the more difficult to believe in since they did him no harm. But he said he had met them. He had also seen a king – a savage this king turned out to be – who claimed descent from Montezuma. This priest had seen a savage Eldorado, where there was a statue of this great king, holding in his mouth an emerald larger than a goose's egg. The statue was of gold. This priest did remark, lest his story should sound too good to be true, that the music in this nation was bad. But that, he said, was only because the instruments were also made of gold, which is not a good metal for a trumpet.'

La Tour again ventured to remind the count about the promised supplies.

'Now we come to it,' said the count. 'Your commission mentions that I shall supply you with carpenters and timber to make a corvette?'

La Tour assented.

'And experienced men to help you navigate the rivers?'

La Tour nodded, and nodded again each time as the count went through the list of promised things – canoes, firearms, spades, axes, other iron tools, guides, food for a year, tents to make camp with, and beads to trade with the savages.

'La Tour, I can give you the beads. I can *perhaps* find you carpenters, but as to their building a corvette, none has ever made anything bigger than a cutter. You must recruit your soldiers as you can, from the garrison. Bribe them well. I can give you some food, though how any food could remain in an edible state for a year I do not know, even if I had it to give you. Which I haven't. The Jesuits eat better than I do. I can give you a few tents. I can give you one good guide, who may know where to pick up others. I will do what I can, La Tour, but that is that.'

La Tour was silent, and then he said, 'Sir, this commission,' – he picked up the parchment from the table, and set it down again – 'does say that I am to bring the light of

Christianity to the savages, and so perhaps the seminary might...?'

The count looked at La Tour. For the length of his virtual monologue he had hardly looked at the man at all. He seldom looked at explorers. Now he did look at La Tour, and saw what was very like amusement in the man's eyes, and was himself amused.

'I think,' he said, 'we may understand each other. We very well may. Savages. Light of Christianity. Fat priests. Supplies. Well, ask them. Ask the priests. I wish you well of it. A letter from me will do you no good with the Superior, except as an introduction, but I'll give you one for that purpose only. Expect nothing else of it. They do not love me. But you may have something to recommend you. Does that commission mention Bibles – for savages? Commissions generally do.'

La Tour regretfully recalled the Bibles he had left to rot in the ship's hold at Martinique, and shook his head.

'Pity. Still, I'll give you two things.'

La Tour waited while the count scribbled a note to the Jesuit Superior, and stood to take it from his hands.

'And the second thing is this,' said the count. He took from a chair beside him a blue robe of Chinese silk, decorated with a pattern of running horses.

La Tour stared at it.

'That *was* brought back by one of the few explorers who ever returned here. He said he had found men trading with the savages, men who might have been mandarins. At any rate, they had whispy beards. He said he got this information and this robe from the savages who had traded with the mandarins. For what my opinion is worth, I will tell you that I did not believe him, but he did have the robe. "Got it from Nantes and brought it over with you?" I remember asking him. But he quietly and earnestly assured me that this was not so. He was not only an explorer, but also a Jesuit. So I had to believe him, and he made me a gift of it, and I now make a gift of it to you.'

La Tour thought the count was dismissing him and

bowed.

'Not yet,' said the count. 'You're no Jesuit, are you?'

'No, I am not.'

'No, because you have two women with you.'

'One of them is my wife, sir.'

'From France?' In Montréal, French women were rare and treasured.

'From Manhattan.'

'Ah. I have told you that few men ever left here and came back, but no man yet has been mad enough to take women, let alone his wife. Think about it.'

'They may be a great comfort, sir,' replied La Tour. 'They are strong, and used to wildernesses, and have seen savages.'

'They sound like Indians. Half-castes?'

'My wife is New England by birth, and half-English, half-Irish by upbringing.'

'Irish. Well, if you left your women here they might very well be gallantly debauched by the garrison. My officers tend to be gentlemen who have failed in France, not of the first water. But consider also the dangers of taking them.'

La Tour bowed again.

'I see Mazarin gives you his written blessing. You have my blessing too. God go with you. Make me governor of China if you can.'

La Tour smiled.

'Stranger things than that are happening,' said the count. 'The king of France is a boy. The king of England is dead – ceremonially murdered on a scaffold in front of his own palace on some trumped-up charge of treason which he would not deign to answer. So, murdered.'

La Tour knew this. The news had reached Québec a few days before he had.

'So stranger things are happening than my becoming governor of China. Take the robe in case you meet mandarins. And look to your women. I see you are determined to take them. I pray they may be a comfort to you, and not fall a comfort to the savages. Good day.'

*

La Tour had not expected to have two women with him. One was Rebekah. The other was Ruth. He had opposed Ruth's coming from the beginning, but always Rebekah had insisted, and always she had her way. When it had first been proposed, by Rebekah, that Ruth should accompany herself and La Tour as far as Québec, to stay the summer there and then return, La Tour had objected, but not strongly. Not strongly enough, as it turned out. Wolsey had been distressed to lose both daughters at once, even if one was going only for a summer. But it had been argued that a summer together would ease the twins' separation. The marriage of one twin is a strange thing to the other, dividing her from a part of herself. La Tour understood this. In the end everyone had given in, and Ruth had come to Québec. There, Rebekah had suddenly demanded that Ruth should come on with them to the interior. To be separated, even for part of the day, had been a trial to the twins. To be separated for a year or two would be intolerable.

'But what of your mother?' La Tour had asked. 'What about her? What of your promise that Ruth should return this summer? What of mine that she should?'

This had swayed Ruth, who had hesitated, but Rebekah was adamant. La Tour was not certain that it had not been her intention all along to insist that Ruth should accompany them. This uncertainty was a cloud in La Tour's mind. But he had been left with no choice. He had written to O'Brien and Wolsey explaining as best he could. The twins had written too, one letter written by Rebekah and signed by both. La Tour had been gentle with Rebekah. Then he had reasoned with her. Then he had become angry. She would not be moved, she got her way, and he had two women to take into the centre of an unknown continent, and no men able to build a ship large enough to give any assurance that this unknown voyage would be safe, and no certain supply of food. The Jesuits listened, and then gave him their blessing and a barrel of salt pork. La Tour's party would have to live off the land. It would not be an easy journey.

23

STARVED ROCK

In a month they were ready. La Tour gathered round him a group of sixteen Frenchmen. Ten were soldiers of the garrison whom their officers were glad to be rid of. 'Dear fellow,' said their captain to La Tour, 'take them, if you will take them, and we shall all be delighted, I to get rid of them, they to escape me. They are insubordinate and reckless, but they are good murderers of savages, which you may need.' La Tour provided them with rough canvas suits and deerskins for the journey, but saw that their uniforms were brought with them in a chest, to be worn if a show of ceremony were necessary. He also collected six civilians, four hunters and trappers who came for double pay, and two carpenters, who came for the promise of a share in the vessel they would build. It was not an auspicious party. Its greatest strength was the guide provided by Villeneuve. La Tour was grateful for this goodhearted gift from a man who, possessing the seigneury of New France, but finding it in reality the governorship of a seminary, remained unembittered and generous. The guide was Henri, who was known only by that name. His father had been a soldier of the garrison, and his mother Indian. He was *coureur de bois*, trapper, hunter, small trader, guide, and had spent all his life in the forests, making twice yearly trading visits to Québec. He was probably about thirty, though no one knew his real age. His features were Indian, and his complexion brown, but his eyes were blue. He spoke the language of the Illinois, and the dialects of five other Algonquin tribes. He could speak the language of the Winnebago, which was in part Sioux. His French was native. He was at home with the forest Indians, and with the French at Québec. He was a pederast. This was no unusual thing among the Illinois, and his mother had been of that tribe. Two years before, a French soldier who had taunted him for his inclinations was found dead. Since the soldier was a known villain, and since Henri was an honest and useful trader, the matter had not been pursued. But the soldiers of the garrison feared him. Those who had been with him on punitive expeditions into the surrounding forest, after some outlying farmhouse was burned, knew that no man was more silent or more uncannily invisible than Henri. No man killed more infallibly. It was fortunate that, like many pederasts, he was gentle with women and considerate of them. The men feared him, but Rebekah and Ruth never did, and he became their natural guardian. La Tour saw this and was glad of it. It was another thing to the credit of the man, who already promised to be everything La Tour could have hoped. He knew the lakes and rivers beyond Montréal, and the savages who lived by the lakes and rivers. He showed a genius for bartering beads and hatchets for canoes and dried fish. He procured, at a fair price, cordage and canvas to rig their ship when they built it, after they came to the cascades which they would first have to find and traverse. With him, Henri brought an Indian boy of twelve, who rarely left his side. So they set out, a party of twenty-one in all.

For two weeks in May they paddled in three canoes across Lake Ontario, camping by night on the shores. Their fires were always seen by savages, whom Henri knew and placated with gifts. This was known territory. Many other men had been this far. On the seventh night they camped and Henri did La Tour a service of which he never spoke. At first light the most dissolute of the soldiers was missing. La Tour wanted to search for him, but the other men were reluctant and curiously sullen. La Tour turned to Henri for an explanation. Had it been Indians?

Henri assured him it had not been Indians. He could not say why he was certain, but instinct told him it had not been Indians.

Why would the others not search for him then, if there was no fear of Indians? Henri shrugged. 'It would be no use. He has slipped into the lake, and the lake is deep.'

The soldier had indeed slipped into the deep lake, after his throat was cut by Henri. In the preceding days, this man and two others had talked with a knowing, boastful lust about the two women. The others had listened, and watched the women like starved men. Henri told them that the first man to do more than look would have his throat cut. The threat deterred most of them. Henri was very well respected. But the night before, the missing man had attempted to approach Ruth. Before she saw or heard him, Henri's quiet knife slit his throat. All the men knew this. None would say. The women were thereafter safe, at least from the Frenchmen.

After two weeks, in the early afternoon, Henri motioned to the men to rest on their paddles, and all listened.

'I hear nothing,' said La Tour.

Henri did not reply. The canoes drifted on soundlessly, and then La Tour heard first a whisper, and then a murmur, and then what might have been distant breakers. But the soft sound was too continuous for breakers. Then the colour of the sky changed from deep blue to a softer colour, which to the south-east was almost turquoise, and then the sound became a roar. They paddled to the shore and carried their canoes on to dry land. Henri motioned La Tour and the two women to follow him. They climbed a steep ridge, with the sound swelling and increasing at every step, until they arrived at the summit and La Tour saw before him the cataracts of his dreams. It was Niagara, and it was beyond his imagination and beyond his dreams.

La Tour looked at Rebekah and Ruth, but they were holding hands, entranced by the twin falls and gazing at the two cataracts which crashed together at the foot of the descent, so that a mist rose twice the height of the falls. La

Tour saw not only the falls of his dreams, but the continent that was his to explore laid out before him – the vastness of a sea beyond, and the immensities of unpenetrated forest stretching into the level distance.

They carried the canoes overland to the waters of Lake Erie. 'They say,' said Henri, when they camped to rest, 'that those cataracts are fed by the waters of four oceans. The savages talk of four oceans. I have seen three. But the three oceans I have seen have been lakes, vast lakes a sea across. Ocean-wide lakes, but lakes. And beyond, there was more land.'

'And the fourth ocean?' asked La Tour.

'The fourth ocean I have never seen,' said Henri.

But the thought of a fourth sea that was a passage to China was in all their minds. There was not one of them who did not expect a fourth sea to be a route westward. For if there *were* three such immensities of water as the one that lay before them, what else could the fourth be but a sea? China was in all their minds.

And particularly, as it happened, in the minds of the carpenters. It was here, where they were to build their ship, that they chose the moment to state their full terms. If the expedition should find only wilderness, the whole ship should be theirs on their return to the spot where they built it. If they found the route to China, then a half share of the ship, and a half share in all profits and rewards should be theirs. These two carpenters had in their minds a vision of gold, spices, silks, high honours, and vast estates. La Tour listened, and after an hour's bargaining conceded them a third share, which was, as he pointed out, a third share, should they succeed, of infinite riches.

The planks were sawn, the keel laid, the ribs shaped, the skeleton erected, the sides planked, the mast erected, the canvas sewn, the sails raised by the intricate rigging of cords, and a ship of twenty feet was theirs. Rebekah and Ruth launched her together, naming her the *Flying Deer*, after O'Brien's ship. They were the first white women to see Niagara, and the first to see the inland ocean, and the *Flying*

Deer was the first rigged ship to sail on it.

They sailed on the first lake, called Erie, and then on the lake of the Hurons, and then south on a third lake, called Michigan by the Indians. The summer squalls and storms on Michigan were so severe that La Tour became imbued with the idea that it must after all be a sea they had found.

He said, 'I have made easier passages than this from Le Havre to north Africa, and we have sailed as far as that on these waters. I never sailed on a lake that got up mountainous seas like this Michigan.'

'I have never sailed on a sea at all,' said Henri. 'I was born in these forests and have never seen anything but these waters, but I know this is a lake.'

'It is easy to miss an outlet, in the dark, or in a storm. And if this is a lake, then it is a lake on which we are more often than not out of sight of land.' But then they found it had been a lake, because they came to the River Illinois, which ran not into the lake, but away from it.

Here they found the Illinois Indians, who were friendly, and made the French gifts of frogs, which were counted a delicacy by both the Illinois and the French. At other times they were given buffalo meat to eat, which they found good. Then for a week there were no Indians, and Henri became uneasy. They slept at night in the ship and then the vessel, which had first seemed so grand, appeared no more than a large ship's boat. Once, when they were running out of food and only the Jesuits's barrel of salt pork remained, a buffalo was seen stuck in a marsh by the riverside. They slaughtered it and ate well, but Henri was unhappy about the campfires over which they roasted it.

By now La Tour trusted Henri in everything. Without him, they would never have come so far. So he said, 'Henri, you don't like the fires, because you think we shall be seen. But you have previously been unhappy because there were no savages. If there are none, who will see us?'

Henri chewed slowly his mouthful of buffalo meat. The French soldiers ate ravenously, but he always ate slowly. La Tour and the women had learned to do the same. 'Because,' said Henri at last, 'this is Illinois country, and there are no Illinois. If there were Illinois, they would come to us. If there are no Illinois, why not? And if there are other tribes, I do not want them to see our fires. I would rather see them first, to know who they are.'

The next day they travelled down the wide, sluggish river through country which on their right, to the west, was flat as far as the eye could see, but to the left was heavily forested with white oak, white pine, walnut, and red cedar. Towards late afternoon, sweet meadows opened out on the right bank. Rebekah and Ruth saw marigolds, foxgloves, and harebells. It was an innocent countryside.

The wind dropped away. The Frenchmen hauled down the sail and were quietly rowing, carried by the current, when Henri, who was crouching in the bow, rose and conveyed to La Tour by signs that they should make for the right bank. He motioned to all but two of the men to ship their oars, took the rudder himself, and they glided into the bank at a spot where the vessel was hidden by overhanging willows. The men all watched him, and understood from his hands, which he held motionless with fingers widespread, that he was commanding silence.

They obeyed.

They were lying in the elbow of a bend in the river. To the right the plains rolled endlessly away. To their left, as they saw when they followed the direction of Henri's silent gaze, taller trees rose from the already high forest. Then they began to see what his sharper eyes had already shown him, that these trees appeared taller because they were growing on top of a cliff. Had they rounded the bend they would have seen a massive rock, the only high point in the landscape, and the highest point for more than fifty miles around, which rose sheer as a sandstone wall from the left bank of the Illinois. It was one hundred and forty feet high, and stood alone in a vast forest, where it had been thrown up by a primeval convulsion. There it had remained, a shapeless outcrop, until its sides were carved sheer by a glacier of the last ice age, which had created the valley of the Illinois.

One man murmured to another, but was silenced by La Tour. Henri's instincts were beginning to communicate themselves to him. He knew there would be a reason. Henri, crouching with his eyes never moving from the summit of the rock, said by his very attitude, 'If you wish to live, watch, and be still.'

But why should a rock menace them?

It was ten minutes, during which time Henri's eyes never moved, before first he saw, and then the sharper-eyed Frenchmen began to perceive, that from the summit, where it overhung the river, a rope was being let down into the water. They were watching from a distance of half a mile, and saw the rope only because at the end of it swung a denser object which stood out black against the sky as it was lowered. The object disappeared into the river, and then reappeared. They saw that it was a bucket or pail. It began to rise, but then plunged down again and splashed into the river. They all saw it fall. The sharper-eyed of the Frenchmen could see the rope still dangling from the summit. Only Henri had seen the hand that had stretched out from the bank and severed the rope with a flashing knife.

They waited for another half an hour, still silent, an eternity of waiting. La Tour caught Henri's glance and asked with his eyes, 'How long?' The reply was a shrug which said, 'As long as we must.'

An hour before sunset the silence was pierced by a single high howl, which was a signal to a thousand voices to take up the howl. This was the attack on the rock. Then there was silence. An Indian battle is not all cannon and clash of steel, but silent hatchets and silent arrows. The only cries were those of the dying. In the first minutes of the battle, many of the Indians assaulting the rock were thrown back by the defenders. But then, when the sun still had half an hour before it set, the battle was plainly over. The Frenchmen, watching from their hidden boat, saw figure after figure plunge from the overhanging summit into the river below. Some were hurled over by their enemies, already dead, and they fell sprawled, bouncing off the rock face in their descent. Then it was plain from the attitude of the falling figures, even from that distance, that they were not falling, or being hurled by their enemies, but were choosing to throw themselves to their deaths. Some ran clear over the edge and fell somersaulting. Others jumped high into the air and then fell with their legs moving, as if running to their deaths in midair, while they still brandished their weapons in their hands and shrieked out their war cries. Others dived like swimmers, stretching their arms forward, arching their backs, and piercing the water one hundred and forty feet below with extended arms, the dying sun gilding their bodies as they dived, and catching the plume of spray that each man made as he entered the water.

Then the whole summit of the rock was set ablaze, and, after it burned out to a red, distant cinder, glowing in the dusk and then in the darkness after the sun had gone, the victors streamed across the Illinois to the right bank, carrying torches. The cries of the succeeding two hours showed that they had taken a few prisoners before the wretches could choose their own deaths.

The Frenchmen did not know it until the next day, but this was the end of a long siege. No Illinois had met the French in the previous week because they had been fighting for their lives against their inveterate enemies, the Iroquois. The last of the Illinois warriors had taken refuge on the rock, which was a natural fortress, sheer on three sides and to be climbed only with difficulty on the fourth. Then the Iroquois had waited. On the summit, there was an acre of land, where a thousand warriors could find refuge from their enemies, and even shade from the sun under the many trees that grew there. But they had little food, and no water. Their food went, and then they endured a week of thirst in the heat of September. Half were already dead when the Iroquois at last attacked. The bucket they had lowered into the river, and which the French had seen cut off as it rose, was the last of many they had lost in that way. The Illinois died within sight of their richest hunting grounds – great plains teeming with buffalo farther by far than a man could see even from the summit of the cliff, and in the sight of the river whose water they were denied.

The French had a miserable night of it, huddled in the boat. They ate hard biscuit, and drank river water. At dawn, Henri went alone to reconnoitre, and returned to La Tour to say that the Iroquois had gone in the night.

'All that remains is a slaughterhouse,' he said. 'The dead were butchered as well as the living, which is the way of the Iroquois.'

La Tour left Rebekah and Ruth with six men, and took the rest forward to the battleground. Many corpses still floated in the river where the weeds had caught them. The current had carried the others far downstream. The Illinois town was on the bank of the river opposite the rock. It was a scene of exquisitely devised horror. The Illinois women had all met their death by ingenious torture. Their men, on the rock, must have heard them die. Illinois children were spitted on sticks. Three men tied to stakes had been flayed alive, and the state of their bloody flesh showed that this was the work of celebration that the Frenchmen heard the night before. The graves of the village had been opened, and the dead killed again so that their spirits should not rise to take revenge against the Iroquois. A few of the recent dead, still recognizably human, were raised on crosses, with their bodies slit from head to belly, every limb mutilated, and the skulls emptied of brains and crushed until bone met bone. The long-dead, who were skeletons, had been disinterred, dismembered, and scattered. Where the hair adhered to skeleton skulls, the dead skulls had been scalped. Wild dogs prowled round, keeping warily away from the Frenchmen, but then returning to gorge themselves.

The French were hardened soldiers to a man, but none had seen the like of this. Only Henri had expected it all. It was the way of the Iroquois. He and La Tour took a canoe which had not been stove in or stolen, crossed the river, and climbed to the summit of the rock. The dead bodies of five hundred men still lay there, grotesquely incinerated.

'Dead before they burned,' said Henri. 'As you heard, any that were taken alive were used for entertainment.'

'Five hundred dead in the brief battle we saw?'

'Five hundred mostly starved and parched,' said Henri, and told him how. That too was the way of the Iroquois, the ancient enemy. His mother had been Illinois. He was half Illinois himself. But the only emotion he showed was at the desecration of the dead. With his boy, he spent four hours reinterring their scattered bones.

At midday, La Tour and his party cast off from the bank of the Illinois, rowed out into midstream, and continued their journey south. As they passed under the lowering sandstone cliff, La Tour marked it on his chart, naming it Starved Rock.

24
THE WILDERNESS WOOING

For another month they travelled south. The river of the Illinois became broader and the Indians they met called it the Messipi. They floated onwards on its wide waters. La Tour knew that unless the course of the river turned westward soon, the great sea which lay before them would be no route to China. But he kept his hopes high. The Indians always assured him that the Messipi debouched into an ocean, though none, when he questioned them, had ever seen it. La Tour pressed on, but his men were weary, and on Henri's suggestion, he agreed to rest them for a week. He looked for a pleasant place.

Since the Frenchmen had left Starved Rock the Indians had been friendly. The travellers had been welcome ashore and offered peace pipes. The French soldiers ritually demonstrated the power of their muskets by shooting game, and La Tour ritually spoke of the power of the great king whose emissary he was – Louis, great chief of France, greatest of the great chiefs, besides whom all other chiefs were childen; Louis the great oak besides which all other chiefs were as saplings; Louis the great chief, terror of the Iroquois. The dreadful fame of the Iroquois had travelled even farther than their widespread slaughters. To the Indians on the banks of the Messipi, the emissary of a king so great that even the Iroquois trembled at his name was to be honoured and entertained. The muskets of his soldiers, killing game far beyond the range of Indian arrows, were evidence of the great king's power.

La Tour had given his great-oak harangue many times when one morning they passed a rock by the riverside which had the look of a good omen about it. The rock was not a huge cliff like Starved Rock. They had seen no other cliffs nearly so high as that. But they had passed countless smaller rocks, twenty or thirty feet high, which carried crude paintings on their sides. They had seen daubs representing red demons, the hunting of buffalo, and triumphal slaughters. Triumphal slaughters were frequent. But the rock La Tour chose to take as an omen was painted with the green emblem of a tree which could, given a stretch of the imagination, have been an oak. At noon they were welcomed ashore at a village of the Arkansas Indians. While six men guarded the boat, La Tour, Henri, Rebekah and Ruth, and the rest of the Frenchmen were fêted. They were given bowls of Indian meal. Then there was fish. Behind the French stood attendant warriors who separated the flesh of the fish from the bones with their fingers, and then conveyed the choicest pieces to the strangers' mouths. Then they were offered a large roast dog, which was fed to them in the same way. The chief explained that the tree was the emblem of his tribe. It was a tree whose branches, extending to the skies, were the ladders down which the many gods of the Arkansas sent beneficent and powerful spirits to fortify their earthly children. And when a chief died, his body was placed high in the branches of such a tree, so that his spirit could ascend to the country of the gods. La Tour then launched into his recital of the greater powers of the great king Louis across the seas, terror of the Iroquois, and a great oak tree compared with whom all other chiefs were as saplings. Louis was an oak tree whose great unfolding branches, stretching into the heavens, were paths to the greatest God of all, to the God of gods.

The chief received these assurances with the greatest show of credulity. The French soldiers once again demonstrated the range and power of their muskets. Henri, having walked round the encampment, told La Tour that he had found a small promontory, overlooking the river and the camp and yet sheltered by trees, which would be an excellent spot for the party to rest in safety. This place, moreover, led down to a small pebble beach on which the ship could be brought ashore. There was even a fresh brook running down to the river there. The Arkansas were friendly. It was ideal.

By early evening the ship was beached, the tents were erected, and the men drew lots to see who should take the first watch. All of them were tired. A few were exhausted. La Tour and Henri stood to one side and exchanged a few necessary words. Only Henri was as vigorous in mind and body as when they set out. It was he who had struck the bargain with the Arkansas chief, negotiating with him the terms on which the French should stay and rest. When he had settled what should be paid, it was La Tour who conveyed the gifts with ceremony into the hands of the chief, but the bargain was essentially Henri's. He had become much more than a guide. He had made himself an admirable second in command. La Tour always took his advice. It was through Henri that La Tour communicated his orders to the Frenchmen, soldiers and civilians. Without Henri he would never have kept his distance and his authority. It was Henri who protected the women, and La Tour knew that very well. By now he understood what had happened to the soldier who had disappeared a few days after their voyage began. He knew Henri was half-savage. He would never forget Henri, half-Illinois, reinterring with his own hands the scattered bones of the Illinois dead at Starved Rock. But he also knew that if Henri had been wholly French, his resource and strength would have carried him to as high a rank in the French service as a commoner could reach.

La Tour looked for Rebekah. He was standing by his tent when he saw her down by the brook. As he watched her, he reflected that though Henri was certainly the only man as strong as when they set out, the women had stood the journey almost as well, and better than the rest of the men.

They still had a spring in their step. Their eyes were not dulled. They had an animal resilience beyond most men's. He walked down towards Rebekah, who was now kneeling to drink at the brook. He knelt beside her, took her in his arms, buried his face in her hair, and kissed her neck. Then he raised his head and, still holding her by the waist with his left hand, dipped his right in the brook and splashed his face with the cool water. When he turned towards her again, he saw that it was not Rebekah he had embraced, but Ruth. It was the first time he had ever confused the two. On the promontory, by the tent, La Tour saw two figures watching. One was Rebekah, and the other Henri, Henri moved silently away. Rebekah stood perfectly still, and waited for La Tour and Ruth as they walked up the slope towards her. As he met her eyes he saw that she was neither surprised nor affronted. On the contrary, she looked more sure of herself than ever.

In summer, the men had slept in the open on the ground, or in the boat, but now that the nights were colder they needed the tents. There were only four, two large and two small. The two large tents were circular. In one of these seven men slept, and in the other six. A fire was lit in the centre of these two tents, which was allowed to smoulder all night. The men slept like the spokes of a wheel, each with his feet to the fire and his head near the outside wall of the tent. There were also two smaller rectangular tents, each of which could be divided by a canvas curtain into two sections. One tent was occupied by Henri and his boy who slept one side of the curtain, and by the two carpenters, who slept the other side. The second small tent was occupied by La Tour, Rebekah, and Ruth. While the men had bivouacked in the summer, the women had used this tent to give them some privacy when they needed it. The men stank. It amused them that even in a wilderness the two women had water brought to them from the river to wash in, and that La Tour also washed. But in the summer neither the women nor La Tour slept in the tent, but beside it, except on the rare nights when it rained.

The first night they spent on the promontory, Henri saw to the pitching of the tents. The two largest were pitched nearest the village, and by them he posted the sentinels, who would keep watch for two hours and then be relieved, and so on through the night. La Tour's tent was pitched on the edge of the promontory, against a clump of trees which protected it from the wind. Between La Tour's tent and the men's was Henri's, to protect La Tour and his women. Not that there was any longer any danger to La Tour from his own men. They greatly feared Henri. He was known to sleep lightly, and so was his boy. And they could never be sure that he *was* asleep. They had all seen him, at various times of the night, throughout the summer, sliding around the encampments, checking the sentinels, checking that no one touched the precious stores kept in the boat, seeing that no one ever approached La Tour or the women.

That night the women retired first. La Tour bathed in the stream, watched by Henri, who saw him to the tent, and then prowled off to inspect the sentinels. As La Tour entered the tent that night he had the sense that he was once again going to Rebekah on their wedding night. He could again hear them softly laughing as they talked. It was all but dark.

He called, 'Rebekah?'

She lifted an arm, and he lay down beside her. Ruth lay the other side of her.

'You are very tired, Pierre,' she said. 'More tired than you thought.'

He knew he was tired, weary, so dog-tired that he had not known Rebekah from Ruth down by the stream. But this was Rebekah now, who took his head in her arms and lulled him. He fell asleep almost immediately.

He awoke at first light, before the sun had risen, when only a quarter-light showed him the figures of the two sisters. He noticed what he had been too tired to see the night before, that the centre flap of the tent had not been lowered as it always had been before. Both women were asleep. Rebekah's arm was laid across La Tour's body, but

Ruth was curled into Rebekah on her other side, with her arm thrown across her sister. It was almost as he had first seen them, but now he was there with both of them. Rebekah was lying next to her husband, but also, again, lying with her sister as she had throughout her life before her marriage. Rebekah awoke, and in waking saw La Tour looking down at both of them. Then Ruth awoke too. Neither woman moved, La Tour lay down again, Rebekah laid her arm across him as Ruth's was laid across her, and thus they remained, still, until the morning came and La Tour rose.

The events of the next two night were the most natural in the world. Rebekah had taken back her sister. Rebekah wanted both her sister and her husband. It was, given Rebekah's will, inevitable, and decorously done. Rebekah lay between them, needing the warmth of both, and at the same time giving La Tour the warmth he needed to recover a strength and courage which had been more exhausted than he thought. When she stroked his head and drew him closer to her, it was the most innocent thing that his arm, laid across her, should meet Ruth's, and that Ruth should not withdraw her arm, but drowsily accept the warmth of his touch and drowsily return it. It was the most innocent thing that Rebekah should place her hand peacefully between her husband's and her sister's. It was most natural that La Tour, again having fallen asleep rapidly and slept deeply, and waking to see the two sisters curled into each other in sleep, should lean over and caress the sleeping heads of both. It was the most innocent countryside of affection.

On the third day they spent there, Henri saw that his commander's vigour of mind was returning. He before anyone else had seen that the man was deeply tired, and was now the first to see the recovery. La Tour minutely inspected the ship, set the carpenters recaulking her seams, sent the trappers hunting, set the soldiers cleaning all their equipment, and resumed the journal which he had neglected for a week. That night it was plain that the amiable drowsiness which had surrounded La Tour and the two sisters could not last.

They were lying together as they had on the previous night, when Rebekah kissed his mouth while the hand that held his was Ruth's. He was wholly aroused, and his hand slid down to Ruth's waist as it never had before and he felt her stir. But the old inhibitions remained, and he took his arm from Ruth and brought it back to Rebekah. They were deep in a wilderness, six months' hard travelling from the most tenuous civilization, and yet for La Tour the old inhibitions did remain. But they did not remain with Rebekah. She took his hand and gave it back to Ruth, and La Tour was lost. He caressed Ruth's waist, and neck and mouth, and hair, and all the while Rebekah subtly caressed him. When he went to kiss Rebekah again, she moved her head away, saying, 'No,' and brought Ruth closer to him, so that he took Ruth's head in his hands and they kissed over Rebekah. Again La Tour broke away, and slid his hand in a familiar caress between his wife's legs. She drew in her breath, moved her head, and could not restrain the low, aroused, thrilled laugh that he knew so very well, but she said, 'No,' and then, softly, 'go to Ruth.'

Now was La Tour's last chance for denial, or at least indecision, but he was only a man. He did make an honest attempt at indecision, but during that moment of hesitation a hand touched his hair, and it could not be Rebekah's because hers were elsewhere. He was after all only a man, so he went to Ruth, and knelt above her, all the time caressed by Rebekah, and entered Ruth with a sweet longing and came with an almost immediate release, and Ruth held him and held him and gently kissed his face.

Now Rebekah was a woman of an instinctive, adventurous lasciviousness, which in a full-hearted woman is a delightful thing. She had a lovely boldness, and she could sometimes be wholehearted. And she had power, and a sense of that power that she could not help employing. Within a week the two sisters were La Tour's most subtle mistresses, and he their happy lover. It *was* an exercise of

Rebekah's power. When she had said, 'Go to Ruth,' and he had, it was not so much that La Tour had lost as that Rebekah had won. But she had done it not only because of a passionate sensuality that was always hers, or out of a sense of adventure that never left her, or in an exercise of power that she could not resist. It was all those things, but it was also a deep instinctive return to the old twin-instinct that everything she and Ruth had was theirs together, theirs alone but theirs together. Rebekah deeply loved her sister. She loved her sister as herself. In the wilderness she had wooed her husband to be Ruth's as well as hers, and therefore to be hers the more. But she did not know what she had done.

When the men were rested, La Tour wanted to press on, and winter farther south. The Arkansas Indians shook their heads, saying that buffalo and other game became scarce away from their lands, and that the tribes farther south were dangerous. La Tour sent Henri to view the country downriver. When he returned, after four days, his advice was that they could not do better than stay where they were. It was true that there were fewer buffalo farther south, and though he had seen traces of Indians, they were of a tribe he did not know. La Tour ordered the salting down of the game they had shot, the purchase of corn from the Arkansas, and the building of a palisaded fort. They would stay the winter.

25
DIVIDE THE WORLD

George Downing strolled from his splendid house in the Middle Temple, along the Strand, towards Whitehall and the illustrious summons. The words 'illustrious summons' ran through Mr Downing's mind. He thought it a good phrase. He had himself invented it, that instant. He was, he admitted to himself, a man given to invention. It was indeed a good phrase, which he would certainly find occasion to write in his journal.

Since he had left New England, Downing had seen much service. First as a chaplain in Barbados, where he had of course been obliged to supplement his stipend by dealings in the sugar and rum trades. He had sometimes reflected that it was often necessary to support one's higher aspirations, and the higher aspirations of humanity, by the profits of a necessary but lower occupation. It was true that the profits of sugar and rum had been great. Well, he reflected, and if that were so? He had ministered long and well to the black savages of Barbados, and even to their scarcely less savage English masters – he shuddered to remember them and their manifold incivilities to a man of his piety – and it had just fallen out, in God's providence, that substantial profits from rum had accrued to his industry, and still remained to him. In short, he was well off. He would say very well off, and thought it not undeserved that he should be so. Perhaps a man in his position had need of a wife? Colonel Howard's daughter was said to have an excellent dowry, and Colonel Howard would be an excellent connection. He must consider.

It was a fine London day in March, not warm certainly, but not cold. Not perilously, appallingly, icily cold as it very likely still would be in New England. He considered that at certain times of the year New England might freeze a man's intellect and chill his entire beneficent inclinations. And, God be praised, England was never as muggily, stickily, enervatingly hot as it always was in Barbados. He reflected that some men did spend many years suffering the inconvenience of severe climates for the entire benefit of others. But he would not rebuke himself for having made such a generous mistake. It had been his duty.

He strolled on towards the palace of Whitehall, acknowledging a salute here, a bow there. He was known. It gratified him that he was known. Or, he would rather say, that his works were known, and that wherever he went his reputation preceded him.

Downing was thirty, a sleek, successful thirty, and what if the sleekness tended to plumpness? A man should eat well. He was grateful that his God set a table before him, not only daily, but also in the higher sense that He had given to Downing great works to accomplish. Had it not been God's will that he (Downing), on his return to England, should serve as chaplain in one of Cromwell's regiments? As it happened it was a good regiment, commanded by men who had advanced his career, but no doubt that too had been His doing, and was evidence of a higher purpose directing the faithful service, and, by chance, the good fortune of George Downing? And now, this fine March morning, the illustrious summons had come, in response to which Downing was at this moment making his way towards the palace of Whitehall. Downing had served Cromwell not only as chaplain to one of his better regiments, Colonel Okey's, but also as an officer in Scotland. He reflected that he had perhaps been too modest in his surprise when the illustrious summons had been conveyed to him. It was perhaps preordained that the Lord should call him to higher things. At any rate, he was ordered to appear that morning at nine of the clock before General Cromwell, saviour of the nation, a man who, Downing thought, should rightly take the title of king, and who was, if not king, then dictator – 'I use the word,' Downing told himself, 'to mean a man through whom God's word is spoken to the people' – dictator certainly, of the Commonwealth of England, Scotland, and Ireland.

The doorkeepers at Whitehall bowed. Downing glanced at the spot where Charles, the unworthy king, had met his just doom – he felt he could properly say *just* doom – and walked into a glorious antechamber of the palace.

He was told to wait.

The doors of the inner room opened and a servant emerged. Downing began to rise, but the man passed straight across the anteroom, not noticing his presence. Downing subsided.

An undersecretary passed in the other direction, entering the inner room.

Downing waited.

At last the inner doors opened again, and this time the undersecretary walked towards Downing, sat beside him, and in whispered tones told him that the general wished his presence at an audience he was granting the Dutch ambassador, and might afterward require his advice on matters to do with the Indies.

Downing nodded wisely, though he had not even been told East or West Indies. His mind flitted to Jamaica, which Cromwell had once proposed should be populated with emigrants from New England, to give backbone to the island. But he did not know Jamaica, which was held by the Spanish. Besides, Cromwell had also proposed that Ireland should be populated with Englishmen from New England – to give Ireland backbone. Downing had never been to Ireland. It must then be the Barbados on which Cromwell wished to ask his advice.

'You will not,' said the secretary, waking Downing from his thoughts, 'make any movement or say any word during the interview, unless the general asks it.'

Downing thought this severe, but assented, and was then led into the presence chamber. The secretary for the navy was already there, and looked through Downing. Downing bowed. He did not see General Cromwell. The great chair was unoccupied. The undersecretary went out, leaving Downing looking around and still standing.

He continued to stand, feeling that this was not so illustrious a summons as he had the right to expect, when a black figure entered the room from a concealed door behind the desk. It was Cromwell, in black coat and with a black scarf round his neck. He took the great chair, but left both Downing and the navy secretary standing. They waited.

Then the ceremonial doors opened and the ambassador of Their High Mightinesses the Lords of the States General was announced. He was an aged man, in rich beaver robes, who walked with difficulty across the width of the marble floor, and made as if to bow to General Cromwell, who stopped him immediately, and cast his first glance towards Downing. 'A chair,' he said.

Downing scurried to bring up a chair for the ambassador, and then retired three paces to his former position.

Cromwell looked up at the ambassador, and as soon as his eyes were seen, the man was seen. Cromwell was no longer a man in a black cloak and a black scarf, a man apparently ill, but Oliver Cromwell, a man who, if not king, was soon to be Lord Protector of England, and was certainly already a dictator. The eyes were the man, and they were luminous.

'Behold,' he said, 'how good and pleasant it is for brethren to dwell together in unity.'

'That,' said the ambassador, 'is a good psalm I have often repeated to myself. Or it is a good *beginning* to a psalm, sir.'

'A psalm it is,' said Cromwell, 'or its first line. And you wish to hear the rest, as it were? So we shall get down to our business, and I will give you the rest of the psalm, which is this.'

The ambassador leaned back in his chair and waited impassively to hear what was in England's mind. Here was he, an aged man, at the end of his life unless God should miraculously spare him further, but still the representative of Holland, the mightiest maritime power of the world. And there was Cromwell, there was England, a great military power, more so than under any king, and a maritime power which was a jealous second to Holland. The ambassador waited. He was Joachimi, who had been ambassador in England twenty-five years before, and had recently been sent back from retirement. He wished he had not been sent back to London, but it had been urged upon him that England was dangerous, and that no Dutchman knew England better. So he had returned. Now he waited.

'Ambassador,' said Cromwell, 'the rest of the psalm is this, and we shall dispense with the herring this morning.'

Joachimi allowed the ghost of a smile to flit across his face. Herrings were a constant curse to both of them. He had met Cromwell's ministers on the subject of herrings, and had conveyed polite nothings in response to bitter complaints. Both the Dutch and English fishermen wanted the herrings in the English channel. The health of both fishing industries depended upon it. He knew nothing and cared nothing about fishing. He did not eat herrings.

'So,' said Cromwell, 'the rest of the psalm. It is pleasant for brethren to dwell together in unity, and to this end I have already proposed a confederation between our two nations.'

Joachimi knew this only too well. It had been this proposition which had impelled the States General to send a man of his experience and age back to London. A confederation had not been wished for by the Dutch. Privately, Joachimi thought it absurdly grandiose, but he said nothing.

'We have proposed a federation, but that was not bold enough. We spoke small, when we should have spoken large.'

Joachimi let nothing show on his face.

'Herring apart, ambassador, our interests are the same.'

Joachimi thought it no harm to agree with this.

'But our interests being the same, they overlap. They conflict. Holland and England both want the same fish. We both want the same islands in the Indies. Herrings. Islands. Herrings do not matter. Islands do. And to put it pat, ambassador, if we both pursue the same things, there may be war, and I am not a man of war.'

Joachimi, remembering Cromwell's iron-clad armies, and remembering their work in Scotland and Ireland, maintained his impassiveness. 'We shall both pray, general, that there may be no war then. War between brethren?'

'Well, then, the rest of the psalm – brief, short, pat – is this.' Cromwell looked over the ambassador's head. He looked up at the high ceiling, as if calling on Heaven to hear and approve his proposal. Gazing upwards, he said, 'Ambassador, let us then divide the world between us.'

Joachimi said absolutely nothing. He allowed his face to show nothing. He did not think Cromwell mad, yet this was a proposal that was so absurd that it must be in earnest.

Cromwell brought down his eyes from the Heavens, and let them rest on Joachimi. He would be more specific.

'The States General, ambassador, would retain the Spice Islands and the rest of the East Indies. We have fought and scrambled long enough over Sumatra, Ambon, Ceram, and our ships together would ensure your enjoyment of the East Indies undisturbed. We should concede Jakarta. The East India Company of London would withdraw.'

'That,' said Joachimi, 'is one half of the world, only the first verse of the psalm?'

'And the second part is this. That England should enjoy the West Indies. We should not wish to disturb your enjoyment of Brazil, such part of it as you have.'

Joachimi nodded gravely.

'But we should ask your help in taking Jamaica and Hispaniola from Spain, and in securing other islands. And you would restore to our Commonwealth the colony of New Netherlands.'

'Ah,' said Joachimi, 'the Manaddos, in northern Virginia?' It was an echo of a conversation nearly a quarter of a century before.

DIVIDE THE WORLD

'Manhattan,' said Cromwell. 'Manhattan. We should require Manhattan. You smile?'

'Nothing,' said Joachimi. 'Nothing.' But his mind was back at Newmarket where the so-recently beheaded Charles, then young, had demanded the Manaddos in northern Virginia, which he would not suffer to be called Manhattan. A king had met him at a pavilion on a racecourse, with bookies and stable boys around him. A Puritan dictator summoned him to a palace. Newmarket was a long time ago. But then, everything was changing rapidly. Joachimi had retired not so long ago from a lifetime of diplomacy, thinking he had seen and heard everything that the magnanimity or duplicity of princes had to offer. Now he had returned, in his very old age, to be offered half the world.

'*Inter Cetera Divina*,' he murmured.

The ambassador's voice was almost inaudible, but Cromwell heard the words and caught the allusion. With those three words a Pope had in 1493 begun an ordinance, a Papal Bull, which divided the new world, and those parts of the world afterwards to be discovered, between the Catholic kingdoms of Spain and Portugal.

'Roughly,' said Joachimi, 'the east went to Portugal, the west to Spain. A line was drawn. Pope Alexander VI, was it?'

'He was a Borgia,' said Cromwell.

'He was, sir.'

'But that's gone and past, and neither States' ships nor English ships have ever taken any notice of that papistical division.'

Joachimi allowed himself a smile. Here was a Calvinist dictator or a purified England doing what a Pope, and a Borgia at that, had done more than one hundred and fifty years before. Times had changed and yet very little had changed, and he had seen everything now. But he brought his mind to particulars, and made a particular answer.

'General Cromwell, I shall relate to Their High Mightinesses what you have proposed. But I must tell you that you are offering us what we already have – that is to say, the East Indies – and demanding in return that we should concede territories which, once again, we already have and possess. I stand under the correction of Their High Mightinesses in this, but we would not concede Manhattan.'

Cromwell stared down at the table. The ambassador began to rise, with difficulty. Cromwell looked up and with a flicking movement of his wrist gestured to Downing to help him. Joachimi took Downing's arm, rose slowly, and then thanked the young man. He did not know Downing, but felt in his bones that here was a fellow who would one day be heard of. He memorized the man's face, and reminded himself to make enquiries. He turned to Cromwell, who rose too, and Joachimi met those fierce and luminous eyes again. Then he gathered his beaver furs around him, and left.

The doors closed after him.

'Now we shall have to take the place,' said Cromwell.

The navy secretary agreed. 'We shall, sir. Five frigates would do. If we are to have the West Indies, we must have Manhattan to begin with. Five frigates sailing from an English Manhattan would take the whole of the West Indies.'

Cromwell considered. 'Five frigates. But we shall need intelligence of the place. We shall send a man to Manhattan. A good man, to look out the fortifications, and sound the strength of the garrison. A good man.'

'This morning,' said the navy secretary, 'will fairly well have told them our intentions.'

'We are not at war,' said Cromwell. 'We are not yet at war. I should mean to send only a peaceful envoy.'

'Whom they will tear to pieces,' said Downing.

Cromwell regarded him directly for the first time that morning. 'Dear Downing,' he said. 'I will risk you.'

26

THE TOWER OF BABEL

'Oh, sir, now don't you take any notice. Don't you give any mind to what those great men say. Tower of Babel! Tower of Babel to them, sir!'

'Take no notice, that's your advice then?' said Peter Stuyvesant, with an amused severity. 'No notice, eh?' He poked with his silver-headed cane, making elaborate patterns in the raked sand path of Wolsey's garden. He had come to pay one of the afternoon visits which were such a pleasure to him. Wolsey was occupied giving orders in the kitchen, and while he waited for her, sitting in the sun, Susannah was entertaining him with her opinions on the conduct of state.

Wolsey came out to them, and Stuyvesant raised a hand to greet his old friend.

Susannah bobbed to Wolsey, and then completed her advice to Stuyvesant. 'Yes, sir, that's what my way would be with them. And sensible, too.'

Wolsey sat opposite the governor. 'And what is this?' she said. 'What are you being told it's sensible to do?'

He said, 'This morning I had a communication from Their High Mightinesses, which had taken four months to reach me, by way of Curaçao. It told me that, according to their information, Manhattan had become nothing so much as a Tower of Babel. I do not know where they got their information, but that is what they wrote. And what, I ask myself, do they propose I should do about it? Dutch merchants, they say, are in great distress, whereas all kinds of foreigners are flourishing. The flourishing foreigners, it seems, are the cause of the Dutchmen's impoverishment. I am asked to send my answer straightaway. I shall send it, but see it takes four months, shall I?'

'I suppose Harry and I are flourishing foreigners, to be blamed?' said Wolsey.

'Their High Mightinesses say nothing about Irishmen. They speak particularly of the Chinese and the Scots.'

Wolsey laughed aloud. There were no Chinese, and she knew two Scots, both in a modest way in the liquor trade.

'And your Susannah here,' said Stuyvesant, 'was giving me *her* opinion of their High Mightinesses' opinion.'

'Oh, no, sir,' said Susannah. 'Oh, no, ma'am, 'tweren't that. That's not my place. But I never could rightly understand that old Bible story about the Tower of Babel. I never knew why it was counted sinful for those poor men, when they'd only just escaped the Flood, to want to build a tower, to get nearer Heaven. That's natural, sir. I never did see why God thought they were taking too much on themselves by building a tower. I never did follow why He said to Himself, "Come on, let's go down and make them all speak different languages from now on, so they won't be able to understand each other anymore, and let's scatter them around the earth, and then they won't be able to build their tower any more."

'I never did understand that. Doesn't stand to reason. If 'twas a Tower of Babel, then 'twas He that made it one, by making them speak different languages. *That* stands to reason. The rest don't, do it, sir?'

'No,' said Stuyvesant, 'put like that, perhaps it doesn't. But you are a heretic for saying it, Susannah.'

'I *was* a heretic in Plymouth,' said Susannah, 'or near to being one, but I won't be in your lordship's colony, so I'll say no more. But all the same, sir, it don't stand to reason, do it?' And she curtsied and left them.

Wolsey said, 'The first day I came here, I heard six languages in the streets. I think it was six. It was a good many. I suppose there are more now. It's no bad thing.

Their High Mightinesses' profits would suffer if there were fewer.'

Then she saw that he was abstracted, and was still making absent-minded marks with his cane. She saw that he had drawn a tower in the sand.

'What is it, Peter?' she said. 'What's the matter? Not that letter?'

'No, you see it isn't that letter, don't you? No. That letter, sealed with the seal of Their High Mightinesses, was the work of some undersecretary with too little to do. It's nothing. It's not that. It's not that letter I'm worried about, it's this whole damned petition.'

He irascibly scribbled out the tower with the tip of his stick. 'It's this petition by the merchants and farmers here, which they're sending off to Amsterdam. They've graciously allowed me to see a copy. I'm a tyrant again, Wolsey.'

'That, Peter, is nothing new. But I've not lately seen any circumstantial accounts of your eating farmers' children for breakfast. So what is it?'

'It's more particular this time, and they've joined together to write it. And, my dear, it can do me no good. Arrests, there've been arrests, they say, and banishments, confiscations, prosecutions, blows, scoldings, reckoning half faults for entire ones....'

At this last phrase Wolsey laughed.

'Well, Wolsey, it *is* ludicrous, but they say it's ruining the colony and estranging the settlers.'

'Have there been arrests?'

'No more than usual. Tower of Babel or not, it's not a city of angels. There've been arrests. Banishments? I've shipped a few ruffians out in the next ship to, oh, Curaçao. They weren't noticed there. A few months ago I made the mistake of shipping a couple back to Amsterdam, where they will have talked loudly. Shouldn't have done that. Stupid of me. But it isn't that. These petitioning serpents, they don't like foreign traders either. No doubt they think of them as Scots and Chinese too.'

She laughed again and then, seeing him sitting glumly, said, 'Oh, Peter, that was thoughtless of me, but it *is* droll.'

'Well, yes it is. There are no Chinamen. They wouldn't know a Chinaman here if they saw one, and nor would I. But the fellow who drafted the petition, van Delft, not a fool, when he brought it to me this morning, said, "Governor, I am not poor. I don't pretend I'm poor. But some of the Dutch here are, and it's these petty traders who're taking the bread out of their mouths. Petty traders, who swarm in with great industry, reap great profits, and impoverish the country, and don't pay any taxes either." I said there was no point in condemning the greater industry of others, and he said, and he had a point, that these foreigners came in, stayed five minutes, skimmed off the cream, and then were off. As often as not leaving bad debts. Wolsey, it can't do me any good when this petition gets to Amsterdam.'

She said, 'It is one side of the case. You can put yours.'

He shrugged.

'Peter, the worst Amsterdam can do is recall you. Would you be sorry to leave?'

Stuyvesant said, quite fiercely, 'Yes, I would. I shall not leave. I do not think I shall ever leave. Yes, I would mind very much.'

He stabbed at the pathway with his stick and then said, 'That's enough of that. Wolsey, I know you would have told me, and you haven't, but have you had any news of your daughters?'

She shook her head. 'Nothing from them since their letter from Québec, and that is almost a year ago. I wish they had not gone on from Québec. Or that Ruth had not gone on. I wish Ruth had come back.'

Stuyvesant met her eyes. He knew perfectly well what Wolsey would not say, that it was Rebekah who had kept Ruth with her. It was Rebekah's doing. Stuyvesant saw Wolsey's pain, but knew that it was not in her nature to admit it. Her courage would hide it.

'But there has been a letter I haven't told you about,' she said. 'Not from them, or from La Tour. But the governor at

Québec. He was very kind. He wrote. By the first ship that got out of the St Lawrence this spring, he sent me a letter. He said La Tour had obviously wintered in the interior, and that he had no reason to think the party had not wintered safely. He said Indians who had come to the fort reported seeing the party on the lakes, and that they were well. He said he had sent his best guide with them, whom he would trust with his life. And he wrote, and asked me to forgive him for saying it, that La Tour had seemed, on short acquaintance, remarkably better than the run of explorers that he saw. He said I would think that was a strange way to comfort me. I *did* think it a strange way to comfort me. But all the same, I was glad to know he thought that. But no, Peter, I have not seen them for more than a year now, and I miss them dreadfully. And now, shall I have some tea brought out?'

They had moved to the shade, and while they took tea, and chatted easily, with the petition gone for the moment from Stuyvesant's mind, and her daughters for the moment from Wolsey's, a messenger came in with a note from the port captain.

He read it. 'An English ship,' he told Wolsey. 'And some Englishman asking for an audience to present General Cromwell's compliments.'

'At least news from London,' said Wolsey.

'You shall meet him,' said Stuyvesant.

George Downing regretted that he could not be styled ambassador plenipotentiary, or ambassador of any proper kind. This would have sounded well, but would never do, since he was sent by the sovereign state of England not as envoy to any other sovereign state but to the governor of a usurping foreign colony. And he was not, he thought, really sent as ambassador, but simply to be pleasant and sniff things out. This was at a time in his life when he had not yet learned that these were the principal functions of an ambassador of any kind. But he did arrive carrying parchments, seals, and good wishes. He was of course afraid that news of Cromwell's indiscreet offer to Joachimi would have preceded him, which would make his reception uncertain if not dangerous. He could not know that Amsterdam commonly sent messages to Manhattan via Curaçao, because that was the usual route of Dutch merchant ships. He did not know that he need not have worried in any case. Joachimi had faithfully reported the meeting with General Cromwell to Amsterdam, where Their High Mightinesses had been amused by its audacity and alarmed, so far as they were alarmed, for the safety of Curaçao and Aruba. It had crossed the mind of a Dutch undersecretary of the navy that Manhattan would be a good base from which to dominate the English islands of the West Indies, but Holland had as yet no ambition to take these islands. Manhattan itself did not appear urgent to the Lords of the States General. Stuyvesant would be told, but all in good time. Downing was therefore received with surprise and courtesy. The governor was, if anything, rather glad of his arrival. It would be something to report to Amsterdam, something of more consequence than a mere reply to some undersecretary's scribblings about a Tower of Babel.

The truth was that Stuyvesant did not expect an attack, certainly not from England. The Anglo-Dutch rivalry was obvious, and had been for years, but mostly in the East Indies. Stuyvesant was aware of the constant bickering and bitterness in the east. He was also well aware that King Charles had asserted that Manhattan was an English royal colony, but that was years ago, and now King Charles was dead. General Cromwell was as good a Calvinist as any Lord of the States General. If Stuyvesant was apprehensive of an attack, it was from the flourishing Massachusetts colonies, but he saw no signs of this.

'You will be going on to Massachusetts?' he asked Downing, and Downing replied that he would not.

'Or to Connecticut?'

'To Barbados.' And this was indeed Downing's intention. He wished to return by way of Barbados in order to look after his own sugar interests on that island, which had been managed for years by a steward.

This was not only true but plausible. It also allowed Downing to express an interest in agriculture, and obtain the governor's permission to view the farms on Manhattan and Breuckelen, and to inspect the fisheries of the North and East Rivers. Altogether, Downing's silky approaches were most successful, and he looked forward to a profitable reconnaissance the next day. As he was leaving Stuyvesant's house that evening, the governor mentioned to him that he must certainly take the opportunity to visit an Englishwoman living on Manhattan, Mrs O'Brien, and scribbled a note of introduction. Downing did not say at that moment that he had met her, and accepted the note.

Next day, touring farms and fisheries, Downing made a careful survey of the town, the beginnings of the defensive wall which, he was casually told by a soldier, was intended to stretch from the North to the East Rivers, though so far only a few yards had been completed. He saw the fort, noting the battlements, the cannon, the demiculverin, the bulwarks, and all other fortifications. The day after that, he hired a boat and circumnavigated the island, marking on a map the isolated farms along the riverbanks, and taking especial note of the safe anchorages in the North River near the fort.

Then, that evening, he visited Wolsey. He regarded the visit as one of courtesy and friendship, and, knowing that O'Brien was a considerable merchant, hoped by means of amiable conversation to learn more about the commerce and shipping of the town. He did not know that Wolsey would regard any visit of his as no courtesy. He did not know that friendship between them was, to say the least of it, wildly improbable. He did remember their first meeting, in the same house in Manhattan to which he now set out. That was when he had brought her the trunk from Plymouth. He very well remembered Wolsey's anger. But he had never understood it. He did not see how the mere holding up of a russet silk skirt, for he remembered the colour of it, had been an outrage. He had taken her anger as a womanly freak. He had never forgotten her look of contempt, which he had thought extraordinarily uncivil and ungrateful. But he was willing to overlook that. He was also willing to forget her coldness to him when he had welcomed her and O'Brien on their visit to the dying Brewster at Plymouth. She must have been upset. They could put those things behind them, he was sure. Now here he was in Manhattan, an Englishman, and here she was, an Englishwoman. He saw his visit as a courtesy she might expect, and as a profitable opportunity for himself to gain more information.

Thus deluded, he presented himself at the house, was shown in by a Dutch servant, and then, before the servant had time to convey to Wolsey the news that he was there, he had the good fortune to bump into O'Brien, who had just come out of the sitting room to walk to his study. The two men met in the hall. O'Brien thought Downing an ass, but would not turn him away, and offered a glass of wine. They went back to the sitting room. The servant, returning to the hall with Wolsey's reply that she was not at home to Mr Downing, saw that the visitor was already in conversation with O'Brien, and withdrew. Ten minutes later, thinking that Downing would have received her reply, hoping that he had taken it as a snub, and confident anyway that the man would have gone, Wolsey came looking for Harry to tell him, and found the two men together. Downing rose with elaborate bows, and she could not escape. They observed each other. Downing saw Wolsey's richness of dress, which he thought would by no means have shamed the wife of a great London merchant, and said to himself, 'How well the woman has worn. And in a colonial climate. Remarkable.' Wolsey saw how sleek the man was, how softly rounded the cheeks, how soft and limp the hand, how quite without wrinkles the forehead.

'I was telling Captain O'Brien the court talk, ma'am,' said Downing, and continued his ingratiating patter of small talk about great men.

He ventured to allow that Captain O'Brien, as an Irishman, might not have understood or approved the conduct of the Commonwealth under General Cromwell.

'Aye,' said O'Brien, 'an Irishman might not. I could agree that an Irishman might not.'

'But the present state may not continue,' said Downing, 'for the monarchy may be resumed. That may well be. It is much to be hoped, and in London, sir, *is* hoped for, and by many gentlemen in the country too.'

'How resumed?' said O'Brien. 'Your man Cromwell has killed the king.'

'But the monarchy may be resumed in General Cromwell's own person, sir.'

'I do not take your meaning. The man has overthrown a king, the man has denounced kingship, and lastly the man has *killed* the king. What should he resume in his own person? What is his meaning? What is yours?'

'That General Cromwell may be king. That the kingdom may be restored. It recommends itself as much the best thing, and is much to be wished.'

'King Cromwell?'

'King Oliver, sir,' corrected Downing, and Wolsey did not hide a smile.

Downing took this as encouragement.

'For you see, ma'am, the question is, is Cromwell to be merely a Regent for Prince Charles? Is he to govern and increase the power of the state merely for a Stuart prince to succeed to an improved kingdom? Or is he himself to assume the throne? The second is the opinion of most gentlemen of power and persuasion in England today.' This was in part true. It had occurred to such gentlemen that a king would be better equipped than a mere dictator, or even a Lord Protector, to bestow upon them offices of profit and titles of honour. They coveted dukedoms and baronies, and there were none to be had without a king. Besides, a restoration of monarchy was pure, disinterested policy, for the good of the nation. So thought these gentlemen, and

Downing was one of them.

'And that is the opinion of *most* gentlemen?' asked Wolsey.

'Of many, ma'am, many.'

'Indeed,' she said.

'For,' said Downing, pursuing his argument, 'a *Commonwealth*, though necessary indeed after the excesses of the late king, does lead to other, though lesser excesses, among the *common* people.' He was pleased with the turn of phrase.

'Excesses, aye,' said O'Brien. 'You could say there have been excesses.'

'Yes, indeed, sir,' Downing sorrowfully confided, conceding as he imagined a little in order to gain a greater thing, O'Brien's confidence. 'Indeed, there have been excesses. You are often in the Caribbean?'

'I am.'

'Then I must confess, with some shame, that men from an English ship, not a Commonwealth ship, sir, but an English ship nevertheless, did throw oranges at coloured statues of the Virgin Mary at San Domingo on the island of Hispaniola. That was an excess. The statues were smashed.'

'I heard that it *was* a Commonwealth ship,' said O'Brien, 'but that was not one of the excesses I had in mind. I am an Irishman from Cork, you see.'

Downing deplored excesses even in Ireland, particularly massacres, assured O'Brien and Wolsey that Cromwell was at heart a peace-loving man and a seeker after peace, and then, saying that he would if he might take Mrs O'Brien's mind back to Plymouth colony, remarked that the Calvinist principles which had inspired that settlement, of which she had been among the founders, were also those that informed General Cromwell's every action.

Imagining that by his placatory addresses he had soothed both Wolsey and O'Brien, and being quite unable to perceive that he had offended Wolsey and irritated O'Brien, Downing began to enquire casually about the trade of Manhattan. Business was thriving? There was a great trade with the sugar islands? Was that a Dutch East Indiaman he had seen lying in the East River? So the river was navigable to ships of that tonnage? Did the Indian depredations continue on Long Island, as he had been sorry to hear? They found Governor Stuyvesant an amiable gentleman? And so on, until O'Brien, having answered in Yeses, and Noes, and Perhapses, and grunts, having answered at any rate almost entirely in monosyllables, asked Downing, 'And what brings you here, sir?'

'Oh, agriculture, Captain O'Brien, and the fishing. Agriculture, sir.'

Neither Wolsey nor O'Brien said a word. Downing looked at the empty glass in his hand, and at the full decanter on the table, and asked, 'You grow wines in the New Netherlands, sir?'

'Only bad ones, Downing. Such as I do not think a man of your taste would care for.'

'But, sir,' Downing protested, 'the wine was excellent.'

'The wine you drank was French.'

'Then the trade with France flourishes, captain?'

O'Brien did not reply. Downing looked again at his empty glass. O'Brien did not offer to refill it. They sat in silence.

At last Downing rose. He was, he said, most grateful for their entertainment. He hoped to have the pleasure of meeting them again before he left Manhattan.

O'Brien curtly nodded, and bounded upstairs to his land cabin. If he had stayed in the same room a moment longer, he knew he would have called the man insufferable to his face.

Downing and Wolsey stood by the street door.

'And I *do* hope,' said he, 'that I shall have the honour of meeting you again soon,' and at this he smiled his courtier's smile and laid a limp hand on her arm. It was in no way a sexual advance. Downing was no womanizer. He was epicene. All the women he had ever known had been mere adornments to his ambition. Throughout his career in London, to be seen with a beautiful woman had been necessary to him as a man of power, and in no other sense.

When he thought of marrying, it was only for the dowry a wife would bring. He had never loved or desired any woman, and it was this coldness, as much as his deviousness and ambition, which repelled Wolsey.

So when he laid his soft, limp hand on her arm, she shuddered, which even Downing could not fail to see. He bowed and left.

Wolsey went to Harry, who sat with his eyes blazing. 'Agriculture, sir,' he mimicked. 'Agriculture, sir, and the fisheries.'

Wolsey laughed and let her own anger evaporate in laughter. Harry took her by the waist with both hands and they laughed helplessly, she first leaning on Harry and then sitting down to brush the tears of laughter from her eyes.

'And for two days,' said O'Brien, 'I've seen that fellow, and my men have seen that fellow, sniffing round every anchorage, wharf, and fortification on Manhattan, and making himself pleasant to every Dutch soldier, and buying rum for every French sailor, to take an exact picture of Manhattan back to King Cromwell. And mighty subtle he is with it.'

More laughter.

'Agriculture and the fisheries, captain,' mimicked O'Brien. 'By God, Wolsey, that man is a George Downing of a liar, and I shall see that it is known. A George Downing of a liar, that he is.'

Wolsey quietly warned Stuyvesant that whatever Downing's purpose might be, it was unlikely to be honest. O'Brien roared it out in the taverns that George Downing was a George Downing of a liar, and told his own men, who roared it out in the doss-houses and brothels. Within a week, Downing was infamous, and any man detected in a lie in Manhattan was called a George Downing. Boys followed Downing in the street, imitating his sleek, plump walk. Thin, dark Anne at the Swan, though she was no longer encouraged to sing in the public house, her voice having gone, still sang in the street when she had drunk too much.

Having learned of Downing's ambitions to crown Cromwell, and observed the self-importance of the man as he went about his sleek business, she achieved a new popularity with a new song, which went:

> *If Cromwell will not take the orb*
> *The sceptre and the crown,*
> *Will Downing be downhearted, lads?*
> *Not on my nelly, lads!*
> *Then Downing will be for crowning*
> *George Downing himself for king.*

The day Downing left Manhattan, he was followed to the quay by a mocking mob of boys carrying a stuffed effigy surmounted by a tinsel crown. In midriver, as he boarded the English ship that was to take him home, he heard his name catcalled across the water. For the entire passage home, the common sailors of the ship turned away laughing whenever they saw him.

He knew at whose door to lay this, and hated Wolsey for it.

27

THE KING'S COMET

After the French had wintered with the Arkansas, La Tour led his party south again the following spring. The sluggish river meandered through swamps and canebrakes. Right down to the river's edge grew thickets of a bamboo-like grass higher and more impenetrable than they had ever seen before, three times the height of a man, and in places higher, taller than the mast of their ship. Now, in the still, stagnant air, the sail was useless, and the men had to drift with the lazy current, or else row, which exhausted them in the sultry heat. They killed two alligators, again the first they had seen, and ate the flesh. At this season it was subtropical country. All the men were burned black by the misty sun, and some were badly blistered. Their hair and beards were matted and long, their clothes filthy, and they resembled wild men. Henri made broad-brimmed rush hats for the women, and for himself and La Tour. The other men were so overcome with lassitude that they would not make the small effort of plaiting hats for themselves. One trapper died of sunstroke, at which the rest took to covering their heads with handkerchiefs which they constantly wetted in the river.

For a week they had seen no Indians, when Henri returned from a scouting trip, which had kept him away for a day and a night, and took La Tour aside. One day ahead of them, he said, he had seen a great gathering of tribes unknown to him. They were the tallest and best formed

Indians he had ever seen. The impaled heads of their enemies decorated the pointed palisades of their town.

'How large is their village?' asked La Tour.

'It is a town.'

'They are more numerous than the Arkansas?'

'More numerous than the Illinois, before the Iroquois got them. And you saw the size of the Illinois town.'

'So there are more of them than there are French at Québec?'

'Many more.'

'Did you get close enough to hear them speak?'

'There were some words of Sioux. I could not follow much.'

La Tour pondered. Should he proceed? Should he take his small force into the midst of such a gathering of tribes? If he did, would the heads of his party join the other heads on the pointed palisades of the Indian town? And yet, if he returned, he would not have carried out his commission, which was to find the Vermilion Sea. He had begun to doubt the existence of such a sea, but he did not *know*.

And this was only one of the reasons, that he did not *know*, that would drive La Tour on. For he would go on. He might ask himself whether he should proceed, but when he did so, the question he was really putting to himself was *how* he should proceed. He was carried on partly by an habitual sense of duty. He held only the rank of lieutenant, but to say just that is misleading. Lieutenant is a poor rank, and yet a lieutenant at sea, in command of a king's vessel, is a god in his power. For months at a time, out of sight of land, beyond any superior authority, he decides the course of his ship and the lives of his crew. That was habitual to La Tour. A lieutenant at sea can exercise more real power in the small world over which he has utter command than a courtier, a great duke, a minister, can exercise at home, where his order may be countermanded the next minute by a superior. And here in a wilderness La Tour's power was immense. He was the personification of all the power of the French king. In this wilderness, La Tour *was* France. So there was his duty, and the power it brought with it, but more than that there was the explorer's devouring desire to know, to discover, to possess. A great continent was his to discover, and this burning idea gave him a strength of purpose far beyond the ordinary. The greatness of the purpose strengthened his resolve. The greater the purpose to be achieved, the greater the man becomes who sets out to achieve it.

So he would go on. There was no real doubt of that at all. But it would be wise to know a lot more before he risked himself and his people in the great Indian town.

'What else about them?' he asked Henri. 'What else about these savages? What did you see?'

'The chiefs were grandly dressed. And thirty round shields were carried before them by thirty warriors, and shone in the sun.'

La Tour would not have been a man of his time if his mind had not leapt to Eldorado, and to shields of gold.

'But not of gold, I think,' said Henri. 'They were too light for gold. A man could not carry so large a shield if it were gold. Copper? Burnished copper?'

'What else?'

'There was a ceremony. They were all taking part in some ceremony, or I could not have got close enough to hear them speak. But I could not see much. I could not stay long.'

'Do you know what ceremony?'

'There was a procession. There were women in the procession. And they were richly dressed.'

'In what colours?'

'White. And the shields were embossed with the heads of women.'

'Have you seen this before? Or anything like it?'

'No.'

La Tour spent the next hour alone with his thoughts. He recalled the fantastic tales of Eldorados, many Eldorados. He recalled the scarcely less fantastic story of Jesuit adventurers who had set out from Québec for this same wilderness, and returned half-crazed. He recalled the mandarin's cloak which one Jesuit had brought back to the governor at

Québec. Perhaps he had not bought it at Nantes after all? Perhaps he had found it in the interior. If the Indians wore rich clothes, had they got them by trading with the Chinese? All was legend. Everything was speculation. Should he turn back, when he might be so close? But to go on to the Indian town would be to risk everything. And from thoughts of women in rich gowns, a thing hitherto unknown among Indians, his mind went to Amadée, duchess of Gisors, Amadée now three years dead. Amadée, absurdly escaping in a brocaded gown splashed with mud. Amadée as he had first seen her at the banquet at Le Havre. Amadée, who had told him, when he asked, that her name meant Beloved of God. Were these richly dressed women of the Indians gods to them? Was that the meaning of the women's heads embossed on burnished shields?

La Tour went to his tent, where Rebekah and Ruth were lying asleep together, taking a siesta in the shade of the canvas awning. To him, it seemed that Ruth's face was softer than her sister's in repose. He pensively turned away from them. If they were sleeping, then Henri would not be far away. He glanced round, and there the man was, sitting on his haunches, with his boy next to him, steadily overlooking the tent where the women slept.

La Tour went to him, and gave his orders. All the men were to trim their beards and hair. The soldiers were to take their blue uniform coats, not worn since Québec, from the chest in the ship's bottom, and brush them as best they could, and shine the buttons. All muskets, swords, and other arms were to be oiled and polished till they shone. As for the trappers, never mind the heat, they were to take out their most sumptuous furs. The fleur-de-lis flag of France was to be taken from the chest where it also had lain since Québec, and washed so that the gold lilies would glisten against the white ground. The ship was to be dressed overall with bunting, signal flags, anything. All was to be ready before the men ate that evening. When it was done, then they could eat. Henri saw what his master was about, and roused the loafing soldiers and trappers to an activity that had for more than a year been unfamiliar to them. Sullenly, they did as they were ordered.

An hour before sunset Henri paraded the men before La Tour. They would not have done for the king's guard at St Germain, but they were a brave sight in a wilderness of swamps. He ordered them to parade again at first light, and dismissed them.

Rebekah and Ruth watched the display.

'And what is this?' said Rebekah, speaking for them both.

'Tomorrow,' he said, 'we shall make an easy, slow progress downstream, and camp early. Then the next day we shall move on again, and by midday arrive at a place where we have a great thing to do. I will tell you your part in it.'

Two days later, at noon, the idle banks of the Messipi saw a more splendid show than in all their previous history. Before the palisades of their vast town, the chiefs of the Natchez and tributary tribes, attended by three thousand warriors, stood in awesome silence to receive the strangers who came in a great ship. The principal chief was in a long white robe, and the lesser chiefs in shorter yellow cloaks. Before each chief sat a warrior carrying a white rush fan. The great chief was cooled by two warriors who stood beside him, making ceremonial passes with fans of feathers dyed to resemble peacock's tails. Before the chiefs crouched thirty warriors each holding a burnished shield which reflected the high sun. Each shield bore the likeness of a woman in profile. La Tour had seen the like only once before, on a voyage to Egypt. At the very front of all stood six women in white robes which covered them from shoulder to ankle. They were the six wives of the great chief, and were guarded by twelve warriors, armed with long spears, who were the tallest savages La Tour had ever seen. Behind them all lay the town, on the sharpened spikes of whose palisaded walls were impaled countless faces. They were not grinning, fleshless skulls, but recognizable human heads with their features baked by the sun to a mummified hardness. The central gates of the town were wide open, and through them could be seen not wigwams, but a thousand wooden huts, stretching into the distance. Each gatepost was decorated with a painted wooden eagle six feet tall.

And facing the great town were the French.

Their ship was moored to a wooden jetty, of a kind Henri had never seen at any Indian settlement. It signified that this tribe's canoes were larger than any Indian vessel yet known. The French soldiers, in vivid blue, were formed in one long rank, standing to attention and presenting arms. On either side of them the trappers stood, sweltering in their beaver furs but making a sumptuous show. Ten paces in advance of them, Henri stood holding aloft the fleur-de-lis, the white and golden ensign of France. His boy was beside him. Immediately behind the flag stod La Tour, between Rebekah and Ruth. The sisters were dressed in swathes of white silk, which had been intended for trade. La Tour wore the blue mandarin's robe bearing the emblem of the flying horse.

The principal chief and La Tour were fifty yards apart. They observed each other closely. The intention of each was clear in his own mind. La Tour's intention was to proclaim the Indians subjects of Louis XIV, king of kings, chief of chiefs, and to take possession of their lands in his name. The Natchez chief's intention was to kill La Tour and all the French. And thus they faced each other.

The first move was La Tour's. At a gesture from him, two soldiers, the one farthest to the right of the line and the one farthest to the left, slowly raised their muskets, pointed them to the sky, and fired into the air. The two reports, one rapidly following the other, cracked out like lightning, and echoed like thunder from the walls of the town. All the Indians gazed up and all round the blue sky, and a murmur rose among them, which was silenced by the chief, who held up his right hand. Once more, Indians and Frenchmen confronted each other, and still the Indians made no move. Then Henri stepped aside, holding the flag aloft, and La Tour with Rebekah on his right and Ruth on his left began a slow advance towards the principal chief where he sat. The chief rose, and, accompanied by an escort of two huge warriors, walked slowly forward to met La Tour.

His intention remained firm, to kill them all. La Tour and the sisters as they advanced, and the soldiers and trappers standing in unwavering line by the shore, were within a minute of their deaths. But then, when he had approached within twenty feet of La Tour, the chief stopped. La Tour and the women stood still too. The chief saw first the pattern of the running horses on La Tour's mandarin robe. Having seen that he looked first at Rebekah, and then at Ruth, saw that they were the same, and fell upon his knees. His escort knelt with him. The Indian women knelt, and the three thousand warriors, in one movement, prostrated themselves. La Tour received the adoration and homage of the gathered chiefs, warriors, and tribes of the Natchez.

The chief alone rose, facing La Tour and the twins, but shading his eyes as if to ward off the too-great glare of the sun. He spoke. La Tour beckoned Henri forward to translate. He said that as far as he could understand, the chief was welcoming La Tour as a god whose brightness extinguished the sun's, and from whose brightness a mere mortal had to shield his eyes. The chief bowed to La Tour, and then first to Rebekah and then to Ruth. The chief's own women followed his example. The warriors remained crouching with their faces in the dust. The great chief offered La Tour his whole domain, spreading his hands wide to indicate the lands which were his, and the city which was his, and entreating them to enter. La Tour, the sisters, and Henri entered and took possession of the great chief's hut, whose lofty roofs rose thirty feet high. La Tour sat on the chief's throne with Rebekah and Ruth on either side. The soldiers and trappers entered the camp two by two, and mounted a guard at the entrance of the chief's house. Then the chief himself entered with five of his lesser chiefs, who prostrated themselves and began with reverential speeches their entertainment of the gods. La Tour sat in splendour and concealed bewilderment, saying and revealing nothing, and learning little from Henri's fragmented translations. There were many things La Tour wanted to know, but he thought it unwise for an all-knowing god to make enquiries, and so kept silence and allowed the Natchez to entertain them.

First there was food, and then the sacred ceremonies of the tribe were enacted before him. The great chief brought in a young girl, his daughter, a lithe girl of perhaps fourteen years of age, and as she came face to face with Rebekah and Ruth, and looked them both in the face, the resemblance between her and them startled La Tour. It must have been a trick of the light, but the Indian girl appeared a younger Rebekah or Ruth. The face was more deeply olive, the hair longer and more deeply black, and the naked figure slighter, but in the dim light of the house she could have been their younger personification. Rebekah leaned forward to touch the girl's face and hair, and the girl returned a grave, unwavering regard, and then stepped into the centre of the house where the sun's high rays penetrated an opening in the roof and shone brilliantly on the baked earth floor. The girl lay on her back, and arched her body upwards, in the attitude of statues of ancient Cretan dancers that La Tour had seen in the Mediterranean. She remained poised in this way so that the sun penetrating the roof beams and travelling downwards in a shaft of golden light through the shady dimness of the house, fell on the silky maidenhair between the girl's shining legs, so that she was penetrated by the sun's rays, and warmed by them. Then she moved with pleasure, until with a cry she arched herself higher upwards towards the sun in a spasm, and then let herself subside to the ground, where she lay in an attitude of abandonment, and they saw that she slept. She was left there to sleep.

Then there was more feasting on wild pig, until in the afternoon, the rain came.

The Indians welcomed this as auspicious, and, so deeply immersed was La Tour in the intoxication of the ceremony that he too took the rain as a fortunate sign, though he had that morning, with his sailor's sixth sense, sniffed at the air and expected rain in spite of the clear skies. Then the rain started, first with the fall of a few heavy drops, so few but so heavy that the splash of each drop was heard on its own; and then with a patter; and then with the drumming of a torrent.

It was then that the chief, in an exaltation, pointed again to the figure of his daughter where she still lay on the floor. The sun had moved, so that the light now fell on her face. Because the sun was obscured by rain clouds it was no longer golden sunlight that fell on her, but daylight nevertheless, which revealed her throat and lips and her closed eyes. But though her eyes were closed, she was no longer asleep. For just as the sunlight had earlier penetrated the high roof, so now a few drops of rain came through and fell in slow, soft splashes on the girl's face and body. Each drop could be seen, as it fell, in the shaft of light. The eyes of everyone were on the girl. A drop fell on her cheek and rolled in a slow rivulet down to her throat, tracing the line of her cheekbone on its way. She extended her arm and caught a drop in her open hand. It rolled over the visible pulse in her wrist, and down the arm to her shoulder. Another drop splashed on her forehead, at which the Indians watching gave a cry of pleasure. This drop, forming its little river, flowed down onto her long eyelashes, gathered there, and then fell onto her cheek, as if it were a tear. This too was auspicious. The raindrops, falling at slow intervals, caressed the girl's body, one running between her breasts, another across her flat belly. When the girl's body was adorned by nine rivulets, which had been nine raindrops, another drop fell on her raised leg, and ran in a meandering river down the inside of her brown thigh until it lost itself in a swift flight into the silky fork of her legs. Then a sigh of completion arose from the watchers, because it was done. The girl's face was radiant in the shaft of light. Her lips moved, and then she slid her hands slowly down her body until they covered the division of her legs. It was done. The great god of the Natchez, who was master of the Sun and the Rain and the Thunder, had first, in the morning, caused the sun to go into the girl, which was a pleasure and warmth to her, and a preparation. She had slept. Then, in the afternoon, the great god of the Natchez in the heavens, had wept involuntary tears of joy, which were Rain, and his tears had fallen on the girl and entered her, and she had conceived a child, and, having conceived, had covered herself with her hands. And while the impersonal great god of the Natchez shed involuntary tears in the heavens, he appeared incarnate among the Natchez on earth in the person of La Tour, honouring the house of their great chief with his presence, and bringing with him to attend him the goddesses of the Sun and the Rain, who were twins. It was the Natchez legend that the great god had, in the beginning, created the heaven and earth with his involuntary tears. That day, with a tear, he had created a child within the girl, and that child would be born a great leader.

This was what the Natchez believed, and what La Tour later came to know through his own observations and Henri's enquiries. Only when he knew, which was much later, did he understand how fortunate he had been that day. The two French soldiers, firing muskets into the air, had created a small thunder, which was marvellous to the Natchez but would not alone have been enough to save the Frenchmen. La Tour, advancing, had worn the mandarin's robe of blue silk, but it was not its richness which struck the Natchez chief, but the pattern of running horses, for such an animal was a legend with them. Though again, that alone would not have deterred the chief from ordering all their deaths. It was the presence of Rebekah and Ruth that saved them all, for twinship was a central myth of the Natchez. The gods of the Rain and Sun, on whom their lives depended, and the success of their hunting and their crops, were known to be twins. So that when the chief saw the perfect twinship of Rebekah and Ruth, he and all his tribe bowed down to the great goddesses who had come among them. And La Tour, being evidently attended by such goddesses, was himself taken to be the greatest of all gods, the great god of heaven whom even the Sun and Rain obeyed, and whose tears had created the world.

By the end of the afternoon, La Tour had only a dim consciousness of all this, but he did know that he was taken for a god. So, through Henri, he made his ritual speech about Louis, king of kings, only this time he named him the Sun King and did not deny, though he did not assert, that he, La Tour, held sway over even so great a king as Louis. Henri translated this into the Sioux dialect of which he had a smattering, and the Natchez understood. Then La Tour went outside, and, accompanied by the goddesses of the Sun and the Rain, and surrounded by his soldiers, trappers, and carpenters, with Henri holding aloft the flag of the fleur-de-lis, carried out the intention with which he had started the day, and made a declaration in French.

This was the gist of it:

In the name of the most high, most mighty, most victorious and invincible Louis, the fourteenth of that name, by the grace of God King of France and Navarre, and in the name of his heirs and successors forever, La Tour took possession of all the lands south and west from the lake of the Hurons to the valley of the Messipi, and all lands lying there beside and around, and all lands farther to the south and west, as far as any savage tribes inhabited the land; and he took possession of all rivers, lakes, bays, lands, villages, towns, mines, fruits, crops, and everything that was within and upon the land, whose peoples by their free will, which they had signified, became thereafter the subjects of the aforesaid Louis, by the Grace of God King of France and Navarre, and now of the Messipi and of American New France.

They cried 'God Save the King,' fired a salute of twenty-one guns with their muskets, and sang the great hymn of the *Vexilla Regis* announcing that the banners of Heaven's king were thus advanced in that barbaric land and that the mystery of the Cross shone forth. And thus, in pouring rain, and in the name of a king not quite thirteen years old, surrounded by a force of seventeen exhausted Frenchmen standing in clothes sodden with the downpour, and attended by two women born in New England, Pierre La Tour, half-pay lieutenant, laid claim, in a voice inaudible at fifty yards, to the better part of an unknown continent.

That night, when the rain had at last stopped, the members of La Tour's party – honoured guests, revealed gods, and acknowledged lords of the earth – lay in their tents by the Natchez town, worn out by long travel, pitiless rain, and their hosts' relentless hospitality. At two hours to midnight, a flaming comet, of the magnitude of the sun, passed across the sky. It appeared not only over the Natchez camp, but in the skies of all the western hemisphere.

In Plymouth, where it was midnight, the ageing William Bradford looked up from his sleepless prayers and out over the surrounding forest, and saw the blazing star as a falling Lucifer. He believed that as surely as a rainbow was a sign of God's favour, such a prodigious sight as this must be a sign of His divine wrath. He had no one with him to comfort him, and saw from his small windows only groups of terrified townspeople gazing upwards at this sign of imminent doomsday.

Over Manhattan, where the clocks still lacked a few minutes to midnight, Peter Stuyvesant, drinking very late with Wolsey and O'Brien, gazed at the comet and repeated an old superstitious verse of his youth:

> *To herdsmen, sheeprot; and to ploughmen, hapless seasons;*
> *To sailors, storms; to cities, civil treasons.*

And then he laughed, full of the wine he had drunk, as Harry O'Brien said, 'Man, take heart. There's always sheeprot enough without comets. And you should make your ministers of religion more useful to you than the darkseeing sort you have in the Dutch church. Now we Catholics can take comfort in anything, and I'll remind you that when there was one comet that caused too much trouble, sheeprot, and the like, why, the Pope just put on his full canonicals and excommunicated it.' And this was true. But Wolsey paid little attention to the talk. Her mind was with her children, wherever they were that night, and she wondered whether the same comet was in their sky.

In London, where it was full morning, George Downing

saw the comet, bright even in daylight, and told his servant, who was babbling a story that at sunrise the comet had lit the city as if it were all ablaze, that men's minds were so eager for novelties that they would seize on a disaster as a welcome change from the ordinry; but that was the view of the common mass of people, he said, and of less weight than a feather.

At the palace of St Germain, near Paris, the boy king of France, Navarre, and, unknown to him, half America, was instructed by disinterested tutors, at his first lesson of the morning, that the comet overhead, which was shaped like a horse's mane, *equinus barbatus*, should be distinguished from those comets that were torch-shaped, *lampadiformus,* and from twenty-five other sorts, the most ominous of which was learnedly known as *monstriferus,* or horror-bringing. At which the boy said, 'We shall not be afraid.'

In the Natchez town, an exultant howl arose, for this comet was the confirmation of all the marvels they had seen that day. But outside his tent La Tour stood, as superstitious as any man of his day, pondering the significance of such a blazing star, and yet at the same time observing, as a sailor and navigator, that, though the head of the comet was dense and fiery, the stars were nevertheless visible through the nebulous tail that followed it halfway across the sky. Rebekah came out to him, saw the doubts in his face, and said, 'But when William the Conqueror, who was a Frenchman, was on his way to conquer England and saw such a comet, and his men were afraid, he replied that it was a sure sign that ahead of them lay a kingdom that wanted a king.'

La Tour looked up at the sky again, and then down at the boughs of yellow pine with which the Indians had encircled the tent, as an act of homage, and saw that in the comet's fiery light the yellow pine glowed red. Rebekah went back into the tent and lay down, and when La Tour came in after her, she opened her arms to him. He went to Rebekah, but as he did so he saw in the comet-lit darkness of the tent that Ruth was awake and that her eyes were on him and full of deep affection and love, which his heart returned.

PART FOUR

28

THE DEPARTURE OF THE GODS

The French American Empire being established, La Tour was left in two minds. Should he go on, or, having done what he had done, return? He had achieved more than any French explorer before him. He had come farther. But he had not found the Vermilion Sea. He knew his latitude: he knew how far south he was. He could measure that by the sun. Wherever this great river might lead him, it would not be to China. That was what his whole reason told him, and yet he could not be sure. Perhaps the great river might sweep westwards and lead him to the Orient. He did not know.

He took Henri aside, and candidly asked his advice.

Henri said, 'I have been talking among the Natchez. Not one of them has ever said that the Messipi turns westwards. No one has ever seen a great river flowing west. There is nothing in the tradition of the tribes that says it does. There *is* a tradition that other gods visited the town long ago, before us, but I can make no sense of it.'

'And our men?' asked La Tour. 'How are they?'

'They will not pass for long as the attendants of gods,' said Henri. 'Their uniforms are sweated through. And they are tired. I would not answer for their health if we pushed farther south. When the Natchez talk about the south, they sound afraid. They say there is nothing but fever and death there.'

'What fever?'

'Men bleed from their skins, fall down, turn yellow, and their vomit is black. I do not know it. But they will not go south where the fever is. They said, besides, that there is a mosquito which breeds in hordes, not in swamps, but in the trees.'

'And yet,' said La Tour, 'they might be concealing an ocean from us.'

Henri shrugged. 'Except that they believe you to be a god, to whom nothing is unknown, and from whom nothing can be concealed.'

But La Tour sent Henri to talk to the Indians again. He told them stories of the cold north, and beaver, and snow, and ice which formed a shining crust on the lakes so that the great god La Tour could walk on the water. In return, they told him the traditions of their history. They did not think Henri a god, and therefore he could ask and be told. But it was not in this way that he gained the single piece of information that told La Tour what he would never achieve. It was the Indians' custom to exchange gifts, rather to their advantage, even with gods. Each evening Henri brought back some token from the Natchez, a carved bow, a bronze shield, a wooden eagle. Each morning Henri took some gift in return. This commerce itself meant that the French could not stay too long. They were running out of merchandise to give. Then on the third evening Henri came to La Tour with a wooden casket from the great chief. It was only a foot long, but it was of sandalwood. La Tour turned the fragrant wood over in his hands, and his heart leaped. He knew of no sandalwood in America. It was a wood that came from India and the east.

'Or from Europe,' said Henri.

La Tour looked sharply at him.

'By way of Europe,' said Henri.

'It is *sandalwood*,' said La Tour, placing the box in Henri's hands. 'Put it to your nose. The scent of it, man. There is no such wood in Europe.'

Henri did not put the box to his nose. Instead, he opened the box, and took from it a dark, skinlike object.

'What is it?'

'I cannot read,' said Henri.

'Read?' said La Tour, taking the skin from him and seeing for the first time that it was an ancient parchment, on which the writing could barely be made out.

'Paulus IV P.P.,' it began, and then continued, reciting these titles in Latin:

Paulus IV P.P., Bishop of Rome, Vicar of Christ, Prince of the Apostles, Supreme Pontiff of the Western Church, Patriarch of the West, Archbishop and Metropolitan of the Province of Rome....

To it was attached a heavy seal of lead, bearing on one side the likeness of St Peter, and on the other that of St Paul. It was a Papal Bull, and whatever it said, it was evidence that white men had been there before, or been near. La Tour's achievement, to have come so far, to have come as he imagined farther than any man before, was dashed from him. He bowed his head in the bitterness of disappointment, and then, with hands trembling, tried to read the rest of the document. It was addressed to a Spaniard whose name La Tour could not decipher, and excused the Spaniard and his party from fasting during Lent in their voyage of holy discovery in the great lands and over the great seas west of Florida. The date was 1555. The Spaniards had seen the Messipi nearly one hundred years before him. La Tour went to his tent, and recorded in his journal the finding of the Bull. 'My God,' he wrote, 'to think that we have come so far, to be so late.' Then he wept.

Henri could not read, and La Tour did not at first tell him the meaning of the document, but he knew what he needed to know. The parchment was no Indian writing. The Natchez might say that it was a gift made to them by earlier gods, but he knew, as well as if he could have read Latin, that white men had been there before them. It did not surprise him as much as it did La Tour. Starved Rock was many months back, but Henri had seen there what no one else had noticed. He had seen the hand that stretched out from the foot of the cliff to cut the rope on which the bucket was lowered into the river. He had seen the glint of a knife in that hand, and had known then that the Iroquois had steel knives. Steel knives could come from far away, from the French or the English, but this small discovery had prepared Henri against the shock of a much larger one. It was his instinct to comfort La Tour. It was also his instinct to leave him alone in his first bitterness. Henri walked away, and Rebekah and Ruth, seeing him go, went to La Tour, whom they found staring at the charts, which had taken him two summers and a winter to make, and then from the charts to the ancient Papal Bull which he had replaced in its sandalwood box.

He told them.

Ruth said nothing.

Rebekah said, 'Then there is a sea, and we shall reach it.'

'There is a sea, but it would not be a sea to China, and, by a hundred years, I would not be the first to reach it by way of the Messipi.'

'No one would know that,' said Rebekah.

'But I should know it. Besides, which is more to the point, it is *not* a way to China. Poor Villeneuve will remain governor of a seminary at Québec, not governor of China. I am sorry for that.'

He laughed, and only Ruth saw his utter desolation, and took him in her arms and comforted him.

The departure of the gods was staged, three days later, with as great ceremony as their arrival. As a farewell gift, the great chief presented La Tour with another box, this time made of the bark of yellow pine. It contained six bones, which the chief had that morning dug up and washed with his own hands. They were the humerus, radius, and ulna of a left arm, and those of a right. They were said to be relics of a god. La Tour wondered grimly if those bones had ever helped human hands to unfold the Papal Bull which he was taking away as another gift. He gravely presented the chief with a copy of the proclamation by which Louis XIV had taken possession of all his lands, and the Natchez made homage in their many thousands to their incarnate gods as they set off, rowing slowly against a steady current which they would have to fight for months. As it happened, La Tour was turning north when the Gulf of Mexico lay only two hundred miles to his south, but the Natchez had not lied to him when they said they did not know of it, and by turning back La Tour saved the lives of his men who would have fallen, as the Spanish had, to the yellow fever. Of that party of Spaniards, a hundred years before, and of all their discoveries, the only remains were the sandalwood box and the Papal Bull which La Tour carried with him. Not one Spaniard had survived to return to Spain. And though he had not found China, La Tour was carrying back to Québec an empire vaster than Europe.

Of them all, Rebekah had lost most. The men rejoiced to be going home, even against the current. La Tour had his charts and his proclamation. But Rebekah had lost everything. When, on the first night of the previous winter, in the camp of the Arkansas, she had given Ruth to La Tour, she had not known what she did. She had done it in an exercise of her own power, but in doing so she had lost that power. If it had been a reasoned, rational act on her part, she might have foreseen the results. She might have seen that to share La Tour would be to share power over him. Even then, had she reasoned in this way, she could not have foreseen that the gentler Ruth would touch La Tour more deeply than she herself did. She could not have foreseen that La Tour would love this gentleness. But what Rebekah had done had owed nothing to reason. It was an act of sheer instinct. Throughout their lives, the twins had possessed together whatever they had possessed. On Manhattan, the greater part of their distinction had been that they were twins. They were both beautiful, but so were other girls. It was because of their twinness that Rebekah and Ruth were particularly distinguished from all other children, and then from all other young women. When they were admired, it was always a shared admiration, and the world *had* admired them. When they went boldly to Breuckelen, it was an adventure that they shared. When they returned they had shared the fame of the exploit, and they had shared the little white deer they brought back with them. It was instinct. In sharing La Tour, Rebekah had for the first time been betrayed by her instinct. In a way unthought of by her, and unthinkable to her, she had lost a power which was habitual to her. The loss was huge, but gradual. The twins were so alike in so many ways, even in the closest ways, or almost the closest ways. Sometimes, in the night, La Tour had not known whose hand it was that caressed him, or whose breast his head lay on. He could not tell their voices apart. It was possible for him to enter one of the sisters, and not know which. But in the deepest of times, he was never in doubt. It was not only that Ruth, though she was as subtle as Rebekah, was often gentler. It was more than that. When the embrace was most profound, and shaking, then it was always Ruth, and he knew it could only be Ruth. And a month after they left the Natchez town it was apparent that a child was to be born, and not to Rebekah but to Ruth.

Henri knew that it was Ruth, but none of the other men could tell the two sisters apart. Neither did the men know that they had travelled so far to reach a place visited one hundred years before by the Spanish. La Tour and Henri thus shared great confidences, which La Tour knew Henri would keep. At first they made haste on their return journey. They passed the camp of the Arkansas, where they could have rested. They did not, but pressed on. Then all events conspired against them. Twice they ran aground in the shallows of the sluggish Messipi. A soldier out hunting was killed by a buffalo that turned on him. Four men suffered from fever, and La Tour called a halt so as to quarantine them from the others. The fever passed. The men recovered, but a week was lost. Then, when frayed rigging needed to be replaced, they found that their stock of cordage was gone. The Natchez had surely not stolen from their gods? Probably it had been the Arkansas. But the cordage was gone. With sail now necessarily shortened, they could not make the best of what favourable winds there were, and had to row nearly all the time. Tired men became exhausted. Exhausted men grew ill. They had not wished to winter again in the wilderness. They had hoped to reach Québec before October. Now it was plain they could not.

La Tour said, as they took another forced rest, 'We are not halfway.'

Henri agreed. They had not reached the Ohio. They were still on the Messipi. The river Illinois and Starved Rock were a month's hard voyaging ahead of them. The Ohio and the Lakes were further still, and unattainable.

'We have to winter,' said Henri. 'We can push on north a while, but then we will winter hard and cold. Or we can stay here, and winter early, and warmer, and start earlier in the spring next year. And there is the child to be born.'

'It is impossible to make Québec this season?' asked La Tour, knowing the answer.

'A man moving fast and alone could not do it now. I could not do it.'

'Then we must stay here. Make camp.'

'No. Rest here again, captain. Then north for just another month, slowly. We should be able to start again very early next spring, but even then you would not want to have to go too far to reach Québec. We do not know that we shall winter as easily this year as we did with the Arkansas. I hope it is not too hard.'

'For the women?' La Tour assumed this was Henri's meaning.

'The women are strong and young. Even with the child to come, they are both strong. No, it is the soldiers. The trappers will not be worried by a winter. It is the soldiers that are weaker than they look. Those who took the fever were soldiers.'

So they continued north for another month, slowly. These early weeks of her pregnancy were bad for Ruth. She was often sick, and could eat only in the evenings, and when she could not eat, Rebekah could not either. Rebekah's old preeminence was lost altogether – her power over La Tour, even her lifelong ascendancy over Ruth. Now Ruth was pregnant, it was she who led, sick as she was. The old bonds of twinship asserted themselves strongly, but now it was Rebekah who, as it were, imitated Ruth. It was Ruth who determined even Rebekah's state of health. When Ruth's hair lost its shine, as it did in those early months, so did Rebekah's. The impending birth of La Tour's child, a child not to be hers, had destroyed Rebekah's love for her husband. As his wife, she was indifferent to him. La Tour was constantly with Ruth, who wanted his presence; and Rebekah, as Ruth's sister, detested the man who came between them. But the early months were the worst, and they passed. By the fourth and fifth months, when Ruth's glow and vitality were restored to her, Rebekah recovered hers.

As Henri had feared, it was not an easy winter. They did not suffer the bitter cold which would have overtaken them on the Ohio or the Lakes. That was a cold which in their present state would have killed them. La Tour, having to keep up appearances, just managed to do so. Henri and his boy maintained their strength, as did the trappers, but the soldiers grew gaunt, listless, and tattered. The carpenters, when they were put to work repairing the ship's timbers, grumbled, and did it only to preserve their share in what they now saw to be a failed expedition. The boy king Louis might have his empire, but the carpenters would certainly not be sharing in the riches of a Cathay they had never found. When they were ordered to build huts for the men as well as themselves, they were rebellious. Henri took them aside and pointed out that the soldiers, wretched as they were, still had muskets, and that what food there was came from the trappers, who could decline to feed the carpenters. The carpenters built the required huts.

On a fine blue winter's day in January, when Rebekah had left them for a while, La Tour and Ruth talked together.

'If the child is a girl,' she said, 'shall we call it Wolsey? If it is a boy I shall call it Pierre, for you, and Robert, after my older brother, who died young. He shall be called Pierre

Robert. Pierre is for you. Robert is for my mother. She never spoke about him unless she was asked.'

'But of course you did ask?'

'We asked. At first she simply said that he had died young. Then, when we were eight or nine, I cannot remember quite when, she told us that our father had taken Robert into the snow one winter's night, when they were at Plymouth.'

La Tour knew this. Not that Rebekah had ever told him, but it was still known to a few in Manhattan, who had known Wolsey for a long time. Dark Anne, who worked at the Swan, the chambermaid who had woken him on his first day in Manhattan, knew.

'Why did he do that?' asked La Tour.

'Our mother told us, because she said if we did not learn it from her we should very likely learn it from others, or from rumours, or from anyone who had been at Plymouth. She said it was winter, and there was deep snow, but that he was a man who never admitted that it could be cold. He had brought them there, you see, and could not admit that it was not always the warm and pleasant land he had promised them.'

'But why harm the boy?'

'Robert?'

'Yes. Why?'

'Because he did not believe that he *was* harming him. To him, the snow was never cold. He was not taking the boy into the cold, only for a walk in the woods.'

'And I have brought you for a walk in the woods, and it has lasted two summers and two winters,' said La Tour.

'Two summers and two winters. But you did not want to bring me. I wanted to come.'

'Rebekah made you come.'

'Perhaps. But I came.'

'And you really wished not to?'

'I *should* not have come,' said Ruth.

'Because of your mother?'

'Because of her.'

They were sitting one each side of a smouldering wood fire.

'And you feel remorse that you did not go back to your mother?'

'I did. I do. But there are two things, two separate things. I know I should not have left my mother. I broke my word to my mother. And to Harry. I made you break your word.'

'No. Rebekah made me do that.'

'I broke my word and I am sorry for that, and more sorry still that I should have left my mother alone. But that is one thing. There is another. If I had not come, there would not have been you, and how could I be sorry to have come with you? And,' she said, putting a hand to her belly, 'there would not have been this. And how could I be sorry for this? A child. Your child. How could I be sorry?'

The words touched him, and he knew this was one of those few moments when the sisters, so much the same women, were so different in spirit. He knew what this difference was. It was that Ruth's was a loving spirit. He had loved two women in his life. Poor Amadée, beloved of God, and dead; and Ruth. Rebekah was his wife, and she had held him in fascination. That might be as great a thing as love, but it was different. He loved Ruth.

And what was to happen when they returned to Québec and Manhattan? La Tour did not talk about this to Ruth. Ruth and her child would be something he would have to account for to Wolsey, and to Harry, when the time came.

'So Pierre Robert then,' said Ruth. 'We never knew anything about that night in the snow until my mother told us. I remember nothing about it. But we were too young, eighteen months old or so. And yet when we look out at the snow together, Rebekah and I, there is something we fear.'

'Fear?' said La Tour. He knew no more than that Wheaton had taken his son into the woods. He did not know that he had also taken the twins. Rebekah and Ruth themselves did not know that.

So when he asked, 'Fear?' Ruth said, 'We are only afraid

when we see snow together. That is strange. Last night, when we *were* looking together out over the snow, we both thought we saw a movement by the riverbank. It was a bird, I suppose. But the moment we saw it, there was a shiver of that old fear. The fear I was talking about. It is nothing. We have both felt it since we were children, as far back as we can remember. It was that old thing.'

La Tour sat with her until Rebekah returned, and then went over to Henri. La Tour had seen no river birds lately. Could it have been a single scouting Indian from a nearby tribe?

'Henri,' he said, asking what he knew was a wild question, 'Henri, are we being followed?'

The half-caste looked into La Tour's eyes. He had not thought his commander had seen the sliding, silent savages who had trailed them. 'All the way from the Natchez town,' he said at last. 'There are two of them. There have never been more than two, and they have kept their distance, so I have let them be. But yes.'

'It is nothing?'

'It is not nothing. But there are only two.'

'Do the others know?'

'I do not want an alarm, and by themselves they will not see. They do not know. Only the two of us. I shall watch.'

The child was born on a day which, by La Tour's reckoning, was the first of March, 1651. It was not a long or a difficult labour. Ruth was brave. Rebekah was intent, devoting herself to her sister and not stirring from her side. La Tour paced up and down, hearing Ruth's cries, and trying to banish from his mind the cries of Amadée, and of her sudden slipping away at Honfleur. Henri stayed with La Tour through the night. At the fourth hour of labour, Ruth screamed, a sound of a different nature from her previous cries, and Henri rose and went silently into the cabin with the two women. Rebekah did not oppose him, and it was his hands that delivered the child. As he later told La Tour, when he was asked, he had done it before in the forest, three times, so he knew a little, which was perhaps more than Rebekah. It had been very nearly straightforward. The mother was well. So was the child, which was a boy.

La Tour himself baptized the child, holding him wrapped in the silk mandarin's robe, dabbing him on the forehead with river water from the Messipi, and naming him Pierre Robert. He recorded the birth and baptism in his journal. Ruth lay in the wilderness with her newborn baby, and was happy. From that day on, Rebekah excluded La Tour utterly. The child should have been hers, but she was bitter not against Ruth but against La Tour. The child, though not hers, was closer to her than La Tour, as being part of Ruth, her twin, and to that extent part of Rebekah herself.

Henri, watching the women closely, seeing Ruth's love for the child and for La Tour, and Rebekah's for Ruth, and Rebekah's deadly coldness to La Tour, would have said that Rebekah hated her husband.

When the child was three weeks old and could travel, they struck camp and moved on. La Tour, looking round at his ruined band, calculated that they would reach Québec by late summer. Henri, seeing the same men embark, thought they would make Québec by September, in time to survive, most of them; three or four of the soldiers would die.

Then it was all very sudden. At dawn on the second day of their voyage north, as they were making breakfast, twenty figures came upon them out of the half light. It did not have the appearance of an attack. The twenty men were walking slowly towards the French, but why at dawn? Then the French saw that the central figure was that of a young chief, before whom was carried a bronze polished shield which, as the line advanced, caught and reflected the first rays of the sun.

La Tour and Henri stood together.

'There were two yesterday as usual,' said Henri under his breath.

'Natchez? Why?'

Henri never had a chance to reply because one demoralized soldier, fearing a massacre, fired his musket and the Natchez fell upon them.

It was never intended as a massacre, but how could the French have known? Henri, had he been given time for a reply, would have told La Tour that the chief wanted to talk. A massacre could after all have been more easily achieved in the night.

But when the soldier fired, it became a rout. Nine Frenchmen died in thirty seconds, pierced through with arrows. Six more ran, and were struck down with tomahawks. La Tour was cut down as he dived to protect Ruth.

In the ensuing silence the river waters could be heard lapping at the hull of the French ship. The dawn birds were singing. The young Natchez chief surveyed the scene and saw only the women alive. His warriors would not have touched them. Ruth crouched over the body of La Tour, and Rebekah was sheltering Ruth. The chief glanced down at La Tour, whose death had not been intended. He walked towards the twins, took them by the hair, and raised them both, looking searchingly into their faces. Rebekah cursed him with wild eyes. Ruth met his stone gaze with silent defiance. The chief jerked his head to summon a warrior. Still holding both sisters by the hair, one in each hand, he again looked steadily at each in turn, and then turned Ruth's head sideways. At this the warrior killed her sacrificially, piercing the temple presented to him with a narrow blade.

The chief released Ruth and she fell dead, unmarked except for a crimson spot in the temple.

He released Rebekah and she stood unmoving.

The Natchez left as silently as they had come. They did not touch the bodies, or the tents, or the ship. They stole nothing. They would not loot the property of gods, or of gods come temporarily down to earth in human shape. The Natchez still believed them to be gods, and that was why they killed them.

When La Tour had left their town, the Natchez were downcast at their departure, hoped that they would return next summer, and confidently expected them to do so. They had followed La Tour's party in order to escort the gods and do them honour. There were twenty Indians, but they had moved so silently and skilfully that even Henri had never seen more than two at a time. They had not disturbed the gods in their winter camp, thinking this discourteous. But when La Tour broke camp and began to travel north into Chickasaw country, the Natchez were no longer friendly. Those whom they had welcomed as gods they did not now wish to see depart from their lands on to the lands of the Chickasaw and of other Indian nations, their enemies, who would be strengthened by the presence of such gods. All their legends told them that the power of the great god came from the twin goddesses of the Sun and the Rain. The divinity was in the unbroken twin, the two in one. If one sister was killed, then the twin would be broken, the power of the gods diminished, and the gods made less capable of assisting an enemy. That morning the young chief intended to kill one twin, and that was all. He did not intend a massacre. He was awed by the death of La Tour, which was farthest from his intention. When he held Rebekah and Ruth by the hair he had looked into their faces to determine which was the stronger of the two, for Natchez theology was that one twin was always stronger than the other, and the source of their joint power. That morning he saw, rightly, that Ruth was the stronger. She had been since Rebekah gave La Tour to her, and especially since she bore his child. So Rebekah, throughout her life until then the stronger, was discarded as the weaker, and it saved her life. The Natchez left her living, having no further concern with her. Theirs had not been a war party sent to slaughter and rob, but an élite band intent on making one single sacrifice.

The Natchez moved out of sight, and still Rebekah stood where the chief had left her. All around her lay the dead. Then there was at last a movement, and Henri, old campaigner, rose covered in river mud from the reeds into which he had thrown himself and the child, Pierre Robert, whom he had, when the agony of the moment was upon him, chosen to save rather than his own beloved half-caste boy, who lay dead with his skull opened by the single blow of a tomahawk.

Rebekah, coming to her senses, gazed down in terror at her twin sister, seeing in Ruth her own dead body, and the death of herself.

29

A FEW SONGS SUNG

Later in the same year that the power of the gods was broken on the banks of the Messipi, an infinitely smaller misfortune overtook a woman in faraway Manhattan. It was a great misfortune to her because she was helpless, and yet she bore it stoically because she had never expected better. What happened was that the ownership of the Swan changed hands, and the new publican had no use for thin, dark Anne – not as a singer, not as a chambermaid. He was not a hard man, and would have kept her as a stable servant, but she was afraid of horses. She had nowhere to go and took to sleeping rough in the streets in the cold nights of late autumn. All her friends had been passing friends, ship's mates staying at the Swan between voyages, and then after a while never returning to that port. Her lovers had been passing lovers of the same sort. She remembered one of them with love, and most of the rest with affection. A few had taken her into their beds for only one night, and then gone, but she remembered them too, if not their names then something about them – a tone of voice, a word, the gift of a ribbon or of a trinket. One sailor, a mate in the Dutch East India service, had remembered her well enough to send her a gift of a skirt-length. He had promised it, but she had forgotten his promise. He had never returned himself, but a year later a sailor from a Dutch ship out of Amsterdam left a package for her at the Swan, and it was the skirt-length, of dark green wool. She had never been a whore. All her men remembered her with affection, as she did them. She still wore the dark green skirt, though she no longer remembered the name of the man who gave it to her. She was still wearing the dark green skirt, now very ragged, in the first few days after she was put out of the Swan. It was the only skirt she had. She also had a worn, stuff cloak, and she huddled in these two garments in the doorways of the main streets until the constables moved her on, and then in the side streets until she was moved on again, and then down by the wharves where the constables never went. The sailors let her stay, and occasionally tossed her food or coins.

She would not go to the doss-houses where she could still have earned a living of sorts by robbing drunken and broken-down sailors. She would not do this. She had never stolen. She would not go to the poorhouse either, or not yet, because she was too proud. The only person in the world to whom she could have gone for help was Harry O'Brien, but he was at sea. She could have gone to Wolsey. She knew Wolsey would not have refused her. But she could not ask help from another woman, and not from O'Brien's wife. She did not approach the house. She kept well away from it. She became aimless. She did not know whether, in sleeping by the wharves, she was really waiting there for Harry O'Brien to return. She was confused and not sure of even that. But she always stayed by the riverside.

It was a cold evening at the end of November when the *Vliegende Hert* came to her moorings. It was almost dark. There had been light enough to come through the Narrows, but O'Brien would never ordinarily have pressed on in near-darkness. He would have anchored far out in the harbour and waited for morning, before coming up to Manhattan. But that night he had news, and brought the ship in himself, with his mates sounding the channels they all knew so well, and making for the lights of the city. He jumped from the cutter on to the wooden quay. Two men with torches, who had half seen, half heard the ship drop anchor in the North River, and waited for employment, came up to him to light him home.

'One of you,' he ordered, 'run to my wife. Tell her there is news. And you, stay with me.' The young man ran ahead. O'Brien followed, attended by the other linkman. Seeing the light and hearing O'Brien's voice, Anne came forward from the porch of a storehouse where she had been sheltering. He did not see her and was hurrying past when she caught his arm.

He looked and saw a ragged woman.

'Sir,' she said, 'I would not ask....'

'Come to the house tomorrow,' he said, not recognizing her.

'Sir....'

'Not now,' he said, and was about to pass on when she crumpled at his feet.

'Bring a light then, man,' he called out impatiently, and the linkman came back and held the torch to show the woman's face.

Now O'Brien recognized her.

'How long has she been like this?' he asked.

'Maybe a week. Since she was turned away from the Swan,' said the linkman. Then the man turned to Anne, who was still unconscious. 'Come on then, my dear, out of the way with you then,' he said, and began to drag her back to the porch.

O'Brien stopped the fellow sharply. 'Don't lug her like that.' He looked round. The ship's cutter had already put back. He could not leave the woman here, and he could not put her aboard the *Vliegende Hert* for the night without more delay than he could afford, so he picked her up in his arms and told the linkman to lead on.

She was easy to carry, she was so light. 'Holy Mary,' said O'Brien, 'she's no more than skin and bones.'

At O'Brien's house the other linkman was waiting with Susannah in the open doorway. Both looked at him unbelievingly.

'Where's Wolsey?' he asked. 'Susannah?'

Susannah replied that she did not know, that she thought she was at the governor's, but did not know for sure. She had taken a Dutch manservant with her, so she would be safe. All the while Susannah was saying this, her eyes were on the woman in O'Brien's arms, whom she well knew.

'Then send to the governor's house. You,' this to the younger linkman, 'run to the governor's. If my wife's not there, find out where. Tell her I'm here. Tell her there's news.'

Then he said to Susannah, 'Is there a room ready?'

She led the way upstairs and opened the door of the room next to hers, near the head of the stairs, and asked, 'Shall I take her, sir?'

O'Brien carried Anne over to the bed. 'Bring some light. Set a fire. See to some food for her.'

A Dutch maid brought candles. O'Brien laid Anne on the bed, gently rolled her over to take the ragged cloak from her shoulders, and then let her lie back again.

The maid watched, stupefied. 'Set a fire,' O'Brien repeated, and she went to fetch wood.

O'Brien looked down at Anne. 'No more than skin and bones,' he had thought as he carried her from the wharf. Well, she had always been light to carry. As she lay there on the bed he remembered carrying her on other occasions, for other purposes, long ago. She had always been light, but he had not thought of her as skin and bones then. She had been a sweet girl, a warm, light girl. Here was a sleeping face he remembered. It was the same face, or what the years had made of it. He remembered her lightness in everything, and her helplessness. She had been helpless when she approached him in the dark at Plymouth on his first visit, twenty-five years before. She had been helpless when she approached him tonight on the wharf at Manhattan. And between, lay the small, remembered events of one woman's life. A few men embraced, a few songs sung. He stroked her hair. Where it had been dark, it was now grey. Where it had been soft, it was now coarse. The lines on her forehead that had once appeared only when she was puzzled, or when she was afraid he would leave her, as he had left her, were now deeply scored even as she lay in repose. Thin, dark Anne.

But now only the eyelashes were dark.

Even the eyes were not dark now, but lighter, and duller. Susannah and a Dutch servant were busying themselves lighting a fire in the room when Anne came fully back to consciousness. She opened her eyes, and he saw that their colour was faded.

'Oh, sir,' she said, 'I was cold.'

'There is a fire now.'

'Sir, I should not have done it. I should not have stopped you. But I was cold.'

He took her hand. It was icy, and he held it between both his hands and chafed it.

'They turned me away from the Swan, and I was cold. I waited for you. I know it was not right, sir, but I had to wait for you.'

'If I was away, you should have come to my wife.'

'It was not my place, sir.'

'Girl!' he said softly. 'Girl! Why not?'

'Girl?' she said, and tears came to her eyes. It was the name by which he had called her in the few weeks they were together. O'Brien had forgotten this, and she saw he had forgotten.

'First,' she said, 'I sang songs. At the Swan, where you got me a place, sir. I sang about getting a husband.'

'Hush. You are all right now. You will not be cold any more.'

'And I saw your fine lady when you brought her home, sir, with the twins. And when you married her, I waited with the others and saw you, when the governor married you.'

'Girl,' he said, 'hush, hush. We'll get you some food.'

'And then the wedding of Mr La Tour and Rebekah, when she was grown up. I was there, sir, and heard the singing, and saw the feasting, and heard the cannons shooting off, and saw Rebekah's wedding gown. Gold thread. Outside, we waited and saw it all, you see, sir, and when the feast was done they gave us all that was left over, sir. I had a quail that they gave me to take away, in jelly, in aspic. I never saw that before, or tasted it since. And then when both twins went to Breuckelen, but that was before.'

'That was before. You helped us find them.'

'They have been gone a long time now.'

'They are all right. They are all right now,' said O'Brien. And where, where, he asked himself, was Wolsey? Where was she?

'You are tired,' said O'Brien. 'You fainted. Now you must eat, and then sleep.'

Anne looked sharply around in alarm, realizing for the first time that she was in O'Brien's house. She tried to get up, but fell back.

Then she said, 'I always sang about a husband, and a sofa with a spring in it, and a man who would bewilder me, and get me half a dozen children. I never got a husband, sir. And oh, Harry, I only ever wanted one man for my husband, sing about it as I might, there was only one I ever....'

O'Brien turned his head, saw Susannah and the Dutch servant standing astonished by the fire, and waved them out of the room.

'I *was* yours, Harry. In your cabin and when you brought me to Manhattan. And ever afterwards, when there were other men, I wanted you. Other men were kind, but I only wanted you. When I sang I thought of you. And sometimes after I sang, and a fine man from a grand ship would dance with me, and give me wine to drink, and court me for the night, it was you who courted me. My night dreams were dreams of you, and my day dreams.'

'Oh, girl, hush, hush.'

But Anne would not be quiet. She raised herself and held O'Brien by the shoulders so that he could not gently release himself. And then, since there is truth in distress, she spoke out her heart.

'Harry, I always told you I was yours. And you said, "Girl, sweet girl," and loved me. And Harry, I gave you everything I had to give, and promised everything I had to promise. And you said, "Girl, girl," and loved me, and I shall never forget it, though it was only for a while. I have seen you at ever so many banquets, sir. But that was afterwards. You did love me, and I shall never forget it, though it was only for a while.'

Anne lay back. She was calm now.

Harry O'Brien stroked her head again, rose to his feet, and saw Wolsey standing in the open doorway. She could have been there since he had motioned the servants to leave.

'I was at the governor's,' she said.

She came over to Anne, who turned her face away into the pillow as if to hide. Harry saw them both together. Wolsey was five years older than Anne, but looked ten years younger. She sat on the bed and turned Anne's face to her.

Anne drew away.

'Anne, how can you be afraid of me? You do not need to be. You shouldn't be. You know me. You know Susannah. She will look after you tonight and give you a drink to make you sleep, and then will you talk to me tomorrow? You should have known you could come here. But we will talk about that tomorrow.'

They left Anne with Susannah. Outside, on the landing, Wolsey held out her hands to O'Brien and he took them and told her, 'Wolsey, listen, the children are safe.'

She came into his arms and he told her what he knew.

'We spoke a French ship off Long Island, off Montauk. Her captain said that the morning he left Québec there was news that La Tour's party had been sighted two days upriver. That was late October. He had no details. But he said, when I asked him, that the women were safe. And he said there was a child.'

Wolsey and O'Brien lay talking late into the night. The news wonderfully restored her. Only Harry and Susannah had noticed it, and perhaps Stuyvesant, but she had begun to despair. That summer, O'Brien had made a passage to Québec on purpose to enquire, and found that the governor had received no reports of La Tour for a year. He had returned and put as good a face on it as he could. Wolsey had said little, and revealed less. But he had known her fears. Now Ruth and Rebekah were safe. It was a blow that a voyage to Québec was impossible at this late season. It was a blow that a few more months of separation had to be faced. But Wolsey's daughters were alive. That was the report, and she was happier than she had been since the day they had left.

When they had talked and talked about this news, O'Brien said at last, 'And there is Anne. I found her by the wharf yesterday evening, when I came back.'

'The linkman and Susannah told me. Mighty astonished they were, to see you carrying her.'

It was dark, and Harry could not see Wolsey smile.

He asked, 'And did you hear what Anne was saying tonight?'

'I think there are some people in Manhattan who could have told you that she always watches for you when she can, and I think I could have told you that she loved you. They all know Anne. I have never heard her called anything but Anne. What is her second name?'

O'Brien said nothing for a long while. Then he said, 'I do not know, and I have never known. And it has been twenty-five years.'

There was nothing more to be said after that. Anne would stay for a while, and then Wolsey would ask Stuyvesant to give her a place in his household. Wolsey remembered that it was Anne who had helped them to find the twins when they went to Breuckelen. She remembered that it was Anne she had heard singing as she drifted to sleep on her first night in O'Brien's house.

Wolsey's last words to Harry, before they both went to sleep, were, 'And they said there was a child.'

And he replied, 'They did.'

30

THE FLIGHT TO
ST GERMAIN

Rebekah sat on a window seat in the governor's modest palace at Québec city, overlooking the St Lawrence and a landscape of ice. Ice piled high on the frozen river; ice in the shrouds and rigging of the ships trapped by the shore for the winter in the grip of the ice; ice on the steep, narrow streets of the town which made them impossible to climb; newformed ice that had to be cleared, swept, and chipped hourly from the baulks of wood laid down between house and house to make pathways; icy rain that fell slanting from the sky and lacerated any part of the face that was left for a moment uncovered; ice that formed in the air before a man as he breathed; ice that kept Québec a city separated from the world and out of the world for the whole of the long winter. As Rebekah looked she saw the bough of a maple split and heard it crack under the weight of ice that had formed along its length. It was a high bough, apparently made of ice because wholly encased in it to a depth of inches, but as it fell from its height onto the ground, which was ice, the bough's casing shattered with the impact as if it were glass, and the living wood of the branch was revealed for the first time since the first snows of the fall. But by next day it would be dead wood, and covered with new ice. No birds flew. No animals were seen. The wind would chill a man caught outside, and kill him in ten minutes. The city was imprisoned by the ice, and Rebekah within it.

She looked across the room at the cradle in which the

child lay, a fine boy now ten months old. By the fire sat Henri, guarding the child and the fire. At her glance he placed another log on the blaze, not tossing it on, but placing it carefully and prudently. In midwinter, wood was precious. Then he went back to his seat and continued to sew the rawhide sole of a moccasin to its soft leather upper with a sinew thread. He was defter with the bone needle than Rebekah had seen any woman.

'How much longer before the ice breaks?' It was a question she had asked many times in the past months.

Henri replied, not looking up from his work, 'In three months it will begin to crack, but there will still be ice floes you could not take a ship through. By mid-April, a channel may be clear. If it is not a late spring.'

It was the beginning of the New Year, two months and one week since they had reached Québec. They had been lucky. A week more, and the winter snow would have caught them. After the Natchez raid, Henri had buried La Tour and Ruth in one grave. He had buried the half-caste boy who had been his companion throughout the long journey with La Tour. The rest of the men he left where they fell, taking from them only two muskets, a pistol, powder and shot, and three coats. In two days he made a birch canoe. From the ship he took enough canvas and cord to rig a lugsail on the canoe. Rebekah had watched all this – the burials, the building of the canoe, and the other preparations – in silent stupefaction, hugging the child close to her and allowing Henri to take him from her only to feed and clean him. On the third day, when all was ready, they set off upriver in the canoe. Apart from necessaries, they took with them only La Tour's charts, his journals, the old Papal Bull, the proclamation of the New American Empire, and the mandarin's robe, in which Henri wrapped the baby.

All other stores, firearms, and powder were piled in the ship, which was unmanageable by one man and useless to them. The moment before they cast off in the canoe, Henri fired the ship, so that it should not fall into the hands of

Indians, and so that its flames should act as a decoy to lurking savages, to distract their attention from the three survivors fleeing upriver.

The journey north had passed Rebekah by as she sat in a terror of grief, clutching the child, and conscious of nothing else. She did nothing to help, and could not. Henri sustained them both, caring for the baby and forcing Rebekah to eat when they had food. It was Henri's wits, strength, force of mind, and unassailable determination that the child should live that got them at last to Montréal. And then they were brought on to the governor at Québec.

At the New Year, as she looked out at the frozen St Lawrence, Rebekah still mourned. She was the picture of mourning, wan and thin. The women at Québec had given her clothes. That day she wore a full, plain gown of purple wool, without decoration but trimmed at the high neckline and at the wrists with bands of black beaver fur. As she looked down at the craft frozen into the ice by the shore, she saw again the receding image of La Tour's ship as Henri had paddled away from it, how it had blazed yellow, and crimson, and white, and then, when they were half a mile upstream, how it had exploded with a force that sent blazing fragments wheeling high into the sky above the Messipi. As they fell to earth, some of the smouldering ashes settled softly on the grave of Ruth and La Tour. By the New Year at Québec, Rebekah had forgotten La Tour, but the sight of Ruth lying dead still lived vividly in her eyes, and she mourned night and day for the death of her twin self.

It was mid-April before the ice broke, and another two weeks before a ship of any size could get up to Québec. By the orders of Governor Villeneuve, O'Brien's ship was hailed at the trading post of Trois Rivières, downstream, and escorted to Québec, where O'Brien was taken straight to the governor.

They knew each other. O'Brien had traded into Québec on and off for years, and though the governor had not met him until the previous year, he had known him by reputation. The previous summer, when O'Brien came searching for news of his daughters and La Tour, Villeneuve had received him, and the two men had taken a liking to each other.

So when Wild Harry O'Brien was ushered in, it did not too much surprise him that Villeneuve embraced him, though he thought it strange when the count immediately turned away and walked towards the windows, clasping his hands behind his back.

'Monsieur le comte?' he said.

The count turned. 'Will you take some brandy?'

'My daughters, sir?' asked O'Brien.

'Yes.' Villeneuve sat, motioned O'Brien to sit, and poured two glasses of brandy. O'Brien took the glass and held it without drinking.

'O'Brien, I do not know what you may have heard. My news is this. I have one of your daughters here.'

O'Brien put his glass down, so that his hand should not be seen to shake. 'One?' he said. 'Which?'

'Madame La Tour.'

'Rebekah?'

'Yes, La Tour's wife.'

'And Ruth? And is La Tour here?'

'O'Brien, this is not news I should have wished to give you. La Tour is dead. And I fear your other daughter is dead. I am deeply sorry.'

O'Brien looked into Villeneuve's face, and knew it was the truth. But he did not quite comprehend it yet, and said, 'But how? We heard the party had returned. Last autumn, I spoke a French ship...'

'There were reports. When your daughter reached Montréal, she was brought on here with an escort, and the news spread that the whole party had returned. But when they came, there were only three.'

'It is certain Ruth is dead?'

'You will see your daughter, who saw her sister killed.'

'Indians?'

The governor nodded, and O'Brien, who had seen

women on Long Island who had died at the hands of the Mohicans, put his face in his hands.

The governor understood. 'No. It was rapid. We know that. There is that at least. We know that for sure. Madame La Tour will tell you that. The guide I sent with them will tell you that. It is quite sure. I give you my word. Besides, they will tell you.'

O'Brien composed himself.

'But there was news of a child that I heard too. That is not true?'

'That *is* true. There is a child. Madame La Tour has a child, born in that wilderness. It is a boy, and is well.'

O'Brien took up his glass again, but his hand shook so badly that he put it down again without drinking. 'How did all this happen? And you said there were three that came back.'

'Three. Your daughter, the child, and the guide. Whatever was saved out of all this wreck was saved by that guide. His name is Henri. He saved your daughter and child, and I know no one else who could have done it.'

'But how?' O'Brien asked again, and Villeneuve told him the whole story, as far as he knew it.

O'Brien listened, taking his glass in both hands to steady it, and draining it. The count refilled it.

'Now, you will want to see your daughter, and your grandson. But before you do, there are two things I ought to tell you. Until two months ago she was nearly out of her mind. She's now much recovered, but she was for a long time out of her mind. Or perhaps I put matters too strongly. She grieved for her sister as if it were her own death she was facing. I was with her twice, and I never saw anyone so afflicted with grief. Henri, who has been with her constantly, says she talked about it as if it were the death of herself. She used those words, that it was she who had died as well. The surgeon here could make nothing of it. She would not eat. For a while she wasted away. But she has come round in the last two months, come round very well. She is strong. She's young.'

'She is twenty-one.'

'Yes. O'Brien, she adores the boy. You'll see that. It's perhaps hardly strange when you think of it, but the fact is she won't let the child out of her sight, day or night. She won't have a nurse. She won't have a maid. She'll only trust the child with Henri. Nobody else.'

'An Indian?'

'Half-caste. French father, Illinois mother. As I said, he saved them, and now she'll trust only him. It *looks* strange. The women think it strange. I don't particularly. But I thought you'd better be prepared.'

O'Brien nodded.

The count took a turn around the room, and then came back to O'Brien.

'Now, there is a second thing. I'd rather tell you later, rather than straight off after all this. But there it is, I think you'd want to know before you see your daughter.'

'I was thinking of my wife. I was thinking how to tell her.'

'Yes.'

'But let's have it, sir.' O'Brien tossed off the second glass of brandy.

'You'll know, I suppose, that La Tour came here with a commission from Mazarin?'

'Yes. I met him first on Martinique, you see. We talked. Mazarin. A route to China. The Vermilion Sea. I said others had tried before him. He said others would try after.'

'It seems to matter very little now, doesn't it? He found no route to China. I sometimes think, O'Brien, that nothing matters *very* much, and all that seems to matter not at all now. I rather think he found a route to Mexico, which is of less use. Well, just before they did return last year, when I must admit I'd given up all hope, I had letters from Mazarin ordering that La Tour should on his return go to Paris to give an account of his discoveries.'

'But the man is dead.'

'Or, that if he should die, those that accompanied him should go to Paris, with all documents, for the same purpose.'

O'Brien stared at the count.

'Captain O'Brien, those who returned and would be able to give an account are Henri the guide, and your daughter, Madame La Tour, who by her marriage is a French subject.'

O'Brien stood. 'You would not keep my daughter. You would not send her to France? What could she say? What use would she be? You could not send her.'

'I have a suggestion, captain. A proposal to put to you.'

O'Brien remained standing, disbelieving but fearful, trying to form in his mind an appeal to the governor against this cruel blow that followed so closely on other calamities. To satisfy a whim of Mazarin's, Rebekah was to be kept from Wolsey longer still?

O'Brien could not find words, and it was Villeneuve who made the appeal. 'Sit down. O'Brien, I have to step carefully between my words. I cannot be that plain with you, do you see? I have my duty to do, and I must do it. But listen. I have a proposal. Will you listen?'

O'Brien sat down.

'Good. Now, it is very clear that I have to send your daughter to Paris. Now, O'Brien, if you will not listen I can do nothing. Will you listen? Now I've said that's clear. But *how* I send her is within my discretion. I can send her by a French ship that leaves here tomorrow, having been icebound all winter, but she as usual goes by way of Martinique. If there were a faster ship, it would be my duty to send your daughter by that ship. Yes? Even if it were not a French ship, I might send her by that ship. Yes? Are we at one?'

'Go on, sir.'

'Supposing there were a ship now lying at Québec, a Dutch ship, whose master offered a passage to France to those two persons I am bound to send – to Madame La Tour and Henri. Suppose that. If that vessel happened to make the passage by way of New Amsterdam, then I should have no objection, seeing that the passage would still be faster than by a French ship. I need go no further, I trust?'

O'Brien rose, took both the governor's hands in his, and clasped them. Villeneuve, sailing as close to the wind as he dared, was letting him know that once such a ship was at Manhattan she and her passengers would be beyond his jurisdiction and his enquiries. And he would have done his duty, just.

O'Brien said gruffly, 'You are generous, and I thank you with my heart.'

Villeneuve looked at his desk. 'I will have you shown to your daughter. You will find her, as I said, much improved from a few months ago. Oh, and when I saw she had recovered, I felt obliged to tell her of Mazarin's orders that she should go to France. I told her that a month or so ago. I said at the same time that in any event she could stay here until you came, and I gave her to understand what I have just given you to understand. So she can have been in no fear on that account. She said nothing to me when I told her. Made no reply at all. Not a word. But she can't have been in any fear on that account. I'm told she's come on marvellously in the last month or so. And there's this, which I'll tell you and you can tell her. From La Tour's charts it's evident that he went much further than any European has before, and I have his proclamation which shows he took possession of vast territories in the name of His Majesty. And you'll be a Catholic, O'Brien, so it may comfort you to know that the Jesuits say Masses for the souls of La Tour and your other daughter.'

'I once said to myself, governor, I once said, "Once a Catholic, always a Catholic," and I was once a Catholic, so it does console me. And, for the matter of my daughter's passage, that *is* generous of you, sir, and I do thank you.'

Villeneuve smiled. 'No generosity on either side, O'Brien. We shall agree a fair price for the passage. All above board. Now I'll have you taken to her.'

Rebekah did not run to him, as he had expected. Perhaps he had been wrong to expect it. But nor was she distracted. She appeared serene, waited till he crossed the room to her, calmly received his hugging embrace, and then stood smiling with steady eyes. She was by a long way more composed than O'Brien, who wanted to embrace her again, but restrained himself. She was not the girl he had known. It was three years, he told himself, and the three years from eighteen to twenty-one made a great change in a woman's life. And she had suffered. Yet there was no outward sign of suffering. If she had wasted, she had since, as the governor said, made a marvellous recovery.

She led the way to the child, and placed him in O'Brien's arms. He was more than a year old now, and robust. O'Brien held the boy up at arm's length to see him better, and the child was not afraid of the great man whose large hands held him, but made agreeable, happy noises.

'Oh, a fine son,' exclaimed O'Brien, delighted for the boy, delighted for Rebekah, delighted for Wolsey and for all that a grandson would mean to her, and delighted for himself.

'A beautiful boy,' said O'Brien, bouncing the child, 'and a great thing for you, and for his father, God rest him.'

He had not intended to mention La Tour. The words slipped out. But Rebekah seemed unaffected, and continued to smile her steady, enigmatic smile. The boy, with his robustness, his green eyes, and his dark brown hair, already plentiful, was Wolsey's son again, the boy he had lifted up in his arms at Plymouth and carried around, so as to make the mother's acquaintance. Wolsey's features, so eloquently present in the child, had come to him through Rebekah, but Rebekah herself, standing there as she did, had little of her mother in her. She kept her distance.

'What is the boy's name?' he asked.

'Robert,' she said. She had always called him Robert, never Pierre. She did not choose to remember La Tour even in his child.

'How is my mother?' asked Rebekah.

O'Brien sat with the child on his knees. 'Your mother's well, and will be lightened in her soul to see you, and will lose ten years off her age and the few grey hairs she has in her head when she sees the boy, and I thank God for it, Rebekah. She thought she had lost you. So did I. She was sure she had lost you. She would never say so, but I knew, and she grieved.'

Rebekah again smiled, and O'Brien was seized by a conflict. He was glad she was recovered, he was glad she had her health, he was glad she was proud of the child, and yet he wished she would weep. For the loss and terror of the last year, or for the joy of going home, or for anything. The Irish in him demanded a rejoicing, or a keening, better a rejoicing, but an open-heartedness which was not hers. And yet, he said to himself, perhaps this was unreasonable to ask. He had heard of men so struck with grief that they could only smile, dissimulating to preserve themselves. Was this Rebekah's case?

He gave the boy a finger, which he grasped and held.

O'Brien turned to Rebekah. 'You mother will rejoice. She wanted to come to meet you, but I would not bring her. An early passage north can be hard, and it was hard. She will be overjoyed to have you safe. But Rebekah, the news was that both of you were saved. She is expecting Ruth.'

'But the governor has told you?'

'He has told me. The news we had was wrong. You were not both saved.'

Rebekah came and took Robert from him, and held the child so close that he cried.

Seeing this urgent embrace, O'Brien began to think that he had done Rebekah wrong. The grief was still too much for her to show. To hide it cost her dearly. At some time she would have to talk about Ruth and La Tour, but he thought it was too soon now.

But then Rebekah did begin to talk about Ruth. She said, 'Do you remember when we went to Breuckelen?'

'Breuckelen?'

'When we were children, we went to Breuckelen. We left a note for you, and you came and looked for us. But we came back on our own.'

'Ah, I remember.'

'And did the governor talk to you just now, before he sent you to me?'

'Yes.'

'And told you about the Indians, who bowed down when they saw we were twins.'

'He told me.'

'Breuckelen was the same.'

The boy had now stopped crying. As she spoke, Rebekah was rocking him to and fro in her arms.

'The same?' said O'Brien.

'Not the same. But like it. When we went to Breuckelen we went to get a white deer.'

'It came up to you.'

'We had some feathers,' said Rebekah, 'turkey feathers, that an Indian gave us down by the wharves. They had been playing a game for them, and one man won, but when he saw us he was afraid and gave us all he had won. We took the feathers to Breuckelen. In the night the Indians found us. We were afraid, but only for a little while. When they saw us, they were more afraid than we were, and we could tell it was because we were twins, because they kept looking. We told them we wanted a white deer. We drew a white deer in chalk on a rock, and we gave them the feathers, and they talked, and then they brought a white fawn and showed us the way to go. That is how we came back.'

O'Brien well remembered. 'But you said the fawn came up to you. You both said that. You always said it and told everybody.'

'We made it up. The Indians gave it to us.'

'Mohicans,' said O'Brien. He still remembered how the Mohicans, that same night, had killed a Dutch family on Long Island.

'It was because we were twins. And it was the same with the Natchez. Other Indians have never cared that we were twins. The Mohicans did, and the Natchez. We never told anyone about the fawn.'

Rebekah fell silent, and O'Brien thought it better to say no more, better just to take Rebekah home.

So, when she put the boy back into the cradle, and lulled him to sleep, O'Brien told her they would sail in two days' time.

She met his eyes quite steadily, but did not reply.

'It will be spring in Manhattan. Nearly summer. You will be away from this wilderness, child.'

'The governor did not tell you I must go to Paris?'

A sweat broke out on O'Brien's hands and face.

'He told me, Rebekah. He told me that he has his orders, and he told me how he means to carry them out. If you know there are orders for you to go to Paris, you must know that too. The governor has told you what he told me. You shall take passage for France, but it shall be aboard the *Vliegende Hert*, and by way of Manhattan. And once in Manhattan.... That is settled. Settled above board, all above board.'

'I must go to Paris.'

'Child, you will come with me, on my ship, to Manhattan. And once you are in Manhattan, you will be your own woman, and the French king's writ does not run in Manhattan. Do you see? Now that is settled.'

'But I must go to France.'

O'Brien stood up abruptly and paced the room, crossed to the window, and looked down on the same view of the St Lawrence that Rebekah had so often seen and so intently regarded during the long winter. Now the ice was thawing, and breaking up. The trees' bare branches were free of ice.

'Now,' he said, breathing deeply to calm himself, 'why would that be? Go to France? For what?'

'For my husband.'

'He is dead.'

'That is why I must go. He took an empire for the French. So I must go. For his fame, and for his sake.'

O'Brien looked narrowly at her. Once again that steady smile, as if what she said were self-evident. He did not know the girl at all. But still, he must try.

He went across to where she sat, and took her hands. 'I liked La Tour. I loved La Tour. If he were living, I tell you I would shout his fame. *But he is dead.* His charts, and the empire he took, will be his fame. They're enough. What could you do more for him?'

'But I shall go.'

'What of your mother? Do you think of her at all? She has not seen you for three years.'

She shook her head.

'What of your mother? Look at me. What of her?' O'Brien took Rebekah's face in his right hand and forced her to look him in the eyes. 'What of your mother? Do you give her a thought? She expects to see two daughters, but Ruth is dead. She does not know that. And now you will not come, and she is to have neither of her daughters again? Now, miss, what of your mother?'

She confronted his anger with a cool gaze, and did not reply.

'You will not take the boy with you,' he cried out. 'I shall take the child. Now think of that. I tell you, think of that.'

'The child is mine,' she said, 'and not my mother's, and not yours. And I shall take the child. I will write to my mother. I am sorry for my mother. But the child is mine. Mine and La Tour's. And we shall go together.'

O'Brien could no longer contain his anger, and threw Rebekah aside. As she lay on the floor her eyes were still calmly on his.

'You are pitiless,' he accused. 'I do not know you. And God help you.'

Slowly O'Brien gathered himself, and saw for the first time that Henri was standing by the cradle.

'Oh, man,' he said, 'the boy is in no danger from me. Would I hurt him?' He badly misread Henri's intentions and sympathies. If O'Brien had taken the child up and carried him to the ship, Henri would not have lifted a finger to stop him. But O'Brien did nothing of the sort. He stormed out of the governor's house and down to his ship, where he drank all afternoon and all night, alone in his cabin.

Next day, when the French ship sailed for Martinique and

Le Havre, Rebekah and the child were aboard. The governor had gone as far as he dared in trying to dissuade her, but once she insisted, he was helpless, and so he told O'Brien. To deflect the purpose of an order, as he had proposed, was one thing. To be seen publicly to frustrate its performance was another. He had to let Rebekah go. With her she carried, under Villeneuve's seal, La Tour's charts, the proclamation of empire, and La Tour's journal. The Papal Bull which revealed that his discovery of the Messipi had been anticipated by the Spanish, and by nearly a century, had long before been dropped into the St Lawrence by the hand of Rebekah during the northward journey of the previous year, and in the sandalwood box she had placed the proclamation of empire. Rebekah had also cut out with a knife the one page of La Tour's journal that recounted the gift of the Papal Bull and his disappointment that he had been preceded. His entry for the child's birth simply read, 'The first day of March, 1651: born, a boy, Pierre Robert La Tour'; and this revealed nothing.

Rebekah and the child were the only passengers aboard the French ship. Henri, not wishing to make a long voyage to a country he had never seen, had vanished earlier that morning into the forests where he had spent all his life. With him he took the knowledge, possessed by no other man, that the Spaniards had been before them at the Natchez town, and that the boy Robert had been born not to Rebekah but to Ruth. During the long winter, he had kept these secrets to himself, telling no one, and he would continue silent for the sake of Pierre La Tour, whose courage he had admired and whose fame he would not harm. As for Rebekah, it was not for La Tour's sake that she would promote his fame, but for her own sake and Robert's, who ought to have been her child and who, in her mind, was hers. This was a pretence – more than that, a firm belief – which was essential to her wholeness of mind, but it was a pretence she knew she could not have maintained with Wolsey, away from whom she therefore took herself and Robert, sailing for France and the court of St Germain.

31

THE NEEDLE IN THE ROSE

For the next two years, O'Brien spent as much time in Manhattan as he could, sending his three ships out under the command of younger men who in their time had served him as mates, and himself staying with Wolsey. For the first week after her husband's return from Québec with the terrible news, Wolsey's mind dwelt entirely on her lost daughters – one dead and the other inexplicably having refused to come back to her – and on the grandson she had never seen. She talked of nothing else. Then, by an effort of will, she did not talk about it at all. She hoped that Rebekah would return, but she hoped in silence. She had always managed O'Brien's affairs in his absence. Now she threw herself into the business, working all the daylight hours.

After three months one letter from Rebekah arrived, sent from Martinique when she was on her way to France. It offered no explanation, and told Wolsey no more than she already knew from O'Brien, except that the boy was still flourishing. She had the consolation of knowing that. No other letters arrived.

War came between Holland and England. News filtered in of sea engagements in the English Channel. O'Brien's overseas trade suffered. He maintained a coastal trade with Québec, and with the Dutch and French West Indies, and had the resources to survive. One New Netherlands ship was taken as a prize by an English vessel out of Antigua. In Manhattan, Dutch and English still lived peaceably together. The war was too far away to break old friendships or to come between old trading partners. Most of the New England colonies stood back from the war. O'Brien still maintained a small trade with Plymouth, but thought it wiser to keep his vessels away from Boston, where a more active and aggressive support was springing up for England and Lord Protector Cromwell. There were reports of English frigates in Massachusetts Bay. Many fewer ships came to Manhattan then, so that there was no way of knowing whether Rebekah had not written at all since her first letter, or whether she had written but found no ship to carry the letter.

In the summer of 1654 the poor began to feel the pinch. The price of grain rose. A mob gathered outside O'Brien's warehouses, murmuring that Dutch grain was meant for Dutch stomachs. It could have been a riot, and Stuyvesant apologized for it to Wolsey. She was now his oldest and closest friend in the colony, and they often walked together on his new Bouwerie, a large farm of about one square mile on the East River, half a mile north of the city proper. That afternoon, as they strolled along a formal avenue he had laid out, two guards followed them at a discreet distance. Stuyvesant regretted their presence, but thought it better to be careful with the town on edge and tempers frayed.

'My soldiers guard me,' he said, 'but I gather they weren't all that much use in guarding your warehouses the other day. I'm sorry.'

Wolsey shrugged. 'It was all over very quickly. There was no need for them. No damage done.'

'There've been tales of Harry holding them at bay waving a sabre.'

'I doubt that. He has no sabre. It was very simple. They roared at him, demanding to know what a damned Englishman was doing profiteering with Dutch wheat. At which he roared back at them that he was not a damned Englishman but a damned Irishman, and explained this essential difference with such heat that they quietened down and listened. He said they became quite abashed, so he told them to go away and come back with bowls, which they did, and he filled them with grain. One of them had a bottle and they passed it round and drank to the Irish nation, long might it endure.'

'They'll never drink to me,' said Stuyvesant. 'I've wanted these few acres all my life, and its only a bouwerie, my farm. But they have to call it the *Great* Bouwerie.'

'Not,' said Wolsey, 'that you could call it small.'

'No, no. But now, by a sort of natural extension, the whole of New Amsterdam has suddenly become known as Stuyvesant's Bouwerie. That's what they call it, Stuyvesant's Bouwerie. Just when Manhattan is really less mine than ever. Take a Dutch colony, put it down three thousand miles from Amsterdam, three thousand miles from civilization. Send a governor, me. The governor governs. Promptly the lower orders murmur, and the few who can write do write, and they send their petitions and their remonstrances to Amsterdam, and call me a tyrant, and say the place is overrun by Scots and Chinamen – you know about that – and instead of sending a battalion of soldiers to deal with the malcontents, Their High Mightinesses send a city charter, creating aldermen and magistrates, so that they can govern themselves.'

'Most of the aldermen appointed by you.'

'As it happens,' said Stuyvesant. 'As it happens. And just as well. And a city coat of arms to come.'

'I have seen no coat of arms,' said Wolsey.

'When the bunglers finish the war. When the war ends. When there's a ship to send it by. Then there'll be a coat of arms. They could have used mine. But they have a new one. I did suggest mine to Amsterdam, and to the aldermen here, but they would not have it.'

'I have never seen yours either.'

'I do not much use it.'

He showed her the design on the knob of the silver cane he was carrying. 'There.'

She looked closely. 'It looks like a rabbit running away, in full flight.'

'Ah. Well, there's a rabbit, but there's also a standing deer.' He showed her the nobly standing deer. 'To signify firmness of purpose. But they chose to see the rabbit instead. Now they have a coat of arms of their own, and I hope it's even less to their liking. But they've never seen it. I've never seen it. It has to wait for its ship, when the war ends.'

There was in fact already peace, the terms of which were humiliating to Holland, but the news of it came only with the Dutch ship that brought the coat of arms. Other ships followed in rapid succession, but still no letter from Rebekah. O'Brien was truly glad when Stuyvesant proposed, since it was necessary that he should visit Curaçao and other Caribbean islands to restore the old trade, that Harry should take him and that Wolsey should accompany them. He would like her to come, said the governor, for the sake of her company, and for her health. They would depart in December, which was a good season for the Caribbean. A sea voyage in pleasant waters might take some of the ache from her mind. On a Wednesday in mid-December the citizens gave a banquet to wish Stuyvesant good fortune on his gallant voyage, and he presented them with the new coat of arms – the three diagonal crosses of old Amsterdam on a silver ground, surmounted by a beaver.

'Absurdly grand for an infant city,' said Stuyvesant, but only for Wolsey's ears. The burghers could not hear his opinion for their own applause of what they saw as a piece of fitting grandiloquence. The arms of great Amsterdam itself and a beaver besides.

'But you love the place,' she shouted to him over the din.

'Of course. But my stag would have done.'

The *Vliegende Hert*, with Stuyvesant aboard and escorted by two armed sloops, sailed for the Caribbean on Christmas Eve.

For Wolsey, the passage south was a healing voyage. She had never been so far south before. As they sailed warmer every day, she walked in the sun on the steady deck, sat for long hours in the shade of an awning, and read and talked. Her most constant companion was Stuyvesant. They talked about their early days in a way they had not since they first met. He told her about his student days in Holland, the same old tales he had told her when he first came to Manhattan as governor. They were now a little embroidered in the retelling. On her part, Wolsey remembered the cold, bitter, pitching voyage that had taken her as a girl from England to Plymouth. She recalled the moment when, for an infinitesimal fragment of time, never forgotten, the ship, after two months of motion, stopped and hung in midair, when the great wave that had tossed the vessel high into the air curled away from under her, leaving her suspended and motionless until she crashed into the trough of the sea. That was unlike the Caribbean, which was soft and calm at that season. Gradually the warmth and rest restored Wolsey, and her old spirit had almost returned when O'Brien announced that they were within a day of Curaçao.

Not, said Stuyvesant, that she must expect too much of that island. He knew it well, had lived there before he came to Manhattan, and was still nominally governor of Curaçao, too. In spite of this warning, she was astonished by what she saw. In parts the island was arid, a desert, and she saw for the first time that a wilderness could be not only a cold wilderness of the sort she had known, but a hot wilderness, a desert.

'A desert with slaves,' she said, 'a desert crawling with slaves.'

'A desert,' said Stuyvesant, 'in part, yes, a desert. Slaves, yes, but slaves very dear to Their High Mightinesses in Amsterdam.'

There were slaves in Manhattan, but only a few hundred. Here there were thousands, brought from Africa in Dutch ships to work in Brazil or on Curaçao itself. Those same ships then returned to Holland loaded with West Indian sugar, molasses, and exotic woods. It was this two-way trade which it was Stuyvesant's business to repair after the war, but he cared to stay only a few days on the island.

Wolsey set foot on it only once, and the stench of many thousands of miserable transported blacks huddled into filthy camps revolted her. It was not a business Stuyvesant was proud of. He assured her that the second leg of their voyage would be more congenial. Barbados had sugar cane, which Amsterdam wanted. The Barbados trade had been quite stopped in the war because the island was British. Now he must restore the trade. He said Barbados was quite the most beautiful West Indies island he had ever seen. Harry must surely know it well? Wolsey, remembering her husband's island women of their early marriage, said she was certain he did. So they sailed east to Barbados, an island where a soothing breeze always blew off the cool Atlantic.

As they came within sight of the new port of Bridgetown, making a slow and careful approach, O'Brien took Stuyvesant aside.

'See that?'

A cluster of masts met their sight.

'So many?' asked Stuyvesant.

'It's too far away for me to see,' said O'Brien. 'What, fifteen, seventeen vessels, all with their sails in shrouds, bare masts. And from the look of them, hardly a man aboard. No movement. Flying no ensigns. I've been coming here thirty years, and I never saw so many at one time.'

'English?' asked Stuyvesant.

'Not English. Not from the cut of them. The two great ships are Spaniards, and the rest I'd say are Dutch.'

'I should be surprised to find Dutch ships here.'

'But they are.'

They were interrupted by a call from the mate. 'Men o' war to windward, sir.'

'There,' said O'Brien, 'are your English ships, governor.'

What they saw was not one frigate but four, flying the flag of Cromwell's Commonwealth. From the leading frigate a cannon flashed, and a shot struck the water a hundred feet before O'Brien's bow.

'In face of that,' he said, 'we heave to, and we talk, governor.'

It was a very young English lieutenant, little more than a boy, perhaps seventeen, who was rowed over from the frigate in a cutter. He climbed the waist ladder of the *Vliegende Hert*, taking care not to trip over his sword, and announced to Wild Harry O'Brien that he and his ship were under arrest, and must strike the ensign of the States General of Holland.

'Do you say so indeed, Mr...?'

'Crashaw, captain. And those two vessels,' the young man gestured toward the two sloops which were also hove to, 'those are yours too, captain?'

'No, Mr Crashaw, not mine,' said O'Brien. At which Peter Stuyvesant, in the full dress of governor – black velvet, silver buttons, abundant lace, and great gravity – opened the door of the aftercabin and stumped to the top of the quarterdeck ladder, where he stood looking down at Crashaw and O'Brien.

'No, Mr Crashaw,' repeated O'Brien, 'not mine, but His Excellency's.'

Crashaw looked up at the apparition on the quarterdeck, saw the silver-topped peg leg, and knew very well whom he was seeing. Stuyvesant did not move. The boy collected his wits, walked to the foot of the ladder, looked up at Stuyvesant, and saluted with his sword. Stuyvesant acknowledged with a flick of his cane, and waited.

'I am sent,' said the boy, 'to demand that you strike your ensign, and to arrest your ship, and the two sloops alongside.'

'So I heard. And by what authority?'

'By that of Lord Protector Cromwell, Your Excellency.'

'Well, it may please you to say that, but I'd put it differently. I'd say by the authority, such as it is, of those four threatening frigates. But I do not think you will care to blow me out of the water, so I shall consider that you have withdrawn your request that I should strike my ensign, and I shall consider that I have not heard the word "arrest" escape your lips. However, I see your predicament, lieutenant, and I suggest that you should return to your commander and tell him that I shall remain hove to for the present to await his explanations.'

The boy saluted again, and retreated.

'Who *is* your commander?' said Stuyvesant, recalling him.

'Admiral Penn, Your Excellency.'

'My compliments, then, to Admiral Penn, for the fishing fleet. Convey that to him. My compliments for the herring fleet.'

The boy had come up without tripping over his sword, but found it difficult to descend.

'Give it to me, lad,' said O'Brien, and the bemused boy unhooked his sword from its hanger and gave it to O'Brien, who returned it to him when he was once more sitting in the cutter.

The ensign of the States General of Holland continued to flutter in the breeze from the stern of the three Dutch ships throughout the afternoon. At five o'clock a more senior lieutenant returned, to ask His Excellency the governor, and those of his officers whom he might care to bring, to take dinner on board the English flagship. Stuyvesant accepted, and took with him not the captains of the two sloops, but O'Brien and Wolsey.

'I may need you for the translation, my dear,' he said.

She smiled. His English was perfect.

There were six at table in the frigate's cabin, the three from the *Vliegende Hert*, an English frigate captain, a civilian in severe Puritan dress, and an Englishman in the uniform of a Cromwellian colonel. He was plainly a gentleman. He introduced himself as Richard Rolls, the frigate captain as Dashwood, and the sombre civilian as 'Mr John Ansell, from Boston, in Massachusetts.' A seventh chair was left pointedly empty. Glancing at it, Rolls said Admiral Penn had received Governor Stuyvesant's message sent that morning, and would be unable to join them. He had full authority to speak for the admiral. Now, should they dine?

Stuyvesant proposed the first toast.

'To our absent host,' he said, and then, while they drank,

added, 'and to his most gallant destruction, with only a small force of men o'war, of the Dutch herring fishing fleet.'

Rolls put down his glass steadily. He and Stuyvesant glared at each other over the table. Wolsey, having lived so long in a city where English and Dutch lived peacefully enough with each other, was taken aback by the intensity of feeling between the two men. But here was the representative of Holland, certainly the richest country in Europe and in the world, but a country that had suffered a humiliating defeat in the recent war, facing the representative of England, a great and growing power, some said greater than France. The Dutch smarted at the defeat. The English did not like it to be said publicly that they had begun their triumphant war at sea with a naval action that was hardly heroic, and which had ended in the slaughter of many fishermen. The English had started by taking the herring waters, had then blockaded the Low Countries, defeated the Dutch fleet, won the war, extracted huge damages for imagined wrongs suffered by the British East and West India companies, and then demanded, as a further condition of the peace, that all Dutch ships should salute the English ensign in Commonwealth waters.

All this news had come to Stuyvesant in dispatch after dispatch and now, when he thought the disastrous war over, he was arrested on a voyage intended to repair his devastated trade. The two men continued to glare at each other, until the Englishman relaxed into urbanity, as he could afford to do. The English naval captain remained impassive. The man from Boston retained an expression of severity.

Rolls waited until the roast was finished and the tablecloth drawn, and they were sitting over fruit and wine.

Then he said, 'Governor, you must allow me to return your earlier toast. I propose, therefore, the continued health and prosperity of Manhattan, that island of which, a few years ago, few had heard, but which is now the talk of the world, and certainly the talk of England.'

Stuyvesant had to drink, but he felt the threat in these words.

'Gentlemen,' said Wolsey, 'we are at *peace*.'

Rolls smiled. That was, he replied, undoubtedly so, and he was very glad, as no doubt they all were glad on Manhattan.

Stuyvesant, who was cool when he wished to be, remarked that since they *were* undoubtedly at peace, he was surprised, as Colonel Rolls would understand, to find a boy in an English uniform coming aboard his ship and purporting to arrest the ship and him in it. Now, except by the power of a few frigates, by what authority was this done, if he could put the enquiry?

The frigate captain allowed himself a half smile as Rolls gravely informed Stuyvesant that he could not have received news of one particular article of the peace treaty, which stated that in future English goods should be carried only in English ships. He could see the inconvenience to the commerce of Manhattan, but the matter was out of his hands. He would have to do his duty. It would not, he hoped, be a grave matter for Manhattan?

Stuyvesant did not reply. There was nothing he could say. It was a bad blow.

Mr Ansell of Boston entered the conversation. 'I have heard,' he said, 'that there are other graver matters on Manhattan which are allowed to go unchecked – as, I have heard, many adulteries.'

Stuyvesant again did not answer. O'Brien growled, but said no word.

'Slipperiness in all things, adultery among them,' said Mr Ansell, 'is to be checked for the spiritual health of a city. I am sorry to say that even in Boston there is much slipperiness. A young woman hanged the day before I left had plainly not repented even at the last. After a swing or two, she catched at the ladder. We had not tied her hands, out of pity. She catched at the ladder, but it did not save her, and all present thought it an evident proof that she had died unrepentant.'

'How old was she?' asked Wolsey.

'Full eighteen. Her adulteries were with many men. She was seen upon the ground with one, in open day. She did it for wine, and other easy gifts.'

O'Brien looked at the man in contempt.

Stuyvesant said smoothly, 'I see *you* do not take the easy gift of wine, Mr Ansell.'

'Sir!' the man protested, pushing his full glass away from him.

'You do not drink to my toast, sir,' said Stuyvesant, 'which I overlooked, thinking you might have interests in the Massachusetts herring trade which would prevent you from commiserating the death of a few Dutch fishermen, who also, no doubt, tried to catch at ropes as they drowned. But then you did not drink to Colonel Rolls's toast. Now, sir, why this slipperiness about toasts?'

Ansell gravely explained. 'This vain business of drinking one to another is an inducement to quarrelling, sir, and a waste of wine, and an idle ceremony, and troublesome to the host.'

Rolls said, 'Not troublesome to me, and I am host.' He liked Ansell less than he liked Stuyvesant, who was his opponent, but an honest one. He could not stand Ansell's canting. Yet he had to have him at his table because Boston had helped Cromwell in the war. Frigates had gathered at Boston, and, had the war not ended, would have attacked Manhattan. Ansell represented Boston, and that was why he was on board, on his way to see Lord Protector Cromwell in London. The views of Boston might commend themselves to Cromwell. They did not to Rolls, but he was a soldier, and did his duty as he saw it.

Ansell would not be stopped. He was at that moment entertaining Wolsey with talk of a plague of caterpillars, one-and-a-half inches long, which, in a year of great iniquity, had wreaked the Lord's vengeance even on godly Boston, eating first the blades of the corn stalks, and then the tassels, whereupon the ears withered. The caterpillars were thought to have fallen in a great thunderstorm.

'And when the corn is spent, the rats leave the barn, and so you are here?' growled O'Brien. Wolsey put a restraining hand on his arm, but Mr Ansell was of a forgiving nature, brushed this remark aside, and embarked on a disquisition concerning slipperiness of the heart, which was of all slipperinesses the most insidious.

'The heart is deceitful above all things, and evil. Oh, the blind corners, the secret turnings, the windings, the perplex labyrinths, the close-lurking sins that beset the heart. Oh, the mystery of self-deceiving. In the very act of prayer I have felt my heart slip into the contemplation of sin, slyly slip away and play with lustful things which our treacherous hearts make us apprehend as delightful, as the heart of David, in his adultery, was seduced by the beauty of the woman he saw.'

No one replied to him. The frigate captain caught Wolsey's eye and raised his eyebrows in apology for the man's gibbering. But Wolsey was not surprised by what she heard. Ansell's was a vocabulary and a cast of thought familiar to her from her early days in Plymouth.

Ansell persisted. 'The deceitfulness of our hearts,' he said, 'is much like that of a rose whose petals hide a needle, which pricks those who bend close to smell the rose's sweet, God-given fragrance. It is the needle in the rose.'

'Very well put,' said Rolls. 'Excellently put, no doubt. But we must pass to other things. There is the matter of Governor Stuyvesant's ships.'

'But this has a great deal to do with Governor Stuyvesant,' said Ansell. 'For Manhattan is, as it were, the needle in the fair rose that is New England.'

There was silence.

'And now,' said Ansell, 'since too-long feasting is an indulgence, I will leave you.'

He went.

Rolls tried to make amends. To his mind, if Stuyvesant sent his herring-fleet message to the admiral, then it served him right if the admiral snubbed him by leaving that seventh chair conspicuously empty. If he repeated the insult in a toast, then he deserved to be told in reply that Manhattan was very much in England's eye. But no one deserved Ansell's harangues about slipperiness. Rolls himself had suffered too much such stuff during a long voyage with the man, whom he thought insufferable. So Rolls, saying that there was now no one to censure their excesses, motioned his servants to pour more wine, and told Stuyvesant civilly that he would be obliged to arrest him for a week. The seventeen ships in the harbour, two Spaniards and the rest Dutch, would be kept longer. He could not say how much longer. Stuyvesant would perhaps not know that the admiral had been scouring the Caribbean. He had taken the island of Jamaica from the Spanish. He had arrested all ships found attempting to trade among the English islands. Those ships would have to remain under arrest. As to the matter of the Dutch ensign, he thought it likely that the admiral would turn a blind eye to any flag flown above the governor's ship. He had seen that she also flew from her topmast yard the flag of the Commonwealth as a courtesy to the nationality of the port she was entering, and that, he was sure he could say, would be enough.

Rolls and Stuyvesant parted on better terms than they had met. But as Stuyvesant's party was rowed back to the *Vliegende Hert*, Mr Ansell was writing to his colleagues at Boston, 'We have met the Dutch governor of the New Netherlands. This man's business was to restore a good trade between Manhattan and Barbados, but we have scotched that as we will one day scotch him.' Stuyvesant lay awake in his bunk that night. He had not known the English were in such force in the Caribbean. He had not known they had taken Jamaica. He recalled Rolls's remark that Manhattan was now very much in the eyes of the world, and that fool Ansell's unctuous observation that Manhattan was the needle in the fair rose of New England.

After a week they left Barbados with an exchange of fifteen-gun salutes. Courtesies were restored. But the English had conceded nothing. Stuyvesant had interceded on behalf of the seventeen arrested Dutch ships, but had achieved nothing. They remained under guard at Bridgetown.

The *Vliegende Hert* arrived back in Manhattan to find she had been preceded by the confident news of Stuyvesant's murder, which had apparently occurred both in Jamaica and in Barbados. Both reports were detailed, and both were believed.

'I need to deny it again, and you see me stand before you?' Stuyvesant snarled at the third alderman who retailed the news to him. He dismally went the rounds of lower Manhattan, hearing tales of Indian depredations and inspecting the wall at Wall Street which was no more than an eight-foot high earthwork with planks shoring it up. At the fort he watched pigs rooting among the crumbling dirt bastions. 'More a molehill than a fortress,' he said. 'More a molehill.'

32

TO VINDICATE HIS FATHER'S NAME

Mazarin's summons, under his seal, took Rebekah to the palace at St Germain. There she was received with cold courtesy by the most under of undersecretaries. The seal of Cardinal Mazarin himself, Regent of France, which she had thought would open all doors to her, opened few, and certainly not that of Mazarin himself. The seal of Monsieur le comte de Villeneuve, governor of Québec, was hardly recognized at all. It was the seal of one French count among so many, and Villeneuve's seal, which authenticated the proclamation of the vast American empire, and La Tour's charts, and his journal, was the less able to assist her because Villeneuve was remote and almost forgotten. Villeneuve? Some recalled the name. But surely he had not been in France for many years? Wasn't he governor of some God-forsaken trading post? 'Of New France,' Rebekah replied. 'Ah,' said the undersecretaries, 'New France. Yes, some icy and forgotten trading post.' Villeneuve had not been seen for years at court, and had no patronage there. And as for Mazarin, she soon learned that Mazarin had summoned many, and forgotten whom he had summoned, and why. 'Yes,' said undersecretary after undersecretary, 'we do see, madame.' But they did not see, because for the most part they never read the proclamation she presented to them at first with assurance, and then with less assurance but more pride, and then with the hauteur of extreme unsureness, and then with inner despair. Still they said, 'I see,' when they did not. They flicked through the journal of La Tour's voyage without comprehending what he had done. They looked at the charts compiled with so much hardship and zeal and love, and did not understand the vastness of the country revealed there. Rebekah was given a grace-and-favour apartment at the palace, but it was the least of the apartments that the court had to offer, and there she would have remained, in obscurity, with the boy Robert and one maid, if her native wit and will had not forbidden her to give up. She everlastingly pestered anyone who could give her access to Mazarin.

Rebekah also had beauty. She found that it was a beauty that shone not only in Manhattan, or at Québec, or in the wilderness, but also at the court of the young Louis XIV, which was the most polished in Europe. She found admirers who saw to it that she did not lack fine clothes, and introduced her to the fringes of the royal court. When she made it plain to them that what she wanted was an audience with Mazarin, two or three wrote long letters on her behalf, and others shrugged. The young Le Febre did most. He was several years younger than she and unusually chaste by the standards of the court, so that she had the luck to become his first mistress, and he prized and loved Rebekah. One day, as she lay drowsily on her bed after a pleasant afternoon, the young man, having dressed, came over to her to kiss her. She held out her warm arms to say *au revoir*, and he said as he left, 'Rebekah, you are very dear to me, and, in the matter of the cardinal. . . .'

She smiled up at him. 'That is sweet,' she said.

'Well, I can do nothing. But perhaps my uncle can. I shall ask him for you.'

He did. The old uncle, knowing why he was being asked, wrote briefly to Mazarin, to whom he was well known. Others had written copiously to Mazarin on the subject. Their letters never reached the cardinal, and the writers received polite and dismissive replies from his secretaries. Old Le Febre wrote four lines, and saw that they reached the cardinal through his valet. Mazarin read the note and rang for a secretary.

'See to this,' he said.

In two minutes the next day, the secretary told him the gist. Mazarin ordered the proclamation, the journal, and the charts to be sent to the abbé Tronson and the abbé Bernon, both of whom had been in Québec. Both were Jesuits. These two priests wrote their opinion but, in the temporary absence of Mazarin in Paris, their statements lay on his table for a few days and were then rolled up, tied with scarlet tape, and placed on a shelf with hundreds more like them. Once again, the matter was at an end.

It was Louis XIV himself who saved Rebekah, and in a most haphazard way. He was then seventeen. He still spent all morning with his tutors or, when Mazarin was at court, with the cardinal as he went through the state papers of the day. Mazarin taught him nothing formally, but was the best tutor of all. The king learned that Mazarin *was* France, and that he, Louis, soon would be. He learned that Mazarin was, and that he, Louis, soon would be, one of the four or five men in Europe who determined the course of events so far as men could control them. He and Mazarin disposed of papers which determined the fortune or ruin of millions of his subjects. Mazarin and Louis determined the etiquette of the court and the conduct of wars. They indicated with a scratch of a pen whether a dowager duchess might display a coat of arms on the canopy of her coach, and whether captured towns should be razed or graciously reprieved.

Most of his afternoons the young king spent with the army, with the regiments quartered close at hand. He loved the military life, rode well, and made his closest friends among the officers of the garrison. But the cavalry was only one of his passions. The other at that time was Maria Mancini, a supple Italian beauty. When he left the cavalry for the day, he was hers. Every afternoon she practically went to claim possession of the young king. When he dismounted, she was there waiting. Maria Mancini was the king's favourite. She was also a niece of Cardinal Mazarin.

It happened one afternoon that Robert was there, too. He was by then five, a very handsome boy, who was attracted to the colour and clatter of the cavalry, the splendour of the horses, and the cultivated dash of the officers. Maria Mancini, having gone down to welcome Louis, saw the boy Robert and his excitement at the panache of the cavalry and of the young king. She saw his vivid green eyes, the like of which she had rarely seen before. And, being Italian, she made much of children.

'*Che bello ragazzo!*' she cried, stooping to ruffle his hair. 'And what do you come to see? The horses and the king?'

'The horses and the king, mademoiselle. And you, because you always come, too.'

Amid the amused laughter, which did not at all confound Robert's self-possession, Maria Mancini said, 'So young, and already so practised? But what really brings you here? The king, and the horses, and perhaps me. That brings you to this courtyard. But what brings you to St Germain?'

'If you please, I have come to vindicate my father's fame.'

This was said with such serious simplicity that it held the attention of all who heard it. So grand an intention, so naturally expressed, and by one so young, amused and yet touched the spectators.

'And who is your father?' asked Maria Mancini. 'Tell the king.'

Robert turned to Louis and bowed. 'Sir, my father is dead. But his name was Pierre La Tour, and he was an explorer. He discovered great parts of New France for Your Majesty. I was born there, sir. But my mother says that no one will look at my father's charts.'

The lookers-on thought to themselves that the old fox Mazarin himself, in the inconceivable event of his needing a favour from the king, could hardly have pitched the request better. The young king, cultivating his two passions of the cavalry and Maria Mancini, had been heard to announce, to a group of young officers, that in his heart he preferred honourable fame above all else, above life itself, and that in the love of glory lay the same subtleties as in the most tender passion. His officers had applauded so noble a sentiment. Now, in the courtyard, they heard the echo of it, and waited to hear what they would hear.

'You were born in New France,' said the king, 'and they will not look at your father's charts?'

'My mother says they will not, sir.'

'Then we shall.'

The charts and proclamation of empire were hurriedly found, and the Jesuits' opinions of them taken down from the shelf, together with the reiterated request of Rebekah La Tour that by way of recognition of her late husband's services a pension should be allowed her for the upbringing of his child, to whom she also begged that some degree of nobility might be accorded.

'All that,' said the old fox Mazarin, 'is perhaps a matter with which Your Majesty might wish to deal?' And so Louis did deal with it.

Robert and Rebekah were shown into the presence. The king said to the boy, 'You have brought your mother? Will you present her to me?'

Robert did. He had been born in a wilderness, but a boy soon learns to live easily in a palace. The manners of St Germain were already second nature to Robert.

Mother and son stood while the king read the opinions, in learned Latin, of the two Jesuits. Both were writing not for the eyes of a young king whose heart was set on glory, but for the canny and worldly-wise Mazarin.

The abbé Tronson wrote that he had been in New France and that some of La Tour's claims could not be reconciled with the observations of previous explorers, including himself. He wrote that La Tour had not pacified savage tribes, which was the least object he had been charged with, but on the contrary had been slaughtered by them. That his discoveries, even if they were what he said them to be, were useless. And that perhaps little more was to be expected of a man who had encumbered himself with two women during his voyage into the interior.

'Madame,' said the king, 'this paper mentions that M. La

Tour took two women with him. Two?'

'One was my sister, sir, and she was killed with the others.'

'Your sister?'

'My twin sister, sir.'

'Then I see this exploration has cost you dearly,' said the king, and read the second opinion. The abbé Bernon took an altogether higher view of La Tour's achievements. For *proof* that La Tour had done what he said, travelled so far, and seen so much, they could only wait until others penetrated so far. But the charts were scrupulous, and the journal either a fabrication or the record of an heroic journey, and the abbé inclined to the second view. The Messipi, by La Tour's own account, was not a route to China, but if it were to lead to the Sea of Mexico that would itself be a great discovery. La Tour had taken in His Majesty's name a vast empire. He was not Columbus, but he had gone farther than any white man before him. However, added the abbé, in a final sentence plainly intended for Mazarin's sceptical eyes, New France was hardly in vogue these days, was it?

But Louis was not Mazarin. A vast new empire established in his name, where no European had ever before penetrated, commended itself to his young ambitions.

He addressed Robert. 'Monsieur de la Tour,' he began, and, by the one word *de*, Robert was raised to the rank of the nobility. To the lowest rank of nobility, to be sure, with no title and no land, but he was enabled to enter the service of the king's cavalry, or the queen dowager's, or the dauphin's, when there should be a dauphin. He could wear a scarlet jacket, and appear armed in the king's presence with sabre and pistol.

Louis, who had made up his mind beforehand, took a paper from the chamberlain and recited that because the late Pierre La Tour had despised the greatest dangers in order to extend the Name and Empire of France to the extremity of the New World, his son, the first French subject to be born in that new empire, was proclaimed Robert, Sieur de la Tour.

'For such,' said Louis, 'is our pleasure, and in order that this shall be firm, stable, and everlasting, we hereunto affix our seal, at St Germain, this fourth day of July, 1656.'

Robert remained a favourite of the court, and was twice allowed to ride with the king. Rebekah was moved to a grace-and-favour apartment grander than the previous one, but neither her good fortune – she having received a pension at the same time as Robert received his patent of nobility – nor her beauty recommended her to the ladies of the court. She was not received again by the king, but was seen by him once at a ball given the next summer by the cavalry officers.

Rebekah was not for the moment dancing. She was sitting on a chaise longue, listening while Le Febre eagerly addressed her. They were in the half light, their faces warmly lit by chandeliers from the ballroom beyond, but their bodies in relative darkness. The light was such that though Rebekah's features were clearly visible, and indeed glowed, the colour of her gown could not be distinguished. She was wearing a necklet of rubies, a gift of Le Febre's, which caught what light there was so that their colour, shape, and movement were reflected richly onto the silken covering of the wall beside her. As she breathed, the reflection of the rubies on the silk rose and fell with the rise and fall of her breasts. When she laughed at some remark of Le Febre's, the reflection danced. When she sat once again in repose, the warm reflection resumed its steady movement, seeming not so much a reflection of mere rubies as of the life of the warm, breathing woman whose neck they encircled.

The king saw this – first the reflection, then the listening face of Rebekah, and then the reflection again on the wall. The reflection, as representing an essence of the woman, was more seductive than the sight of the woman herself. The king saw Rebekah, and saw this. Others saw that he saw. One of these was Maria Mancini. The king moved away. No word was spoken. Rebekah was unaware of his having passed so close. But Maria Mancini was not unaware.

Nor was an Englishman who had lately come to the court. Not that he saw exactly what the king had seen. He did not see the woman imaged in breathing spirit and warm carnality by the shimmering movement of reflected rubies on the silk-lined wall. He saw the king, for it was his business to notice the king, and then he saw that the king passed near a sitting woman and glanced at her. The Englishman saw that the woman was handsome and enquired her name. Having discovered by indirect enquiry who she was, how long she had been at court, and for what reason, and with what recent and fortunate result, having informed himself in short as a subtle courtier should, he introduced himself to her as George Downing. They danced a figure together. Then, over supper, Mr Downing engaged in the most civil conversation with Rebekah and with Le Febre.

When, two months later, Maria Mancini formally received Rebekah at a soirée, she was noticeably condescending, and was afterwards heard by half the court to say, 'That woman, my dear, we have done so much for her, and for her son. Her son is truly charming. No doubt he inherits his late father's disposition in that way. Madame La Tour has charm, of course, perhaps of a different sort. She has a certain hauteur, as if she were of noble birth, which of course she is not.'

Her listeners agreed with Maria Mancini. The king's favourite always found ready agreement with her opinions.

'She has,' said one lady, 'already found the means to provide for herself.'

'The pension,' said Maria Mancini.

'And Mr Downing from England,' said the second lady. 'She also has Mr Downing, by whom she is *said* to be kept.'

'And M. Le Febre?'

'Is superseded.'

'Kept by Mr Ambassador Downing,' said Maria Mancini. 'Do you say so? It sits well with her. They deserve each other. Though how *any* woman can be said to be *kept* by that man, in a way any woman should properly be kept by any *man*, is beyond me.'

But Rebekah was kept by Downing, and it was a relationship convenient to both. He was ambassador from England,

and her liaison with him gave her an entrée she had not previously enjoyed. Whereas she used to be only on the fringe of the court, now as the ambassador's mistress she went everywhere with him. She loved the gaiety, the richness of Turkish carpets and Aubusson tapestries, the brilliant glitter of mirrored chandeliers, the music of flutes and oboes, the display of her own beauty among all this, and, above all, the envy she knew she excited in others who a few months before had barely condescended to notice her. But to say this alone would be unjust. Rebekah did love these things. But she did not become Downing's mistress only for these things. She was also acting out of necessity. She had to survive. She was a woman alone, except for a young boy, at a court where she was more tolerated than welcome. She needed a protector, not only for herself but for Robert. And Downing, though no one liked him, was English ambassador, and therefore a man who could protect her. He was a surer protector than a young French nobleman who might rapidly tire of her. Le Febre loved her, and would not grow tired of her, but he had little power, and had already done as much as he could for her. So Rebekah accepted Downing, who asked principally that she should be *seen* to be his, and that her beauty should reflect glory upon him.

Downing was well pleased. He had married well. His wife Frances had brought him a good dowry, though there had been no children. He had left her in London. He was pleased to have as his mistress the woman who, after the king's favourite, was the most striking at St Germain. He had always felt that a beautiful woman was a necessary appurtenance to a man of power, which he now was. Cromwell had looked on him with favour. He was Member of Parliament for Edinburgh, and, while still retaining that office, had been sent by Cromwell to France to protest to Mazarin about the slaughter of Protestant Vaudois in Provence.

When Mr Ambassador Downing finally attained his audience with Mazarin, his reputation was not increased by it, and an account of the audience, whispered by an indiscreet undersecretary, was soon common currency.

The matter of the Vaudois was soon settled. On the one hand it was made clear that this was the business of France and not of England. On the other hand, it was intimated that fewer Protestants would be slaughtered for a while. Mazarin asked that his respects should be conveyed to Lord Protector Cromwell. Then, the business being concluded, Mazarin said, 'And you, Downing, are the man who wishes to make a king?' This was true, since Downing was now the leader of the group that urged Cromwell to take the crown.

To which Downing replied, referring to the young Louis whom Mazarin had instructed so well, 'And you, Eminence, are the man who *has* made a king.'

The presumption and deep sycophancy of this reply was smiled at for weeks thereafter. During those weeks, Maria Mancini and her circle discovered that though Rebekah was, in whatever way, kept by Mr Ambassador Downing, the young Le Febre had not quite been superseded. Rebekah appeared constantly with Downing, and in public no longer recognized Le Febre. Once, walking across a ballroom to the corner where Downing was holding his own little court, she affected not to see Le Febre as he approached her, and the world saw this. But the poor young man loved her, and went to her when she wished it, which she still did. She insisted that he should come and go unnoticed, which cut him to the heart, but he did it because he loved her.

He pleaded with her, 'Rebekah, this is not you. This *was* not you. You bring me here, when you need me. At other times I do not exist. Downing and you, it is....'

She mocked him. 'Is it so grotesque, Downing and me?'

'It is,' he cried passionately. And yet he still returned when she called him. It was an agony to the man's spirit, but though he loathed himself for remaining her lover, once he was with her he forgot everything.

There was one evening when Downing had not been expected to return from Paris, but did. Le Febre was with Rebekah, in bed with her, when she heard carriage wheels upon the gravel. She listened, lay still, slid from under her lover, and left him lying on the bed while she went to the window to look. It was Downing. She ordered Le Febre to be silent by a wave of her hand. She stood still at the window, with a sheet from the dishevelled bed wrapped round her shoulders. Downing, seeing no lights, walked towards his own quarters.

Rebekah returned to Le Febre, and threw aside the sheet. 'There's half an hour before I need to go to him,' she said. Le Febre stayed, and despised himself for it.

This heartless incident nearly brought about her downfall. That night Le Febre's departure, and then Rebekah's going to Downing, were seen. At St Germain everything, sooner or later, was seen.

Maria Mancini and her friends, assisted by their gallants, resolved to treat Rebekah and Downing according to their deserts. On the evening of a masked ball in September of 1657, on the occasion of the king's nineteenth birthday, they arranged a mock bridal night for Rebekah and Downing.

That evening Maria Mancini was more than usually civil to Rebekah, inviting her and Downing into the inner circle. By midnight the brilliant gathering was intoxicated with wine, and with the charm of its own company. Soft invitations, declined with a smile an hour before, were now accepted. Couples drifted away. The king retired to carouse with half a dozen of his military friends. Maria Mancini, who would join him later, proposed to her circle a stroll in the gallery which overlooked the illuminated fountains, and there they all went. As the group moved off, a secretary of Mazarin's, who had been discreetly watching all evening, called Downing aside. Downing bent to listen to what the man had to say, and waved Rebekah to go on with the others. He would follow.

Maria Mancini, followed by her own entourage, Rebekah among them, walked up the long staircase to the gallery. Off the gallery was one of the state bedrooms, in which, by arcane etiquette, royal princes and their brides were put to bed on their bridal night. The prince was prepared for bed by his gentlemen-in-waiting and the bride by her ladies, they were viewed by all as they sat side by side in the canopied bed, and then blessed by a cardinal who prayed that their union might be long, happy, and fecund.

The door to the state bedroom was thrown open, and Maria Mancini saw that all was ready for the parody of the First Bedding which she had devised. Gentlemen-in-waiting stood with a lace nightgown intended for Downing after they had stripped him of his clothes, which they hoped would require some force. A courtier in the scarlet cope of a cardinal, wearing the ceremonial broad-brimmed and tasselled hat, and also, for this ceremony, a scarlet mask, stood with a censer ready to sprinkle the bed with holy water. To the right of the bed stood the ladies-in-waiting, holding a mocking nightgown. It was of black, widow's velvet, to suit Rebekah's widow's status, and open down the front.

Into this stage-set of a room, grotesquely lit with red candles, Rebekah walked innocently, at first smiled at what she saw, and then realized that it was intended for her.

'A black gown,' said Maria Mancini softly, 'for a widow-bride.'

Rebekah looked round, seeing the mocking faces of the young favourites who had paid court to her all evening, and now intended to pay this further court to her. She looked round again, feeling the beginnings of panic.

'You are looking for your bridegroom?' asked Maria Mancini. 'He will not be much delayed. We shall prepare you for him. But first, look.'

She indicated the window nearest the bed, which was half open and in which a dummy had been so arranged as to resemble a man escaping in his breeches.

'Monsieur Le Febre should not be forgotten,' said Maria Mancini. 'Or not by us.' Then she made a gesture, inviting Rebekah to place herself in the hands of the waiting women who would disrobe her. Amid low laughter from her friends of the evening, Rebekah did take a few steps forward. This surprised no one. They had expected Downing to fight, but then the man was English. Rebekah they regarded as French, and on the fringes of the court if not of it, and it was a strange truth that previous victims of such parodies had always played their parts without protest, obeying etiquette to the point of humiliation and beyond. But the young courtiers had not understood the nature of Rebekah. Having taken the first few steps towards the waiting women, who held up the mocking nightgown for her to see it the better, she turned and met the eyes of each of her tormentors, doing this so slowly that the laughter petered out and died away and they waited to hear what she would say. She said nothing. With rapidity and force she hurled herself at Maria Mancini, seizing her gown at the neck and tearing it from her shoulders so that it was the cardinal's niece who stood naked to the waist, with bloody scratches across one shoulder where Rebekah's nails had caught her in tearing the dress from her. Then Rebekah hurled the girl towards the bed so that she sprawled against it.

Rebekah did not touch her again, but walked straight through the assembled courtiers, and down the length of the gallery to the stairs. They were all so astonished that Rebekah was followed only by Maria Mancini's scream of outrage and a string of Italian curses.

At the foot of the stairs Downing stood waiting for her in the hall. The cardinal's intelligence service was everywhere in the palace, and the secretary who had taken Downing aside had given him the cardinal's compliments and suggested that it might be wiser not to follow the group. His Eminence wished to save the Lord Protector's envoy from annoyance. So Downing coolly waited, suspecting the nature of what he was warned to avoid, but not attempting to save Rebekah. As she descended the stairs and saw him waiting there, she too understood. She would have done the same herself. She took his arm.

It was fortunate that Cromwell soon required Downing's services elsewhere, to be English ambassador at the Hague. It was the most powerful post in the foreign service of the Protectorate. He took Rebekah with him.

Only Robert was sorry to leave St Germain. He was much liked by all, and had made many friends among the officers of the royal garrison. As a parting gift they gave him a boy's sword. Rebekah was glad to go. After the affair of the First Bedding, Maria Mancini had ensured that she never again came into the presence of the king, however remotely, and that she was shunned by the ladies of the court. As for Downing, what could he do but rejoice? He was to have the most coveted ambassadorship in Cromwell's gift. He also had the consolation of Rebekah. He was glad to have her principally because she was on almost every occasion the most beautiful woman in the room. He was also glad to possess the daughter of a woman whom he well remembered to have insulted and slighted him. He had never forgotten Wolsey's shudder when he touched her, or her scorn, or the laughter that had pursued him across the North River when he last left Manhattan. Having been so insulted by the mother, he was glad to possess the daughter. He thought it poetic justice.

Few assembled to see Downing's party leave, but among them was young Le Febre. Downing had a notion of the part the man had played, and cut him dead. Rebekah did not. She had shunned him before, and shamed him. Now that she was about to go, she was glad to see him for one last time, and touched that he should come to say good-bye. She knew what such an action would have cost her own pride, if he had so shamed her. She forgot that Le Febre loved her, and that when a man loves, his pride counts for very little.

She kissed him on both cheeks, and said, 'I am sorry. I despise myself for it. You know what I mean.'

He knew. He had never forgotten the sound of Downing's carriage wheels on the gravel, her abandoning him at such a moment, her stealthy approach to the window which overlooked the courtyard, and then her return to him.

She could not bring herself to say that in this and other things she had wronged him, but she knew she had, and much of this showed in the few words she spoke to him. 'I am sorry. I am deeply sorry.'

As she was about to leave for the Hague, towards what promised to be her most brilliant success, Rebekah began to see her own treachery for the first time. She had not thought it treachery. She had not thought. Now she saw.

Le Febre said good-bye to Robert, too. All the time Downing sat upright in the coach, refusing to acknowledge the man. As they drove away, Robert fought not to cry. He did not cry. But he did not want to go. He had so much liked Le Febre and many of the officers, and he did not like or trust Downing at all.

33

THE LETTER

Wolsey walked slowly home from visiting Peter Stuyvesant, sat for a while in her garden in the warmth, and then, only half rousing herself from her thoughts, called out absent-mindedly for tea. 'Susannah?' she called. No one came. She recollected herself, walked inside to her sitting room, took a sheet of paper, and began to write:

My dear daughter,

I have just come from Governor Stuyvesant, who is recovering from a slight fever that has been about the city this spring. He tells me he has a ship bound for Amsterdam tomorrow by which I shall send this letter to a friend of his at the Hague, a merchant, who will have the means to deliver it into your hands. I have not heard from you since you were at St Germain, but the governor knows from his dispatches that Mr Downing is ambassador at the Hague and that you are with him. So I will trust to that, and address this to you there.

Here then is my news of more than a year. Harry and I are both well, and we do well. As for the rest of my news, I wish it were better. The fever has taken away only a few, but one was Susannah. She was more than seventy years of age, but strong, and had shown no signs of failing. I am sorry to bring you such news. She was your nurse through all your childhood. In her last hours, when she knew she was dying, though the doctor told her, and himself firmly believed, that she was not dying, and would mend, she spoke of you and Ruth as a great joy in a happy life. She did not remember, or if she remembered she did not speak of it even then, that her husband had died so young, carried away in the first winter at Plymouth, and that her daughter Leah chose to leave her and return to Europe soon after we all came here from Plymouth. Susannah talked much of you on the last day. I told her, and the doctor told her, that she would recover. When the doctor had gone she smiled and said she only wished he could be right, so that she could see you again, and your son, but that she knew she would not. That was a month ago, I have lost a dear friend, and I resist the loss. Just before I began to write this I was sitting in the garden, with no thought in my head, when I called her, wanting some tea, and only then remembered that she was not there and could not answer. She helped dress me for my wedding the day I married your father. At the last she talked much of that. 'Turn round,' she said, 'turn round,' and I knew she was far away and thinking she was dressing me for my first wedding again, for it was an old belief that a bride should turn to the four corners of the world, to bring herself good fortune. It was the custom at Scrooby in England, where she knew me when she was as young as you are now, and I was a little girl. When her mind wandered back to Scrooby she revived for a moment, and took a sip to drink, and then died. I believe she was happy.

We rarely hear from Plymouth now. William Bradford has died. He was governor for many years, a good man. There are few left that came over on the first ship.

But to other things. New Amsterdam has changed since you saw it. Governor Stuyvesant says it is become very like a Dutch city, and though I have never seen a Dutch city you will have done, and will know better what he means. The town is now all high gables, and the gable walls are brick, though ours remains one of the few houses built wholly of brick. The rest, for their other walls, and for their barns, still use timber. And though Manhattan may look more Dutch, there are as many languages as ever spoken in the streets, and I believe more English than ever before. There is a Mr Maverick here from the Massachusetts, who has now lived here some years, and who is full of praise for the town and its situation which he calls delightful, and for the harbour which he declares the most magnificent he has ever seen, and so I have heard him say at the governor's table; but that is an opinion, as to the harbour, that Harry has always had. The Dutch here do not share this high opinion of their situation, and several families have lately shipped for Amsterdam and home. Many English, principally I believe from Connecticut, have settled large parts of

THE LETTER

Long Island, so that the place you know as Heemstede is now Hempstead, and Vlissingen is become Flushinge. Utrecht and Breuckelen remain Dutch, though some English have taken root there, too. But those of whatever nationality who settle Long Island have to fortify their townships, for the Carnarsie Indians, when they come by any brandy, as lately they have, prey on lonely farms, and several Dutch men were slaughtered only last week.

But this talk about the town and Long Island is chatter, and you will know it is not what I am writing to tell you. The matter, my dear daughter, is that it is many years since I last saw you, which is a great grief to me and to Harry. He never understood why you did not return from Québec, and I have never known why. You have never written why. I have never seen your son, my grandson. You wrote that he was a favourite with the officers of the garrison at St Germain, and that he had twice ridden with the young king, but this, together with Harry's description of him as a child in arms at Québec, is all that I know. I long to see him here.

We receive little news of the outside world here, and very late, so all I know of you comes indirectly, since Mr Downing is often mentioned in Governor Stuyvesant's dispatches. The actions of Mr Downing are material to us here in Manhattan because he above all other men has been the strict enforcer of the new laws that English goods shall be carried only in English ships; this has ended the old Manhattan trade with Barbados, to our great injury. It has hurt Harry's trade. It has hurt others' much more. But again I am straying from my matter, which is this. You have been much reported with Mr Downing first at St Germain and then at the Hague. You have never written his name to me once, and I know too well how reports can garble the truth, but many dispatches have said the same. I have known Mr Downing. He may be a changed man. You may be a changed woman, but although I have not seen you since you were a girl, I did not mistake your spirit then, and cannot think it that much changed. The spirit does not change. Lord Protector Cromwell is dead. Mr Downing still serves Cromwell's son, but there is much talk, even here, and in the English colonies of Connecticut and the Massachusetts, that the old king's son may return to England and be restored to the throne by Parliament. And what then? Except that he wished to make the Lord Protector king, which may the more go against him, Mr Downing has never been a king's man. He *may*, if the Stuart heir is restored, escape with rewards. He has always been rewarded before. But I beg you to think. I urge you to think. I cannot say that I am writing this dispassionately. I know that I am arguing as much for myself as for you. I am no longer young, and I wish to embrace you again, and to hold my grandson in my arms.

In due course Rebekah did receive this letter at the Hague, where Downing was still the detested ambassador of England. But events had flown. Downing had survived the death of Oliver Cromwell. During the brief second protectorate of Cromwell's son, he retained his post and his confidence, even boasting to the Lord Chancellor, on a visit to London, that his were the best spies in all Europe.

'I have,' he said, 'bribed De Witt's servants, the servants of the Dutch first minister himself, and had his men so much in my pocket that they picked *his* pockets and took his papers while he slept, and brought them to me.'

'That is of service to England,' said the chancellor, 'but there is no conscience in it. And though it were well done, it would be better not spoken of. Tell me the contents of the papers, but not how you sharked them into your sight.'

Then the younger Cromwell fell. Still Downing retained his preferment. Parliament recalled him to London, but only to renew his appointment. Before he returned, he offered the post of undersecretary at the Hague to a young man called Samuel Pepys, but Pepys declined, not wishing to leave England in such days of turmoil, and besides not wanting to leave his wife, whom he held in affection. Downing thought him a man likely to be useful in the future, and so, to put Pepys in his debt, procured him the post of Clerk of the Acts, which effectively made him secretary of the navy board.

They were indeed tumultuous days. At the Royal Exchange in London a royalist crowd gathered round the plinth from which the statue of Charles I had been toppled ten years before, and cheered as a painter whitewashed out the inscription cut into the plinth by the Commonwealth, which read, 'Here Stood the Last Tyrant King.'

It was said in Parliament and in the army that a new king would soon sit on the English throne, and a new statue stand on the plinth.

At the Hague, Downing was jeered whenever he drove out in his carriage. Once, on his return, he had to run the gauntlet of a derisive crowd, and made a run for the embassy door as he left the coach, keeping his head down. 'Down, down, down,' chanted the mob. When Downing protested to the civil authorities, they regretted that they were unable to stop the mouths of so many citizens, or prevent the utterance of what appeared to be a universal, though regrettable, sentiment.

In London, Samuel Pepys, as navy secretary, wrote an order for silk flags, a rich barge, scarlet waistcoats for the bargemen, and for a noise of trumpets and a band of fiddlers, to bring the new king up the Thames when he returned from exile.

Outside the English embassy at the Hague, mobs chanted 'Down, Downing.' Rebekah and Robert watched from an upper window, she with fear, for she had never seen such a mob, and he with excitement. For a nine-year-old boy it was an entertainment, and he waved at the crowd until a solitary stone smashed a pane of glass and Rebekah drew him back.

In his study, Downing sat at an elegant marquetry desk, brought at great expense from St Germain. He ran his fingers over the smooth wood. The Dutch, he thought, might be rich, but enjoyed their wealth like animals, whereas the French had tastes similar to his own.

'Down, Downing,' yelled the brutish mob.

Downing sat on, coolly assembling in his mind the phrases of the loyal address he intended to present to the future King Charles II of England.

34

THE *ROYAL CHARLES* AND SIR GEORGE

In the late spring of that same year, George Downing stood in a cabin of the *Naseby*, an English first-rate ship of the line, as she lay hove to in the English Channel in company with two other first-rates, the *Richard* and the *Speaker*. The ships were dressed overall, the ensigns they flew were those of the royal house of Stuart, and they were attended by seven frigates and a flotilla of smaller craft. All morning, at intervals of twenty minutes, cheers had broken out on ship after ship around the fleet; and from each of the other capital ships, the *Richard* and the *Speaker*, twenty-one gun salutes had pounded out and echoed across the water. Now, on board the *Naseby*, the silence of expectation was everywhere. The king was coming. In an antechamber of the admiral's cabin, Downing stood, feet apart, bracing himself against the sway of the slight swell. He heard the lapping of water on the ship's sides and the creak of the timbers at each roll, but above all lay the silence of the officers and crew as they waited above on deck. All eyes were on the gilded pinnace approaching from the *Richard*. Downing watched her through the quarter lights of the stern cabin as far as he could before she disappeared to cross the bows of the *Naseby* and come up to her starboard quarter, for the king to make the ceremonial boarding of his flagship. Even when he could no longer see the pinnace, Downing could hear the dipping oars and the boatswain's calls as she came alongside. Then came the shipping of oars, and then the weird, shrill pipe calls as the king, having climbed the waist ladder, came on deck. Downing heard the orders of the admiral to the flag captain, the orders of the captain to a lieutenant, of the lieutenant to the master gunner, and the cries of midshipmen to their gun crews.

'Run out!'

The eight cannon-royal of the flagship thundered on iron wheels across wooden decks to the gun ports.

'Make ready!'

The crews crouched at their stations beside each great gun.

'Royal salute. Fire!'

The crashing out of the cannon shook the timbers of the ship. In the cabin, Downing saw heavy chairs leap with the impact. Decanters rattled inside their brass swivels on the table. The terrestrial globe rolled inside its gimbals. Then the cheers arose, but Downing was too deafened to hear them. Inside the cabin the thunderous reverberation was greater even than on deck. He heard only a singing in his ears, and saw only the swinging globe.

The king had come, thought Downing, and the world had moved. And what of his world? Once more he braced himself against the slight roll. Were his fortunes on the down roll, or on the up? He did not know. He waited.

He was by no means without hope. As he had sat in the embassy at the Hague, while the crowds jeered outside and Rebekah and Robert looked out at them, Downing's thoughts had not at all been concerned with their safety but rather with his wife's connections. His wife Frances was in London. He had left her there on his missions abroad. She was not a wife who could be shown off like Rebekah. She had brought him a good fortune, but she was a plain woman. But she did still have one asset of great worth. She was the sister of Charles Howard, and Howard, though he had once commanded Cromwell's bodyguard, had since ingratiated himself with the party that had wished to restore the Stuart heir. Howard was a man who had access to Prince Charles in exile. Downing, acting with considered audacity, had approached the prince through Howard, expressing in a written memorial his loyalty to His Royal Highness – or, could he dare venture to say, His Majesty? – and hoping to be allowed to serve his king with as great fidelity as he had served the cause of England during the late and regretted interregnum.

The prince had become king. His Royal Highness had become His Majesty. Charles II, the restored Stuart king, had that day taken ceremonial possession of his fleet, and would that afternoon, before supper, dispose of George Downing as best suited His Majesty's interests.

From his antechamber Downing could hear everything that passed in the admiral's great stern cabin. First the admiral's servants came, making sure that all was ready to receive the king, and chattering about the day's ceremonies. Then the chattering ceased abruptly. Downing could see nothing, but clearly heard the admiral's flag lieutenant, who had come to inspect the preparations and detected one man helping himself to a glass of rum, call out irritably. 'Afterwards, Johnson, and not where I can see you.'

Then the king's aide-de-camp entered. 'Ten minutes,' he said to the lieutenant, and then a languid conversation ensued about a horse which was an acquaintance of them both. Downing fumed that he should be obliged to wait, suffering the chatter of servants and the drivel of underlings. He felt the indignity. Then the king came, with the admiral, the flag captain, and other officers. Ringing loyal toasts were drunk. Downing's presence was still not asked for. When he had already been waiting three hours, the officers departed. Downing could now hear only murmurings, the rustle of papers, and the scratch of a pen. The rustling of the paper came to him more clearly than the few words spoken. He surmised that the king was signing papers put before him by his aide. Then he could have sworn he heard his own name spoken.

'Downing, sir.' It was a subdued murmur, but he could have sworn it was his name. He strained his ears and leaned close against the dividing wall.

'A blank sheet,' said a deeper voice. Downing recognized the voice he had heard responding to the toasts. It was the king. The rustle of paper followed, then a sigh, then footsteps, and then the communicating door between the cabins was thrown open so suddenly that Downing was discovered crouching against it to hear better. He was quick to recover his composure, but the aide, who had thrown open the door, smiled broadly, stepped aside, and motioned him to enter. The king was reading. Downing could see that it was his loyal address. The aide attempted no introduction.

The king at last raised his head.

'Downing,' he said thoughtfully. 'Well.'

Downing bowed lower than he had ever bowed before, and stood facing the king. He might have been found halffalling through the door, but he would not lose himself without a fight. He faced the king with fear in his heart but boldness in his eyes.

'Interregnum,' said the king, indicating Downing's paper. 'You say interregnum, late lamented interregnum.'

'Much lamented, Your Majesty.'

'We daresay it is, now. You lament it, now. You say so. We do not doubt you do lament it, now. But it was an interregnum which began when our father's head was struck from his shoulders. Yes? D'you see, Downing? That is how we see it.'

'It is how it must be seen by any man of conscience, Your Majesty.'

'Conscience? Conscience now, we daresay. But take your mind back to the interregnum. Whom did you serve in the interregnum?'

'My country, sir.'

'Whom, Downing, whom?'

'A usurper, sir, but through him, England.'

'Usurper? Do you say so? Even we call the man by his name, Cromwell.'

Downing said, 'I lay the blame for my engagement in the Commonwealth service on my early training in New England, where I was brought up and nurtured on principles that experience has shown me were erroneous, and most wrong. Dissenting principles.'

'Ah, Downing, what changes there are today. We have been round the fleet today, you see.'

Downing inclined his head.

'Yes. And the *Speaker* we have renamed the *Mary*. A ship named after the Speaker of the Parliament, we suppose, is now named for my sister Mary. The *Naseby*, on which we find ourselves now, is renamed the *Royal Charles*. The officers assured us, when we asked them, that they would be as good sea boats under new names as under the old. Better, they said. That was drinking talk. But they'll fight as well under a changed name as with an unchanged, as you would no doubt serve your country as well with a changed conscience. Would you say that?'

Downing protested earnestly that a man's conscience could not be changed so easily as a ship's name, that he had some time before seen the error of his ways, and that he had then hidden his true beliefs so that he might continue to serve his country.

The king sat back and waved this away. Then he said, 'Your former convictions having been put away, no doubt after anxious self-examinings, we see you, Downing, as a blank sheet of paper.'

Downing froze. He now took the meaning of the allusion, as he had not when he first heard the king's voice mutter 'blank sheet' through the cabin wall. When the king's father, Charles I, was sentenced to death eleven years before, the present king, then Prince of Wales, had begged Parliament for his father's life and sent to the Commons a blank piece of paper bearing only his signature. It was an offer to accept any terms to save his father's life. But Parliament had offered no terms. The royal *carte blanche* had been scorned, and the king executed.

'We see you,' said the king, 'your conscience being changed, as a blank sheet on which we may write what we wish.'

It was a blank sheet on which the king, as Downing well

knew at that moment, could write a death warrant. It was a long, black moment before the king smiled and held out his right hand. The aide-de-camp drew his epée and gave its hilt into the king's hand.

'We shall need you first at Whitehall,' said the king, 'and then later at the Hague again.'

Downing knelt, as the aide motioned him to do.

The king touched him with the epée on the right shoulder. It was a light touch, but the sword did not move, but remained on the shoulder. Downing knelt in silence for a full thirty seconds, feeling the touch of the sword, and then looked up at the king standing above him. The king still waited. The sword still remained. At length Downing looked the king full in the eyes. Charles was smiling with an urbanity which he never allowed to leave him. Still smiling, he moved the tip of the epée to the point where Downing's ruff met his bare neck, and then, as if at a fencing lesson, delicately moved the epée, held between thumb and forefinger, so that the point drew from Downing's flesh the smallest prick of blood.

Then he returned the epée to his aide.

George Downing thus became Sir George. The knighthood was entirely practical. The new king did not love the Dutch. Downing knew the Dutch, and did not love them either. Downing would do very well to traduce a likely enemy. He would do it by experience and instinct. The knighthood was necessary to give some credence to his return to the Hague, so that the Dutch should believe he was indeed changed and held in special favour by the king, which he was not. The king merely had a use for him. This is how Downing escaped with rewards.

Sir George Downing moved for the moment to London, where he lived no longer in his old lodgings but in a house in Whitehall given to him by the king. The house, like the knighthood, was a gift of policy. The king had learned much from his exile and was resolved never to go on his travels again. He had learned that the loyalty of some men came from their hearts. For this he was grateful, and these men he rewarded. He saw also that the loyalty of others had to be bought, which was their nature. Downing was such a man. He bought Downing.

In his house in Whitehall, Downing lived with his wife Frances, for the sake of appearance, and for the sake of her brother's good opinion, through whom he had made his approaches to the king. He was glad when his wife's brother flourished in the king's favour and was created Earl of Carlisle. He rejoiced, he told himself, for his brother-in-law's own sake, but also, he admitted, because it brought himself a little closer to the king, as having the friendship and the ear of a favoured earl. Just as, for appearance's sake, he kept a wife in Whitehall, he also kept Rebekah, in a smaller house, in Buckingham Street. It was good for a man of substance to be seen to keep a mistress. The boy Robert lived with her. It was an altogether satisfactory arrangement.

Downing congratulated himself that he had prospered as he deserved. He had quite forgotten his former fears, which came to him only when he remembered, which was rarely, the prick of blood drawn by the king's sword that knighted him. But even then it was not exactly fear that came to him, but rather a need to reassure himself quite firmly and unequivocally that this had been an unintended, trivial accident. He reasoned with himself that the king had not even noticed that tiny scratch, and certainly could not have intended it. Had the king intended it, it would have been a slight. He considered it inconceivable that the king would slight a man whom he so evidently trusted, and had honoured with a knighthood and the bestowal of high office. Thus Downing reassured himself. He also, by instinct, cultivated the friendship and company of those able to advance his interests. His brother-in-law, of course. His wife, of course, to whom he was now more civil than he used to be. And Samuel Pepys, who owed his preferment to Downing. True, Pepys's clerkship had turned out to have raised him to a position of greater consequence than Downing had intended. The man as good as spoke for the navy board. He wrote a kind of shorthand, and the king, learning of this, had dictated to him an account of his adventures in exile. Yes, Pepys had risen high, and might be of service even to so great a man as Downing.

So Sir George, meeting Mr Pepys one morning in Whitehall, proposed to him that they should take a stroll to Buckingham Street, and drink a cup of chocolate.

'I keep a place there,' said Downing. 'You must see my boy.'

Pepys assented. He privately thought Downing a scoundrel, though a capable one, but was pleased to accept the chocolate and the confidences even of scoundrels. He knew of no boy. Downing must be about to impart a confidence. Mr Pepys was a good listener.

But on their way, Sir George talked first about matters of state.

'You will know I am to return to the Hague?'

'The king has let it be known. I am glad for you, sir.'

'It will come to war with Holland. The City merchants are crying out for it. The Dutch are great thieves of our commerce.'

'Indeed?' said Mr Pepys, reflecting that the navy, as he was discovering more and more certainly every day, as his knowledge of the admiralty grew, was in no state to engage in a war. Rotting timbers, fraying rigging, men laid off, officers on half-pay. He said nothing, and listened with attentive amiability.

'And when it comes to war,' said Sir George, 'it will need men to manage it. It will need men to take care of it.'

'We shall not lack such men,' said Mr Pepys, inclining a bow towards Sir George.

Downing, taking the bow as a recognition of his own evident capacities, reflected that the man Pepys had perception. He had done well to procure Pepys his appointment.

'Those who take care of a war,' Downing continued, 'must have power. They must have a free hand. It must not be power to be taken away at the least word of another, at the word it might be of a woman, spoken to the king.'

Mr Pepys, reflecting that a word from Barbara Palmer to the king would be enough to sink the chancellor himself, let alone Downing, and thinking that Mrs Palmer was a mighty fine, sparkling woman, murmured his assurance that the royal power, once given, would not lightly be withdrawn.

'One would hope not,' said Downing. 'Power once given should not be contradicted. That would be the loss of everything. Those that know should have the managing of a war, without words from other quarters.'

They turned from the Strand into Buckingham Street, descending a flight of stone steps. It was a street which led straight down to the Thames. From the other end of the street more steps led down to a jetty from which a ferry ran upriver to the houses of Parliament, and downriver to St Paul's. The tide was high, as Downing had known it would be. At high tide the air was fresh and tonic. At low tide, refuse and sewage lay stagnant on the exposed mud, and stank. He would not have taken Mr Pepys there at such a time, or gone there himself. He was sorry Rebekah had to endure this inconvenience, but it was a good house which he had taken at a frugal rent.

He stopped and pointed out to Mr Pepys the small craft busy on the river – a sight Pepys had seen a thousand times. He breathed deep of the sweet air and remarked that it was sweet, to which Mr Pepys assented. Then Downing said, 'Now you must see my boy.'

Robert was nearly ten. At the house, he greeted Downing with a formal bow, and a formal 'Good morning, sir.' Cool for a son, thought Mr Pepys. But then Downing was cool for a father.

'He has ridden with the French king,' said Downing. 'When we were at St Germain, at court.'

Then to the boy: 'Tell Mr Pepys how you rode with the young king.'

'It was only twice, sir.'

They had been let in by the maid, who had disappeared.

Downing went off, calling impatiently for the maid, for chocolate, and for Rebekah, leaving Pepys and Robert in a sitting room.

'Your father is a great man in the kingdom,' said Pepys. 'And that is a great thing for you.'

Robert replied. 'Will you take a seat, sir?' He would not deny that Downing was his father. Rebekah had told him that Mr Downing liked it to be thought so. But neither would he admit that he was. The fame of a real father he could not remember was dear to the boy's mind. He would not deny Mr Downing outright, but would not call him father.

Mr Pepys courteously accepted the boy's invitation to sit, and spoke to him as an equal.

'You have seen the French king. Ridden with him. Have you seen King Charles here in London?'

'Only once, from a distance, in Whitehall.'

'Once is more than most men have seen him,' said Pepys, and began to tell Robert the stories of the king's campaigns and escapes as they had been told to him.

The boy listened with fascination.

'But do you know,' said Pepys, 'he has never told me the story of his hiding in the oak tree, and Cromwell's men standing underneath, and not finding him.'

'That is a story I know,' said Robert.

'It was a story I knew too, but when I asked the king he could not remember. He said he could not deny it, but he could not remember. Out of a thousand adventures, he said, the one he could not remember himself was remembered by everyone.'

Pepys was in full flow when chocolate, Downing, and Rebekah appeared. Mr Pepys, when presented to Madame de la Tour, took her hand and raised the fingers to his lips. 'There is no "de,"' she said. She wished Downing would not consistently give her the name which the French king had given only to Robert.

She sat, smoothing her wide skirt over her lap, and Mr Pepys thought her beautiful.

Throughout the polite nothings of their exchanges he became warmly conscious of Rebekah. They talked of New England, which she said she had known, as Mr Downing had.

'I had a cousin there,' said Mr Pepys.

'I was born there,' said Rebekah.

'Then,' said Mr Pepys, 'we have been well rewarded for all our trouble in planting and nurturing those colonies.'

She smiled. It was a nothing, but a pleasant nothing.

'My cousin there,' said Pepys, 'was Richard. Richard Pepys. He was at Boston in the Massachusetts, but he returned.'

'I have never been to Boston, but very near.'

'It is a fine town now, so I am told. But in those days not fit for a gentleman. I remember my cousin saying, not fit for a gentleman. But then he was harsh in his judgments. He is older than me. Not fit for a gentleman, he said, and very likely he was wrong, but he never could forget he was son of a Lord Chief Justice of Ireland.'

'There's grand for you,' said Rebekah, laughing for the first time in weeks. Robert went across and hugged her, happy to see her happy.

Downing, none too pleased to see the boy show an affection to Rebekah that was denied to him, and none too pleased either that Rebekah was so much entertained by Mr Pepys, rose and said they must be on their way. Matters of state demanded their attention.

Mr Pepys, very sensitive to men's moods, was careful not to kiss Rebekah's hand when she offered it to him again on parting, but merely took the fingers for a second, and gave a formal bow. But he ruffled the boy's hair, and they parted already firm friends.

Downing returned to his house in Whitehall, where he ate in silence with his wife, attended by four footmen. Mr Pepys after two hours at the admiralty reading papers which revealed even further naval deficiencies, went home mourning the state of the fleet but pleased to see the maid who opened his door to him, whom he patted so that she stifled a squeal, and delighted to see his wife, who greeted him with affection.

Late that night, before going to bed, he wrote his diary in the tiny shorthand he habitually used. Transcribed from the shorthand, but leaving in the occasional words of maimed French and Italian that he employed, that day's entry reads:

Up and to Whitehall, where fell in with Sir G. Downing and with him to Buckingham St. to see his son, as he said, and his kept woman. Sir G. spoke on the way, by indirection, against His Mjty's mistress, exclaiming that a word from her could bring a man down, as indeed *half* a word from Bab Palmer would work his destruction, and heartily I wish it would, though he did get me my place, for he is a sider with all times and changes, a crafty fawning man, full of stingy treachery. His lady, Mme. La T——, not French but from New England, mighty fetching in a flowered tabby silk gown, and I besar su main, and she merry in talk, but Sir G. not pleased to see it so. The boy, who has ridden with the French king, very grave and pretty, and loving to her but, showing uncommon sense in one so young, cold to Sir G.

Then to the Office, where all confusion, and two hours with dispatches showing the fleet less fit for any action than was feared, the main courses of the *Royal Charles* having split at a puff of wind at Gravesend, and two new cannons burst their barrels on the *Mary* at the first firing them.

So home early, having thought to be very sparing of my discourse, not giving occasion of any enquiry where I had been, but my wife being delighted I was early, and greeting me sweetly, I pleasured her in our new great bed, and hazer very well con ella to her great content, though with Mme. La T—— in my mind, which God knows runs that way, and on her cunny, which thoughts may God give me the grace to forbear, though ella is comely and my heart full of surprise and disorder on that account. As to the boy, Sir G. says it is his son, but, query, is there capacity in such a sleek, fawning scoundrel to get such a son, or any?

My mind still running on La T——, to bed and prayers.

35

THE PALACES AND DUNGEONS OF THE HEART

But Mr Pepys did not need God to give him grace to forbear. Within two weeks of his meeting with Rebekah, and before he had opportunity to renew the acquaintance, the exigencies of European politicking removed Downing to the Hague once more, nominally as ambassador to a friendly power, but in reality to spy upon and harass an intended enemy. Once again he left his wife at home, and took Rebekah and Robert with him. Rebekah went with reluctance, but it seemed her only course. In London she was no better than a kept woman, and a woman kept apart, in a house which had none of the grandeur to which she had become accustomed. At the Hague she would once again be in the centre of society. Downing was detested, but the representative of Charles II could not be shunned, and she would be mistress of his house. Had she wished to stay in London, she had not the means to do so. She *had* thought, since Wolsey's letter, of returning to America. She had debated this with herself. But she was still not sure she could face her mother and pass Robert off as her own son and not Ruth's.

She had asked herself at the Hague, when she first received her mother's letter, 'Can I return?' And the answer had always been, 'I cannot.'

Now in London, when Downing once more expected her to go with him to Holland, she asked herself the same question, and gave herself the same answer. 'I cannot.'

In any case, had she wished to do so, it would have been next to an impossibility. A party of pilgrims, given all the strength of their faith, and the comfort of each other, could cross the ocean. But for a woman and child to cross alone and unescorted was almost unheard of.

So Rebekah went to the Hague, and the second period of her acquaintance with Mr Pepys, which was to have momentous consequences for her, was delayed by eighteen months.

In truth she had been much less affected by Mr Pepys than he by her. His visit had entertained her, even rallied her spirits, but she was used to the amusing attentions of courtiers. She did not forget him, but nor did she particularly remember. It was Robert who occasionally asked after the man who had talked uncondescendingly to him and ruffled his hair. As for Mr Pepys, for three weeks he was desolate, but then comforted himself with Mrs Jopp at Rotherhithe, whose husband was a brewer, and with the piquant Jane Sandell at Greenwich, whose husband was frequently absent on long sea voyages. But he did remember Rebekah.

Sir George Downing's mission to harass Their High Mightinesses of the States General on behalf of His Britannic Majesty Charles II was so successful that after eighteen months the two countries were fast slipping into another war. Downing was for the moment recalled to help plot the war. He brought Rebekah and the boy with him, and they took up residence at the old address in Buckingham Street, where, after a few days, Mr Pepys called, ostensibly to see Robert, who had twice written to him from the Hague.

He did see the boy, who was pleased and excited. Rebekah also received him with pleasure. He kissed her hand, and gave her the gossip of the town and the court.

'It's all who's in, who's out, Mr Pepys,' she said.

'That is the game called politics,' he replied.

'But the navy is not a game to you. I see it is not.'

'It is not. The fleet's reformed. Or part reformed. Almost

half of it is fit to sail. It is a great satisfaction to me that it should be so.'

On his second visit he affected to notice that her cheek was a little flushed and solicitously took her pulse, leaning over her with the gravest attention and holding her wrist with two gentle fingers. She did not take back her hand, and before he at last withdrew he kissed her forehead and told her she was as fine a woman as he had seen that month, and it was *his* heartbeat that was rapid. Hers, as he had ascertained, was calm. That night he confided to his diary a more than eloquent plea for grace to forbear. On his third visit, the very next day, he found a pretext to measure the length of her hand against his, and on the next presented her with five pairs of silk gloves.

'Five!' she exclaimed.

It was necessary, he assured her, to try on one glove of each pair. She laughed, seeing very well how he intended to assist her to do so, and thus their intimacy grew. For the greater part of each visit Robert was with them, so that moments alone had to be stolen and connived for, Robert being sent to fetch this and that about the house, and then on errands to tradesmen in the Strand. Then Mr Pepys proposed that they should take supper together at the Heaven.

'The Heaven?'

'At Westminster Hall. There are alehouses there. They are called the Purgatory and the Hell. They are outside the walls of the hall. The Heaven is an eating place, where one may eat well. It is inside the walls. It is known as the Heaven at the end of the Hall.'

Rebekah had not seen Downing for a week. His visits had become less and less frequent. She knew he would be engaged with the king at Richmond on Tuesday and Wednesday of the following week. Supper on Tuesday was agreed, at the Heaven, where one could eat well and discreetly.

Yet Mr Pepys was not discreet when he chose to arrive on Tuesday in his new gilded coach, drawn by four bays. He had possessed it only for a week, and was ingenuously proud to show it off to Rebekah and to the town. Next day it would be the talk of the town. She did not care. She was overtaken by a kind of recklessness, and let Pepys hand her up the coach steps while a liveried footman held open the door.

'You are doing mighty fine,' she said, looking at his new brocaded coat as she sat opposite him.

So he was. The coach was fine. His clothes were fine. Even an honest secretary to the navy board had vast patronage, which it would have been thought unnatural not to use.

'Strange,' he said as they clattered over the deplorably cobbled roads, 'strange how these people do promise me anything. One man a rapier: he wanted to build a navy sloop in his yard. Another a hogshead of claret: he wished a licence to sell grog in Plymouth docks. Another a gown, another man a silver hatband to do him a courtesy. Anything. They promise me anything, without my once asking.'

'Then pray,' she said, 'that God keeps you from being too grand to take such things.'

The footmen standing on the back of the carriage heard laughter from within.

'Or,' said Rebekah, 'from being too much lifted up when you do accept them.'

More laughter inside.

The coach had left the cobbles of the Strand for the packed dirt road that was Whitehall, and then they were in the narrow streets where a hundred houses were crammed in between the towers of Westminster Abbey and the thick Norman walls of Westminster Hall, once a royal palace, now the meeting place of Parliament and the law courts, but surrounded on all sides not only by the Purgatory and the Hell but by a dozen other alehouses and coffeehouses whose ramshackle buildings had been tacked by generations of builders on to the very walls of the great hall itself. The footmen dismounted, bullying a way through the ragged, gawking crowds, and the coach turned into Palace Yard. There they dismounted, entered by the south door, and walked the echoing length of the longest hall in Europe, between walls already six hundred years old. At the end, torches flickered and voices were raised in laughter.

Mr Pepys took Rebekah's arm. 'Heaven,' he said, 'at the end of the hall.'

The keeper of the eating house, a Mr Peters, expected Mr Pepys, knew him well, and came up all obsequiousness, protesting that he was honoured by the visit of so great a man.

'As you directed, Mr Pepys, sir. As you directed. All is as you directed.' He led them through the crowded outer Heaven towards an oak door. They passed a table of six men, a couple of them young, the others grizzled. One of the older men raised a glass to Pepys.

'Your health, Mr Secretary,' he called out.

Pepys acknowledged the toast by raising the hand that was not guiding Rebekah.

'And your lady's,' cried a younger fellow. Pepys took no notice of this.

'Half-pay captains,' he whispered to Rebekah, 'drinking their half pay. They think it is in my power to find them ships. It is in my power to find one or two of them ships. I will do it for Richards when I can. He is the one who toasted me.'

Another group greeted them. Mr Pepys was a rising man, a man to be greeted cordially, but there was perhaps a touch of derision in their friendly calling-out to him.

'Members of the Parliament,' said Pepys. 'Of no account, save for Nicolls, who is not a Parliament man properly, but just drinks with them. He is the Duke of York's man, the king's brother's man, whom the duke will see go far.'

Pepys called out to Nicolls, 'A good evening, sir,' and Nicolls raised a glass.

Peters ushered them through the oak door, and into his private room. It was a small room, ten feet square. A fire crackled at one end, warming the cool air. The only light apart from the fire was from two candles, set either side of the places set at table. A sofa stood against the far wall, and, on the wall opposite, a tapestry hung.

Peters saw that Rebekah's eye went to the tapestry. 'From France, ma'am,' he said. 'It is from a set whisked out of a

Lord's house in Cromwell's time, as many things was whisked. There was six of them, I was told, but I have only the one. It was pictures of a hunt, but I never saw all six together, and there's no hunting on that one, only a tame beast by the look of it.'

Rebekah said, 'It was a hunt. They were right to say it was a hunt. That is nearly the end of the chase. The tame beast is a unicorn, but it is not tame at all. It is wild. Only it has been tamed for the moment by the maid who is holding it by the leash. In the next tapestry it will be killed by the hounds that will take it now it is tamed.'

'Are you from France, ma'am?' asked Peters. 'And have you known unicorns there?'

'No,' she said, 'not in that way.'

She sat. Mr Peters buzzed around. 'I shall wait on you myself, sir. Everything is as directed, and the claret warmed. As directed.'

He took a bottle which had been set to stand near the hearth, and poured wine into crystal glasses.

They took their first sips, and were warmed by the wine.

Peters brought in a dish of marrow bones, and left them.

'His name is Peters,' said Pepys. 'And as this is the Heaven, he is called St Peter at the gates.'

They ate. Pepys pressed Rebekah to more wine. Both were comforted by the drink, the flickering fire, the scent of the woodsmoke which from time to time blew back into the room, and by the presence of each other.

'That,' he said, indicating the tapestry, 'covers the very wall of Westminster Hall. Eight feet thick, and, until they built Whitehall, part of the palace of all the English kings since Rufus.'

She smiled.

'Kings have been here,' he said. 'Kings have eaten here. Kings of the Houses of Normandy, and Blois, and Plantagenet, and Lancaster, and York.'

At this he took her hand. 'And princesses, too,' he said.

Peters entered with a dish of a dozen larks, which they ate with relish, dismembering the little birds with their fingers.

Pepys held a leg between finger and thumb, ate the meat from it, and tossed the bone onto the rush-strewn floor. He watched as Rebekah stripped the delicate meat from a lark's breast with her teeth. She felt him watching, met his eyes, and tossed the carcass over her shoulder. He took a lark from the dish, tore off a leg, and held it across the table to her. She leaned forward and took the meat from it with her teeth as he held the bone.

She looked round for a finger bowl, and dipped both her hands into it. Mr Pepys saw the slender fingers paddling beneath the water, and, taking the opportunity to assist her, found his hand covering hers, and then the fingers of one hand entwined in her fingers.

Mr Peters entered again. Rebekah held her hands high in front of her, shaking them so that the drops of water fell onto the table, and Mr Pepys held out a napkin to her, folded her hands in it, and dried them finger by finger.

Mr Peters moved silently and quickly about his business of removing the dish of larks. He saw that they had eaten seven between them. He saw that everything was going well.

After Peters set before them apricots from the king's greenhouses at Kew, Pepys said, 'I have not enquired how you were in Holland. I was sorry you returned to Holland so soon after we first met. I was stricken when you went to Holland.'

'Yes?'

'How were you at the Hague, then? There were reports that Sir George was not held in so high esteem as an ambassador should be. The king was displeased at this discourtesy of the Dutch. The report was that Sir George himself felt obliged to address the States General, Their assembled High Mightinesses themselves, and tell them to their faces that he was not received with the same respect now that he was when he served Cromwell.'

'He did tell them that.'

'There were reports that he said he was not received with so much respect as when he served "the *traitor* Cromwell."'

Rebekah and Pepys had never once spoken of Downing before. On his visits to Buckingham Street, the very mention of the name was avoided. But now they were free with each other.

She replied, 'He said "the *traitor* Cromwell." Cromwell, from whom, I suppose, he got all he has in the world, and knows it, and the world knows it.'

'Save only his knighthood,' said Pepys.

'And he got that from the king only because Cromwell had raised him so high at the Dutch court that there was no one better fitted to harry them on the king's behalf, as Sir George has harried them.'

'And on account of Cromwell's having raised him so high,' said Mr Pepys, very daring, 'on account of his being at the French court, he first got you? Which I hold against him.'

Rebekah said steadily, 'I was at the French court. He was at the French court. But I do not know he *got* me.'

Pepys poured more wine.

Rebekah looked at the filled, red, glowing glass. 'You like your wine, Mr Pepys.'

'Lord, not so much as I did. I am temperate. There was a time, when I was young...'

Rebekah smiled. Mr Pepys was just thirty, a year or so younger than her.

'There was a time when I was young, when I was a three-bottle man. Sometimes, rising to piss when it was half dark, between night and day, I would not know whether it was sunset or sunrise.'

She laughed.

'But, forgive me, I must rise for a moment now, though I am a changed man, and I know it is dusk, not dawn.' He bowed his way out of the room, leaving Peters to clear the fruit. The man left the remains of the fourth bottle of claret, and put another log on the fire. Mr Pepys returned as Peters left. This time as he withdrew, he pulled a long red curtain which hung inside the door. He would not disturb them again.

Rebekah sat back. She knew how this evening would end. She was sure she knew how it would end. She had known when he caught her hand in the bowl, and when he dried her fingers one by one in the napkin. No, she had known much further back than that. She had known the day in Buckingham Street when he took her pulse. No, she did not know when she had known. But she had long ago abandoned herself to the events of the evening, and was happy.

Pepys was standing behind her chair. He said, 'That is not your new flowered tabby gown.'

'Tabby?'

'The gown you wore the first time I saw you.'

'That is now an old flowered tabby gown. But no, this is not it.'

She took a last sip of wine and then walked over to the unicorn tapestry.

'I am a twin,' she said.

'You are a twin?' he said.

'I am one of two twins. Twin sisters.'

She said this quite composedly, but as it seemed to him, apropos of nothing.

'Twins. Ah,' he said. 'I saw a stone once, a commemoration stone, in a church in Holland, which said that two hundred years ago a noblewoman was accosted by a beggar-woman, who was carrying twins in her arms. She begged some coin from her. But the noblewoman would not give her anything – I remember, it was Margaret, a countess of Hennenbeck who refused. At which the woman cursed her, and said that for her pitilessness she should bear at one lying-in as many children as there are days in the year. And she did, nine months later. Three hundred and sixty-five children. The stone said so, in the church wall. Half of them boys and half girls. I do not know what the odd one was. Three hundred and sixty-five.'

'Three hundred and sixty-five,' Rebekah repeated, and then Mr Pepys took her boldly by the hips.

She smiled with closed eyes, and looped her arms round his neck. He embraced her with his hands, softly talking.

'Not your tabby gown, but Piedmont silk.' He caressed her back. 'I had the ordering of the silks to dress the king's fleet overall. Yellow silks. Scarlet silks. Blue silks.'

She nodded her head, content to be held in his firm hands, which went from her hips, to her waist, to her breasts, and then again to her hips.

'Piedmont silk,' said Mr Pepys, and his right hand eased beneath her petticoats. To do this he had practically to kneel, and when he rose he had still penetrated only two layers.

'More,' she said; 'more to get under.'

Mr Pepys took stock. They were standing, swaying together, on the further side of the room from the sofa. He had counted on the sofa. He was about to take her hand with great aplomb and lead her to it, when she, feeling herself sway a little too much, took two short steps back, so that her shoulders rested against the tapestry. Since her hands were still clasped, though loosely, round Pepys's neck, he had to go with her. She leaned against the tapestry, lips apart and eyes closed, and held him in a fierce embrace. Now the sofa was indeed lost to Mr Pepys. He had hoped not to have to be this resourceful, but he cast one backward glance at the now useless sofa, then mercifully abandoned all lamentation for the loss of it, and followed necessity and strong instinct. Desisting for a moment from his conquest of the petticoats, he looked at Rebekah's face and tousled hair and kissed her in pure affection. He felt her hands tighten on his back in response, and kissed her again. Then to the petticoats, both hands adventuring in a sweet lust of affection.

'Oh,' he said, raising the first, 'the mainsail.'

'And oh,' slipping under the second, 'topsails.'

And so on through topgallants and royal topgallants, with Rebekah assisting and gathering yards of petticoat at her waist and tossing them to one side, until Pepys arrived at her bare waist, bare hips, and parted legs, and she, leaning against the tapestry-covered wall, uncovered him as little as he needed to be uncovered, and Pepys, all afire but with a trembling agitation – Could he enter her? Could he

not? She was slipping away. Could he? Oh, he could –
entered her standing and was proud, and gratified, and
mightly pleased as he had not been since he was a very
young man indeed, and embraced her with utter open affection, and called her sweet Becky, sweet Becky, and came too
soon. But she kissed him and held him, and still embraced
him and spoke softly to him. 'Hold me. Keep your weight on
me. Hold me.'

He did, and they stayed there. Still staying close to her as
she wanted, he assembled his clothes again, and she let her
many petticoats fall from her waist and cover her. He kissed
her and told her she was a lovely woman and felt, with the
purest proud ingenuousness, that he was a pretty fine man,
too, of which her soft caressing hands assured him as she
folded him against her and stroked his head.

The pell-mell of it all did not matter, the lost sofa did not
matter, the brevity of it did not matter. The affection and
loving-kindness of it were all that mattered, and that was in
abundance.

Mr Pepys stayed with her, murmuring to her, until he felt
cold. The fire was at the far end of the room. So he made as if
to move, but she did not wish it. 'Rebekah?' he said.

She held him tightly, and began to shake.

'Rebekah?' he asked again. She did not answer, but
shivered as if she had a fever. She shook through her whole
body. When at last it seemed to have gone, he raised her
face, he saw that she was not crying. There were no tears on
her face. He was comforting her, thinking it had passed,
when she began to shake again, with a racking shudder, and
said again and again, 'Hold me.'

He hugged her to him. He stroked her hair. He held her
hands. He held her for long minutes until she at last recovered herself and could walk across to the sofa, where
again he comforted her as well as he knew how.

What had happened? So many things, and so complex.
Pepys's wooing of her, and his open pleasure in her, had
aroused Rebekah from the long barrenness of her association with Downing, which she now thought shameful

because it was all expediency. She was not ashamed to be a man's mistress, but with Downing it was hardly even that. As she had once told him in a fit of anger, she was, with him, barely worth the name. It was a pitiful façade. The man rarely touched her, and never at all in kindness. And as her spirit revived with Pepys's visits, she knew she had found someone who was closer to her than anyone had been since her sister Ruth. At supper that evening she had said, 'I am a twin. I am one of two twins,' and would have told him more. She did not know how much she had been prompted to do so by the sight of the unicorn tapestry, which had taken her mind back to Breuckelen and the white fawn, and into the wastes of New France. Then Mr Pepys in his boldness coaxed her and caressed her, and raised her petticoats with a desperate commentary about topgallants and royal topgallants, and had her in a scuffle against a wall; and his deep affection, honest desire, and warmth of spirit had touched her to the soul. Then she regretted her treachery to the young Le Febre at St Germain, whom she had betrayed for so worthless a man as Downing and for the sake of her ambition. And she had never before felt so strongly the enormity of her betrayal of La Tour. She did not regret her giving of Ruth to him. To Rebekah that had been as natural as night and day. She would do it again if Ruth were alive. But her abandonment of her husband when Ruth bore his child now seemed terrible to her. Until Mr Pepys, no one had shown her again the loving-kindness that had always been La Tour's. And enormous as she now saw that betrayal was, she saw that her deception of her mother, her coming to Europe, her bringing of Robert, and her claiming him as her own, were greater sins. She had abandoned her husband and her mother, and she was ashamed.

The warmth of Pepys brought out in Rebekah a warmth she had never in her life shown. She longed to make what reparations she could. She longed to see Wolsey, and the continent where she and her son Robert had been born. She still said to herself, 'My son Robert.' That was perhaps too old a deception to be recanted. She did not know. But the rest she would repair as far as she could.

At the Heaven, Pepys waited with Rebekah, and, when she was recovered enough, gave her his arm and walked her bravely through the outer Heaven, receiving the obsequious thanks of Mr Peters, and once again running the gauntlet of the now-drunken naval captains and Parliament men. His coach was waiting, and he took Rebekah home to Buckingham Street.

At her door he raised her hand to his lips.

She kissed his cheek, and said, 'Thank you for the Heaven. Thank you for that. Thank you for holding me, and staying. Thank you from my heart for that.' Then she went in.

When he returned home, Mr Pepys's wife was angrily tearful, but he won her round with contrition, and she came to bed and read to him.

Rebekah lay awake. The Heaven at the end of Westminster Hall was in what had been once a palace, though from the thickness of the walls it could have been a dungeon. She saw now as dungeons the palaces she had inhabited with George Downing. Supper with Mr Pepys had taught her more than she had ever before suspected about the palaces and dungeons of her own heart.

36

GOOD NIGHT, MANHATTAN

It was really on account of his brother James that Charles II, by the Grace of God and of Parliament King of England had summoned Sir George Downing back from the Hague to plot mischief and war. Charles was happily treating with France to form an allegiance against Spain, whose ships the English had in any case been plundering since Drake and before. The old fox Mazarin was at last dead, and the young Charles, in his early thirties and relishing his new power, got on well with the young Louis XIV, who in his mid-twenties had at last come, with the old cardinal's death, into sole enjoyment of his realm. England's old enemy was Holland, and it had to be said that Downing's diplomacy had excellently maintained the old enmity and bitterness, but on the whole it was James, Duke of York, who was the immediate cause of Downing's being summoned from the Hague. The Duke was the king's younger brother and Lord High Admiral, and he had suffered from the Dutch.

So after preliminary conferences with the chancellor and others, Downing found himself summoned one morning to the palace at Whitehall, where he waited in company with three gentlemen he had come to know well in the previous few days. They had talked much together. They were Samuel Pepys, a man, thought Downing, whom he had made and on whom he could therefore rely; Samuel Maverick, a New Englander who had also lived in Manhattan, a man, thought Downing, who was discontented and ambitious, and on whom also he could therefore rely; and

Richard Nicolls, of whom Downing was not sure, since he was the Duke's man, and reticent. Nicolls was a straight, honest man. He was the officer Pepys had seen drinking with the Parliament men in the Heaven, and had pointed out to Rebekah.

The four men rose first for the entry of the Duke of York, who waved them down, took snuff himself, and offered the others snuff as a matter of form, which was as a matter of form declined, and then took Nicolls aside and talked with him in undertones.

The king entered, and surveyed them as they made their bows. Pepys, good fellow, Downing, serviceable tool. Maverick, a man whose name he remembered simply because it was unusual, and sounded like mischief.

'Well, brother,' said the king, 'we know what we are about.'

'We do,' growled James, a solid, stolid man. 'Downing will have told you.'

Downing had written to the king, and written often.

'Refresh me, Downing,' said the king, whereupon Sir George went at length into the matter, how the States General had grown insolent, insulting the king through the person of his ambassador, how they had frustrated the lawful trading adventures of his Grace the Duke of York along the African coast, and how they had fired on three of his ships. The king heard him out.

'Nothing new there, Downing.'

The duke replied. 'And that's mostly the trouble of it. It's the continued insolence of many years, on and on. But the firing on my ships *is* new. The firing on those particular three ships of mine is new. The fact is, there's not enough trade in the world for the two of us, not enough for Holland and England, so one must go down.'

'And that is war,' said the king, reflecting that war cost money.

'But there can be war without war,' said Downing. 'That is our proposal.' That was in truth *his* proposal, assiduously put to the duke and the others over the previous few days.

'How war without war?' demanded the king.

'By taking what is ours,' said Sir George, and he brought forth his argument. There was an island, the possession of which would give an easy command of all West Indian islands. It was an island which His Majesty's father, many years before, had sworn to be his own royal colony, which he would cherish and maintain entire. It was an island which even the pretender Cromwell had intended to take. If, asked Downing, His Majesty would forgive such a reference?

The king smiled a bland smile.

'This island,' said Downing, 'is Manhattan, which all the world knows was discovered by an Englishman, Henry Hudson, and is therefore English by right of first discovery.'

The king smiled again. This was known. It was also known by every man in the room that Hudson had made this first discovery in a Dutch ship under Dutch patronage. Still, there was no need to labour that.

'Furthermore,' said Downing, 'there is a gentleman here, Mr Maverick, who is able to state on his oath that the savages near Manhattan swear that the first white men they ever saw were English, not Dutch. So that is more.'

The king, calculating how long ago this must have been, merely observed, 'Then they must be ancient savages, to live so long to remember it.'

'There is an English title to the land,' Downing persisted, 'which goes beyond the memory of man.'

'Evidently,' said the king. 'And your war without war is to take something which is ours, and has been ours beyond anyone's memory, but of which we have never yet entered into possession?'

'Your Majesty,' said Downing, 'puts the matter more pithily than it lies within my power to do. And Mr Maverick here, if Your Majesty will please to hear him, will state what he knows, of his recent knowledge, about your colony of Manhattan.'

Maverick spoke. 'It is, Majesty, a most delightful situation, between two rivers, a very delightful situation....'

'Yes, yes. There are many situations, Mr Maverick, which are delightful but which we do not want. We do not lack delight. Descend to particulars.'

Maverick described the ruinous state of the Dutch defences, finishing his account by saying, 'And on my last day there, before sailing for England, I spoke to the master gunner, whom I had contrived to know by drinking with him at the inn, the Swan.'

'Yes, yes. The Swan.'

'Majesty, he said there were eighteen barrels of powder in the fortress, each containing only fifty pounds in weight, and so old and decayed and damp they would rather smother a bonfire than explode it, if thrown onto the flames.'

The king nodded and looked at the duke. 'Brother?' he said.

'Manhattan lies clear between the colonies of New England and Virginia. With it, we should possess the whole of the eastern coast. Without it, we suffer a constant check to our trade. The New England colonies, no less than Virginia, are bound by law to trade direct with us, but they do not. They trade through Manhattan, and therefore with the Dutch, and so evade our proper profit and our proper excise.'

'And who will be captain of your expedition?' asked the king.

The duke indicated Nicolls.

Downing said quietly to the king, 'Sir, give us five frigates, and it will be Good Night, Manhattan.'

The king looked at Nicolls. 'Do you agree with that estimate?'

'I do.'

'Mr Pepys,' said the king, 'tell me, can the navy dispose of five frigates?'

Mr Pepys thought of his half-a-fleet that was capable of putting to sea. 'It can, sir.'

'Then,' said the king, 'Good night, Manhattan.'

*

The delightful island whose taking the king so lightly approved was going through a bad year. It was so hard a winter that the East River froze over. The cold chilled Governor Stuyvesant, who lay in bed for weeks with a fever. Then came the earthquakes. When the first tremor was felt, Wolsey was in the kitchen with the cook, and both stood amazed and afraid as the battery of brass pans hanging on the walls at first vibrated, and then swung and chimed against each other. Stuyvesant saw the earthquake as an omen. He saw the hand of God in vibrations that shook a city built on granite. As it happened, his picture in full uniform shook off the wall, the fall smashing the frame and flaking paint from the portrait's nose and brow. He saw this as an omen too, at which Wolsey gently told him that at that rate omens were begetting omens. He could have one omen if he wished, either the earthquake or the falling of the picture, but to make two of it was nonsense. He took temporary courage from her sympathetic common sense. Then in the summer there were two scourges – the smallpox and Indian raids. The smallpox abated, but the Indians became more and more audacious, murdering outlying farmers and their families. Stuyvesant posted proclamations offering rewards for volunteers to hunt down the killers, but few came forward, and in the end the first scourge relieved Manhattan from the second, when the smallpox spread to the Indians and ran through their villages.

Then Englishmen from Connecticut set up the town of Westchester a bare six miles from Manhattan, plainly within the Dutch jurisdiction, which they defied. Stuyvesant could do nothing, and paced about his house exclaiming, 'And only twenty men.' It was reported that it had needed only that number of Connecticut men to defy the authority of Stuyvesant, and, indirectly, of Their High Mightinesses themselves. Smarting from this defiance, but thinking it tactful to maintain friendship with his English neighbours, Stuyvesant visited Boston, taking passage there with Harry O'Brien. He found a city of seven thousand men and women, neat houses, Puritan industry, full warehouses, a flourishing trade, and bare civility. On his arrival he was met by a ceremonial guard of three squadrons of cavalry, but that was a show of force rather than of courtesy to a governor who knew he could not himself have raised a single squadron. He complained of the taking of Westchester by Connecticut, but was told that Connecticut was not answerable to Massachusetts, or Massachusetts to him. He returned to Manhattan in a fury, and stumped straight to his house.

Harry, going to Wolsey, told her, 'He was received with sweet nothings, and less. When a ceremonial welcome was read out to him, he was addressed as "Governor of the Dutch plantations in America." Not as Governor of New Netherlands, or of New Amsterdam, or of Manhattan. It was as if they were telling him these places only existed on the map, or in his mind, and were not facts, not real places, with real boundaries.'

Wolsey listened. She had expected no more. Then she said, 'Harry, I have a letter.'

'Letter?'

'From Rebekah. It came by an English ship a week ago.'

He turned and waited. He knew from her voice what her news would be. As he waited for her to tell him – and it could only have been a pause of a few seconds – he observed her more clearly than he had for a long time. They had been man and wife for many years. When a man and a woman live together for so long, they hardly notice the change in each other, until a change is suddenly seen, and then it is as if it has only at that moment taken place. In his cabin that morning, as he rose, Harry had caught sight of himself in a looking glass. His strong, short beard was now not so much grizzled as grey all through. His hair, which, when he last noticed it, had been red flecked with grey, was now grey flecked with red. His face seemed no more weather-beaten and lined than it had appeared when he was forty, but that is because a sailor's face takes on a fixed, weatherbeaten cragginess younger than other men's. He was no longer forty. He was more than sixty, and so was Wolsey. Her eyes were as vivid as ever, but it was in noticing this that he saw that other features had not remained as they were. There was no changing in the high set of her cheekbones, and the firmness of the chin. But the skin was no longer supple. And though her figure was not greatly changed from the time of her young womanhood, for she had always been compact and solid, her body too had lost suppleness. She was less quick. But the eyes were the same, and they shone as she told Harry, 'They are coming home. It is a strange letter, so long. Rebekah tells me things now that she has never written about before – St Germain, and the Hague, and stories about Robert she never wrote before. And of La Tour, so long ago, but she suddenly writes about him. She says she will be coming home. She cannot say when, but she has been promised a passage, and will take it.'

'And the boy?'

'She will bring the boy, too.'

Harry took Wolsey in his arms and lifted her from her feet. He could not lift her as easily as he used to, but he could still lift her.

'She will be coming home,' she said.

And so it was. Downing, a few days after the meeting with the king, the duke, and the other gentlemen, when the first preparations for the invasion were made, had visited Buckingham Street, where he was by then a stranger. He was tired of Rebekah. Furthermore, he did not want as his reputed mistress a woman who had been seen with Mr Pepys. If she had become the king's or the duke's mistress, or the mistress of any great man, that would not have troubled him. It would have reflected glory on him, and he would have been content. But he would not keep a woman who was seen with Mr Pepys. On the evening of supper at the Heaven, Mr Pepys's new coach, and Rebekah in it, had been very much noticed in Buckingham Street and near Westminster Hall. Watching eyes had then seen other visits. Rebekah's acquaintance with Mr Pepys was plainly no longer a formal one. And so, when he made his visit, Downing announced that if Rebekah had at any time thought of returning to Manhattan, he could probably provide passages for her and the boy.

She looked sharply up at him.

'It will be a king's ship,' he said. 'And the captain will have my orders to look well after you and Robert.'

Rebekah accepted this offer, and a gift of one hundred guineas. Downing's dealings with Rebekah were completed, and hers with him. It was then that she sent the letter to Wolsey. 'Robert and I,' she said, 'will be coming home.'

Still she did not say, 'My son and I.' She knew that would be assumed, but did not dare to write the words.

37

THE HEAVENS INFINITELY HIGHER

The good ship that Downing knew would be sailing was the *Elias*, a man o' war of thirty-six guns. She sailed from England in the summer, in company with three other vessels, to seize the usurping Dutch plantation on Manhattan in the name of the Duke of York. That it was an English royal colony, no one at the English court or in the English Parliament doubted, or would express the doubt. The king had made a present of the place to his brother the duke, stipulating only that if he wanted to take it, he must pay for the ships, officers, and men to do it. The duke grumbled but paid, and the fleet sailed under Nicolls, who was promoted general for the occasion. The duke himself remained in the comfort of England, awaiting the result of his expedition. Downing returned to the Hague, with tacit orders to foment more mischief. After his visit, and the gift of the hundred guineas, Rebekah never saw him again.

She and Robert were conveyed to the ship in a closed carriage, where a young officer escorting them handed sealed orders to Nicolls. He did not allow himself to be curious. There were greater matters in hand. But he knew, as all the court knew, that Rebekah had been Downing's, and he remembered her also from the evening he saw her with Mr Pepys. It was Pepys's signature that appeared on the orders. The paper had been put in front of him to sign, as navy secretary, and he had signed it with a heavy heart. He at least had seen her off from London, hugged her in affection, tousled Robert's hair, and then turned quickly away. Rebekah watched him to his carriage. He was the one sincere mourner of her departure and her only cause for regret at leaving England. Nicolls, knowing Rebekah's connections, feeling pity for her loneliness, and liking Robert, gave her as good quarters as he could, turning the flag lieutenant out of his cabin for her, and accommodating him with the other lieutenants.

The first many days of the passage were in fair weather. Rebekah stood silently on deck watching the sea, talking to no one. Robert ran about, making friends with the sailors, asking endlessly about the continent where he had been born but never remembered seeing. The sailors, anxious to give information about a continent most of them had never seen at all, told him with great authority that in America lay lions, and tigers, and three-headed savages, and gold, and that they were going to take it all for the English king. 'When shall we be there?' he asked, and they always replied, 'When shall we make a landfall, sir? Tomorrow, you count on it. Tomorrow.'

Nicolls himself passed a word with the boy now and again, wondering about him but never asking. So on the eighth day, when the lookout called, 'Land, ho!' it was to Nicolls, who was standing on the quarterdeck, that Robert ran.

'Is that America, sir?'

Nicolls shook his head. It was the coast of southern Ireland.

The cumbersome English fleet kept in convoy and made a slow passage. It was only halfway across the Atlantic when Manhattan was already buzzing with rumours. The departure of the English fleet had been noticed by the Dutch, whose enquiries had been answered in London with evasions and at the Hague by Downing's lies. Fast Dutch ships brought the news to Stuyvesant. All inhabitants of Manhattan were ordered to work one day in three at strengthening the city fortifications. A pound of powder and a pound of lead were issued to each member of the militia. One half of Stuyvesant's entire force of one hundred and fifty soldiers patrolled the city by day, and the other half by night.

Another Dutch vessel made port, bearing fresh news. It had been reported at the Hague that the English fleet was indeed bound for America, but only for the English colonies, to impose episcopal rule on them. King Charles wanted bishops in his colonies as well as at home. For a day or two Stuyvesant believed this, and foresaw with wicked amusement the dismay this would cause to the deathly rigid Puritans of Boston.

But an Englishman called Edward Welsh, who had lived many years in Manhattan, showed what credit he gave to this report by parading drunkenly, wearing on his head a bishop's mitre, and carrying in his hand a loaded English musket.

'These,' he said, 'are the bishops you can expect.'

Stuyvesant sentenced him to be tied to a post outside the city hall, with a bridle in his mouth and a placard round his neck saying, 'Slanderer and Disturber of the Peace.' But while the poor man was still standing tied to his post in the hot summer sun, another Dutch vessel brought news that the report about the bishops had as its source none other than Sir George Downing. Stuyvesant in disgust released Welsh, saying he would keep no man at a stake for Downing's sake. Then he ordered the brewers to brew no more malt beer, to conserve grain, and all Manhattan knew that the English threat was real.

When the English came, the fleet anchored off Gravesend on Long Island, the town which had once been s'Gravesande but was now entirely English. Here Nicolls met representatives from New England, who had been required by dispatches sent by fast, small ships, to provide forces to aid him. The Massachusetts and Connecticut men were ready. Nicolls listened to the New Englanders, who told him New Amsterdam was no more than half Dutch, if that.

'A ragtag mix of all races,' said a Bostonian, 'unfit to fight, except among themselves, and moreover Godless.'

Another elder concurred, informing Nicolls that the inhabitants of Manhattan were united only in their ineluctable damnation: of that, and that only, they could be sure. A more down-to-earth political man from Connecticut told Nicolls that New Amsterdam had enjoyed the advantages neither of an efficient despotism nor of self-government. Nicolls did not much like his New England allies, and declined their offer to represent his cause in Manhattan to demand the city's surrender on his behalf. He would, he said, at least do the governor the honour of going himself.

So he did, taking a cutter under flag of truce up the harbour to the Battery and there coming face to face with Peter Stuyvesant. Soldier and gentleman met soldier and gentleman. Courtesies were exchanged, but courtesies could not last indefinitely.

At length Nicolls said, 'Excellency, I must be brief. It is better that I should be brief. I do demand the town.'

'What town? New Amsterdam?'

'I cannot know the name New Amsterdam. Excellency, I do demand the town situate on the island commonly known as Manhattan. This town.'

Stuyvesant sweated in the sun. He was pale, and had been ill, which the Englishman could see. The governor said, 'General Nicolls, according to any equity, and any law, this will be seen as an enormous proceeding. It will stink to the world.' He hesitated, lost for words. 'It is opposed to all rights and reason, and all good-neighbourliness.'

Nicolls lowered his eyes. He wished he could have dealt with this old man in a better and more honest cause.

'Sir,' said Stuyvesant, 'it is all rights and reason gone. It is flagrant and open war.'

Nicolls looked round at the Dutch soldiery drawn up, and saw they were a ragged bunch. He looked at the civilian men and women, many of them richly dressed. If Their High Mightinesses had devoted half the energy to arming and fortifying the place as they had to its exploitation for profitable commerce, he knew he could not simply have come to the governor and demanded the town. But now he knew he could, and it was his duty.

'I beg you to read my terms,' said Nicolls, holding out a parchment.

Stuyvesant did not take it. 'I cannot know your terms,' he said.

'I wish you would,' said Nicolls. He had made them as generous as his commission would allow him.

'I cannot know your terms,' Stuyvesant repeated, but as he said this a Dutchman came forward and took the parchment from Nicolls who, assuming the man to be an officer of the governor's, let him have it.

But the man was not an officer but a merchant. Stuyvesant wheeled on him, jerked the paper out of his hand, and tore it in pieces, which he let drift to the ground.

Nicolls watched the pieces flutter down. Slowly he said, 'Excellency, there will be precious little honour in making this a bloody business. Precious little honour for either of us. My ships will stay in the bay, but I shall have to come up soon. I will not fire first, without receiving an answer from you. I beg you to consider.' He saluted, and returned to his cutter.

Stuyvesant stood his ground bewildered, surrounded by a murmuring, mutinous mob. Wolsey and Harry O'Brien saw him sway and were about to go to him when dark Anne darted out of the crowd, saying, 'Come home, sir. I'll see you home.' She had been a servant in his household since Wolsey found her a place there years before. 'No, no, woman,' said Stuyvesant, but all the same he did go home to the cool of his high rooms.

The long afternoon dragged on. Nicolls's fleet came up into the harbour but there, as he had promised, the ships hove to and lay at anchor. Meantime the principal merchants assembled the fragments of Nicolls's torn-up parchment which they had picked up from the ground, and glued the bits together on a board. Harry O'Brien was one of those invited to read the terms. They were indeed generous.

'Shall I go to him?' asked Wolsey.

'And tell him what?' said Harry. 'Tell him to give away his town? If I were governor, I would not thank any man, or any woman, who told me to give away my town.'

In the end it was old Van Delft and his son who demanded an audience with Stuyvesant, which he had no choice but to give. The two men came bringing their wives and children with them.

Stuyvesant glowered at them. Van Delft was the merchant who fifteen years before had drafted the remonstrance to Their High Mightinesses, protesting that Stuyvesant was ruining the colony and estranging the settlers. He had then called Stuyvesant a tyrant, and Stuyvesant in return had called him a serpent. Since then they had come to an accommodation, and even to a sort of friendship. Van Delft was not a fool, and Stuyvesant knew that. But still he said scornfully, 'I say I will see you, Van Delft, and you bring your children, too. Will they speak for you?'

'Perhaps they will, better than I can. But I'll speak first. We have pieced the English general's paper together. The terms are good.'

'His terms are simple,' Stuyvesant replied. 'He said, and you heard, "I do demand the town." That is generous?'

Van Delft said, 'We have read the paper. The terms are that all Dutchmen are to be treated as if they were Englishmen, that the old laws and magistrates are to remain, and that each man shall keep his own property. Each soldier is to have passage to Holland, or land here if he wishes to stay.'

'But he demands the town. "Give me the town or I will take it. But if you give it, you shall keep some small other things." Those are his terms? That is the gentleman's agreement we are offered?'

'And if we fight?' said Van Delft. 'We cannot see that anything is to be expected but misery, sorrow, the burning of our houses, the rape of our women, the death of our children, and destitution. The absolute destruction of fifteen hundred men and women, not two hundred and fifty of whom can bear arms or have as much as a pistol to fire.'

'You forget the garrison,' said Stuyvesant.

'How many?' said Van Delft. 'Two hundred? We know there are not so many.'

Stuyvesant paced fretfully back and forth, and turned angrily on them. 'This is treason.'

'No. It is sense. And it is all that is left to us.' The older Van Delft glared back at Stuyvesant. There was deadlock. Then Van Delft's son, a sane, handsome young man stepped forward, and spoke more quietly than his father had.

He said, 'Excellency, if there was the smallest chance of help from Europe.... But there is not.'

Stuyvesant did not deny this.

The young man continued, 'You know in your own conscience that we are incapable of holding out for three days against such an enemy. Grant that it would be different if we could hold out for six months, three months, or even a month. But we cannot. We cannot save the smallest part of this entire city, or, what's dearer to us, we cannot save our wives and children.'

Stuyvesant replied, 'Ah. I see how your children speak for you now. But the English general is not a Turkish barbarian.'

'But the sensibilities of the English general are not those of his hired soldiers,' said the elder Van Delft, and then he bowed and they left, and as they did a child, a girl of three or four, looked back at Stuyvesant, and bobbed a frightened curtsey.

'Oh, God help me,' said the governor, and stood staring at the door through which the child had passed.

Through the door he saw a soldier running towards the Battery on the southernmost tip of Manhattan, and then heard others. Their muskets clanked against their breastplates as they ran, and their pikes trailed on the cobbled streets. It was the sound of a garrison in disarray. Men were deserting their posts on the east and west of the city, and running like an undisciplined mob towards the Battery to see the English ships.

There they still lay in the harbour, not attempting to stop the fishing boats that sailed close to them, in the main channel, returning with their catch to Manhattan. The fishing skippers, when they landed, passed on a garble of information got from their own observation and from gossip with fishermen out of Gravesend. The English ships, they said, were the *Guinea*, which carried thirty-six twelve-pounders; the *Elias*, forty-two guns counted on her decks, and eight more said to be stowed in her hold; the *Rear-Admiral*, eighteen guns; the *Martin*, sixteen guns; and one other unnamed ship, thought to be not a fighting vessel but only a small merchantman. Altogether the ships carried four hundred soldiers, and six hundred New Englanders were drawn up on Breuckelen.

Stuyvesant waited alone in an agony of mind.

Then a cry arose from the Battery which came clearly through the open doors and windows of his house, and he leapt into the street, shouting for his officers. No one replied, so he propelled himself madly with his wooden leg and his one good leg to the fort, and mounted the steps to the bastion. Two of the fleet, the flagship *Guinea* and the *Elias*, had broken out sail and were coming up to Manhattan. Slowly they approached, changing course to enter the North River and sail under the very guns of the fort. The mob had now run there, and all eyes were on Stuyvesant as he called to the master gunner, who alone had remained at his post. The man was holding a lighted taper, which Stuyvesant took from him. The crowd moaned, and then, as Stuyvesant lowered the taper to the cannon touch-hole, fell into terrified silence.

What Stuyvesant would have done he never knew, but he heard a voice and found himself looking across the cannon's breech at Wolsey.

All she said was one word, 'Peter.'

While he looked up, the moment passed. The *Guinea* and the *Elias* had glided upstream, and lay no longer in his cannon's field of fire. They were still well within range of other cannon on the bastion, and the master gunner looked enquiringly at Stuyvesant. The governor shook his head, and lowered the lighted taper to his side. The ships had passed, with not a shot from either side.

'They will say,' he murmured, 'they will say in Holland that this place was taken by four little frigates and a merchant bark. Only four little frigates, they will say.'

Wolsey shook her head. 'No one will say that.'

The surrender was as good as accomplished, and Stuyvesant faced the fact. 'But I will have it colours flying,' he said.

It was agreed. When Nicolls and Stuyvesant met again, Stuyvesant put his hand to the hilt of his sword, to draw it and offer to the Englishman. Nicolls stopped him, taking Stuyvesant's sword hand and pushing the blade back into the scabbard.

'Oh, no,' said Nicolls. 'No, Excellency. Oh, no. I will not take it, and you shall not offer it. Yours was the braver part today.'

So the garrison marched out with arms at the port, drums beating, and colours flying. Nicolls made his proclamation before the city hall, taking in the name of Charles II, by the Grace of God King of England, all lands, rivers, soils and harbours, and ending with these words:

And whereas the possession and freeholding of this town has been bestowed by His Majesty on his right royal and beloved brother James, Duke of York, it is now ordered and commanded that from this eighth day of September in the Year of our Lord 1664 this place shall not be called otherwise than by the name of New York, on the island of Manhattan, in America, forever.

At this a great cheer arose. The British soldiers cheered. The Dutch burghers cheered. Peter Stuyvesant, standing by Nicolls, looked down and could not cheer. Neither could Wolsey or Harry O'Brien, and neither did the Van Delfts, father and son, though they had urged the necessary surrender of the town.

The business of the day was over. Now it was time for feasting. But Nicolls did not want a riot. He had replaced Stuyvesant's garrison of one hundred and fifty men with a British contingent of the same number, and kept the rest of his men aboard the ships in the harbour. He had also seen to it that the New England troops would remain on Breuckelen and not cross to Manhattan. He told Stuyvesant all this, and the late governor thanked him.

'It is only prudent,' said Nicolls. 'Now, one other matter, and we are done. I have passengers from England. They are on board my flagship. I'll have them brought ashore and hand them over to you. I believe they are known here.'

He gave the names of a young woman and a boy, and Stuyvesant, as almost his last official act, went to meet them and took them to Harry O'Brien's house. The boy wore a suit of brown velvet, too warm for Manhattan. The woman was richly dressed in a gown of lustrous silk, called lutestring, with a light cloak of scarlet satin over her shoulders, gold bracelets and lace ruffs at her wrists, and a silver chatelaine and scent box hanging at the waist. Her whole manner of dress was undoubtedly Dutch, but of a cut and fashion that had yet to reach America. Her gown and cape were made the last time she had been at the Hague. Only her gloves were English, and these she had from Mr Pepys.

It was Rebekah. As she stood she did not look round at the tapestries and panelling of the hall, but at the boy, who stood to her right. And the thoughts running through her mind were those that had occupied her for a good part of the voyage, and even while the ship lay at anchor in the harbour earlier in the day.

'Shall I say,' she asked herself, 'that Robert is not my son but Ruth's?'

And she answered herself that, if she did, then the truth would have been told, for what the truth was worth for its own sake. Against that, she would have to tell Wolsey the story of the wilderness wooing. In the wilderness, to Rebekah's mind, this had been as natural as night and day, but would it seem so to Wolsey, in Manhattan? Would

Wolsey comprehend? Would she forgive? To tell would ease Rebekah's conscience. 'But what,' she asked herself, 'of Robert himself? If I tell Wolsey, shall I tell Robert too? All his life he has known me as his mother.' She had not told Robert, but even as she waited in the hall she had not resolved what to tell her mother.

At last Wolsey and Harry came down, expecting to see only Stuyvesant. But then they saw the woman and child.

Wolsey stopped, and glanced at Stuyvesant, expecting him to explain who the two visitors were.

But the young woman herself stepped forward towards Wolsey and said, 'I am Rebekah.'

Wolsey was bewildered. She had known her daughter was coming, but had not expected her to arrive with a fleet of men o' war. She stood immobile until Rebekah ran to her, and mother and daughter embraced. When they parted there were tears in Rebekah's eyes. She went to Harry and kissed his cheek, and then called the boy to her.

'This,' said Rebekah, 'is Robert, my son.' As she said it, she trembled for the lie, and for the wrong done to La Tour and Ruth, but she said it. The truth was something she would keep to herself for the rest of her life. The easing of her own conscience would have cost others too much.

When the boy stepped forward into the light, Wolsey recognized him instantly. The candid green eyes, the hair worn long and so dark as almost to be black, and the carriage of the head, were hers as she remembered herself. And Harry, looking at the boy, saw the young Wolsey in him too, as he had first seen her. But there was more than that. The boy was Wolsey's grandson, but he was also the image of the son she had lost on the forest floor in the New England snows two generations before. He was named Robert, as her lost son had been Robert.

She held out her arms to the boy and held him close.

'So you are home?' she said.

'Yes, I am *home*.' His voice was hers too. 'General Nicolls is an Englishman, and reserved, and so we did not talk at first. But when a sailor called "Land, Ho!" and I asked the general if it was America, and he told me it was only Ireland....'

'*Only* Ireland?' said Harry. 'Did he say *only* Ireland? Nicolls is an Englishman all right, if he can say "Only Ireland."'

'I beg your pardon, sir. He said it was Ireland. After that we talked often, and he told me that my mother and I were very likely the only true Americans on board, having been born there, and would very likely be some of the truest Americans in Manhattan even when we arrived, having been born here.'

Stuyvesant spoke. 'I feel somewhat American, having lived here as long almost as I can remember. And so does your grandmother, and Captain O'Brien. And so, I suspect, will General Nicolls, now he has taken the place.'

'He did talk about that too, sir,' said Robert. 'But he said he would only be a tenant. That was his word. He said the Dutch had been tenants, and the English would only be tenants. I said I was French by birth, and he said, begging my pardon, that the French were tenants too. But that those who were born here would be the true Americans.'

'He is a generous man to see himself as he does,' growled Stuyvesant. 'A generous man, I'd say.'

It was now dark, and the night was full of fireworks. They all went out into the warm, soft darkness and saw rockets lift into the sky from the English ships in the harbour and in the North River, from the contingents of New Englanders camped on Breuckelen, and from the Dutch inhabitants at the Battery. The largest bonfire was that lit by Harry's sailors, down at the wharves. Robert saw it, and, when he heard it belonged to Captain O'Brien's men, wanted to go to it. The men were singing and roasting two deer the Carnarsie had brought over from Long Island thinking to trade with the English victors. The Indians had been surprised to see neither the massacre which would have been the proper end of an Indian victory, nor even great dances and feasting by the victors. Instead it was the Dutch who were lighting bonfires and dancing. They sold their deer and went uncomprehendingly back to Long Island. Harry's men had acquired two, in exchange for two dozen fishhooks and a knife.

Wolsey stood with Stuyvesant. She said, 'It wounds you to see the Dutch feasting like this, all over your town?'

'No longer my town. But yes it does. And yet, why shouldn't they celebrate an escape from what they feared would be misery and murder? I am no longer governor. It wounds me, yes. But I shall stay here, and die here. I have my bouwerie.'

Wolsey looked towards the bonfire made by the men of the *Vliegende Hert* and Harry's other ships. 'Peter,' she said, 'my grandson wants to go and join them, and I think we shall all go. It's not a Dutch bonfire, Peter. Harry's men are a scratch lot – a few Dutch, but some from Barbados, and some French, and even a few Irish.'

'And Scots and Chinese?' asked Stuyvesant.

'And Scotsmen and Chinamen, as Their High Mightinesses once feared. Will you come too? It's not a celebration for what happened today, except for the return of my daughter and grandson. It's a Thanksgiving for them, if you like. It's that. Will you come?'

He offered his arm, and she took it. She called Robert to her. When he saw her and Stuyvesant together, he too offered an arm to his grandmother and they started off. Rebekah, who had changed into plainer clothes, came up behind with Harry. One of Harry's mates busied his men to find them benches, and they sat drinking ale and eating the roast venison carved by Harry's boatswain.

'Who is she?' asked the boy. He had seen a figure flitting on the edge of the circle of light created by the bonfire.

Wolsey looked, and called out, 'Anne? Is that you? Will you come here?'

Thin, dark Anne emerged hesitantly from the shadows, curtsied to Wolsey, to Stuyvesant, to Rebekah, at whom she stared in puzzlement, half recognizing her, and to Robert. Then, with timorous eyes, she bobbed to Harry.

'Come by me,' he said, making room. After a pint of ale

her timidity went and she did as the sailors repeatedly demanded and gave them a song, standing before the semicircle of listeners, and singing as she once had at the Swan.

> *Step into my canoe,*
> *Ah come on, Johnny, do.*
> *The river is wide,*
> *And down we shall glide,*
> *And discover a new countrie,*
> *Our new-found Americky.*

The bold, timorous, plaintive notes died away, and Robert applauded with the men. Harry motioned Anne back to him, and Rebekah recognized her, and the three of them talked about the Breuckelen adventure, when Rebekah was a girl.

Wolsey took Robert by the hand and led him a little way apart, so that they both looked across the North River at the mainland, towards the far interior of the continent where he had been born. It was a clear night. The stars stood out brilliantly, and to Wolsey, remembering Francis Wheaton, it seemed that the skies were now, indeed, infinitely higher. She and Robert looked round at the bonfires, at the surge of people, and at the fireworks which traced brief arcs and spirals in the sky.

It was the first night of New York, but still, as she watched the rockets flare and then fall and die, they seemed to her to personify figures of the past: one personified William Brewster, her beloved mentor; another William Bradford, for so long governor at Plymouth; another Dorothy May his wife, who had slipped into the sea in Provincetown harbour before she ever set foot on the Promised Lands; another Susannah, who dressed her for her first wedding and remained her friend for years; and another poor La Tour, murdered in a wilderness. And a Catherine wheel, which spun on and on and refused to die, was Peter Stuyvesant, who would stay on and retire to his bouwerie.

She said, 'It is strange. When we first set out from Plymouth in our big ship, years ago, our patent was to come here, to the mouth of this river. But we were blown off course and could not reach this far, and it was winter, so we went to Plymouth instead. Now we are here.'

'I did not know that,' said Robert.

'It is true,' she said.

The boy gazed westwards across the river at the land. Wolsey said, 'General Nicolls was right about tenants, you see. There are different kinds of tenants, though. If a man comes here, and stays, with the intent to live and die here, as Governor Stuyvesant will stay, then he is a tenant with a very secure lease.'

'And you will stay, grandmother?'

'I will. I have seen many kinds of tenants. I have lived in this country more than forty years, and have seen many people come here. Not every man can make a new country. We all knew that before we came. At least we were told it before we came. Now we know the truth of it. Those who missed old friends, old loves, old ways, never thrived. Those who were English and remained in their hearts English, never thrived. Maybe the forests were too deep for them. Those who were French, and thought of themselves only as transplanted Frenchmen, never really did take root. Though your father would have taken root. And with the Dutch, it has always been the same. For so many men and women the plains were too broad, or the heavens too high, or the snows too cold, or the wine not what it was back at home, and they never took. But some did, and they were the ones who knew they were in a new country and set their hearts to it. They thrived. And their children, who were born here, thrived.'

'And shall I thrive?' asked Robert.

She looked at him in the flickering bonfire light, and then back into the fire, and the scenes of her own life played across her mind. The first meeting with Francis Wheaton at Scrooby, and how in the half darkness of the courtyard she had lifted her hand high to pluck grapes from trees. The long Atlantic passage, and the never-forgotten moment when the ship stood still, and then fell into the trough of the waves. The night of the first Thanksgiving, after the venison, when she had decked her bed for Francis, with meadowsweet. Her departure from Plymouth, and the grief of her beloved William Brewster, to see her go. The exhilaration of first sailing through the Narrows and up to Manhattan, and her drifting asleep that night with the voice of dark Anne in her ears, singing at the Swan, as she had just sung to the men around the bonfire. And dear Harry, her shy, bold lover, and her second husband, whom she still cherished as he did her. Then her daughters seen together in their bed by the light of Harry's candle as he showed them to La Tour – 'Now you've seen them both, both ways.' Then her daughters leaving her, and the pain of that. But now Rebekah at least had come back. And beside Wolsey stood her grandson, who was her own lost son returned.

She murmured, 'A full life, I'd say.'

Then she came to herself as she heard Robert's voice at her side, asking his question again. 'And shall I thrive?'

She looked at him. A boy born on the banks of the Messipi, the son of a French father and a New England mother. Her grandson, the grandson of a girl brought up like the daughter of an earl by the canons of York cathedral. She remembered the decayed hall of the archbishop's palace at Scrooby, and the hanging, faded, cardinal's hat, inside which the spiders of nearly a hundred years had spun their webs as if to construct a skull where the head of a man, her ancestor, had once been.

Wolsey looked at her grandson and across the river. Nothing was faded there.

She said, 'It is a new country, still in its morning. As you are. And you will thrive together.'

A NOTE AND ACKNOWLEDGMENTS

Thanksgiving is a novel, not a history, though I hope it is true to the spirit of its time and of the places in which it is set – Scrooby and Plymouth in England, Plymouth in New England. Manhattan, and the wildernesses of the Illinois and Mississippi. Some of the principal events of the story did happen. The Pilgrims landed at Plymouth in 1620. Manhattan was bought by the Dutch in 1626 and taken by the English in 1664. The French did constantly, bravely, and very early prospect the midwest. Some of the people are real – William Brewster and William Bradford, Charles I and Cromwell, Peter Stuyvesant, Samuel Pepys, and George Downing. Downing, who was one of the first graduates of Harvard, rose to be esteemed the most devious diplomat in Europe, and Downing Street in London is named after him. Pierre La Tour bears an admitted resemblance to Robert Cavelier, Sieur de La Salle, one of his several successors. But Wolsey Lowell herself is a creature of the imagination, as are the hearts and souls of the other people of the book.

But still, novel though it is, *Thanksgiving* is a picture stretched in a frame of fact. So I must thank the following institutions, where I learned what I could about the history of the times:

The New York Public Library, surely the best public library in the English-speaking world, for whose books, hospitality, and comfort I am more grateful than I can easily express.

The British Museum Reading Room in London.

Pilgrim Hall, Plymouth, Mass., whose generosity in putting into the hands of a stranger such a book as Governor Bradford's own Bible, as well as many of Brewster's books, is astonishing.

Plimoth Plantation, which faithfully re-creates the topography, speech, and I think the spirit of the pilgrim village of 1627, and also exhibits, on the waterfront, a full-scale reconstruction of the *Mayflower*.

Starved Rock State Park, Illinois.

There is little point in appending a vast list of books, pamphlets, letters, commissions, and mad tracts about the portent of comets, the will of God, and the slipperiness of the heart, which I have read for information and pleasure. Any historian will know of them. No one else will want to know. But I believe that to attain the smallest understanding of early British settlements in New England, a reading of Calvin's *Institutes* is essential and, as it happens, entertaining. And more can be learned about the Dutch and French in seventeenth-century America by reading an explorer's commission from Louis XIV, or a Dutch governor's bitter complaint to The Hague, than from ploughing through a thousand doctoral theses.

I was constantly stirred as I visited the places of the book – tracing the site of the archbishop's palace in the sodden wastes of Scrooby, Nottinghamshire; climbing the Hoe at Plymouth, Devon, and then descending to the Jacobean houses of the old town; following the course of the town brook at Plymouth, Mass., and then, not so far along the shore, stretching up to pick grapes from tall trees; trying to hide somehow from the winds of Québec in winter; scrambling up the precipitous walls of Starved Rock and watching the wide Illinois flow past below; wandering around those bits of London which are still more or less as they were in Pepys's and Downing's time; and sailing through the Narrows up to Manhattan which is now, among other less splendid things, the most exhilarating of cities.

Last, I wish to thank Rose Briggs, Jean Mills, Nancy Orton, Charles Strickland, Bob Marten, and the Reverend Charles C. Forman, all of Plymouth, Mass., though none of them is to be held responsible for whatever use I have made of the information and help they so kindly gave. I also thank Alice E. Mayhew of Simon and Schuster, New York, James Cochrane of Hutchinson, London, and Michael Sissons, who one day over lunch suggested to me the beginnings of this book. Without him I shouldn't have written it.

Nyon, Plymouth, Starved Rock,
Manhattan, Lavender Hill
1978–81